The SIN of Addison Hall

The SIN of Addison Hall

By Jeffrey A. Onorato

A Block Island Book

Published By Bryant Park Press Inc.

BLOCK ISLAND BOOKS

An Imprint of Bryant Park Press Inc.
100 Park Avenue 16th Floor
New York, NY 10017

Published in the United States by Bryant Park Press Inc., New York, NY
www.blockislandbooks.com

Author's photograph by Anna Shender.

Cover design by Burnt Sky Media.

Book Design by Kiwi Creative.

First Edition

ISBN-13: 978-0-9796816-4-6

ISBN-10: 0-9796816-4-2
LCCN: 2009928145

12 11 10 9   10 9 8 7 6 5 4 3 2 1

Printed in the United States of America.

This book is dedicated to Max and Sam,
the two sweetest souls in my world.

thick fabric of her tunic. She was obviously enjoying this little flirtation. As Addison watched her interact with this handsome man, his courage began to wilt. What was he thinking? Mimi would never go out with him. Sure, Mimi was facially unattractive and her hair looked like an unraked pile of straw, but her body was exceptional; she could easily attract a man much better looking than him.

The queue moved forward again. Three customers now stood between him and Mimi. Addison's brow was wet with sweat. He couldn't approach Mimi doused in perspiration. He needed to project confidence. How could he play it cool if he looked like he was hot? He hid from Mimi's view by ducking behind the broad-shouldered man standing in front of him. He quickly wiped his forehead with his right hand, and then dried his hand on his trouser leg. HAIR-SPROUTING FACIAL MOLE! He had wiped it too close to his crotch! Now, it looked as if he had urinated in his light blue trousers. It flickered through his thoughts that he needed to add some fresh profanities to his repertoire. He began browbeating himself… I'm as smooth as the underside of a glacier. Why don't I think before I act? Do I have a subconscious desire to continually make a fool of myself? His self-loathing thoughts were cut short; it was his turn to order.

Addison walked tentatively toward the service desk, his hands folded awkwardly over the stain on his trousers. He was grateful that the height of the desk made it impossible for Mimi to see his shoes. When he got to the desk, he gave Mimi a close-lipped smile.

"What do you require?" Mimi asked brusquely.

"Th-Th-Th-Three espresso tablets please," Addison sputtered. His throat tightened. While Mimi turned and prepared his order, Addison admired her heart-shaped derriere. Gorgeous god, it was perfect! She turned back around with a scowl on her face. Either Mimi had caught him ogling her or she had somehow divined what he was about to ask her. His courage steadily waned. What should he do? His instincts screamed for him to abort.

Mimi handed him a small chrome plate with two glossy white square tablets placed on it. "Th-Th-Th-Thanks," Addison said, and then in an instant of foolish pluck, he blurted, "M-M-M-Maybe we could go out sometime… for a saunter." A saunter? Wh-Wh-Why did I say saunter? "I meant a walk… you know… a walk around Grand Square… or m-m-maybe along the river… How about tonight? No, tonight's too soon… you probably have plans… m-m-maybe tomorrow… or the day after?" Addison felt as if his heart had vaulted to the top of his tonsils. He didn't expect Mimi to say yes, but now that he had asked her, it was at least a possibility. Even this grain of hope was more than he was used to, and for a moment, he was exuberant; however, this good feeling swiftly vanished.

Mimi's scowl deepened and she waved forward the next customer. Without looking at him, she said flatly, "I have no interest in taking a s-s-s-saunter, walk, trek, tramp, trudge or any other type of ambulation with you. Spending time with you would be a waste of time for me."

Addison was humiliated. He turned to leave. Was that second of hope worth this overwhelming shame? Predisposed to blushing, Addison's face and neck now tingled. A dull ache banged around his stomach like a moth in a lampshade. Cleft palate! Club foot! Alopecia! Why had she rejected him so harshly, so maliciously? She had even mocked his stutter! Her cruelty astonished Addison. He left the Caffeine Depot, and walked toward the nearby transport station with slow, heavy steps and his head hung low. His face and neck burned and his temples throbbed. He knew she was going to say no when he saw her expression as he approached the service desk. Why, in gorgeous god's name, did he still go ahead and ask her?

Addison Hall was an unattractive man living in Wakork, the second largest city in the country of Alpdon. Wakork was a modish city located in the southern part of the country, bordered on the north by the Luvista River. Most mornings, as it was this morning, the city was shrouded in a soupy mist that wandered off the Luvista. It gave Wakork a grimy feel, as if it needed a good downpour to wash it clean.

Addison arrived at the transport station and stood amongst the crowd waiting for the 08:16. Although surrounded by a gaggle of commuters, he felt alone and self-conscious – believing that each one of the waiting passengers was looking at him and either laughing at the stain on his trousers ("It's only sweat from my hand!" he wanted to shout) or recognizing him as the pitiable one just socially annihilated at the Caffeine Depot.

Mimi was the latest in a string of romantic failures. He thought back to Lenina, the woman from his complex with the pretty face and a posterior the width of two transport seats. Three months ago, he asked her if she wanted to go to the Depot for some espresso tablets. She turned him down, telling him she had a "severe case of projectile diarrhea." Before Lenina there was Julia – a concave-chested woman with narrow hips, who worked as a sales clerk at the Ye Olde Trouser and Tunic – who told him that her genitalia were smothered with herpes blisters… and the list went on. Why did women in his caste find him so unappealing? And why did they give him such disgusting excuses? He had observed men he considered uglier than him coupled with caste-appropriate women. Why couldn't he attract any? Any? How about one?!

Addison fixed his eyes on his sullied shoes while he waited for the transport. Two women behind him were having a hushed conversation. They looked familiar. Didn't he just see them in the Caffeine Depot? He could hear them whispering, but he couldn't make out what they were saying. Were they talking about him? Addison's face warmed, and a droplet of sweat trickled down his temple and dripped into his left ear. As he fingered the fluid from his ear, one of them laughed. Addison was convinced; they were talking about him! Why else would they be whispering? Addison put his left hand into the pocket of his trousers and rolled his fingers over three polished rocks he carried with him at all times. He kept his eyes on his shoes and hoped the transport would arrive soon. At that moment, a strong gust of wind disheveled his hair. He let out a protracted sigh; he felt more air on his scalp and knew that more of his bald spot was now visible. In the breeze were the faint but recognizable fumes from the incinerators at his current place of employment, Camp Sycamore. Located thirty kilometers southwest of Wakork in the agricultural town of Shawcuzit, the camp was a six-minute ride away on the high-speed transport. Addison was a camp worker (or Menial), and while it wasn't a job that took full advantage of his above-average intelligence, it aligned well with his blunted ambition.

Addison was not entirely to blame for his lack of drive; there were few employment options for someone who looked like him. For while it was obvious that god had blessed many citizens in Alpdon, it was also obvious that Addison was not one of them, and the prevailing belief in Alpdon was that god had preordained it that way. Addison was angry with god for his lot in life; however, he suppressed his feelings as he believed express-ing anger toward god, even the diluted version of this age, would incur the almighty's wrath and bring him more tribulation. Addison's god was vindictive, not loving. He was an omnipotent punisher who was unpredict-able, unsympathetic and unjust. He hadn't cursed Addison; that was too harsh an assessment. It was more appropriate to say that god had turned his back on Addison, forcing him to live a Burdened life – a life best described by its shortcomings rather than its virtues.

Addison was bright, but he was not the nimblest of thinkers. Solutions to problems and clever comebacks came to him, but usually after the appro-priate moment had passed. From an early age, he loved geology and was fascinated with history and ancient literature.

He suffered from a steady low-grade anxiety, which was probably the reason why his hands and forehead were usually damp from sweat. It was definitely why he stammered whenever he spoke to someone. This anxiety was fueled by his subconscious – a merciless predator that collected, tagged and filed for future use against him every humiliation he had ever experi-enced. That Addison lived a Burdened life was not just a conclusion to be drawn from the substantial evidence; in this age and in this country, it was considered an irrefutable fact.

The holographic clock floating in the center of Grand Square read 08:14. (August 14th, Addison thought, the date Japan surrendered to the

Allies in World War II.) The transport would arrive in two minutes. It was never late. Addison stood waiting; his shoulders hunched forward and his back rounded as if he were carrying a heavy bag in each hand. His hands were empty of course; the burden of his overstuffed emotional baggage was weighing him down. He continued to fondle his rocks. He had found these rocks as a child during a family trip to the beach, and he carried them with him at all times. In stressful situations he found it comforting to rub them, although he couldn't explain why.

Addison heard the rush of the arriving transport. He took a deep breath, attempting to fortify his will for the approaching day. The smell of brackish water from the Luvista soothed him some, but there was another scent in the air that Addison couldn't identify. It wasn't the hint of fumes from the Camp Sycamore incinerators; it wasn't the occasional whiff of wet clay and dead fish that wafted off the banks of the Luvista during low tide. It was an unfamiliar and foreboding smell, and it stirred a premonition of dread that tugged at his psyche. The 08:16 transport arrived, right on schedule. With his eyes still cast downward, he jockeyed with the other commuters and passed through the transport portal. He immediately turned and faced the lushly carpeted caboose wall, blocking his sweat-stained crotch from the other passengers' view.

As he waited for the caboose to depart, he was unable to exorcise this ominous feeling. Something significant was going to happen to him – somehow he knew it – but he wasn't sure what it was or when it would occur. All he was sure of was that his life, until now a neglected dust-covered snow globe sitting on the back of god's divine shelf, was about to be picked up and shaken vigorously. ■

CHAPTER TWO

❖

"WERE YOU MISTREATED AS A CHILD? Was your birther too busy dashing off to the hair salon or soaking in a tanning balm immersion chamber to nurture you properly? Or perhaps, when your POP disciplined you, he favored the titanium fist over the velvet glove? Whether you were reared in a milieu of dysfunction or you suffered through occasional spurts of abuse or neglect, your negative childhood experiences burrow into your subconscious and sabotage your interpersonal relationships..." Addison looked disdainfully over his shoulder at the apparition talking to his back. The caboose was packed with commuters and the holographic saleswoman chose him – bad luck followed him like a stray black scimitar-toothed cat. This iteration was nice to look at however; a voluptuous blonde (naturally) with protuberant nipples that poked through sheer white breast cups like brown fingertips, obviously programmed to sell to men only. "For a trivial amount of commerce credits, we can flush out the emotional sludge that inhibits you from experiencing full relational joy..." Abruptly the voice stopped and the holograph vanished. The transport had arrived at the Shawcuzit station.

Addison dismounted the transport and walked through Camp Sycamore's main entrance. He looked at his crotch. The sweat stain was still visible, but less noticeable. Located inside the entrance was a Recognition Unit (RU), a waist-high chrome fixture with a vertical goose-necked arm. Addison waved his right wrist under it. "Hall, Addisoy acknowledged at 08:27," an androgynous voice announced. (On their 18th birthday, all Alpdonians were required to have a microchip embedded in the capitate bone of their right wrist. The chip was used for identification and for payment on commercial transactions. Addison's name had been misspelled during registration, and he had never gotten around to visiting the Bureau of Records to have it corrected.) A shrill beep signaled the deactivation of the security field, causing Addison to flinch.

He had passed through the RU hundreds of times over the past four years, yet the beep always made him flinch. Addison walked to the locker room, put his uniform on and entered the campgrounds.

Camp Sycamore was the oldest camp of Alpdon's Four Beautification Retreats. (The others were Camp Poplar, Camp Hornbeam and Camp Willow.) Alpdon's chancellor, Bormann Brock, erected these camps after he took office to make Alpdon's grotesquely obese citizens "less unsightly" by forcing them to lose significant amounts of weight in a compressed time frame (typically ten kilos a fortnight). Sycamore was a converted military barracks left over from a double-digit century when wars were still unscheduled. It was comprised of two dozen or so red brick buildings, all in varying stages of disrepair. The building edifices, especially those facing the Luvista, were all missing bricks. Addison thought they looked menacing, eerie, like poorly carved jack-o-lanterns.

Addison entered the campgrounds at 08:34. He spotted his old friend and fellow camp worker, Nigel Puddlepacker, at the eastern part of the compound and walked over to him. Nigel was supervising a group of campers digging a trench. "G-Good morning, old friend," Addison said. "I-I don't think it's hyperbole to say that I made a complete fool of myself this morning."

"Made a fool of yourself? You didn't trip and fall again, did you?" Nigel asked in his usual croaky voice. It sounded like the voice of a man who had inhaled too many burning nicotine rods, but Addison had known Nigel since childhood and was almost certain that Nigel had never even tried one.

"N-No, not this time," Addison said, grinning. He was prone to physical clumsiness.

"Then could you please tell me what you did? Don't leave me in suspicion." Addison grinned again. Nigel was prone to verbal clumsiness.

"W-Well I-I asked out Mimi from the Caffeine Depot this morning… you know the one with breasts like Mercurian melons who works the service counter?" Nigel nodded; most of Wakork's lower caste males knew of her.

"A-And I am sure you are not surprised to hear that she declined my offer faster than hydrochloric acid dissolves talc."

Nigel looked momentarily confused. "Anyway... Addison, why did you go and do that?"

"What do you mean? She's in my caste; it's socially acceptable for me to ask her for a date."

"She might be in your caste dear friend, but she is way out of your league," Nigel said with a warm smile.

"W-Well I certainly can't argue with you. Her body is lip-licking luscious. What was I thinking?!" Addison said, shaking his head remorsefully.

"I have to say, however, that I do admire your moxie. It takes courage to ask out a woman as well-bodied as her. In fact, I hear that she will only copulate with well-endowed upper caste men," Nigel said. He had a tidbit of gossip on just about anyone Addison mentioned.

Addison changed topics. Talking to Nigel took some of the sting out of his embarrassment, and it flashed through Addison's thoughts how fortunate he was to have him as a friend. "What vitally important project are we working on today?" Addison asked sarcastically. The guards referred to most camp projects as being "vitally important."

"Today we are eliminating more 'sacrilegious materials,'" Nigel said, making quotations with his long knotty fingers. Addison responded with a mocking snort. Chancellor Brock was on a crusade to gather up all types of "appearance-improving aids." Just two nights prior, Brock delivered a speech, classified by the Bureau of Information as mandatory viewing for all Alpdonians, and with the zeal of an evangelist the night before Judgment Day, he condemned the blasphemy of unattractive mortals attempting to alter their god-given looks. "Attempting to become attractive when our perfect god preordained you to be visually unappealing is not only sinful; it has the very real possibility of stalling the momentum of our recovering economy."

This was blasphemous to Brock because it was an attempt to invalidate his core belief that those who were beautiful were smart and those who were ugly were not. "Completeness of Creation" he called it, the tenet being that a perfect god cannot do an imperfect work. If he "blessed" you with comeliness, it was axiomatic that he also "blessed" you with intelligence. A wholly infallible god could not partially bless someone with either good looks or smarts. He either gives you both or he gives you neither.

During the last six fortnights, Camp Sycamore had burned or buried all different types of "appearance-improving aids" including ampoules of anabolic steroids, vials of Human Growth Hormone, hair restoration creams, hair-eliminating lotions, wrinkle putty, lip plumpers, waist trimmers, breast-building gels, cellulite-reducing ointments and facial-enhancing powders (once known as "makeup" because they allowed the user to construct or "make up" a visage that bore little resemblance to their actual appearance).

"When I have gathered up all of this paraphernalia," Brock had said, "I will only allow the finest-looking citizens, those most Blessed by our flawless god, to have access to them. We must make certain that those preordained by our creator to be beautiful remain beautiful and those he preordained to be unattractive stay as such. Then we can place our most attractive, our most intellectually gifted citizens, in occupations where they can generate the maximum economic benefit to Alpdon. The torrent of failed businesses that boosted unemployment, bloated our welfare system, and ultimately bankrupted our economy is a result of the ham-fisted job performance of our unappealing-looking laborers. A little yeast works its way through the whole batch of dough; hence not a single lower caste citizen will be permitted to hold a job that is mission critical to our economic recovery. Let me be clear. It is not that they don't have the desire to do quality work, certainly some of them do; however, they have not been divinely equipped with the necessary intelligence to do important work well. They are not to be disparaged for this. One cannot defy one's god-given nature. They are like the goat. No amount of desire or effort will ever allow a goat to best a stallion in a race because god did not create it to be fleet of hoof. Only a jackass enters a goat in a horse race, and our previous Chancellor, because he naively believed that 'all people are created equal,' was a jackass disguised as a Leader."

Addison thought the logic supporting Brock's Completeness of Creation theory had more holes than a boulder of pumice. After all, the goat would easily beat the stallion if the race was over a rocky mountain. For the time being, however, he was a "goat" forced to work in an unskilled job, but he didn't find it burdensome. He got to spend time with his friend, and he was outdoors getting fresh air, instead of being walled up in an office pushing graphite etching rods and writing foil. Besides, once the economy recovered, once the citizens were confident that steady jobs and plentiful food were not the result of a short-term fix, he knew Alpdon would return to normal and his employment options would expand.

He and Nigel supervised the campers as they torched these appearance-improving aids in large thermonuclear ovens. The charred remains of the items that didn't burn and the ashes from those that did were then buried in long narrow ditches. Nigel pointed to a black tarp covering a group of pallets stacked a short distance from the digging campers. "These are today's 'victims,'" he said, again making quotation marks with his fingers. "I was told that burning this substance will create a stench that could knock a crow off a compost cart so the 'sons of bitches' (he did it again) running this 'circus' (and again) have decided that these materials are to be buried without being incinerated first." Addison was counting; Nigel made quotation marks four times in less than three minutes.

Addison had been friends with Nigel for twenty-five years. In all that time, they had never had an argument; they had never even raised their voices at each other. However, Nigel had recently acquired two habits that irritated Addison – Nigel made quotation marks with his fingers way too often, and he used the phrase "sons of bitches" to describe any group of two or more people.

A gust of wind blew up a corner of the tarp revealing neatly stacked containers of Super Creatine Anabolic Muscle Milk (SCAMM). The friends laughed derisively when they saw the recognizable containers. "Th-This stuff is about as effective as a fishnet condom," Addison said. Both men laughed again. It was common knowledge that muscle-building supplements like SCAMM were useless; nothing more than a well-marketed swindle like Scientology, snake oil and sea monkeys. Using questionable research, retouched "before" and "after" photos, and testimonials from long-forgotten celebrities in desperate need of consumer credits, the public was duped into believing that ingesting whey protein, nonessential vitamins, minerals, shark cartilage, amino acids and ground-up bull testicles would help them build a great body with minimal effort.

Nigel returned his attention to the campers. "These sons of bitches are exceptionally fat, even for this place. Which one will be the first to faint or vomit?" he asked, initiating a game the friends occasionally played to help pass the time. Nigel was older and uglier than Addison. He had oversized ears and a thick pelt of carbon-black hair with an unfortunate cowlick that caused a tuft at the center of his hairline to poke straight up. Nigel told Addison that frequent washing made his cowlick worse, so his hair was often greasy. He had a blotchy red nose shaped like a gherkin, teeth that were usually caked with honey-onyx-colored plaque, and an egg-shaped body that reminded Addison of one of those punching bags that always returned upright when knocked flat. All of these were secondary characteristics, however; what one noticed first about Nigel was that he walked with his feet pointed outward, unnaturally so, like those of a duck.

Addison scanned the group of seven campers, a wretched bunch of obese men digging at a snail-smothered-in-molasses pace. "Th-That one over there; that breathing lump of lard hunched over his shovel, panting like an overheated dog." Addison pointed to a humongous man with a humongous stomach that spilled out from the bottom of his uniform top, obscured his crotch and extended halfway to his knees. (How did he urinate?) "H-He'll do one or the other any moment now... probably both." The words had barely cleared Addison's lips when the man spewed mud brown vomit over the front of his uniform and onto a pile of shovels and pickaxes lying near the ditch. Addison whooped triumphantly.

Nigel smiled, "You know what 'they' say," he said, making air quotations for "they," "unlucky in love, lucky at guessing which fat man will heave."

Addison clapped Nigel on the back and laughed. The two friends walked over to the nearby Sanitary Shed to get a disinfectant spray gun and a container of drying agent. Nigel walked faster than Addison and arrived at the shed first. He grabbed the disinfectant spray gun and cackled softly with delight. Nigel always grabbed the disinfectant spray gun because he found it fun to use. Addison, who didn't find the spray gun as entertaining, grabbed the container of drying agent and affected a disappointed look for Nigel's benefit. Nigel aimed the spray gun at Addison, shot a dollop of disinfectant onto Addison's boots and grinned. Addison shook his head in mock disgust. Nigel then turned and shot some disinfectant on his own boots and feigned a look of surprised annoyance, as if what he had done was an accident. The expression on Nigel's face made Addison laugh. Since they were school boys, Nigel had the ability to make Addison laugh, quite an accomplishment given Addison's usual glumness. More importantly, Nigel made the effort to try and make Addison laugh, which Addison interpreted as a sign of a true friend.

The friends walked to the back of the Sanitary Shed, dipped their left hands into a vat of liquid polyurethane, then waited for it to harden, clenching and unclenching their hands and wiggling their fingers as the composite congealed to ensure they remained flexible. Once their hands were dried and sheathed, they walked back to the stained camper. With his right hand, Addison scooped up some drying agent, a white powder that looked like talc, and threw it overhand at the stain on the camper's uniform. He unintentionally aimed too high and some of the drying agent entered the camper's mouth, causing him to vomit again, this time on his own shoes. "O-Oh please!" Addison shouted, "T-try and control yourself! You are revolting!" Addison suddenly felt awful. It wasn't the camper's fault he had poor aim. Addison scooped up some more drying agent and tossed it softly, underhand, making sure it landed below the lowest of the camper's four chins. Meanwhile, Nigel was liberally spraying disinfectant over the vomit puddle, the tools and now the camper's shoes. The disinfectant smelled of bleach and citrus, and it reminded

Addison of his birther; she used a similarly-scented solution to sanitize their living unit when he was a child.

Even though it had been fifteen years since his birther, Primary Optimal Provider (POP) and sole sibling had been mortally desiccated during the Third Quarter of World War VI (the war to end all wars… again), the thought of her still brought tears to his eyes. Addison was never sure if they were from grief or guilt.

On the day of the desiccation, Addison's birther angered him by forcing him to clean his personal living area, even though he was engrossed in a digital digest on geology. ("You are always reading about rocks. You must have rocks in your head!" his POP had said, the last words spoken to Addison by anyone in his family.) When his living area was clean to his birther's satisfaction, Addison went for a walk along the Luvista, hoping to punish her with his sudden disappearance by making her worry. A helium blister bomb struck their neighborhood fifteen minutes after he left, turning each of his family members into a pile of fine gray ash, which he discovered when he returned a few hours later.

Addison turned his face away from Nigel, hoping his friend wouldn't see his display of emotion, but he had no need to worry. Nigel was too consumed with spraying disinfectant to take notice.

Nigel covered all the vomit, but continued to shoot away, obviously enjoying himself. When he finally finished, he pretended to holster the sprayer like an ancient gunfighter. He looked over at Addison with a wide plaque-layered smile. Disgusted, Addison averted his glance. Why didn't Nigel brush his teeth? Addison often mentioned this apparent hygienic oversight to Nigel, but he always insisted he brushed them regularly. Comely christ, did his brush have bristles?!

The friends waited for the defiled areas to harden into glittering mica-like sheets, and then picked up the pieces with their sheathed hands and dropped them in a silver disposal sack. Addison was careful not to get too near to his close friend; Nigel's mouth smelled worse than it looked. As Addison cinched up the sack, a muscular camp guard wearing a tight black uniform approached him from behind and barked, "What in Lord Brock's name are you blubber butts doing?!" The campers had stopped digging to watch Nigel and Addison clean up. Addison was startled by his bellow and flinched. The guard looked at Addison condescendingly, as if to say "Be a man!" and continued, "Recommence work now before I introduce you grotesques to the business end of my baton!" The campers resumed digging immediately at a much faster pace.

The camp guards did not tolerate work stoppages – not only because the work was "vitally important," but because suspending movement, even for a few seconds, prevented the campers from burning the maximum calories. "I want to see those fat faces shining with sweat!" was a popular exhortation from the guards, which is why they were commonly known as "Sweat Sergeants" (or SS), and why Alpdon's Beautification Retreats were called "Perspiration Camps."

The SS turned to Addison. "Hall, Addisoy, report to the western end of the camp at once. A group of unsightlies are laying the foundation for a structure that is critically important to our camp expansion project. The Grand Commander wants you to ensure the velocity of effort complies with the revised SS work standards. This project needs to be completed expeditiously." Addison took a step forward, and then stopped. Intimidated by the SS, Addison momentarily forgot which direction was west. "West is that way, you intellectual dwarf," the guard shouted, pointing with his baton while he (inadvertently?) flexed his prominent triceps muscle.

The camp expansion project had been a hot topic of gossip among the Menials for the past few fortnights. Nigel claimed he had overheard two SS talking about how the threshold of camp inclusion was being expanded to include others besides the morbidly obese – "all the remaining unsightlies," Nigel had said with air quotations. The camps had a quick and positive effect on the immensely obese, but how would these camps help someone ugly? It didn't make sense. Even in his limited travels around Wakork, Addison had seen plenty of citizens who were not morbidly obese, but fat enough to benefit from a tour through a Perspiration Camp. It made more sense that Sycamore was being expanded to accommodate these people.

As Addison walked toward the western end of the camp, he again saw the series of vertical supports erected just outside of the camp barrier – the stanchions for a new building. When the chrome beams first appeared two fortnights ago, Addison wondered why campers weren't being used as labor; after all, it was being built practically on top of the camp fence. The more he thought about it, however, the more he understood why they hadn't been used. Laying the foundation was backbreaking work, not well suited for the poorly conditioned campers. He guessed the campers would be used for the less strenuous interior construction once the frame was completed.

When Addison arrived at the western end of the camp, a small group of the stockier and stronger-looking campers were hauling dusty bags of cement from a nearby transport to a mixing area. A couple of the campers were using long chrome poles to mix the cement with large vats of boiling water. (It was communicated to the Menials that concrete produced with purified water was 24.4593845% denser than concrete produced with untreated water, and was therefore less prone to chipping and erosion.) A third group of campers funneled the mixture through chrome guides placed in a bedding of sand, broken red brick and gravel. A small, neatly etched sign stuck in the ground identified the area as "The Sauna." Addison smiled when he saw it. "This commander is confounding," he thought. When Addison started working at the camp, he was initially surprised that there wasn't a sauna – it was a great tool for enabling rapid weight loss –but over the past four years, Sycamore consistently surpassed its monthly weight loss quota without one. After four successful years, the camp commander had *now* decided to build one?

One of the campers working the cement bag line was loafing, walking with heavy, plodding steps. Addison's brow furrowed in anger. He pulled his zinc-dipped whip from his holster and cracked it on the ground a few centimeters in front of the camper's feet. A shard of broken brick shot up into the camper's face, making a small laceration on the third of his five chins. "St-St-Start jogging!" Addison shouted, but with a slight waver in his voice – the voice of a man trying to sound authoritative, but not sure if the person he was yelling at would accept it. To Addison's mild surprise, the camper obeyed. Then Addison saw what he had done to the camper's face. He scooted over and said "S-S-Sorry. It wasn't my intention to injure you."

"Your behavior is unacceptable, Hall!" an SS hollered. Addison nodded without looking at him; he knew it, but compassion momentarily suppressed his reason. "We're not here to make these bloated bastards feel good, Addisoy; we are here to make them look good..." he paused. "No, good is a 'flagrant' overstatement... pun premeditated," he said, making quotation marks with his fingers as he smiled smugly. "We are here to make these swollen simians a trifle less disgusting." The admonished camper reached the mixing area and dropped his bag of cement. A chalky cloud lifted from the bag covering his cherubic face with white powder and caking on the trickle of blood from his wound. The SS laughed, "You need a suntan fat man."

A hydrogen horn honked indicating the end of the workday. As the campers gathered up their tools, the setting sun bathed their sweaty faces in crimson. They look suntan now, Addison thought.

Once they returned to their barracks, the campers received their dinner – two slices of soy bread and three slimy strips of tofu. After they ate, Addison and the other Menials served each one a drink the SS called a "Hot Toddy" – named not for its temperature but for the thermogenic properties of the drink's ingredients, which included green tea extract, kola nut, chromium picolinate and a heavy-handed portion of ephedra. The body-quaking tremors caused by these stimulants, combined with the draftiness and overcrowding of the barracks, made sleep difficult for the campers. Addison guessed this was done purposefully as a sleeping body burned fewer calories than one awake and shaking.

Addison served the last Hot Toddy, left the barracks and lumbered toward the Menial locker room. It had been an unusually hot day and he was exhausted. The sun had set and yellow spotlights set high on chrome poles now illuminated the camp. The mist from the Luvista returned with the evening's cool, cloaking each light in a moist, spooky haze. Like a child passing through a graveyard, Addison whistled nervously as he walked.

Addison approached the jade-colored waste container across from the SS locker room, and was startled by three loud thumps. He stopped. Two more thumps. The noise was coming from inside the container. Addison resumed walking but gave the container a wide berth. What could be in there? Perhaps it was a bear. He had never seen one, but he heard that there were man-sized cave bears living in the nearby Trata Mountains. He decided to take cover from a safe distance, hoping to get a look at whatever was rooting around in there. This would even the score with Nigel, who had been raving for the past fortnight about witnessing an eagle killing a muskrat by the main guard tower. Addison ducked behind four old rusted barrels. Loud chewing noises were coming from the container. Whatever was in there had found food.

An SS walking by the container heard the noises and stopped. Addison recognized him. It was the new SS commander assigned to supervise the camp expansion. Nigel had told Addison that his name was Hans Starck, and that he had been personally chosen by Brock for this project.

Starck was an athletically muscled man with short blond hair that extended only a few centimeters from under his black visor cap. He was the most powerful and the best-looking man Addison had ever seen. Even in the muted light, Addison could see Starck's strong jaw, harmonious nose and pronounced cheekbones. Looking at this perfectly formed man made Addison aware of his own physical shortcomings and he seethed with envy.

Starck unsheathed his graphite baton and gave the container a few quick raps. The chewing noises stopped. Starck banged his baton again, but whatever was in the container remained silent. With an annoyed grimace, Starck pounded harder and a huge head popped up from the container. Addison brought his hand to his mouth in shock. It wasn't an animal; it was a man! And from his blue-and-gray-striped collar, Addison could see he was a camper.

The camper looked annoyed, as if a portal-to-portal sales-droid had interrupted his evening meal. His hair was wet and stringy, and a link of tubular meat dangled from his gaping mouth. Then he saw it was an SS. He abruptly stood up, sheepishly let the meat drop from his maw, and stepped gingerly until he found something sturdy enough to support his ample weight. "Sorry, sorry, sorry... I know I shouldn't have done that," he said in a whiny voice. He placed both of his hands on the container edge, swung his left leg onto the top of the container wall and started to climb out. Starck didn't give him the chance. He grabbed the front of the camper's uniform and pulled him out, held him over his head with one hand, and then in one swift move, slammed the camper to the ground. Starck straddled the camper's legs and beat him about the head and upper body with his baton, grunting with each strike. The camper thrashed about trying to avoid Starck's blows, but Starck was too quick; each one he delivered found its mark. The camper whimpered for help, but his weakening voice was stifled by the brackish mist. The barrels Addison was cowering behind were only ten meters away, and yet he could barely hear the camper's pleas.

Starck continued to beat the camper with mad abandon. His eyes were opened wide, and he smiled with a disturbing expression that reflected both ecstasy and anger. The camper was silent. Starck stopped swinging, looked down at the camper contemptuously with his hands on his hips, then raised his right foot and stomped on the camper's stomach. The camper rolled onto his side, panting for air. Blood trickled from the corner of his mouth. Starck crouched down and placed two fingers on the camper's neck. He straightened up, cocked back his right leg and delivered a devastating kick to the camper's head, spinning the fat man's body forty-five degrees clockwise. Addison could now see the camper's face. He sucked the air in horror. The camper's eyes were half-open; his tongue had lolled from his mouth and was coated with gravel. Addison couldn't take his eyes off the camper's face, which looked translucent in the amber light. In his thirty-plus years, Addison had never seen a dead body; he was looking at one now.

Starck grabbed the camper's flaccid body by the right arm and right leg, lifted it over his head and tossed it back into the trash container. Addison was amazed. That corpse had to weigh at least 150 kilos, yet Starck handled it as if it were a sack of soiled uniforms. What strength! What frightening strength! Starck dusted off his hands and walked toward the SS locker room with a maniacal grin plastered on his gorgeous face.

When he was absolutely certain that Starck was gone, Addison came out from behind the barrels and walked to the Menial locker room. His heart was pounding and his breathing was rapid and shallow. Addison couldn't shake the image of the dead camper's ashen face. His color had changed so quickly! Was that what was meant by the pallor of death? One thing was certain – he would have a difficult time sleeping tonight. Whenever he closed his eyes, the camper's alabaster face would haunt him. As he left the camp and headed for the transport station, he decided he would sleep with his lights on tonight. He also decided that he should be extremely vigilant around Starck and never give that madman any reason at all to punish him. Starck's unbalanced response to the camper's indiscretion, and the ferocious way he delivered his discipline, led Addison to believe that committing even a minor infraction in Starck's presence might just cost him his life. ■

CHAPTER THREE

❖

ADDISON STOOD AT THE SHAWCUZIT transport station awaiting the next caboose. The image of the dead camper's face was branded inside his eyelids, and no matter how hard he tried, no matter what pleasant image he tried to invoke, he couldn't get rid of it. His heart continued to beat hard and quick. Feeling lightheaded, Addison stabilized himself by leaning his right hand on a nearby billboard, sending a shower of rotten wood pulp all over his trousers and shoes. Addison lowered his head and sighed. While he brushed off the debris, he glanced up at the decaying billboard – an advertisement for gasoline that was obviously decades old. (Urea, extracted from human urine, had been the primary fuel source for more than twenty years.) The poster adhered to the billboard was faded, and tatters, like miniature pennants, snapped in the evening breeze. At the beginning of Brock's regime, a graffiti artist had painted over the ad in bulbous black letters: FORGET THE PAST AND YOU ARE CONDEMNED TO REPEAT IT.

Addison recognized it as a bastardized quote from Santayana's *The Life of Reason*, but he had read it so many times now, that like a street sign on a frequently traveled road, he no longer took notice of it.

The caboose pulled into the station, on time as always, and Addison mounted it for the short ride to the Wakork station. His left hand was buried in his trousers' pocket and he rubbed his rocks. A virtual saleswoman at the other end of the caboose was nattering on about a penis enhancement lotion ("go from a needle to a knockwurst in one fortnight!"), but Addison tuned it out; his mind was locked on Starck. What had pushed him to such anger? The camp had strict rules regarding extracurricular eating, and while the camper had violated the rules, it was a minor infraction and incongruent with Starck's rage. No, there had to be another reason. If Addison believed in such twaddle, he might have thought that Starck was demon possessed. The expression on Starck's face as he beat the camper certainly looked demonic. Or perhaps Starck's POP and birther hadn't shown him enough love as a child, or maybe his diet consisted of too many glucose-rich foods. Addison smirked. The soft-hearted apologists of this age always tried to rationalize acts of unrestrained violence rather than acknowledge that some people were simply evil, and it was natural for evil people to do evil things.

The transport pulled into the Wakork station. Addison dismounted and walked northeast through Grand Square to his living complex. He entered his building foyer, a dark square room with threadbare gray carpeting, passed by the bank of mail servers and waited for the lift. The scents of peppermint and chamomile were pumped into the room from the air purification unit in a feeble attempt to mask the mildewed stench from the carpet. But decades of neglect created a reek too powerful to be disguised. Addison crinkled his nose and breathed through his mouth. He was grateful when the lift arrived.

Addison entered the lift, and as he turned to face the portal, he saw the mustachioed Thaddeus Pankewitz, a former college professor, walking briskly toward the complex entrance. Addison glanced down and acted as if he didn't see him. If he made eye contact with Pankewitz, he would probably signal for Addison to hold the lift, which meant that Addison would have to follow WASP (Widely Accepted Social Practices) and talk with him about something trivial. Addison did his best to avoid interacting with people he didn't know well (or at all) as it became yet another opportunity for him to say or do something foolish. And Addison's stammer, made worse by the anxiety he experienced in these types of social situations, practically guaranteed that he would wind up embarrassing himself.

Addison had to get the lift portal to close before Pankewitz entered the building. "Please articulate your floor," the lift interfacing system prompted in an inviting female voice. The muscles in Addison's neck tightened.

"F-F-F-Five please," he sputtered.

"I cannot process your response. Please re-articulate your floor," the dewy voice replied.

Addison's palms started sweating. "F-F-F-Five," he said again. He had encountered this problem before; his stammer frequently confused the system.

The interfacing system replied, "I *still* cannot process your response. Please re-re-articulate your floor." Did he detect a hint of irritation in the reply?

Addison took a deep breath. He had one last chance to activate the lift before Pankewitz reached the foyer. While continuing to look down, Addison said for the third time, "F-Five please!" As soon as he spoke, his shoulders drooped. In his haste, he had spoken too loudly. He knew what was coming next.

"Please temper your volume and re-re-re-articulate your floor," the system said. This time Addison was certain it had used an admonishing tone.

Pankewitz walked through the foyer and entered the lift. "Thank you for detaining the lift Mr. Hall," he said graciously, although both men knew Addison hadn't tried.

Pankewitz was new to the living complex and Addison had only seen him on two other occasions. Both times the Professor was wearing a brown corduroy tunic, and both times it smelled of mothballs and parchment. Today, Addison detected the subtle odor of spirit gum as well, but he wasn't sure if it was coming from Pankewitz, or more likely, from the adhesive used to attach the new carpeting to the lift floor. The Bureau of Shelter had mercifully replaced the old carpeting three days prior. That germ-saturated mat had smelled even worse than the carpet in the foyer.

Pankewitz was a member of the Burdened caste (like everyone in Addison's living complex), but for a Burdened he was uncommonly distinguished looking. He had thick white hair, blue opal eyes, and an aquiline nose dotted with three small moles, each one sprouting some coarse black hairs. Pankewitz's unsightly nose was the only reason he was a Burdened, however; he was tall and maintained an excellent physique, especially for an older-looking man.

"M-M-My pleasure, Mr. Pankewitz," Addison replied. He knew the Professor's name because he was the only new tenant assigned to the living complex in over a year.

"Mr. Hall, before I was removed as an educationalist from The Wakork Academy of Science and forced to work there as a filing clerk, I spent ten annums obtaining my doctorate in Global Studies. Kindly address me as 'Doctor' or 'Professor,'" Pankewitz said, the deep timbre of his voice magnified by the tight confines of the lift chamber.

"S-S-Sorry, Doctor," Addison said. What a pompous boob, he thought.

"New arrival, please articulate your floor," the lift interfacing system asked in a deferential tone.

"Kindly transport me to the Eighth level please," Pankewitz said, drawing out the word so it sounded like "Aaaaayth."

"Floor Eight recognized," the voice replied. Addison took mild interest that Pankewitz had said eight – that used to be Addison's favorite number as a child. He remembered that his favorite color was orange and his favorite animated show on Saturday mornings was *Spooky, The Sociable Apparition.* "Original passenger, do you wish to attempt to articulate your floor for the fourth time?"

"F-F-Five please," Addison said again. Flecks of spittle shot from his mouth. Once more, he was told that his floor was not recognized. Sweat formed on his forehead; he furrowed his brows as the briny moisture stung a cluster of pimples over his left eyebrow.

Addison wasn't going to try again. It would be easier to ride up to Pankewitz's floor and after the Professor dismounted the lift, he could vocalize his floor in pressure-free solitude. Pankewitz intervened – either he felt sorry for Addison or he was in a rush to get to his living unit. "My companion wishes to go to the Fifth level please."

"Floor Five recognized," the voice replied.

Pankewitz turned to Addison. "Mr. Hall, I hope this evening finds you as robust and healthy as our revitalized economy," he said, giving Addison the latest WASP greeting approved for the lower castes.

"I-I-I am feeling well, and it is my hope you feel even better than I," Addison said, giving an older, less elaborate, but still acceptable WASP reply. "Th-Th-Thank you for articulating my floor. I-I-I don't know why I am stammering so much today. I must have ingested too many espresso tablets," and then in a stilted voice, "M-M-May your evening be as pleasant as your demeanor," Addison said clumsily complying with WASP. He slid his left hand into his pocket and stroked his rocks, hoping their conversation was over. It wasn't.

Pankewitz waved his hand as if to say "not a bother," then in his deep voice said, "The word 'well' is relative, isn't it Mr. Hall?" Pankewitz paused thoughtfully. He didn't make quotation marks with his fingers but emphasized "well" by changing the inflection of his voice. "What I mean is that without the sufficient context it is difficult to quantify the degree to which someone is 'well.' Proclaiming you are 'well' when you have just spent a half-day having polyps plucked from your colon is quite different from saying you are 'well' after receiving a massage with a botanically scented lubricant. Would you agree?"

"I-I-I most certainly do. Wh-What you have put forward is intriguing," Addison fibbed. He found Pankewitz's point as interesting as watching liquid polyurethane hand-sheathing coalesce.

"The word 'free' is also a relative word," Pankewitz continued. "I would venture that you consider yourself a free man, Mr. Hall. Is my assertion accurate?" Addison nodded, not sure where Pankewitz was going with all these questions and getting increasingly nervous that he was on the threshold of another humiliation.

"After all, Mr. Hall, your appendages are not shackled. You are not incarcerated or housed in a small cage like a veal calf. You are able, if you so desire of course, to enter and exit your living unit as often as you please." The lift stopped at Addison's floor. Addison was relieved; however, Pankewitz wasn't finished talking. When the portal slid open, Pankewitz positioned himself in front of Addison, keeping the portal from closing and Addison from leaving.

"E-E-Excuse me, Mr. er, sorry... I-I mean Professor Pankewitz," Addison said as he tried to step around the broad-shouldered academic. Pankewitz repositioned his body to prevent Addison from passing. "Pr-Pr-Professor Pankewitz, if you could just move a bit..." Addison broke off in midsentence. He could see that Pankewitz wasn't listening. Like many intellectuals, Pankewitz was an A-plus talker but a D-minus listener.

Pankewitz continued. "You are a free man indeed, Mr. Hall. However, when you are compared to a similar-looking citizen living in United CanAmexico and Eurafrica, you don't appear free at all. Citizens from those countries who share our appearance can dwell wherever they want, can toil at whatever occupation they desire and can enhance their appearance using all means available. They have choices, Mr. Hall, but we do not. The government tells us where to live, they constrain our employment options, and they make it unlawful for us to use external aides or cosmetic surgery to improve our appearance. So you see that you are not free, Mr. Hall. As a Burdened citizen of Alpdon, you are not free at all! We cannot mimic the Ornithomimus[1] and conceal our heads in a mound of sediment! We need to be vigilant and vocal to ensure this maltreatment doesn't intensify. If we don't, there is no predicting what they are capable of doing. Remember, Mr. Hall, man's wickedness is only constrained by his courage, and even though *Our Leader* has liabilities, cowardice is not one of them. Mull that over as you consume your porridge this evening," Pankewitz said, finally stepping aside and allowing Addison to pass.

Addison brushed past Pankewitz and steadied himself by placing his hand on the Professor's upper arm. Gorgeous god, it was as solid as granite! As he left the lift, Addison mumbled over his shoulder, "O-O-OK. G-Good afternoon... er... I mean evening...O-O-OK...Mr.... Doctor... Teacher... N-N-Not Teacher, sorry, Professor...." He sighed with relief when the lift portal shut. Good-looking lord, that man could talk! Quieting an academic

---

1   Ornithomimus is a bipedal dinosaur from the Late Cretaceous epoch that resembled an ostrich.

like Pankewitz was like flossing a scimitar-toothed cat's canines. It could be done, but it sure wasn't easy.

As Addison walked down the hallway toward his living unit, he reflected on what Pankewitz had just said. Addison agreed that freedom is a relative word, but he disagreed with the Professor's assertion that restricting freedom was inherently bad. Sure, the citizens of the UCAM and Eurafrica had more choices; they lived in countries with thriving economies. When Brock took office, Alpdon's economy was dying; immediate and dramatic action was required to rescue it. Sure, some freedoms had been limited – a competent doctor will place a cast on a broken leg, temporarily restricting its movement in order to let it heal. Was this any different? As soon as Alpdon's economy woes were cured, Addison was certain the restrictive social "castes" applied by Brock would be removed.

Addison entered his living unit and smoothly said "Illuminate." He loved talking when no one else was around. How easy it was! After a momentary flicker, the lighting system bathed his unit in a flat white light that was better suited for a warehouse than a living space. He despised the lighting system; it made his face look pale and accentuated his blemishes. Exhausted, Addison plopped down on the corner of his sleeping platform. He stole a quick glance in his only mirror and groaned. He despised his mirror even more than his lighting system. He stood up and put his face a few centimeters from the mirror. Encountering that sadistic but perfectly formed Starck had put Addison in a masochistic mood, so he decided to inventory his faulty features.

He focused first on his face. He had no visible cheekbones; so his face not only looked puffy, it also drew attention to his recessed chin. Next were his teeth. To get a better look, he extended his lips like a braying mule. They were not even close to white, but they were too dark to be classified as yellow and too light to be brown – their color was similar to a pale lager. After a brief deliberation, he settled on petrified amber. And what was the matter with his gums tonight? They were swollen and white, and they receded from his teeth so that even more of the amber enamel was visible. He didn't think it was possible, but his smile looked even worse.

Addison stepped back and wiped the foggy patch his breath had left on the mirror with the sleeve of his tunic. He surveyed his arms and his legs. They were too thin and too long for his squatty torso. To illustrate this, he reached down and scratched his kneecaps without bending at the waist. Impulsively, he lifted up his tunic to reveal his midsection, which looked to him like a cheesecloth sack filled with curdled yogurt. He suddenly felt a whole lot worse. His stomach hung over his beltline, causing the elastic band of his undergarment to fold over. "Scrawny everywhere except my belly," he said derisively. He grabbed a handful of blubber and dug his fingernails into the soft flesh until it hurt.

Of all his perceived flaws Addison was most sensitive about his teeth, a side effect from the hefty dose of tetracycline he received as a toddler to heal an ear infection. In his early teens, he had employed some extraordinary measures to try and whiten them; brushing his teeth with mashed strawberries, rinsing his mouth with diluted bleach – he even tried rubbing the discoloration off with sandpaper – but nothing worked. Addison learned to smile, talk, sneeze, cough, belch, drink and eat without showing his teeth.

Addison turned from his mirror and grabbed a can of French Vanilla HastyTasty, a ready-to-eat meal that was especially popular with students, bachelors and birthers with newborns. HastyTasty came in two other flavors – Bavarian Chocolate and Asian Plum; however, French Vanilla was his favorite. As he held the can, the image of the dead camper's face flashed again through his thoughts. He started humming, a lame attempt to distract himself from the ghastly vision. He pushed the button on the side of the HastyTasty can to activate the "EZ Release" top, but nothing happened. He pushed a bit harder, but still the top failed to yield. His third attempt was no charm, and he angrily slammed it back onto the cupboard shelf. Like the occasional pistachio nut, some cans of HastyTasty were never meant to be opened. He grabbed another can and this time it opened on his first try. He dropped the lid into his refuse incinerator, a chrome tube located next to Addison's food pantry, and quickly closed the flap. This system was convenient, but it had a malodorous drawback – the incinerator regurgitated burning garbage fumes up the chute, causing all of the units in his living complex to smell of smoldering trash. He grabbed a hermetically sealed container preloaded with diatomic hydrogen gas and placed it in his tarnished Oxygenator. The appliance beeped and a burst of hot air expelled from the vented top. Addison removed the container and took a tentative sip. He frowned. As usual, the hydrogen and oxygen failed to bond completely and his instant water tasted like flat tonic. He shoved a spoonful of HastyTasty into his mouth to eliminate the bitter taste.

HastyTasty lived up to the first part of its name – it came ready to eat – but to call it tasty was an overstatement. HastyTasty had the consistency of lumpy pudding and was high in unsaturated fat, which gave it a greasy aftertaste and left the diner's tongue coated in a white film that was difficult to remove, even when scraped with a HastyTasty container lid (Addison had tried). However, the oily porridge also functioned as an effective laxative, and the joke amongst those who enjoyed indelicate humor was that HastyTasty looked the same whether it was "entering" or "exiting" the body.

A short musical interlude chirped from Addison's communication portal. Addison faced the center of his room and watched for the holographic clock floating in the middle of his unit to morph into his caller's identity. During the half-second delay between the first note and the caller's name, Addison held his breath in anticipation. Perhaps it was Mimi calling to say she had changed her mind! "N. Puddlepacker, Cursed" appeared. Addison exhaled, mildly disappointed, even though he knew there was a better chance of all of the earth's three moons turning to cheese than there was of Mimi calling him.

Addison said "Answer" and activated the image emulator. A life-sized, three-dimensional representation of Nigel rose from the holographic origination panel embedded in the center of his living unit floor. When communication traffic was high, as it usually was during post-work hours, it wasn't uncommon for the image to stutter or even freeze. Tonight the wipe was smoother than Classy HastyTasty (a premium version only available to the upper castes), and Addison was soon looking at the smiling face of his good friend… attached to the body of a voluptuous woman wearing a white crotch panel and matching breast cups. Addison smiled.

In an earlier age, Nigel would have been labeled "good with tools." He had a natural curiosity for how things worked, and anytime Addison visited his living unit, it was littered with bric-a-brac from different household appliances that Nigel was either trying to fix or improve. Nigel had recently figured out how to manipulate his holographic image – not the facial representation, which was protected by seven positronically encrypted firewalls and virtually impossible to penetrate, but the body representation, which had a single firewall and was as easy to breach as the Maginot Line. Over the past two fortnights, Nigel had appeared as a beauty queen adorned with a gold holographic crown and wearing a tasteful single-string black swimsuit, a muscular man wearing only a white penis sling, and a morbidly obese man wearing the same penis sling. Addison had laughed uncontrollably at the last iteration and had actually drooled on his living unit floor.

"Greetings, my friend," Nigel said, sounding concerned. "Is all well with you? I fancy this to be one of my funnier manipulations and I was hoping it would have you laughing so hard you would wind up dribbling on your floor, like the time I appeared as a fat man in a penis sling. But all I get is a smile? Are you still upset over Mimi's rejection?"

"N-No, no," Addison lied; however, he appreciated Nigel's concern. "Th-Thanks for asking, but I have moved past that incident, old friend. However, I did witness something rather disturbing tonight at the camp as I was returning to our locker room, and I am afraid it has harnessed my humor."

Nigel's holographic image shimmered and his usual egg-shaped physique replaced the voluptuous female. He gave Addison a questioning look, tilting his head like a confused dog.

"On my way to the locker room tonight, I heard some loud noises coming from a waste disposal container… the green one right outside of the guards' locker room. Do you know which one I am referring to?" Nigel nodded. "I hid behind some barrels, hoping to catch a glimpse of what was roaming around in there when the new commander, Starck, walked past the container and heard the same noises I did…" Addison gave Nigel the details of what he had witnessed.

When Addison was finished, Nigel paused and then said, "You are correct. That is disturbing, but I am not surprised. I have heard that Starck often has fits of anabolic anger because he is more 'attached' (making quotation marks) to his intravenous steroid drip than he is to his own birther."

"D-Do you think I should inform the Sycamore Grand Commander about this?" Addison asked.

"Negative, negative, negative!" Nigel said excitedly. "It's best if we keep this to ourselves. There is no corpse, and therefore, no proof. The contents of that trash disposal unit are incinerated every four hours, so by now that camper's body is charred powder."

Addison interrupted, "Y-Yes, but the camper is not going to be present for the morning roll call. Isn't that sufficient proof?"

Nigel held up his holographic hand, "Please let me finish. Even if you were able to produce a body, which you can't, unless of course you have suddenly acquired the divine ability to create a man from dust," Nigel's image grinned, "it would still be your word against Starck's, and who do you think the Sycamore Grand Commander is going to believe?" Nigel shrugged, as if the answer to his rhetorical question was obvious to Addison. It was. "If you make an attempt to get Starck disciplined for this, he'll find out you were the one who snitched on him and someone will get punished all right, but it will be you… by him!"

His bowels quivered. Curly back hair! The absolute last thing he wanted to do was invite Starck's wrath. "E-E-E-Excellent point. Y-Your logic is tighter than a Blessed's bottom," Addison said nervously. "I-It is best then if this remains our secret," he said. He put his right pointer finger up to his pursed lips, and then ran the finger across his throat, a figurative of the age signifying that it would "remain a secret till I perish." Nigel's image did the same.

Nigel's holographic face glanced from side to side cautiously, as if he were checking to see if anyone else was in the room. Then he spoke in a hushed voice, "I eavesdropped on two SS talking over caffeine tablets in their break room today, and I distinctly heard one of those sons of bitches say 'when we conclude the expansion project and the camp population is extended to include the unsightly as well, we are going to be so diffused with work…'"

Addison interrupted and said snobbishly, "D-Diffused? Diffused with work? Perchance you mean *deluged*?"

"Whatever, great master of the lexicon," Nigel said, rolling his holographic eyes. Addison couldn't tell if his friend was truly annoyed or just playing with him. Nigel continued, "Anyway, if you are done correcting me, what this SS was saying was that they would be so deluged with work that he would have to eliminate one of his extracurricular coitus companions. He confirmed what I have been telling you, Addison!"

"N-Nigel, 'worry not about tomorrow for tomorrow will worry about itself. Each day has enough trouble of its own,'" Addison said, quoting a verse from the Gospel according to Matthew in the Bible's New Testament, even though he knew Nigel would not know the reference. "Of course they are expanding the camp. Take a look around next time you are out and about. There are overweight people everywhere! There are plenty of Alpdonians who would benefit from a short stay at Sycamore."

"Of course I agree with you, but that is not what I've been hearing. I distinctly heard the SS say 'when the camps expand to include the unsightly…' Look at the size of these mud flaps," Nigel said tugging on his virtual lobes. "Do you honestly think I heard incorrectly?"

"N-Nigel, you're not approaching this rationally," Addison said. "How would weight loss benefit someone who is simply ugly? The purpose of the camps is to make the disgustingly obese less repulsive looking; it is certainly not to make them attractive. Are these malformed going to be more bearable to look at if they lose weight? I think not. It makes no difference if they are large or lean; they will still be ugly."

Nigel sighed, "Your reasoning is solid. I couldn't poke holes in it with a diamond-tipped awl, but I'm telling you what I heard, not what I believe." Nigel paused. "I heard something else you might find interesting. May I proceed?"

"Go ahead," Addison said, smiling, "regale me with another one of your fables, Aristotle."

"Aristotle? Perchance you mean Aesop?" Nigel said with a satisfied smile. "Two nights ago I bootlegged the Blessed news feed and a ruby-eyed propagandist, a real crotch-throbber, reported that Brock's Security Agents are investigating a rumor that an older looking lower caste citizen, a former educator, is smuggling people out of the country with a special emphasis on the so-called lower caste intelligentsia. Didn't you tell me that a Professor Pattycake moved into your living complex a short while ago? You said he was older looking. Could this be the 'professor' the penis-perpendicularizing propagandist was talking about?"

"Th-That is preposterous," Addison said, letting the fact that "perpendicularizing" wasn't a word pass. "F-Firstly, his name is Pankewitz not Pattycake; and secondly, there are probably hundreds of older looking lower caste educators in Alpdon. The chances of it being that pompous Protoceratops'[2] posterior from my living complex, *Doctor* Pankewitz, are about as slim as the chances of Mimi doing a handstand sans clothes on my sleeping platform."

"Fine, so it probably isn't Pankewitz, but I tell you, my friend, that someone is sneaking artists out of this country. Chagall and Masson, two painters from my complex, both vanished four fortnights ago. And remember the sculptor Jacques Lipshitz? (Addison couldn't help but smile at the name.) He went missing two fortnights ago!"

"N-Nigel, I am surprised at your naiveté," Addison said aloofly. "Creative types have a propensity to be peculiar. Haven't you ever visited the artists' district in Zodl? A few annums ago I fell asleep on the transport

---

2 Protoceratops is a dinosaur from the Late Cretaceous epoch that resembled a horse.

and ended up there. They are an irregular lot. I saw men with long braided beards that extended beyond their knees. I saw a woman wearing a sleeveless tunic with braided underarm hair! And you should have seen the clothes some of them were wearing – V-neck trousers that exposed their genitalia, long conical hats covered with images of crescent moons, stars and the twelve planets of our solar system... Yes, they are a colorful bunch. All three of the artists you mentioned are probably living in a Zodl kibbutz swapping coitus companions and licking horned toads."

"You have an answer for everything, my friend," Nigel said with a wide smile. Addison noticed that Nigel's holographic teeth were clean and white as talc. "It is time for me to go. May I have the pleasure of meeting you again with the new day's sun," Nigel said, giving a standard WASP goodnight wish, but with his tongue placed between his teeth and cheek.

Addison chuckled at his friend's sarcasm, and replied with the corniest WASP response he could think of, "Till then. It is my hope that you have a wonderful night's sleep and dreams sweeter than a mouthful of cane sugar confection." Nigel smiled. His holographic image retreated back into the origination panel. Addison mounted his sleeping platform. If he fell asleep within the next thirty minutes, he would log seven hours' sleep; he would feel good the next day; and he wouldn't have basalt-colored circles under his eyes. The moment his head hit his memory foam pillow, he started to doze. Then he remembered the dead camper. Nigel had diverted his attention, but the horror of what he had witnessed earlier returned. He couldn't keep his eyes closed. What a dreadful image! He stared at the water stains on his white puckered ceiling. He counted all the stained tiles, then all the untainted ones, and then tried to calculate the percentage of untainted versus stained tiles. After two hours of these mental gymnastics, fatigue finally overthrew his gruesome thoughts and he drifted off into a shallow and agitated sleep, clutching a fistful of bed sheet in each hand. ■

CHAPTER FOUR

BEAUTIFUL BIRTHER OF GOD! Why did he always dream about his teeth?!

Addison was seated in the penultimate row of a dark theater. He couldn't recall how he got there, but there he sat, his sweaty palms resting on his knees. A moving image was being shown, although he was sitting too far away to see it clearly. Even when he narrowed his eyes, it was still fuzzy, but apparently he was the only one having this problem as others scattered in the seats around him watched with no complaint.

Addison pried his feet off the tacky floor and slid forward in his seat. Gorgeous god! It was a naked woman! At least he thought she was naked – she was either naked or wearing a tight flesh-colored garment. One thing was certain; she had titanic breasts and they were bouncing up and down while she moved in a vertical motion. Was she climbing a rope? Or riding a horse? He deepened his squint but still couldn't tell. She flickered in and out of his focus like the last line of an eye chart. How frustrating! How badly he wanted to see her! He unconsciously clenched his teeth and slowly slid his lower jaw from side to side. Was she using an exercise stepper? Jumping on a trampoline? He saw two prominent shadows on her breasts. Could those be her nipples? If so, they were enormous! He slid forward even further in his seat. He was now dangerously close to touching the head of the man sitting in front of him, but he didn't care – he had to get a good look at this woman's body. Magnificent looking messiah, how he loved large nipples!

Addison became aware of a crunching sound. Was the woman walking with tap shoes on gravel? No, the noise wasn't coming from the image panel but from somewhere in the theater. Was someone in the audience eating something crispy? Perhaps thrice-fried dollops of HastyTasty? Or maybe it was… Ouch! Something pricked the roof of his mouth. He explored the area with his tongue and with a jolt of horror realized what had caused it

– broken shards of his teeth! He had clenched his jaw so violently that some of his teeth had shattered. He rolled his tongue around his mouth. Most of his molars were cracked. He ran his tongue over the jagged craters left in his gums and he tasted blood. Cautiously, he ran his tongue over his front teeth – two of them were damaged as well. A bolt of pain shot through his stomach. Oh horror! Facial birth blotch! Using his tongue, Addison pushed the pieces of shattered teeth to the left side of his mouth and then spit the mess into his right palm. His handful of broken teeth, saliva and blood looked like chewed corn and catsup. Addison moaned with grief; his broken teeth had broken his heart. He was now even less attractive.

He needed to get to a dentist. Would this be considered a cosmetic procedure? Would the Bureau of Health deny him care? He guessed this would be classified as a functional repair; after all, he couldn't chew food with his teeth in this condition. They wouldn't be concerned about aesthetics, however. They would repair them using a cheap material – probably an amalgam composite recycled from the mouths of ancient skeletons – and he would be encumbered with a metallic smile for the remainder of his life. How many more tribulations would god hurl at him? Hadn't he endured enough?

A high-pitched chirping sound interrupted Addison's thoughts. He looked around but no one else seemed to hear it. They were all still watching the image panel. How could that noise go unnoticed? It was deafening! Addison decided to get up to try to find the source and stop it. As he tried to stand up, however, an invisible restraint hugged tightly across his beltline, clamping him to his seat. The restraint gave a little and Addison sensed that if he really exerted himself, he could break free. The chirping got louder. If he didn't have a handful of broken teeth and blood he would have clapped his hands over his ears. Chirp! Chirp! Chirp! Pushing down hard with his elbows on the armrest, Addison gradually raised himself up until the restraint popped and he broke free.

Addison was laying on his sleeping platform. The brilliant morning light slapped him across the face and involuntarily his eyes snapped shut. This violent contraction of his ocular muscles sent a wave of pain from his brain stem to his eyebrows. He now recognized the chirping noise. It was his waking device. Addison growled and buried his face in his memory foam pillow. Another dream where his teeth were destroyed. What was the irritant in his subconscious that continually gave rise to this dream? He rolled over onto his back. His headache was historic. He found it difficult to quiet his mind and random, yet related, images bubbled up to its churning surface – Starck's enraged face, the dead camper's gravel-coated tongue, three piles of gray ash, his tarnished Oxygenator, Mimi's bouncing breasts, Nigel's plaque-coated teeth, three espresso tablets on a chrome plate (with no doily), Mimi's scowl, the nipples on the holographic saleswoman, and then, unexpectedly, the image of Dana – a precociously voluptuous girl with blonde hair and flat features – his partner for his only sexual experience. Memories from that encounter flooded back and stilled his roiling thoughts.

It took place at a social event during his third year of tertiary school. It was called a "dance," but most of the students were more interested in drinking the alcohol-augmented solutions they hid in their tunics than they were in dancing. Addison had never attended a dance before; however, his birther had badgered his cousin for a fortnight to bring him to this one and his cousin eventually and begrudgingly consented.

Addison's cousin was a good-looking early bloomer who had been sexually active (and bragging about it) since their final year of secondary school. He promised to bring Addison to the dance, but he didn't say he would stay with him. The moment they entered the school gymnasium – where these "dances" were held despite the slippery floor and horrible acoustics – he abandoned Addison. Overwhelmed by the loud music and flashing lights, and feeling awkward and self-conscious, Addison drifted to the wall and clung to it like a static-charged balloon. He watched with envy as the attractive and (therefore) popular students flirted with one another. Dana, his cousin's most recent coitus partner, was one of the few students actually dancing. Her ability to gyrate her hips in time with the music mesmerized Addison and he gawked at her with desperation, hunger and desire – a discordant leer that only a virgin adolescent male was capable of affecting. Dana obviously noticed him staring, it was hard not to, and she danced toward him smiling brazenly. Addison couldn't believe his luck! His cousin had discussed their latest trysts and one comment he'd made had wedged into Addison's thoughts – *She loves to go all the way.* Go all the way where? Addison wasn't sure, but it must have been a desirable destination as his cousin talked of it frequently and always with a triumphant smile on his face.

Soon she stood alongside Addison gyrating her hips, her left hip repeatedly brushing his left leg. Addison panted like a dehydrated dog. He could still remember her fragrance – roses and freshly tilled soil – the smell of promiscuity. The rose – bloomed, ripe and ready to be picked; the soil – plowed open, fertile and eager to be implanted. She leaned over and whispered in his ear, "Salutations, sexy. Do you mind if I ask you a question?"

"O-O-Of course," Addison stammered, careful to keep his head tilted downward so she couldn't see his teeth.

"Does your amazing looking cousin ever talk about me?"

Addison was crestfallen. "Y-Y-Yes he does… quite often actually," he answered, his voice trailing off in disappointment.

"Oh my heavens! He talks about me! He talks about me!" she said, leaping up and down with glee. On her fourth leap, the spiked heel of her shoe landed on Addison's big toe and he yelped in pain. Dana stopped jumping. "Act like a man and grow some fur on your testicles," she said, annoyed. "It couldn't have hurt that much. I only weigh forty-six kilos," she said, but then her tone abruptly changed. She twirled her hair with her finger and inclined her head coquettishly, "Addison, if you could tell your cousin how nice I was to you even though you are unattract… I mean, unfortunately not my type looks-wise, he would think I am a kind and caring person and he might choose me to be his girlfriend." (Strangely, that was the term used for a regular coitus companion back then even though girls often said "Let's just be friends" when they *didn't* want to engage in sexual activities with a male pursuer.) "Oh, if you promised me you would do that tonight, before the dance was over, I would be so grateful to you…

why, I would do anything, and I mean *anything*, for you." She said the last "anything" in a throaty whisper. Addison promised he would talk to his cousin and Dana delivered on her pledge, in an empty Societal Ethics classroom, which Addison considered poetically appropriate for their sordid transaction. All these years later, Addison couldn't recall every detail, but he did remember that he had finished the coital act only seconds after they had started. (Did she snicker afterward or was that a cough?)

That uncomfortable recollection kindled thoughts of another girl from that time in his life – "Fancy" Nancy Arnott, the object of his first secondary school crush. Nancy was a playful little brunette with a delightful face, a voluptuous figure and magnificently smooth skin the color of pure copper. Addison adored her. What he remembered best was that she had a unique way of flipping her head back to remove her hair from her face. Every time she did that head-flip, his heart jumped.

It had taken him the entire semester, but he finally mustered up the courage to ask her out. She had declined his offer with no hesitation, simply saying "No, thank you." However, Addison made the mistake of pressing her for a reason. After some protesting, she relented and, in an apologetic manner, said, "Well, Addison… The truth is that I just don't find you attractive. Nothing gets my hormones hopping more than a guy with a spectacular smile… Addison, I hate to break this to you, but your smile is light annums away from spectacular. Why don't you brush your teeth more often? Have you tried flossing with steel wool? Maybe then your smile wouldn't repulse me." She'd actually used the word "repulse." Fifteen years later, Addison was still dumbfounded by her cruel language. The appearance of his teeth forced her to move away from him, as if they were similarly charged poles from different magnets. He knew his smile was bad, but he never realized it was *repulsive*. To this day, every time he heard that word – that devastating word – his entrails ached from shame.

Addison dismounted his sleeping platform. His stroll down destructive memory lane had put him behind schedule. He would have to forgo his shower. He brushed his teeth with four strokes in two seconds, threw on the same soiled tunic and trousers he had worn the day before and left his living unit, paying no mind to how his hair looked or how much of his scalp was visible.

His first stop, as it was every morning, was the Caffeine Depot – a square building with an oxidized copper exterior and tinted gray glass – located south of his living complex and conveniently on his way to the Wakork Transport Station. He entered the Depot and saw Mimi working at the service desk. Why was she working? Today was supposed to be her day off. He considered turning around and walking out before she saw him, but he decided to stay. The only other place he could get caffeine would be at the Camp Sycamore cafeteria and he didn't want to wait that long for his daily fix. A caffeine-withdrawal headache was already gathering behind his left eye and he needed his espresso tablets to stave it off. No, he would stay and suffer the uncomfortable consequences of interacting with her.

Addison stood at the back of the queue and stayed out of Mimi's sight by slouching behind the man in front of him. He licked his fingers and ran them through his hair – a futile attempt to rearrange his hair and conceal his bald spot.

When the queue advanced, Addison saw that a Blessed woman with blonde hair and a delightful freckled face was now standing next to Mimi. Addison couldn't stop staring at her. Gorgeous god, he was a sucker for a cute face! Then he remembered. She was the new proprietor. With all that had happened the day before, he'd forgotten she was assuming ownership of the Depot today.

After four years of managing the Depot, Mr. Bentley, a good-natured Burdened with a round ruddy face and a potbelly that stuck out past his shoes, announced he was retiring. That was the official reason and the one communicated to the Depot customers by the Bureau of Commerce, but Addison knew it wasn't the real reason. Jolly old Bentley was forced to quit. The Wakork Commerce Secretary told Bentley that having a stunning, young-looking woman manage the Depot would put customers in "a mood more conducive to prolific procuring."

The new proprietor posed behind the service desk, her hand on her hip and her back arched, drawing attention to her breasts. They weren't large; they were perfectly proportioned to her sleek athletic figure. "Anything more than a mouthful is wasted anyway," his cousin used to say. He hadn't seen his cousin in at least five years – why did he think of him so often?

A strapping SS with a dazzling smile walked over to the service desk and started chatting with the new proprietor. Addison gasped. Sexy savior! It was Starck! He hadn't immediately recognized him. Starck's chiseled cheekbone-to-cheekbone smile revealed prominent dimples; he actually looked approachable and friendly, nothing like the frothing behemoth Addison had seen the previous evening. Starck was enamored with the new proprietor – Addison was certain of it – as he leaned toward her like a sun-starved plant to a day-lit window.

There was something unusual about the new proprietor. She was exceedingly beautiful, all Blessed women were, but she looked approachable. Usually exceedingly attractive women made him self-conscious, uncomfortable, aware of his own inadequacies, and he typically wanted to avoid being in their presence. But this woman didn't intimidate him. Her accepting eyes and adorable upturned nose put Addison at ease long before he made it up to the service desk. He watched as she greeted a disgusting Cursed man who was a few positions ahead of him in the queue. Addison was shocked. She was nice to him! Not just the typical counterfeit friendliness shown to customers by those who own retail businesses – she was *genuinely* nice to him (at least she appeared to be genuine). And the Cursed man had a goiter protruding from his neck that looked like a second head! Addison found it difficult to even look at the man, yet she was standing a few meters away chatting with him. What a remarkable display of humanity and kindness! What a strong stomach she must have!

Addison observed something else – the new proprietor's presence bothered Mimi. It was plastered all over Mimi's pinched face. And Addison thought he knew why – Mimi was envious of the new proprietor because she was no longer the most desirable woman in the Depot. Until today, most male customers, even upper caste ones, flirted with Mimi because even in her loose-fitting tunic, it was easy to see she had a wonderful body, definitely the body of a Blessed. There were a number of coital positions she could assume that would allow a man to enjoy her without having to see her face. But the new proprietor, with her blonde hair, mesmeric beauty, and lightly tanned and tightly toned body, was desirable from scalp to foot and enormously more attractive than Mimi. She would look fetching in any coital position.

As Addison got closer to the service desk, he could smell the new proprietor's perfume, an intoxicating scent of jasmine and espresso that made him feel confident and calm. The espresso with its pungent, nutty smell gave him a slight caffeine lift; the jasmine's soft, sweet aroma relaxed him.

She was wearing what Blessed women typically wore – a tight pair of shimmering super-micro-mini-shorts and scalloped breast cups. (How did those things stay on?) She had a small tattoo of an albino tiger on the cap of her left shoulder. Addison found her tattoo appealing even though he usually didn't like body art. He approached the service desk. "I-I will take three tablets please," Addison said to Mimi, who was servicing the queue minus her usual swagger. Seeing Mimi's obvious uneasiness brought Addison a perverse pleasure and removed the awkwardness of seeing her again. The new proprietor smiled at him, then said something to Mimi, who immediately turned and prepared his order. Addison breathed deeply, taking in her scent of jasmine and espresso, enjoying it so much that he felt as if he were in some way violating her.

She turned back toward Addison. "Delightful morning to you! Permit me to introduce myself. I am Otka, the new proprietor," she said effervescently. She focused her gold-flecked turquoise eyes on Addison's mud brown ones with such a look of sincerity that Addison averted his glance. She seemed to look into the core of Addison's essence.

When she finished talking, she narrowed her eyes and fixed her gaze on Addison's mouth. Oh no, his teeth! A tremor passed through his bowels. Did he inadvertently smile at her and show his teeth? "You have a bit of loam on the entrance to your oral cavity, sweetie," Otka said. She licked her finger, and then reached out toward Addison. He pulled back. Otka smiled and retracted her arm. "Aren't you a darling?" she said. "I'm not going to inflict harm upon you, sweetie. I just want to eradicate that unpleasant looking stain from your lip." She reached out again and gently rubbed his lip. "There, I have successfully removed it. Now you are copacetic."

Addison flicked his tongue over the area she had wiped. He could taste the jasmine and espresso from her finger as well as a dried dollop of HastyTasty that remained on his lip from his previous night's dinner. Although out of his field of vision, he could feel the angry glare from Starck, who had backed off a bit but was still within arm's length of Otka. Addison quickly glanced sideways and saw the face of that same enraged behemoth he had observed the night before. What a rapid change! A palpable fury radiated from Starck, sending another tremor through Addison's bowels. One more such tremor and he would have to make haste to a waste disposal facility.

Addison took his tablets from Mimi and nodded clumsily to Otka. "Th-Th-Th-Thanks. Have a bright day," he said, and turned and headed for the exit portal. What had he just said? Why in the luscious lord's name had he used the phrase "bright day"? What did it even mean? Absorbed in self-deprecating thought, Addison forgot to say "Open" when he approached the portal and he crashed nose first into the glass panel. The Depot instantly fell quiet.

"It is an antediluvian model, sweetie. You have to speak to it to open it," Otka said with pity in her voice. A male voice shouted "canker!" disguised as a cough and the Depot erupted in laughter.

"I-I-I know. I-I-I just forgot," he replied. He said, "O-O-Open," and the glass panel yielded. Addison walked through the portal with his eyes on his shoes and his shoulders slumped. His cheeks and neck now matched the ruby red roses that brightened the Depot entrance.

Addison popped two espresso tablets into his mouth. His nose still burned from the impact with the glass panel, but he dared not rub it.

Numerous similar experiences had taught him that doing so would probably set off another round of snickers. Why did people take such pleasure in the misfortune of others? He had to admit that he found it amusing whenever he witnessed someone committing a faux pas. Just last fortnight, a Cursed man stumbled as he entered the transport caboose and tumbled face first into the shapely derriere of a Favored female passenger. Laughter filled the caboose and although Addison felt sorry for the Cursed man, he laughed right along with everyone else. Why had he laughed? He thought for a moment. He laughed because it had made him feel better about his own embarrassing moments; he laughed because it really did look funny; and he laughed most of all because that time it wasn't him. But this time it was… and it hurt.

Addison bit down on his tablets and swirled the pieces between his cheek and gum. He had discovered that this was the quickest way to get his beloved caffeine into his system. After his public humiliation, he needed some chemical assistance to boost his mood. As the caffeine took effect, it improved not only his disposition but also his posture. Like one of those pictorial timelines depicting the fable of Darwinian evolution, the caffeine transformed Addison from a hunched-over, knuckle-dragging *Homo habilis* to an upright *Homo sapiens*. He walked to the transport station with his back straight and his head up.

He thought of Otka. He had never been treated with such kindness by such a beautiful woman before. No, that wasn't entirely accurate. Beautiful women had been nice to him in the past, but it was always so contrived, so deceitful, and he knew they were trying to manipulate him into doing something that served their purposes, not his. Otka was different. She seemed authentic, and from his limited observations, she appeared to see something of value in everyone she interacted with, no matter their caste.

Meeting Otka had improved Addison's mood well beyond the effects of the caffeine. As he waited for the transport, he spontaneously smiled. For the first time in a long time, he forgot all about hiding his teeth. ■

CHAPTER FIVE

❖

ADDISON SAT ON A PARK BENCH at the northwestern end of Grand Square. When he dismounted the transport at the Wakork station, the weather was so nice and the breeze so refreshing that he decided to enjoy the arriving dusk by doing a little lady-looking in Grand Square. He found a bench right near the entrance to the Blessed compound – a prime location for ogling gorgeous women. Rather quickly, however, his disposition soured. Sure, there were plenty of attractive women to admire, but each one was affixed to a good-looking man! And watching all these happy couples traipse by with their hands on each other's derrieres depressed him. When would he find a woman to cohabitate with? Would he *ever* find a woman to cohabitate with? I'll find someone, he thought, just as soon as my bald spot sprouts new hair, my teeth whiten and the plump in my belly migrates to my biceps. He found his last condition funny and he snorted sarcastically. Why wasn't he attractive? Did god really predetermine who to bless and who to pass over? Or were Addison's bad looks simply the result of bad fortune? If one of his POP's other sperm had fertilized his birther's egg, might he have been a Blessed... or at least a Favored?

A gorgeous couple walked past him. Look at those tanned and toned legs; not a hair or a blemish on either pair! Addison burned with envy. They were both looking right at him, but neither of them made a friendly nod or gesture. In fact, the expressions on their beautiful and tanned faces reminded Addison of the way people regarded transport seat lickers (an unusual fetish of the age) and personal injury lawyers (often the same ones who engaged in this fetish) – a sneer expressing both physical disgust and moral disdain. Just then something brushed up against Addison's leg. He pulled his leg back instinctively and glanced down to see what it was. He laughed with delight. It was a dog! Addison loved dogs. During his childhood, he'd had two – Pots and Difo. Pots was his first – a black-eared beagle Addison had found wandering around Grand Square without identification. Difo was his second – a small, black-haired poodle given to him by Nigel during their primary school years after Nigel's poodle had a litter of seventeen puppies.

Addison crouched down to pet the dog – a new designer breed that was a popular accessory for many Blessed couples – a rainbow-colored Affenpinscher infused with rabbit DNA. This cute creature was bred to be easy to care for and tidy. Its coat barely sheds and it is coprophagous.[3]

The dog was attached to a long leash held by a statuesque Blessed woman who was walking toward Addison with an ugly glower on her beautiful face. Addison barely took notice of her, however, as he stroked the animal's long pink ears and cooed to it softly. The dog's left ear was flopped over and Addison straightened it out by gently stroking it upward. The dog's garnet-colored eyes were half closed and its orange and green pom-pom tail wagged; it was obviously enjoying what Addison was doing. When the dog's owner got closer to Addison, she barked, "Next time ask before you lay a hand on my pet, you subhuman Cursed troll!"

While he continued to caress the dog's bent ear, Addison shot back with uncharacteristic forcefulness, angered that this Blessed woman not only dropped a prejudiced remark, but that she also got his caste wrong. "I-It is called a 'pet' for a reason. I am simply engaging in an act the dog enjoys. Do you see the look of contentment on its face? Maybe if you gave it some attention rather than use it as a way to draw attention to yourself, it wouldn't run over and solicit affection from complete strangers!" The woman gave Addison a startled look. She apparently hadn't expected him to bark back.

"Let's go, Blondie," the Blessed woman said. She jerked the leash toward herself and lifted the dog into the air, away from Addison. The dog

---

3   Feeds on its own dung.

yelped in pain. The poor animal landed in front of her and she kicked it in the ribs. The dog yelped again. Addison seethed with rage as he watched them exit the Square. How could she treat an animal that way? What a pitiless bitch! The dog was named "Blondie," the same name as Hitler's pet German shepherd. How sadly appropriate, he thought. He fantasized about running up behind this cruel woman and punching her in the back of her head. Oh how satisfying that would be!

Located near the entrance to the Blessed compound was the new four-dimensional holographic tribute to Brock. Addison walked over to it. This latest iteration had been active for five fortnights; however, this was the first time Addison had approached it. As he stood amongst a small group admiring the presentation, he was struck by how life-like the rendering appeared. The tribute was a depiction of a crouching Brock welcoming a small group of gorgeous and blonde children. Brock was speaking to them in such a soft tone that Addison had to step closer to hear what he was saying. Even up close the rendering looked incredibly real and Addison felt a surge of awe, as if he were actually in Brock's presence. He was surprised by his reaction. He completely disagreed with Brock's ideology, but as the leader of the country, he was still someone who commanded respect, whether Addison agreed with him or not.

Brock's mustache quivered as he drew his breath to speak. "All that we do now, we do for you," Brock said, smiling. Addison caught a whiff of something sweet and noticed that a freckled little girl standing next to Brock's bent right knee was licking a red and black sugar shaft.

To the left of Brock was a scroll with the transcript of his inaugural address. It had been a little more than four years since Brock seized office. Addison had watched his inauguration from this same Square. Addison waved his hand over the top portion of the speech. The subtle change in temperature from the heat of his hand highlighted the text. Addison chuckled, surprised, as Brock stood up from his crouch and the children morphed into a chest-high podium constructed from lacquered blond wood (naturally).

Brock began reciting the text Addison had selected. "As I take office today, there are more than six million citizens of Alpdon that are out of work. Our economy has suffered a protracted depression that has dropped our Gross National Income ranking from tenth to ninety-seventh. Ninety-seventh! Alpdon has already met two of the three criteria necessary for third world nation classification. Fellow Citizens, now is the time to speak the truth, the whole truth, frankly and boldly. Our nation is floundering and without decisive leadership, and unwavering support of this leadership, this nation will not endure.

"Values have shrunk to fantastic levels; taxes have risen; our ability to pay has fallen; the withered leaves of industrial enterprise lie on every side; companies find no markets for their products or services; and the savings of thousands of families are gone. More importantly, a host of unemployed citizens face the grim problem of existence and an equally great number toil with little return. Only a foolish optimist can deny the dark realities of the moment.

"This is because our past leadership has failed. True, they tried. But their efforts have been cast in the pattern of an outworn tradition, taking the form of government assistance – welfare – which has now become so bloated that one out of every five citizens accepts some form of it. And since we are speaking the truth, let me say that those populating the welfare docket are not Alpdon's best-looking and brightest; they are not the ones blessed by our god with beauty, intelligence and ambition. Those who take assistance require assistance and this must change now, right now, if we are to survive! Welfare is not an investment in Alpdon's future, but rather a Class IV hemorrhage that is bleeding our country to economic death.

"Today I declare a new revolution – a revolution against the old system of inclusive politics that put the needs of the incompetent and incapable alongside the needs of the talented and productive. Therefore I say that this last election was the election to end all elections!" Brock slapped the podium with the palm of his right hand for emphasis. "We are now one party, one people, with one common purpose – to restore this nation to its former glory!" When Brock finished reciting the passage Addison had highlighted, he stood motionless.

Addison waved his hand over the next passage and Brock resumed speaking, "The cost of this revolution will be high and it will require much sacrifice; but to stand by and do nothing is to sacrifice our prosperity and our way of life. To stand by and do nothing means that we are passing this burden to our offspring, and to their offspring. Are we going to take the easy way out and let them live in a third-world or even a fourth-world nation? Of course we aren't. Providence has placed me here; I am the right man at the right time. I will do what is necessary, no matter how distasteful, to ensure a flourishing economic environment for our beloved and beautiful offspring."

Addison sneezed violently. A dollop of mucous flew from his nose and passed through a later portion of Brock's speech. The warmth of the mucous highlighted the text and Brock's image talked in hyperspeed until it caught up. Some onlookers laughed – Addison wasn't sure if it was because Brock's high-pitched voice sounded humorous or because he had done something so disgusting. He sighed. No one would be foolish enough to laugh at even a holographic representation of Brock in such a public place. No, they were laughing at him. Hardly a day passed when he didn't embarrass himself in some way. "Thanks again god," he muttered sarcastically.

The holographic image of Brock resumed speaking normally, "If you are equipped with the god-given abilities necessary to help this nation pull itself out of this economic death spiral, it will be visible to all. And for whatever divine reason the almighty has withheld his blessing from you, and this nation is forced to expend its valuable resources to support you, this too will be visible to all." Addison passed his hand over the text and paused Brock's speech. He stopped it there because activating the finale of

Brock's speech would just stir up a painful memory. It was during the last part of his speech that Brock announced his plan to conduct an Evaluatory Census of each Alpdonian. Even now, four years later, Addison's cheeks prickled warmly when he thought back to the humiliating experience of his evaluation.

The day following Brock's inauguration, pairs of trackless, white-paneled transports appeared in every major population center in Alpdon. Addison was summoned early in the census, before word of mouth on what to expect had time to spread.

He arrived early on his assigned day. Two transports were positioned one in front of the other, fifteen meters or so apart, on a vacant strip of land just outside the Blessed entrance to Grand Square. A large Lucite desk mounted with a Recognition Unit was set up ten meters in front of the fore transport and a small, four-post, metallic canopy provided the desk with shelter. Sitting behind the desk was a stern-faced but unusu-ally attractive woman. Her hair was pulled back in a tight ponytail and she sat perfectly erect even though she was sitting on a bench with no back support. She was smartly dressed in a tight brown spandex uniform. Her nipples poked out from under her uniform top so prominently that Addison was embarrassed to look for fear that she might rebuke him for gawking. It was the standard uniform for Brock's Security Agents (or SA familiarly), a paramilitary group responsible for overseeing activi-ties that fell under Brock's domestic agenda. The woman had dazzling sulfur-colored eyes, but Addison only looked at them briefly; he was too intimidated to make eye contact with her.

Addison approached the desk cautiously, with his hands in front of him, fingers up and palms out in a defensive posture, as if he were half expecting the sulfur-eyed beauty to leap out from behind the desk and scratch his eyes out. "Present your right wrist for scanning," she said in a voice as taut as her uniform. She grabbed Addison's wrist and pulled it toward the RU more forcefully than Addison expected and he nearly lost his balance. Her fingers were feminine but strong and they smelled of cloves and spent gunpowder – a manly scent for such a beautiful woman. Addison found the dichotomy alluring.

After registering Addison, she ordered him to report to the SA standing in front of the fore transport. He was an implausibly handsome man, tall and blond with angular features and a lean and athletic physique. Addison, still intimidated and feeling insecure, fixed his eyes on the SA's highly polished black boots. With mild surprise, he noticed that he could actually see his reflection in the buffed leather. After a few seconds, Addison redirected his gaze, bothered because the contours of the SA's boot distorted Addison's face like a fun house mirror and made his nose look like an eggplant with blackheads.

The athletic SA directed Addison to take a seat in the front transport, which was fashioned as a waiting facility. It was a windowless room with gleaming white porcelain walls. Concealed lamps flooded it with cold light and a shallow chrome bench ran along the wall. As Addison entered, the SA shouted at him through the entrance portal, "Sit on the ledge and wait quietly!" Addison sat down on the ledge directly across from the door. He dropped his chin to his chest and stared lazily at the floor, letting his vision meander in and out of focus on the cross-laid tiles. The athletic SA entered the transport and shouted, "Hall, Addisoy, on your feet now!" Startled, Addison let out an involuntary squeak sending the SA into a raucous fit of laughter. For the first of many times that day, Addison's face and neck flushed warm from humiliation.

Addison was led to the rear transport. It was larger than the front transport and equipped with two equally sized chrome-finished examination tables. A flimsy changing screen was located behind each one. Equidistant between the two examination tables stood a polished chrome chest of drawers. The same gleaming white porcelain from the front transport adorned the floor, ceiling and walls. Inscribed on the long far wall in sleek sans serif black letters was a list of physical characteristics. Addison would learn shortly that these were the appraisal measures for the evaluation. Under the FEMALE column were listed skin quality, facial shape, lip density, cheekbone height, hair density, eye color, eyelid density, nose width, head size, body fat percentage and height. Under the MALE column were listed facial shape, skin quality, eye color, hair density, hair coverage, eyelash density, chin prominence, body fat percentage and height. Below that was the following table:

	MALE	FEMALE
Blessed	< 20	< 25
Favored	20 - 40	25 - 40
Burdened	41 - 70	41 - 70
Cursed	> 70	> 70

Cold air was blowing in the room although Addison didn't see any vents. The athletic SA entered the room behind Addison and said, "Go behind that partition and change into this." He tossed a neatly folded examination gown to Addison. "Put your tunic and trousers on the hooks. When you are dressed, take a seat on the table to my left." The SA spun smoothly on his right heel and exited the room. Addison walked behind the screen and put on the diaphanous paper gown. It fit horribly. One sleeve was a bit longer than the other and the gown hung down around his neck just short of his nipples. Once dressed, he quickly walked on the balls of his feet over the cold floor and took a seat on the edge of the examination table, pinching the two ends of the gown together behind his back to ensure that his bottom rested on the thin material and not directly on the cold metal. Addison looked down with disgust at the dozen or so scaly eczema sores that ran from his ankles to his knees. He crossed his feet in a futile attempt to hide them.

A shorter SA entered the transport. He was clad in a white smock so bright that it made Addison's eyes hurt. Addison assumed he was a doctor. Following a bit too closely behind him was a younger-looking male SA, dressed in a tight ivory spandex uniform – Addison guessed he was some sort of nurse or assistant. Addison noticed that, like the comely woman sitting at the Registration Desk, this man's nipples were poking through his tight shirt as well – a consequence, Addison guessed, of the coolness of the room. This SA was slender, effeminate and attractive, although he was more beautiful than handsome. In his delicate hands, he carried a digital input device. "Stand!" the doctor commanded. Addison stood and winced as his feet hit the cold floor. The doctor pulled a quartz-coated card out of his breast pocket and read it to Addison rapidly, with no inflection in his voice. "By allowing your wrist to be scanned, you have given your approval to undergo this Sanctification Evaluation. Failure to finish this evaluation or abide by the final results will be considered a prime crime and punishable, as all prime crimes, by lifetime incarceration at a labor camp or extermination." The doctor paused, apparently letting Addison digest the magnitude of what he had said.

"This Sanctification Evaluation has been instituted to create an objective standard that quantifies, in an atmosphere devoid of bias or emotion, the amount of blessing our god has bestowed upon each citizen of Alpdon. You will be given a score of one to ten for each appraisal category. Do you acknowledge reading the list of measures posted on the interior walls of this room?" Addison didn't answer; he thought the question was rhetorical.

The nurse standing behind the smocked SA yelled out in a drag queen's whinny, "Answer, you malformed ninny!"

Addison quickly said "Y-Y-Yes" and his neck and face began to burn again. The doctor continued, "Since you are a male, the perfect score for you would be nine. Your actual score, which will obviously be significantly larger, will then be multiplied using Dr. Leegmen's Bilateral Symmetry Coefficient.[4] An explanation of how that is calculated is available at the RU

---

4   The Bilateral Symmetry Coefficient (BSC) was an empirical measure of facial attractiveness created by Longwood's Minister of Health Services, Dr. Leegmen. It was a summary measure that utilized the "Rule of Fifths" for frontal facial evaluation – the Ricketts E (esthetic line) for the nose to lip to chin relationship, the Holdaway H (harmony line) for lip positioning, the Nasofacial angle, the Nasofrontal angle, the Nasomental angle, the Mentocervical angle and the Frankfort Plane for lateral facial evaluation. A perfect bilaterally symmetrical face had a BSC coefficient of 1.0; less symmetrical faces had BSCs of greater than 1.0 with the maximum coefficient capped at 4.0. It was the institution of this system that led to the labeling of Leegman and his political philosophy as Face-ism.

desk, but given your appearance, it is more than probable that you would have a difficult time understanding it. This final number will constitute your Sanctification Indication Number or SIN for brevity's sake." The doctor returned the laminated card back to his pocket. "Let me simplify this for you as it is obvious to me that you have not comprehended what I have just said – the lower your SIN, the higher your level of blessing."

The doctor crouched down, grabbed the hem of Addison's gown and lifted it, revealing the eczema sores on Addison's legs. He said, "Acute eczema; probably caused by overt insecurity and the inability to cope with slightly elevated levels of stress." While he spoke the nurse's fingers moved frantically over the keypad of his handheld digital input device. Shame stimulated Addison's adrenal gland and caused his heart to beat faster, once again rushing blood to the capillaries in his neck and face. His cheeks flushed and a bead of sweat rolled down his neck. Instinctively, he reached down to rub his polished rocks but he wasn't wearing his clothes. He would have to endure the remainder of this evaluation separated from his comforting stones.

The doctor grabbed a fistful of Addison's gown, in the area right above Addison's stomach, pulled swiftly upward with one strong move and ripped the gown off. Addison now stood naked. The nurse made a slight noise; it could have been a cough or it could have been a snicker. Addison assumed it was a snicker as the cold temperature in the examination room had caused his manhood to shrivel as if he had just stepped out of an iced-water soaking chamber.

The doctor reached into the chest of drawers and retrieved a chrome caliper. He used it to pinch folds in Addison's skin; first at his ankle, then at his knee, then his waistline, and finally on the back of his upper arm. The doctor clucked his tongue after each pinch and called out Addison's results with the same tone a school administrator uses to call out a detention list. The doctor put aside the caliper and pulled from the open draw a device that looked like a pair of copper binoculars with five laser pointers mounted between the lenses. He pointed the peculiar-looking device at Addison's face and depressed a small white button over the left lens, sending needle thin beams of ruby red light in a zigzag pattern all over Addison's face. Starting at Addison's (receding) hairline, he worked his way down Addison's face, slowly pointing and clicking the device, all the while calling out cryptic sounding measurements to the nurse, "one dot four millimeters, three over six over five, seven to the seventh over seven…" He pointed the device at Addison's nose, and then stopped. He exhaled in disgust and lowered the device. "How am I supposed to read the beams if you keep blushing like a coital neophyte on her initial night of cohabitation? Settle down, you weak-minded fecal midge!"

The doctor paused for a few seconds and then tried the device again. He raised it to his eyes and immediately lowered it. "If I have to wait for this fecal midge to un-blush, it is going to put us off schedule!" Muttering to himself, the doctor reached into a lower drawer and pulled out a clear container of white powder. He shook the powder generously onto a gauze pad and swiftly slapped Addison across both cheeks with it. Addison's head was engulfed in a chalky plume and some powder entered his mouth, causing him to gag. "Don't get sick on my floor!" the doctor warned. Addison's face was coated in white powder, evidently allowing the doctor to use his device effectively, and soon he finished his evaluation. After a few moments of inputting data, the nurse looked up and announced in a falsetto voice with tight lips, possibly suppressing a smile, "His final SIN is 49."

"Burdened!" the doctor shouted. He spun on his heels and left the examination transport with the nurse still following a bit too closely behind. ■

CHAPTER SIX

❖

ADDISON SAT ON THE CORNER of his sleeping platform leafing through *The Directory of Rocks and Minerals*, a printed handbook given to him by his master POP. With practically all media in digital format these days, Addison found it pleasurable to run his fingers over the smooth paper. The pages were slightly yellowed and the volume smelled musty, so Addison turned the pages carefully; a few had already broken free from the threadbare binding. This morning he had been reading the profile on quartz. It was his favorite mineral because it was attractive yet tough. He wished he was the same.

He studied the different images – one that showed the mineral's typical prism and pyramid crystal habits; another that showed a scientist making a scratch on a specimen's surface with a diamond-tipped awl, illustrating why quartz was ranked seventh on the Mohs Scale of Hardness. Addison was trying to commit these images to memory, making sure he would be able to recognize the mineral in the event he should stumble upon some specimens during his occasional walks down by the Luvista River. He had two other printed volumes, *Lessons Forgotten – A Comprehensive Account of All Seven World Wars* and *The Origin of Species*, a book that his master POP had called the "greatest piece of fiction ever published." Besides some undergarments and one outfit, these were the only personal items he was allowed to bring with him when the Rehabitation Initiative occurred soon after the SIN evaluations were completed.

Early one morning (Addison couldn't recall the time, but he remembered that it was still dark), three tremendously muscled and surprisingly courteous SA had entered his living unit, roused him from his sleeping platform and told him he was being relocated. He was asked to get dressed (Addison put on the clothes he had worn the day before), then choose one piece of personal property (the SA in charge, perhaps because he was a bibliophile, had generously decided to count all three books as one piece of property). He was taken via trackless transport a few blocks away to his new living quarters, a recently renovated student dormitory from the bankrupted University of Wakork. The night before the move, Addison had forgotten to remove his three polished rocks from his trousers and so he was able to surreptitiously bring them along.

While his new living unit was significantly smaller than his previous one, it contained a number of upgrades that made it an enormous improvement. It was equipped with a security system (a Recognition Unit), a new sleeping platform, a holographic receiver and decoder, and best of all, a pantry stocked with a fortnight's supply of HastyTasty – a new, inexpensive food staple developed by Brock's Bureau of Nourishment. In this new living unit, Addison was more secure, more comfortable, more informed and better fed than he had been since the country officially announced its bankruptcy and defaulted on all international and national debts five years prior. With his new living unit also came steady employment – a job as a camp worker at the newly opened Camp Sycamore. Although Addison wasn't thrilled with the idea of watching after those the government classified as physically unfit for public appearance, it allowed him to spend some time in the fresh air and was much more desirable than some of the other jobs assigned to lower caste members – factory production line worker, farm worker, sanitation worker, or a horrible job that Nigel had told him about, "pipe unclogger" at the Biological Solid Waste Removal Plant. Of course given Nigel's penchant for practical jokes, Addison wasn't sure if that was an actual job.

For the past five years, Addison had been fortunate enough to get occasional work as a day laborer in the legal department of the Bureau of Economics – spending twelve hours a day filing away notices of bankruptcy from citizens of Alpdon, as well as the numerous subpoenas and liens issued from countries and international businesses owed money by Alpdon. Even though the work was tedious, Addison was glad to have it, especially since more than forty percent of the country was unemployed. But even this steady part-time work meant he could only afford to eat harvest bread, at that time a staple of Alpdon. Harvest bread was cheap to buy and plentiful. Made from dark brown or black dough, it was the consistency of pressed sawdust and smelled and tasted like damp cardboard. In fact, Nigel claimed he had actually found a small piece of cardboard in one of the loaves he had purchased.

Like most citizens, Addison ate this bread for every meal. And like practically all of those citizens, he was tired of it. So while initially Addison had felt a bit violated by Brock's reforms, the steady employment and the plentiful (and more palatable) food he now received allowed him to overlook restrictions that might have upset him in more prosperous times. And what was true for Addison was true for all the citizens of Alpdon, no matter their caste.

Addison shut his book and glanced over at his holographic timepiece. It was 09:12 –Addison smirked at his ability to recall historical dates – the month and day America surrendered to the CanaMexican alliance to end World War IV.

Today was Sunday, his day off, and riding a rare wave of spontaneity, Addison decided that this morning he would attend a church service. During his travels around Wakork, he had recently seen huge crowds at the local diocese and he was curious as to why there was such a surge in ecclesiastical fervor. Addison hadn't shadowed a church entrance portal in twenty years, but he still remembered how boring the service had been – the jaded, ill-tempered priest, his face set in a perpetual frown, performing the service in a passionless rote to a small group of regulars who participated with unbridled apathy and spent most of the time looking around the sanctuary to see who showed up and how they were dressed. What he remembered most was the unique smell of the church – the odor of sweat and mildew from the priest's seldom-washed garments commingled with the smoke from hundreds of tiny candles lit by parishioners praying for a lottery win, a better job, a better-looking coitus companion, or for those who considered themselves especially "holy," all three. Church attendance had declined steadily over the years and when Brock took office it was estimated to be at an all-time low. What had changed to warrant the sudden popularity? Why was interest in religion born again? And why were citizens so focused on looks attending a place that focused on spiritual matters? He wanted to find out.

At 10:15, with two espresso tablets dissolving in his mouth, a back-up tablet in his right pocket and his polished rocks in his left, Addison stood in the long queue that weaved into Our Lady of the Immaculate Reflection. As he watched the other parishioners enter the rather ordinary looking chrome building that just four years prior had been a convention center, he thought back to the political parties Brock and his supporters often held here prior to the last election. They were always raucous affairs, and the attendees, nicknamed "Zanies" due to their rowdy behavior, used to keep Addison up most of the night. They chanted party slogans and sang bawdy nautical-sounding songs, but the loudest noise came from thousands of leather-soled boots slapping the concrete as the "Zanies" goose-stepped around the Square in perfect unison.

Addison didn't notice too many lower caste citizens entering the church. As he scanned the crowd, he was shocked to see Starck entering the church with Otka. And they were definitely together as he had his massive hand planted firmly on her tight little derriere. Bulbous hooknose! Addison swore silently. What was she doing with him anyway? She seemed to be too kind to be doing "the nasty" with someone as wicked as Starck.

Addison entered the church nave. The good-looking parishioners were dipping their fingers into a small brass dish of holy water located just inside the entrance portal. Addison did the same. Uggh! Addison jerked his fingers back. It wasn't water! Addison looked at his fingers – he had dipped them into a clear gel that smelled of witch hazel and Omani frankincense. He glanced around at the other parishioners – the good-lookers were putting it on their faces! He observed them a bit longer and then realized what they were doing. They were dabbing the gel on the corners of their eyes and mouths... they were "anointing" their wrinkles. As Addison looked down at his wet fingers, a tall male usher with platinum blond hair walked over and grabbed his wrist. "Hey! Your kind can't use that," he said sternly. "Wipe those fingers clean on that ill-fitting tunic of yours." Addison did as he was told. "Now, you go there," he said, pointing to a set of dilapidated wooden bleachers at the back of the auditorium. When the usher extended his arm to point, his short sleeve rode up, revealing a well-defined triceps muscle that looked as hard as a Jupiterian diamond. A large sign was suspended over the bleachers that read "Court of the Neglected." How charming, Addison thought sarcastically. Why not just call it, "Seating Area for the Repugnant?"

Addison walked down the narrow aisle toward the bleachers feeling self-conscious. Should he swing his arms a little less or even more? How long should each step be? Did Starck and Otka see him? By the time he arrived at the bleachers, he had droplets of sweat soaking his forehead and dripping down his temples. This service was already much different – the ones he had attended as a child were never this stressful. He found a spot on the first bleacher next to a co-Burdened – an overweight man, fat but not grotesquely obese, who appeared to be in his early forties (although it was quite possible that he was much older as wrinkles were usually not as prevalent on puffy faces).

The auditorium was sparsely decorated. A large chrome altar sat at the front of the cavernous room on top of a short platform. Suspended high from the ceiling over the altar was a life-sized golden statue of Jesus. Jesus was on a cross, but rather than being nailed to it as Addison remembered, the cross was laid flat and Jesus was standing on top of it. Something else was different. Jesus was much better looking than Addison remembered. He had outstanding cheekbones, muscular arms and legs, and an extraordinary set of "virtuous" abdominal muscles. Even his hair looked different. Addison recalled it being matted down with sweat and blood and topped with a crown of thorns; this Jesus had thick, wavy hair billowing out from a bronze crown studded with large purple crystals. (Addison guessed the crystals were amethyst.) The gold plating actually made the savior's hair look blond. Addison noticed another oddity. Like the Jesus Addison remembered from the church services of his youth, this Jesus was posed with both arms raised to shoulder height, parallel to the ground; however, he was not pitifully splayed with his chin resting on his chest and nails driven through his hands and feet as Addison recalled. This Jesus held his head high, his palms and feet were nail free, and he affected a powerful, defiant posture. It looked to Addison as if he were about to say, "You *wish* you looked as good as me." Inscribed in polished chrome letters below the cross were two passages of scripture:

I AM PERFECT IN BEAUTY — Ezekiel 27:3

THE LORD'S FLOCK WILL SPARKLE IN HIS LAND LIKE JEWELS IN A CROWN. HOW ATTRACTIVE AND BEAUTIFUL THEY WILL BE. — Zechariah 9:16-17

A gong sounded and the ushers closed the metal doors to the sanctuary. The lights dimmed, a single drum began pounding slow and steady, and a single white spotlight shone on the gold-plated Jesus. It waxed and waned in time with the beating drum. The beam refracted off the buffed statue and sent flecks of brilliant light out in every direction. A large inflatable silver ball the size of a nuclear summer squash appeared from somewhere near the altar and was repeatedly pounded high in the air by tightly formed clusters of toned and tanned arms. A particularly big hit brought a collective "ahhh" from the parishioners; however, everyone in Addison's section remained quiet.

Feeling uncomfortable, Addison wedged his hand into his left pocket and rubbed his rocks, wondering briefly if doing so in a house of worship was in some way disrespectful. He glanced around and noticed that others in his section looked uncomfortable as well. While lower caste members were not discouraged from attending, they certainly weren't encouraged

- their special section, poor seating conditions and great distance from the altar made it clear that the service was not intended for them.

The metallic ball was pounded back and forth across the auditorium by those closest to the stage and the tribal drum continued to beat faster and faster until it was impossible to differentiate one beat from another. A broad-shouldered man with sandstone-colored skin ran onto the stage wearing a snug brown bodysuit that matched the color of his skin so closely that for a moment Addison thought he was naked. The man (Addison assumed he was the priest) looked handsomely distinguished. His white hair was curly and short and he wore a closely trimmed white beard. He appeared to be in his mid-thirties, but Addison got the impression that he was older, perhaps even in his mid-fifties, as he moved with the grace and poise of a much older man. The parishioners clapped in unison (except for those in Addison's section) as the priest stomped around the altar flexing his blocky muscles. A white spotlight was aimed at him and Addison noticed that the priest was following the spotlight rather than the other way around and that he was always a beat or two behind – his routine was obviously choreographed but not well rehearsed. This continued for three minutes or so, and then the priest suddenly silenced the drum and the clapping parishioners with a long sweep of his right hand. When he spoke, it was in a deep melodic voice with a wide range of inflection.

"In the Old Testament, the ancients were instructed by god (he pronounced it as "gaaahad") to sacrifice an unblemished lamb, one without any visible defect or flaw, to atone for their congenital waywardness." Some of the more expressive parishioners put their hands in the air and shouted over and over what at first sounded to Addison like "amen, amen, amen," but as he listened to it longer, he realized they were shouting "what a man, what a man, what a man." The priest continued, "In the New Testament, this old covenant with god was replaced, superseded by a new, more merciful covenant. Now god commands his followers to strive for perfection in order to honor and worship Jesus, who serves as the propitiation for our sinful ways, and as such, has become the new sacrificial lamb for god. The apostle Paul further clarifies our duties to god by urging us to express our love and adoration for our 'lamb of god,' our perfect savior, Jesus, by offering our bodies as *perfect sacrifices* to him. Heavenly offspring, I ask you, is my offering perfect?" The priest grabbed the front of his shirt and in one swift movement ripped it off, revealing a taut and muscular physique that, given the complexion of his skin, looked like chiseled russet-colored marble. He spread both arms high and wide, flexed his pectoral muscles and flapped his hands up and down, imploring the crowd to cheer. It wasn't necessary. They cheered wildly; many of the parishioners sitting close to the altar leapt to their feet with their arms held high up over their heads and their palms pointed skyward. The priest allowed this to continue for about five minutes, then quieted the noise with another wave of his right hand. "Now then, let us rise and perfect our bodies together as we strive to create an unblemished offering that will be pleasing to our flawless and immutable god. Let us begin our exertion of faith."

The priest led those who were standing in a bizarre yet strangely familiar form of calisthenics. Those seated on the floor of the auditorium joined with the priest – kneeling, standing, genuflecting, and then all together they shouted, "One!" Kneeling, standing, genuflecting, shouting, "Two!" To Addison's relief, none of the wretched-looking parishioners in his section participated, although the forehead of the fat man next to Addison was sopped with sweat apparently just from watching. He definitely smelled like stale urine, Addison decided, and with that he had had enough. The odor of the man sitting next to him was making him nauseous and this service wasn't edifying – in fact, watching all these gorgeous people exercise their beautiful bodies was depressing. With all of the parishioners in the lower sections moving, now was a good time for him to make an inconspicuous exit. Addison rose quickly from his seat and the question again flitted through his thoughts as to why "gaaahad" had not created him as a Blessed... or at least a Favored. It never occurred to him to be grateful that he wasn't a Cursed.

As he started to walk, he felt a stabbing pain in his posterior. He reached back and found a small sliver of wood sticking out of his trousers – a splinter from the dilapidated bleachers. Addison removed it while he whispered an expletive-laden prayer of thanks to god. He walked quickly and carefully down the aisle of egress, which took him through a different part of the auditorium. As he neared the large sanctuary door, he allowed himself a quick glance at the Blessed parishioners sitting close to the altar. A few aisles up he saw Otka. She was sitting in the seat nearest the aisle, wearing an appropriate black micro-mini halter with a matching velvet crotch panel. Her head was bowed deeply and her hands were tightly clasped, apparently in intense prayer. Addison accidentally banged his right leg against the pew immediately behind Otka and broke her spiritual trance. She looked up, saw Addison and gave him a little wave. Addison's heart bounced; she remembered him! And if it were possible, she looked even more adorable than he remembered. She beamed a brilliant smile at Addison. He sighed; his knees wavered. He was hopelessly infatuated. Her smile was so genuine and her wave so sincere that Addison truly believed she was happy to see him. Addison gave her a short wave back. Bell's palsy! Starck was sitting next to Otka and had witnessed their exchange. He gave Addison a menacing look, actually raising the corner of his upper lip, mimicking an angry dog. If Starck wasn't so scary, the gesture might have looked funny, but comedy was the farthest thing from Addison's mind. Addison was frightened – he had seen firsthand what this beast was capable of doing. Quickly looking away, Addison took the last few steps and reached the sanctuary door. He pushed against the large door, but it didn't budge. He pushed harder and as he did, his feet slipped out from under him on the smooth floor and his body slid down until he landed softly on his hands and knees. Addison heard a few chuckles from some of the Blesseds sitting nearby. He turned around and saw Otka looking at him with a hurt expression on her excruciatingly beautiful face. Embarrassed, Addison quickly turned back around and got to his feet. An usher with a thick muscular neck and shoulder-length wavy blond hair walked over smiling. "Having difficulties with the heavy door? Watch this," he said and he pushed the door open effortlessly with one hand. Addison brushed past him and left the church so fast that he forgot to anoint himself with anti-wrinkle cream on the way out.

Addison walked quickly toward his living complex. All he wanted was to be alone, to get away from all people, especially good-looking ones. He thought back to Otka. Of all the people sitting in that sanctuary (he guessed there were around two hundred), Otka was the only one who looked as if she were taking the service seriously. All of the other Blesseds he saw were treating it more like a social event than a religious service. They appeared to be more concerned with being noticed than actually engaging in worship. And the priest was the worst offender of them all! Addison found it strange that someone as beautiful as Otka could be so spiritual. It was incongruent. Given her incredible beauty, why would she even care about such things?

As Addison walked toward his living complex, he noticed a small crowd gathered around one of the crystal pits in Grand Square. There were six pits in the Square; similar pits were scattered all over Alpdon's other large population centers. Each pit was filled with crystal balls and prisms that sparkled brilliantly when touched with even the muted light that squeezed through the typical leaden sky. The crystals in these pits looked expensive and Addison initially thought it was a slothful use of funds, given the country's bad economy. But Nigel heard that they were deemed a justifiable investment by the Bureau of Economics because they "raised the 'morals' of the people." His explanation made sense to Addison. The Perspiration Camps made the grotesquely obese citizens a bit less disgusting and the crystal pits created beautiful reflections that made the city a lot less gloomy. From his tertiary school economics classes, Addison knew the outlook of the people had a significant effect on the economy. He figured that Brock's strategy was to boost the spirits of all Alpdonians to beget their confidence, which would then create a fertile environment for growing a thriving economy. Brock had thought of everything.

Some in the crowd were pointing into the pit. Addison walked over to see what was drawing their attention. He crinkled his nose as he got closer as he caught a whiff of the foul-smelling water that pooled in all of the pits. The recent rains had flooded the pits and they drained slowly. Nothing was done to correct the problem, however, as the water reflected off the balls and prisms and conjured up miniature rainbows.

Addison stood at the edge of the pit and looked in. Handsome lord! A small dog with big ears, similar to the one Addison had been admonished for petting a few days ago, had fallen into the pit and was struggling to get out. Like all dogs, it had been declawed. (Claws damaged the poly-blended spandex clothing worn by all Blesseds.) Without nails, the dog was unable to gain traction on the pit wall and it had no chance of getting out. After a few moments of watching, Addison could see that the animal was tiring, and if no one rescued it soon, it would most certainly sink under the water and drown; but no one made any move to help it.

"Wh-Wh-Wh-Why doesn't somebody do something?" Addison asked to nobody in particular.

A slightly overweight Favored man with thick dark hair and an unshaven but handsome rogue's face answered, "To prevent the balls and prisms from being stolen, the entire basin is equipped with electronic sensors. If a significant amount of weight is placed on the walls of the basin, it will trigger a powerful electric shock. Because the basin is full of water, an electrical shock will instantly electrocute the dog. The little critter's weight hasn't yet been sufficient to trigger the sensor. It could happen at any moment, however." Addison was surprised that his manner was banal, matter-of-fact, as if he were talking about a stuffed toy rather than a living animal.

"Wh-Wh-What happens if someone jumps into the pit, but doesn't touch the walls?" Addison asked.

The Favored man responded in the same prosaic tone, "That would present two problems. Not just the walls are outfitted with sensors; the basin bottom is as well. If the force of the landing exceeds twenty kilos per centimeter, it will trigger one of the sensors. However, if by some miracle the landing didn't set the sensor off, getting out of the basin would require contact with the walls and that would also exceed the pressure constraints and trigger the sensors. Face facts; the animal is doomed. We are all just watching to see if its demise occurs via electrocution or drowning."

Quickly Addison reached down and removed his belt. He had put on so much weight over the past year that his belt was useless anyway. He fed the tapered end through the buckle, fashioning a noose, then leaned over the pit and tried to ensnare the dog. He couldn't reach. The dog had moved to the middle of the pit and Addison's outstretched arm wasn't long enough. "C-C-Can someone please hold my hand so I can lean over further?" Addison asked desperately. A few of the onlookers recoiled with disgust, as if Addison had just asked them to lance a boil on his buttocks.

"S-S-Someone... anyone!" he pleaded. The dog sunk under the water and a stream of tiny bubbles floated to the surface. Still nobody moved to help him. Addison looked around the crowd standing at the rim of the pit, but no one made eye contact with him.

Then from behind, he heard a commanding female voice, "I will assist you, sweetie. Take hold of my hand!" Addison turned. It was Otka! He grabbed her hand and cautiously leaned over the pit. "I've got you, sweetie," she said. The strength of her grip surprised Addison. Just then the dog bobbed his head up from the water. Addison deftly slid the belt loop over the dog's head. Apparently sensing what Addison was about to do, the dog placed its front paws through the loop. Addison pulled up, the belt tightened around the dog's midsection, and Addison lifted it out of the pit. Once the dog was on the ground, Addison removed the belt. The dog shook itself off and its long left ear flopped over. Addison recognized it immediately – it was the same dog he had been admonished for petting just a few days ago! The dog approached Addison and buried its head affectionately between Addison's shins. Addison looked around, but the dog's Blessed owner was nowhere in sight. Addison bent down and scratched his head, a bit surprised that the dog's short curly hair didn't feel wet. Otka tapped Addison on his shoulder and he glanced up. "Aren't you a resourceful chap?" she said coyly and winked at him.

Addison pet the dog for a few seconds more, then stood up. "Th-Th-Thanks for your help," he said. When he turned back toward the dog, he saw it scurrying back toward the Blessed entrance, its left ear flopping up and down like a palm frond in an intermittent breeze.

Addison turned back to Otka and smiled slightly – afraid to be too friendly, as Starck was standing right next to her. Otka turned and walked away with Starck, their hands resting on the other's derriere. Otka never looked back at Addison; however, Starck looked back at him twice – the last time, he ran one of his fingers across his throat. Addison pretended he hadn't noticed, but he did and the gesture terrified him. He reached into his pocket and fingered his rocks vigorously. What did Starck have against him anyway? And was his menacing mime a threat or a promise? ∎

CHAPTER SEVEN

❖

ADDISON WALKED ON THE PATHWAY that led to his living complex. The tall pine trees clustered at the northeast corner of Grand Square rustled loudly, descending into the oxidized green copper dune they sprouted from, revealing a large metallic media screen with a brushed nickel finish. A news update was about to be delivered. A brass fanfare brought the panels to life with an image of the red, white and black Alpdon flag waving heroically against a cloudless aquamarine sky. Addison turned toward the panel and waited. Others quickly joined him and soon he was awash in a sea of personalized fragrances; he smelled notes of salt-peter, ginger, leather, wet wool, wet leaves, wet ink, oil paint, cloves, musk, peppermint, freshly shorn grass, huckleberry, boysenberry, strawberry, new rubber, witch hazel and cedar wood shavings. He marveled at the odd scents people chose for themselves, scents they thought were flattering. Some he could understand. Many found the scent of ginger, leather, strawberry and cedar wood shavings pleasurable. But new rubber? Who would want to smell like a transport bumper factory? And who would find that appealing? The fanfare ended and the waving flag dissolved into a close-up of Brock.

Brock's face was pale. Slate-colored semicircles hung beneath his bloodshot eyes; it looked to Addison as if he had been crying. Brock spoke in a slow and measured voice, "Fine-looking citizens of Alpdon, I address you tonight with my life essence saturated in intense grief. My dear com-rade and my ambassador to Farce'n, Ernst Van Rath, was assassinated a short while ago on the steps of the parliament building, within ear and eyeshot of my personal offices." The image cut to a lean man, with thick salt-and-pepper hair, lying facedown on the parliament steps with his right arm bent over his head and his left arm pressed to his side. His tight white spandex tunic and tight white trousers were splattered with blood. The crowd gasped. The image cut back to Brock. He continued, "Two enemies of the state were captured at the crime scene as they brazenly stood over the body of my fallen friend, laughing." Brock paused and then repeated with an incredulous shout, "laughing!" He lowered his head, apparently overcome with emotion.

"Ambassador Van Rath was assassinated while leaving a late morning breakfast meeting. He was heading back to his living complex to visit with his beautifully formed offspring – offspring who will now tragically be left without a Primary Optimal Provider. This is a calamity of the highest magnitude as this man was truly blessed by god. He had a powerful and lean physique, beautifully thick hair that was the perfect pigment given his advancing age, ideal facial bone structure, and a rugged yet symmetrical nose. He was a devoted cohabitant and an exemplary Primary Optimal Provider. He loved his offspring almost as much as he loved himself – maybe even as much. He was a treasured comrade of mine; a man I have been acquainted with since I was in secondary school."

The close-up of Brock cut to an image of two ugly men. Brock continued, "The two men you see here are responsible for this dastardly act. The man on your left was the initiator. His name is Herschel Greenspan and he is one obviously Cursed by our infallible creator." No doubt about it, thought Addison, as the man had a large pulpy nose that looked as if it were sculpted from regurgitated red meat and oversized ears that stuck out perpendicular to his tiny head. "The man on your right is obviously a Burdened and is not only a co-conspirator, but also the initiator's POP!" More gasps from the crowd. This was a much older-looking man with a protruding stomach, a round face with a flattened nose and full head of gray hair. The image cut back to Brock. "Good-looking citizens of Alpdon, let me assure you that these men will be dealt with most harshly." Brock paused and licked his lips, which were so thin and colorless that his mouth looked like an incision on a pale melon. Someone out of image was speaking to him. As Brock listened, his right eye twitched. After a lengthy pause, he continued, "I am being told that some of our productive citizens are already expressing their outrage over this heinous incident by engaging in impromptu acts of vengeance against the castes that spawned these two killers. And while I do not condone this type of behavior, I can certainly understand it." Then, with a slight smile on his face, "in fact I can't help but reluctantly admire such examples of patriotic fervor. After all, the ancient scriptures tell us that a little bit of yeast works through the whole batch of dough. Are these two, who have been so neglected by our creator, the only two who harbor ill-will toward my regime? We would all be naive indeed to believe that. And if this is how the enemies of this state treat my fruit, what are they capable of doing to me, the vine that produced and nourished this fruit? That is a frightening thought, fellow good-looking citizens, a frightening thought indeed." Brock paused and again licked his lips. The corner of his right eye and the right corner of his mouth twitched simultaneously, as if connected by an invisible filament. The tight image of Brock pulled back slowly. "Soon, very soon, my good-looking brethren, this will no longer be a problem. Plans are already in motion to ensure the safety of this country's leadership and the safety of our critical producers," Brock paused, as if he wanted everyone to absorb the importance of what he had just said. He continued with a warm smile, "Stay tuned, my beautiful ones. Something significant is going to happen – significant and long overdue – and it will guarantee prosperity for my unblemished flock for at least a thousand annums! We live in exciting times, brethren. God has appointed me to be your shepherd and I have made a covenant in my own blood promising him that I will protect and feed his sheep so that none of you shall ever want again. I will make your cups runneth over... Runneth over? My fabulous looking flock, your cups are not just going to runneth over, they are going to 'poureth' over until you are standing waist deep in the intoxicating juices of prosperity!" Brock started laughing in a way that suggested to Addison something diabolical underpinned his words. The laughing grew in intensity until even some of the Blesseds around Addison looked at one another uncomfortably. Brock, perhaps sensing he was sounding borderline maniacal, ratcheted down his laugh until once again he was smiling warmly. "May our gracious and gorgeous god continue to smile upon the productive citizens of this great nation," he said calmly and his image faded to black.

Brock was not a handsome man, Addison thought. He had soft facial features and sallow and puffy cheeks; his only striking facial characteristic were his grayish-blue eyes. Brock and his ministers spoke constantly of the Blesseds and Favoreds and the critical role these citizens played in Alpdon's economic recovery, but they never made mention of their own SIN. You didn't need an expert's eye to see that most of the men in Brock's cabinet were unattractive. Maybe they weren't Curseds, but there were certainly more than a few Burdened in the bunch. For instance, William Gringo, Brock's Minister of Economics, had a receding hairline, a visible stomach bulge, and an ample and smashed up boxer's nose; while William Firk, Brock's Minister of the Interior, had a wide puffy face that looked like it would flatten out like a saucer in a stiff breeze and a rosacea-infested nose that stood out on his pale complexion like a blood stain on a snowman. Surely Addison wasn't the only one who noticed this? Why hadn't anyone else mentioned it? Was it because Brock's plan was actually working and Alpdon's economy was starting to recover? Maybe Brock's regime was hypocritical, but no one could argue with the results. Alpdon's economy was recovering much quicker than predicted. When Brock first seized office, the country's currency was so devalued by inflation that Addison had to hold his wrist under the commerce scanner for seven seconds just to buy his morning espresso tablets. Today, the transaction took less than two.

Addison recalled Franklin Delano Roosevelt's belief that true individual freedom cannot exist without economic security and independence. Were the citizens of Alpdon willing to ignore Brock's hypocrisy because they were so desperate for economic security? FDR also said that citizens who were hungry and unemployed were the kindling for dictatorships. Before Brock took office, Alpdon was teeming with the famished and unemployed.

Addison's thoughts were interrupted by staccato pops that sounded like bursting balloons. The noise was coming from the direction of the Cursed living complex. At first Addison wasn't sure what he was witnessing. A dozen or so good-lookers were fetching balls from a nearby crystal pit and throwing them at the edifice of the Cursed living complex. Then he realized they were trying to destroy the complex windows. The balls were shattering against the two-story windows that faced Grand Square, but they weren't causing any damage. Apparently the mob didn't know what Addison knew – the Cursed complex was a converted psychiatric prison and the windows were ten centimeters thick. It would take a lot more than a crystal ball to break one. Undeterred by their lack of success, the good-lookers kept picking up balls and hurling them at the windows. After impact, the slivers of crystal sparkled brilliantly as they fell to the ground, reminding Addison of the flickering trail of depleted uranium flakes left by a megaprotonic nuclear missile. (A localized missile, of course; the vapor trail from an intercontinental missile would stretch half a kilometer!)

Finally realizing that their throws weren't breaking the windows (for intelligent people, it sure took them a long time to figure that out), the attractive mob began throwing balls at the third-story windows; but those windows held as well. They tried the fourth-story windows, but they also held. An exceptionally tall male good-looker, wearing a white fishnet body stocking with a white satin panel covering his bulging crotch, launched an impressive throw at the fifth floor, the top floor of the complex. The crystal ball passed easily through one of the windows and the mob shouted with glee. Encouraged by the results, more good-lookers stepped up and lofted crystal balls at the fifth story, but none had the arm strength to reach and their throws fell short. The exceptionally tall male good-looker stopped the others from throwing with a sweep of his long arm. When all had stopped, he grabbed a crystal ball from someone standing nearby, took a short skip, and pitched the ball through the center of one of the fifth-story windows, shattering the glass so completely that the window pane was left empty. The crowd cheered again and others passed their balls to him. The tall man then proceeded to shatter all twenty of the fifth-floor windows facing Grand Square, making just one errant throw and that was only because he was distracted by a low-flying pterodactyl just as he released the ball.

Addison watched the throwing prowess of the little muscular man with a combination of envy and marvel. He spotted an older-looking Cursed man walk through the exit portal of the living complex. The man had a round body with long legs, a knobby bald head and big bulging eyes. He reminded Addison of a large toad. Addison clenched his hands nervously. What would the mob do when they saw this toady chap?

The toad man noticed the mob about the same time they noticed him. Addison watched with horror as a few members of the mob started walking toward the toad man. He saw that one good-looker was concealing an arm-length-long prism behind his "V-shaped" back. The toad man saw the large amount of shattered glass and the purposeful walks of the good-lookers approaching him and evidently thought, as Addison did, that he might be in danger. With a look of panic, the toad man quickly turned around and tried to go back in through the exit portal. There was no activation pad on the outside of this portal, so he tried to wedge his fingers into the narrow canal where the portal opened. It wouldn't yield. The approaching good-lookers walked toward him a bit quicker. When they were twenty meters or so from the toad man, they fanned out to prevent him from outflanking them and escaping. Then they pounced on him. Addison gasped and brought his hand to his mouth. He could see a flurry of arms and hands but the broad shoulders of the good-lookers blocked his view. What were they doing? Finally, with big smiles on their faces, the good-lookers turned away and walked back toward their crowd. When Addison could finally see what they had done to the man, he gasped again, struck by the cruelty of what they had done and shocked by the vulgarity of what he was seeing. The good-lookers had stripped the toad man naked, tied his hands and feet behind his back with his stained undergarments, and placed him facedown on the ground. And as if leaving him helplessly naked in public wasn't humiliating enough, they had inserted the crystal prism into his buttocks. As Addison was wondering how the toad man was going to remove the prism, a Favored brunette (for a change) approached the man, delicately removed the prism and placed it on the ground. Then she freed his hands and feet. The mob of good-lookers, obviously disappointed that she had undone their handiwork, responded by pushing up their noses and serenading her with a chorus of swine snorts.

Having broken what glass they could at the Cursed complex, and having violated a Cursed citizen in a most humiliating way, the good-lookers turned and walked in Addison's direction toward the Burdened complex. Was the mob going to wreak havoc on the Burdened complex or were they coming after him? He had been so engrossed in watching what they were doing that he hadn't even considered his own safety. He wasn't going to wait around to find out their intentions. Where could he go? He could run into town and get lost among the pedestrians in the shopping district. He quickly dropped that idea – the shopping district was at least a kilometer away and given the obvious superior physical conditioning of the mob, they would catch up with him rather easily. His best option was the Caffeine Depot. He turned and walked toward it briskly, keeping his eyes locked on the mob the entire time. They continued walking toward the Burdened complex, taking no notice of him. Then an icy bolt shot up Addison's spine. One member of the good-looking group, with a mischievous smile on his strikingly handsome face, started running toward him. Then he abruptly stopped and walked backwards slowly, until he rejoined the walking mob. A few seconds later, he did it again; this time taking more strides and getting closer to Addison before retreating once again. What kind of game was he playing? Was he simply teasing Addison? Or was he doing to Addison what a cat does to a mouse – sadistically toying with him as a prelude to harming him? Addison couldn't be sure. Afraid that the mob might decide to do to him what they had done to that unlucky Cursed man, he started walking faster. Even this moderate increase in intensity caused him to breathe heavily and sweat profusely. I am pathetic, he thought. He wasn't even running and he was out of breath. I am going to start an exercise program real soon, he thought. He immediately smirked because he had pledged to start such a program more times than he could ever possibly remember and he never once followed through. Why bother? Would it make much difference to his appearance if he were in good physical shape? Is a malformed, feces-covered troll any less revolting because he is skinny rather than fat? Whether he was lean or heavy, he would still be balding; he would still have a puffy face, a weak chin and amber-colored teeth.

Addison kept his eyes locked on the mob. The good-looker continued to taunt him – sprinting toward him, stopping, and then returning to the mob. He was making Addison increasingly nervous. Addison decided it was best to get to the Depot as quickly as possible, so he started running. After ten seconds, his lungs and thighs were burning. Was he being chased? He didn't dare turn around to look; he remembered hearing somewhere that looking back, even for an instant, would slow him down. But his desire to take a look grew until it took all of his discipline to keep his eyes forward. Rashly and without breaking his running stride, he turned and glanced over his shoulder. He was immediately filled with relief. The good-looker was walking with the mob and wasn't even facing in Addison's direction; he had apparently grown bored of his sadistic game. As Addison snapped his head forward, he stumbled over a raised brick and tumbled headfirst to the ground, severely scratching his hands and knees. He let loose with a string of obscenities that would have mortified a two-toothed, trashy-tongued transport driver, "knobby-kneed, hairy-backed, thick-legged, flabby-bottomed, needle-thin-penis-toting, pus-leaking, acne-infested dwarf! With a deformed arm and six hammer toes on one foot!" He glanced back at the mob. Many were now looking in his direction and pointing, but were they mocking him for his clumsiness or making a plan to get him? Addison was too far away to hear them. He decided not to wait around to find out and he resumed running at a slower, more careful pace. In a few moments, he was standing in front of the Caffeine Depot entrance portal. "O-O-O-O-pen," he sputtered. To his relief, his stammer didn't confuse the voice recognition system and the portal opened. Addison entered the Depot and bent over, putting his bloody hands on his scraped knees, trying to catch his breath. Otka ran out from behind the service desk. "Are you copacetic, sweetie? You looked rather flushed."

"I am fine," Addison said, although his head was spinning. As he straightened up, his left hand fumbled clumsily for his pocket. After a few attempts, he found his pocket and rubbed his rocks. Strangely, the rocks felt larger than usual. He found it difficult to catch his breath. He tried to relax and slow his breathing, but he was just too winded.

"Sweetie, are you sure you are not suffering from some malady? Your face has changed colors at least three times in the past thirty seconds," Otka said, her voice echoing in Addison's ears as if she were speaking to him from a deep cavern.

"Well, maybe I should sit down for a bit," Addison said feebly. Suddenly his knees morphed to marmalade and he was falling.

"Oh, he fainted just like a bean-sprout-eating uber model... how precious!" Addison heard Otka say right before he collapsed in a sweaty heap on top of her espresso-and-jasmine-scented feet. ■

CHAPTER EIGHT

❖

ADDISON WAS LYING ON HIS BACK on a substance that was spongy yet supportive. His eyes were closed, but he was awake; he knew when he lifted up his head it would hurt. Already he had a dull throbbing pain just behind his right eye. The pain was always in the same spot, behind his damnable right eye. A verse from the Gospel of Mark wisped through his thoughts – "and if your eye offends you, pluck it out." Slowly he opened his eyes and took a deep breath. He smiled and sighed... jasmine and espresso. He propped himself up on his elbows and looked around. Each heartbeat brought a new wave of pain. He reached up and pressed firmly on his eyeball, as if it were possible to shove the pain right out of his head. Where was he? Again he breathed in deep; the scent of jasmine and espresso was so strong he could taste it in the back of his throat. Then he remembered. He must still be at the Caffeine Depot. He sat upright, keeping his head tilted slightly to the right; for some reason, this lessened the pain.

He was in a small room. He swung his head to the left to look at a holographic timepiece. It was 21:05. Holding his head in this position made his headache worse, so he slowly rotated it back to the right.

A bright yellow spotlight shone down from the ceiling, illuminating a small, square, chrome-finished table positioned in the far right corner. Addison stood up slowly and walked toward the light, not seeking an alleged destination for transmuted souls, but because he was curious about a folded piece of writing foil placed in the center of the table.

Addison picked up the note – it also smelled of jasmine and espresso. He closed his eyes and breathed in the scent. It made him peculiarly optimistic. Handwritten in perfectly formed uppercase letters was the following:

SALUTATIONS, SWEETIE:

SHORTLY AFTER YOU ENTERED MY DEPOT YOU FAINTED
RIGHT ON TOP OF MY NEW OPEN-TOED, SCIMITAR-TOOTHED
CATSKIN SHOES. THANKFULLY YOUR TORRENTS OF PERSPI-
RATION DIDN'T DAMAGE THEM. I PLACED YOU ON THE NAP-
PING PLATFORM IN MY OFFICE. REST AS LONG AS YOU NEED.
YOU CAN EXIT THROUGH THE SERVICE PORTAL LOCATED
IN THE NORTHEASTERN CORNER OF THIS ROOM. THE EXIT
CODE IS D-503. — OTKA

Addison punched in the activation code. The security unit chirped
louder than he expected, causing him to flinch, and he left the Depot. The
brackish breeze blowing off the Luvista was cool and refreshing; it lessened
the pain of his headache. He walked around to the front of the Depot and
toward his living complex. Incredibly, there were no signs of the earlier
destruction. All had been cleaned up and restored – the trenches were even
refilled with crystal balls and prisms. Had it not been for his skinned hands
and knees, what he witnessed earlier might have been just another one of
his disturbing dreams.

To get to his living complex Addison had to pass by the social clubs
that ringed Grand Square. Vacant and limp during the day, these clubs
awakened after sundown. Each one Addison walked past was engorged
with Blesseds and pulsating with excitement. The good-looking cohabitating couples he saw were scandalously attired – naked except for a few
strategically placed dabs of latex paint. Seeing them made Addison angry.
What arrogance to parade around in public like that! And if their near
nudity wasn't offensive enough, these perfectly formed counterfeits spent
their entire evenings feigning interest in their partners as they furtively
ogled every opposite-sexed person they could see. What a gaggle of pho-
nies! And while outwardly Addison despised them, deep down, residing in
a cobwebbed corner of his subconscious was an envy blazing so strong that

had it been possible to trade ten years of his mortality for just ten days as a Blessed, Addison would have done it without hesitation or regret.

Addison walked quickly toward his living complex. What he had witnessed earlier was indeed disturbing, but Addison was more curious than scared. He hadn't realized that the upper castes were harboring such anger toward the lower castes. What he had witnessed earlier in the day was not just a response to the assassination of Brock's attaché. Had that been the case, Addison reasoned, a single act of destruction to either a person or property would have been enough to even the score. The length of the outbreak and the display of sadism revealed that their anger toward the lower castes had been festering for quite some time. The assassination was merely the sliver of vine that broke the llama's spine. But Addison couldn't understand why. No one could argue the fact that the bloated welfare system had crippled Alpdon's economy, but were only the unattractive to blame? There had to be at least some good-looking citizens who relied on welfare during those bleak days. Conversely, there were plenty of economically productive, self-sufficient citizens in the lower castes. After all, Addison had never taken a government handout. How could the lower castes be universally blamed for Alpdon's economic demise? Then two morally bankrupt individuals murder a public official and the castes they belonged to get blamed for the crime? This was madness! It made no sense, but Addison realized he was discounting the emotional factors. The reality was that practically every citizen of Alpdon had suffered through many long and lean days. Although the economy had started to recover, memories of those horrible days were still fresh in the citizens' minds. Once the currency stabilized and the economy rebounded, Addison still believed life in Alpdon would return to normal.

Addison walked past one of the more popular social destinations in Wakork, The Eagle's Nest. Buttressing Grand Square was The Eagle's Nest's outdoor gathering area – a fenced-in enclosure twenty meters across by ten meters deep – reserved only for those with single-digit SINs. Guarding the enclosure was an enormous SA wearing a red and brown kepi hat. Two couples dancing in the enclosure caught Addison's eye – four blondes with angelic faces so beautiful that Addison was only able to tell the sexes apart because the women were wearing chrome nipple wafers. The couples were gyrating to the latest chart topper – the passionate grunts of two copulating baboons accompanied by a continuous sequence of whispered ancient French profanities. Although he was not a fan of this musical genre, Addison found the guttural groaning of the primates rather catchy and he bopped his head in time with the song as he walked past the enclosure.

The taller of the two women undulated her stomach like an ancient belly dancer. She immediately captivated Addison not only because of her overtly sexual style of dancing, but primarily because she had a huge diamond adorning her navel. He couldn't believe how large it was – it was as big as one of his pocket rocks! The woman danced with her eyes closed and her head tilted back as if she were experiencing the same pleasure as the rutting apes. Increasing the intensity of her gyrations along with the music, she rotated her hips, causing the large stone in her navel to refract one of the overhead spotlights. The reflected brilliance shined directly into Addison's eyes, momentarily blinding him. Addison snapped his eyes shut and didn't see another slightly raised brick in the walkway. (Who was the incompetent mason who laid these bricks anyway?) He tripped over it and fell. Instinctively, he protected his scraped hands by pulling them to his side. He landed hard on the left side of his face, a few meters in front of an approaching Blessed couple. Blood and saliva oozed from his open mouth.

The couple stopped walking. The Blessed woman raised her foot and tapped the sole of her scimitar-toothed cat skin shoe on Addison's bald spot. (Did every Blessed woman own a pair of these shoes?) "Watch your way, you ill-formed oaf!" she said. "These shoes are worth more than your life. Why, you almost got some of your disgusting bodily fluids on them!" The tall, blond bucket-jawed man walking with her laughed at her rebuke. "You are in my way, you parasite. Move!" she yelled as she pushed her foot down hard on Addison's head. A pebble embedded in the sole of her shoe dug into Addison's scalp and he squealed in pain. Everyone within earshot roared with laughter. A wave of humiliation crashed over Addison.

"You are not moving fast enough," the bucket-jawed man said and he kicked Addison hard on the cap of his left shoulder. Addison scrambled to his feet and walked briskly toward his living complex. He frantically fingered his polished rocks as he walked; even that trivial motion aggravated the shoulder the Blessed man had kicked.

Addison bolted upright from his sleeping platform and looked over at his holographic time device. It read 04:01. (The last day of the Sportugal Civil War... or was it still known as just Spain back then?) His sleeping tunic was soaked with sweat and his heart was pounding. Adrenaline coursed through his body. His hands and feet prickled. Another nightmare. For a change it didn't involve the destruction of his teeth. This dream was much more disturbing; Addison had dreamed of his own death.

This dream had been especially lucid, much more so than the typical dental disasters his subconscious conjured up. He was standing in a circle of people. A short man with dark eyes and a baritone voice was speaking from a dais on top of a tall platform erected just outside of the circle. Although he was physically small in stature, his booming voice gave him authority. In the middle of the circle was a pile of books, stacked as high as the platform. Even from his distance, twenty meters or so from the pile, Addison could make out a couple of the titles, including a best-seller from a few years back – *Lose Weight, Look Great and You'll No Longer Need To Masturbate*.

The short man on the tall platform was talking passionately, as if he was preaching, but he was wearing a military uniform not an ecclesiastical vestment. Addison could clearly hear him, but he was speaking in a foreign language with a harsh chunky cadence and plenty of hard consonants – so hard that spittle occasionally flew from his mouth as he spoke. Every time he finished a sentence he pounded the dais with his right fist. The crowd around Addison understood his language and cheered wildly every time the short man paused. The short man then pulled a flaming torch from under the dais, held it over his head with an outstretched arm, and dramatically tossed it onto the pile of books. The pile became an instant wall of flames; sparkling embers floated over the crowd like swollen fireflies.

An angular-faced man standing next to Addison grabbed the top of his head, yanked off his toupee and hurled it into the fire. A petite woman standing next to him removed her sapphire-tinted contact lenses and threw them like Frisbees toward the blaze. Another woman reached under her micro-mini dress, slithered out of her support garment and threw it onto the fire. Soon a flurry of debris from all directions was landing on the burning pile – false eyelashes, push-up bras, shoe lifts, hair extenders, more toupees, jars of wrinkle putty, handheld lip plumpers, ampoules of blond hair dye, even a pair of derriere cheek-lifters. The short man on the tall platform watched with open-mouthed delight.

As the flurry of debris subsided, the now-inflamed crowd looked for other items to burn. Heads rotated frantically from side to side as the crowd searched for other appropriate items to toss on the fire, but nothing could be found. Seconds passed; then a full minute passed. Addison sensed the crowd's building agitation. The fire slowly dwindled; if it wasn't stoked soon, it would burn out. A loud cheer erupted from behind Addison. He spun around to see what was happening and the steel tip of a dirty shoe knocked him in the nose. Three husky, sandy-haired men carrying a plump bald man pushed past and headed toward the fire. With a synchronized heave, the three he-men tossed the plump man into the fire! The crowd roared and they looked around for more ugly people to burn. Screams of delight burst forth from a section across from Addison. A scrawny man with a beaked nose and stringy black hair was thrown high onto the flaming pile by four brawny Blessed men. The short man on the tall platform tilted his head back, his skinny body heaving up and down from laughter.

Addison was nervous; he needed to get out of there... quickly. The beautiful people standing nearby turned towards him. The glow from the fire gave their skin the appearance of unblemished copper, making them even more attractive.

As he turned to leave, two thick-necked men with heavily muscled arms stood in front of him, blocking his path. They were tall – so tall that Addison couldn't even see their hair color, but he guessed they were blond. Addison stepped to the left; the men shifted their feet and blocked him again. Addison turned and headed right, banging into onlookers as he frantically tried to escape the two behemoths. As he moved through the crowd, he expected at any moment for a strong hand to grab him from behind, but none came. He could see open space. He was going to make it! Just then a broad-shouldered man came out of nowhere and lunged toward Addison. He grabbed Addison around the chest, pinning his arms to his side. Someone else grabbed his legs. They carried Addison toward the fire headfirst, like a human ramming pole. The temperature on Addison's bald spot increased with each step. He tried to squirm out of their grasp, but it was no use; they were too strong. The fine hairs scattered around his bald spot started to smolder; the pungent aroma caused his eyes to water. The two men threw Addison toward the bonfire. Addison screamed, but the cheering crowd was so loud that he couldn't hear it. It was at that moment he had awakened.

Returning to sleep would be difficult, especially with his heart beating like a pneumatic jackhammer, but he had to at least try. Addison laid his head back down and started counting his shortcomings. He had tried counting his blessings, but he couldn't think of any. Counting sheep would just make him hungry for lamb chops, which he wasn't allowed to eat since the Bureau of Sustenance had outlawed the slaughter and consumption of "attractive" animals.[5] He drifted off to sleep soon after he thought of shortcoming number twenty-one – his hideous testicles – two purple-skinned sacks covered with tufts of wiry gray hair – that hung much lower than what he considered normal – four centimeters during the cold months and seven centimeters during the warmer ones. ∎

---

5   "Attractive" animals included lambs, rabbits, fawns, joeys and the occasional lipstick-wearing pig.

CHAPTER NINE

❖

ADDISON'S AWAKENING APPARATUS ACTIVATED,
filling his living unit with bright light and loud, irregular beeping. He commanded the system to stop and let out a protracted groan. He'd had another horrendous night's sleep – he guessed he had gotten about three-and-a-half hours. He had been engaged with Nigel on the communications portal until well after 02:00. (Nigel was regaling him with some fifth-hand gossip about Brock's alleged same-sex proclivities.) Addison rose from his sleeping platform and dragged his weakened body to the waste elimination chamber. On a masochistic whim, he sneaked a quick glance into his only mirror. "Look at those dark circles under my eyes," he said aloud to his haggard reflection. Again he found it odd that he never stammered when he talked to himself. Why couldn't he talk like that when he was around people?

Addison felt so putrid he decided to skip his shower – seeing his flabby naked body would only worsen his mood. He grabbed his empty tube of toothpaste and squeezed hard, trying to extricate a drop, a trickle, some residue from the spray – anything to apply onto his pneumatic toothbrush. He wasn't frugal; he was procrastinating. He was too lazy to make the fifteen-minute walk to the Hygiene Hut to purchase a new tube.

When his toothbrush finished its work, he put on the same clothes he had worn the day before. He stumbled out of his living unit and headed for the lift. Addison rarely cursed out loud (although he often cursed to himself); his birther had conditioned him to believe that bad teeth looked worse in a "dirty mouth," but when he waved his right hand over the scanner to requisition the lift, he suddenly yelled, "Alopecia!"[6] He cringed. It sounded so

---

6 Of the genetic anomalies that could dramatically alter appearance, this was one of the worst; therefore, it was one of the more obscene epithets of the age. This malady was so feared that birthers developed a prayer, which they recited every night from fetal verification through fetal liberation, "Good looking lord above, before I rest I make of you this one request. Form my fetus symmetrical and fair, and bless it for its life with beautiful hair."

❖

crass. He hoped nobody had heard him or if someone had, that they hadn't recognized his voice. Addison turned around and stormed back to his living unit. For the second day in a row, he had forgotten to put on his mandatory jingler. He was angry that he had to go all the way back to his living unit to retrieve it and livid that he was being forced to wear it.

A fortnight had passed since Ambassador Van Rath's assassination and the accompanying upper caste disturbance (or what the media had labeled "The Day of Shattering Crystal"). In response to the crime, a new law had been passed during an emergency session of parliament to ensure that "no additional acts of treachery are perpetrated against Chancellor Brock or his cabinet by any member of the lesser castes." Addison found the law not only unreasonable, but degrading. To prevent any lower caste member from "surreptitiously committing an act of treachery," each Burdened and Cursed citizen was required to wear a small chrome jingler on a suitable length of twine or chain around the neck. Failure to wear the jingler, to keep the jingler shiny, or to keep the clapper functional were all considered tertiary crimes and were punishable by thirty days' imprisonment.

Addison hated it. Already hyper self-conscious, the high-pitched ringing drew annoyed looks from any Blessed or Favored within earshot.

With his jingler on properly – it had to be worn on the outside of the outermost garment and the jingler crown was not permitted to hang lower than six centimeters below the larynx – Addison walked toward the Caffeine Depot. He stepped on the sensor pad to activate the Depot entrance portal and immediately groaned. The queue was especially long this morning; there had to be at least twenty people ahead of him. He guessed that it would take him at least ten minutes to get his caffeine. He sighed and glanced down at his shoes. They were still scuffed. He really had to get around to polishing them soon. Good thing his POP wasn't around to see them. He frequently badgered Addison on the poor first impression unpolished shoes made. Something struck Addison hard from behind, almost causing him to lose his balance. He spun around to see what it was. Hair-sprouting facial mole! It was Starck! He was pushing his way past people to get to the front of the queue and he had shoved the person behind Addison, causing him to crash into Addison's back. Addison turned back around, lowered his head and hid his face by pretending to scratch his eyebrow. As Starck passed by, Addison breathed a sigh of relief; Starck hadn't noticed him. Starck bullied his way to the front of the queue. He received some angry looks once he passed, but no one was brave enough to confront this heavily muscled titan. Addison felt a surge of panic. He kept picturing Starck's threatening gesture that day in Grand Square. Would Starck say something, or horror of horrors, do something if he spotted him? Should he leave now and forgo his morning caffeine? That wasn't an option. The Depot was too crowded for him to turn around and go out through the entrance; to leave the typical way, via the exit portal, he would have to pass directly in front of Starck. His only hope was that Starck would do what he came to do and leave quickly. Addison watched Mimi give him a plate of tablets (presented properly on a white doily, of course). He couldn't count how many tablets Starck was given, but he could see there were quite a few of them. It struck him what a large amount of caffeine that was, but then again, Starck was a gargantuan man. He watched with disgust as Otka hurried over to greet him, almost knocking Mimi over in her haste to get to him. Mimi gave Otka an exasperated look, but Otka had already locked eyes with Starck and took no notice. Addison suddenly felt bad for Mimi. Otka's presence had completely eroded her self-confidence. Mimi rarely made eye contact with him when he ordered. If she did, it was only for a brief moment; she would quickly cast her gaze downward. Addison knew with absolute certainty that if he asked her on a date now, she would readily accept. But he no longer had any desire to be with her. As her confidence waned, so did her appeal.

Otka grabbed Starck's hand and led him behind the service desk until he was standing shoulder to shoulder with her. Starck bent over and whispered in her ear. Addison watched with a pit in his stomach as Starck kept whispering. What could he be telling her and why was it taking so long? Whatever it was, Otka seemed to be enjoying it; her beautiful face was beaming. Addison noticed that Otka had the type of face that looked even better with a smile, as if the muscles, ligaments and bones were specially constructed to accommodate that expression. He shook his head quickly from side to side, trying to regain his composure. Gorgeous god, she was spellbinding!

Starck continued whispering and then it occurred to Addison that he wasn't whispering to her at all – he was nibbling on her earlobe! Addison was crestfallen. He had hoped that Otka's dalliance with Starck would be a brief one, but it was obvious that it was still going strong. So strong that Otka was now letting him engage in public acts of affection at her place of business. Starck finished with her ear, gave her a long, open-mouthed kiss, grabbed his caffeine tablets from Mimi, and stomped out of the Depot.

Addison was initially relieved to see Starck leave, but his overwhelming envy – the envy that accrues only from encountering someone superior to you in every way imaginable – caused him to become enraged. He subconsciously decided to vent his anger on Otka. When he got to the front of the queue, he would tell her exactly what he thought of her lewd behavior. He wouldn't shout at her or be nasty – that might betray his fondness for her. No, he would calmly point out to her how unprofessional her actions were and how bad it was for business. There were four people between him and the service desk. While he waited, he rehearsed his rebuke. "Otka, as one of your habitual patrons, I think it is not only inappropriate but also detrimental to commerce to conduct yourself in such a lewd manner." No, that wasn't good; it sounded too scripted. "Otka, as one of your better customers, I think it is inappropriate for you to be flaunting your fondness for your coitus partner in your place of business." It wasn't perfect, but he was out of time and it would have to do.

His throat tightened as he stepped up to the desk. He trained his eyes on the polished chrome countertop of the service desk and said, "Th-Th-Th-Three tablets please," to Mimi. Addison could see in his peripheral vision Otka sidling over to the desk. He smelled her strong scent of jasmine and espresso and his courage began to wither.

"Look at me, sweetie," Otka said. She put her fragrant fingers on Addison's chin and lifted his head. He looked into her gold-flecked turquoise eyes and his nerve capitulated faster than Bertrand during the Blitzkrieg. "Three tablets this morning, sweetie? Did you experience a restless night in your cradle?" Was this an allusion to the dark baggy skin under his eyes? His neck and face flushed instantly and sweat formed on his pimpled brow. Otka apparently noticed his sudden change in condition, "Oh my! What's the matter with you? Mimi, please hastily acquire a container of instant water from my Oxygenator. I think he is going to swoon again!"

"I-I-I am fine, Otka. I-I-I am not going to faint. I'm just a little warm, that's all. Don't you condition your air in this establishment?" he said and he forced a casual laugh.

Otka smiled at Addison. "I am happy to hear that, sweetie. Your profuse sweating and ruddy complexion made me anxious. I don't like seeing one of my favorite customers in distress," she said and she winked at him. Impetuously, Addison reached into his left pocket and pulled out the first polished rock he felt – his piece of obsidian. He held it out to Otka.

"H-H-H-Here. A gift for you," he said apprehensively. As the words left his mouth he instantly regretted them. What was he doing? That was his favorite specimen! Did he secretly harbor some infinitesimal hope that Otka might actually have romantic feelings for him and that this trivial gift would somehow amplify her feelings? He was such a fool!

Otka looked surprised, but not happy. Addison pegged the look as bordering on offended, as if his action had crossed the line. "What's this?" she asked flatly.

"I-I-I-It is a piece of obsidian," Addison replied, embarrassed.

"Obsi...what?" Otka asked, in the same tone.

"Ob-Ob-Ob-Obsidian," Addison said. "It is a natural glass made by volcanoes. It's formed when felsic lava cools rapidly and freezes without sufficient time for crystal growth. It's usually found on the margins of lava flows where cooling happens faster. People often mistake it for a mineral, but because it is not crystalline, it is actually only mineral-like, in fact..."

"Aren't you a smarty-tunic," Otka interrupted, but in a manner that suggested she might actually be impressed. She gave Addison a wink, said "Thanks," placed the rock on the back counter and greeted the next customer in the queue in her usual cheerful voice.

Addison felt as if he had been kicked in the groin. That was it? That was the thanks she gave him? It couldn't be. Addison waited uncomfortably at the service desk. She would come back over to him and show him some more appreciation; he was sure of it. Addison waited, shifting his weight awkwardly from foot to foot while he frantically worked his two remaining pocket rocks. Why did he have to pull the obsidian out of his pocket? Why couldn't it have been the piece of granite that looked like chewed raw beef? A man with a deep voice yelled from the back of the queue, "Hey, tingle boy! She's done interfacing with you. Move already! You're holding up the queue!" Addison turned and walked briskly with his head down toward the departure portal. His neck and cheeks burned hotter.

He walked by a young-looking SS with broad shoulders and a baby face – Addison guessed he wasn't even twenty years old. The young-looking SS jumped out of the queue as Addison was passing, timing it perfectly so he collided into Addison's shoulder, knocking him hard into the nearby chrome-finished wall. The queue burst into laughter. "Oh, pardon me," the young-looking SS said, with a smile bubbling just under the surface of his puffy lips, "but you must be more careful. Those are quite a pair of well-maintained shoes you have there and I understand you wanting to admire them, but you need to keep that subhuman head of yours upright while you ambulate." The queue burst into another chorus of laughter.

"Hey, you there – with the masculine shoulders and the adorable face," Otka shouted from behind the service desk, "All my customers are to be treated with equal esteem. You will remove your gorgeous body from my Depot immediately!" The young-looking SS stood motionless, apparently shocked by Otka's scolding. "Move! Now!" she shouted. The young-looking SS looked embarrassed and his flawless face soon matched the color of Addison's. Addison turned toward Otka and she gave him a big smile.

Addison returned her smile with a grateful closed-lipped one and started for the exit portal. He heard slow footsteps behind him; the young-looking SS was also leaving, but obviously not too eagerly. The pace of his steps reminded Addison of a mischievous schoolboy walking reluctantly to the principal's office to receive his punishment. He imagined the young-looking SS now regretted what he had done – no one liked being reprimanded in such a public setting – and this pleased Addison. Distracted by his thoughts, it slipped his mind once more that the exit portal was voice activated and again he walked nose-first into the glass. For the third time in three minutes, the queue burst into laughter, some laughing so intensely that tears ran down their faces. He glanced back at Otka. She gave him the same sympathetic look she had given him after he had been unable to open the heavy door at the church service.

Addison turned back around, said "O-O-O-Open," and walked out of the Depot.

Addison dismounted the transport and headed toward Camp Sycamore. Ten strides or so from the entrance gate, Addison heard someone shout his name. He stopped and turned around. Needle-thin penis! He was snookered. Remy Noodlespine, a co-Menial, was calling to him. Addison exhaled in resignation and tried to hide his obvious annoyance. To adhere to WASP, he would now have to engage Remy in sincere-sounding dialogue for at least a few moments. Addison didn't want to; he didn't like Remy. As far as Addison knew, none of the other Menials liked Remy either. Remy's favorite pastime was SS bootlicking. The other Menials avoided him the way Parisians avoid cheap wine, pasteurized cheese and good manners.

Addison thought for a moment about disregarding WASP. After all, most of the upper castes did nowadays. But he knew that ignoring Remy's advance would embarrass Remy, especially with so many people around, and Addison had felt the brutal sting of humiliation so many times that he couldn't bring himself to inflict that pain on another person, even on someone he genuinely disliked.

Remy was a plump and untucked-looking Cursed with a pasty face that was usually set in a vapid but pleasant expression – a countenance that gave Addison the impression that Remy was not prone to much introspection. He looked to be in his mid-thirties; he had a severely receding hairline, bucked teeth the color of petrified wood and bushy eyebrows. He was usually sweating profusely, even in cold weather, and he had a habit of wearing too much cologne – a sickeningly sweet scent that commingled with his perpetual sweat and caused him to smell like a freshly wetted urinal patty. What really pounded Addison's schnitzel was that in spite of Remy's obvious shortcomings – and on Addison's ledger Remy had quite a few more than he did – Remy appeared to be completely comfortable in his own skin. This flummoxed Addison. Didn't Remy own a mirror? Remy was repulsive looking; what kind of sleight of mind allowed him to generate such self-acceptance?

Remy caught up to Addison by taking a few long and effeminate-looking strides, as if he were leaping over some invisible puddles. He stood by Addison's side, breathing heavy. "Where is the conflagration, Addster?" Remy had a habit of taking the first syllable of someone's name and creating a nickname by adding "ster" to it; this annoyed Addison tremendously. He also used the Blessed dialect whenever he spoke; this annoyed Addison even more.

"Y-You know what they say, Remington," Addison replied, hoping that Remy would find his impromptu nickname equally bothersome, "the late lark gets no larvae," he added, teasing Remy by doing his best Blessed impersonation.

"Well, Addster, I am not going to allow you to arrive before me and make me appear slothful to the camp commander. I have siblings and a committed coitus partner who rely on me for provision. If I were to get sacked, who would supply my dependents with victuals and libations? Are you going to bring over a fresh case of HastyTasty each week if I am unemployed?" Remy gave a few contrived-sounding laughs, apparently trying to give Addison the impression he was joking. Addison knew he was not.

"W-W-Well, I wouldn't want to make you look slothful, Rembrandt (surely that nickname would irritate him), but registering three seconds after me will not have a deleterious effect on your career. Trust me." Addison had fulfilled the requirements of WASP and he was now free to go. As he turned to resume the short walk to the camp entrance, Remy brushed past him with surprising speed for such a portly fellow, scanned his dimpled wrist and shrieked with delight as he entered the camp.

As Addison entered the locker room, he glanced over at Nigel's locker. Nigel's work smock was still hanging in it, which surprised Addison. Nigel was always prompt and usually beat Addison to work. As they had been up late interacting, Nigel was probably just running behind schedule. Addison took off his tunic and reached for his work smock. At that moment, the entrance portal slid open and a blast of cold air blew against his bare back. "A-About time you graced us with your presence. C-Close the portal, will you? It's colder than a woolly mammoth's testicle out there," Addison said, assuming Nigel had entered the locker room. Addison turned to greet his friend and gasped. Starck was standing in front of him.

"I bid you a good morning, Lord Starck," Remy said. "It is my wish that you are feeling as magnificent as you look. Your level of conditioning is quite spectacular. You have obviously been...," Starck interrupted Remy's toadying.

"Menial Hall," Starck bellowed, his voice reverberating through Addison's chest cavity. "Get on your feet and face me now!" Addison was half-dressed; his work smock was bunched around his ankles and he had to pull it up before he could turn around. Starck didn't seem to care. He unsheathed his baton and whacked Addison across the back and shoulder blades. Addison yelped like a whipped dog, wriggled up his smock and turned to face Starck. "First, let me inform you, *Addisoy*, that I expect my orders to be fulfilled most expeditiously," Starck said as he re-sheathed his baton.

Starck continued, "Today is your lucky day, *Addisoy*. I have personally selected you for a special assignment. The rules of the camp dictate that I cannot order you to participate in special work if there is no corresponding increase in compensation. No, you must volunteer for this work. So I ask you, puke scrubber, do you volunteer for this special project? Before you answer, let me remind you that it would be quite easy for me to extricate a yes from you by simply delivering some physical punishment, which is well within my rights as a camp official. You could save yourself a heap of hurting if you were to volunteer on your own." Starck rubbed the shaft of his now-holstered baton while he waited for Addison to answer. He didn't have to wait long.

"Y-Y-Y-Yes, Lord. I volunteer," Addison said, his eyes cast down at his bare feet. He noticed that his toenails desperately needed clipping... and cleaning. "Just tell me what task you want accomplished and I will do it."

"I had a strong premonition that you would accept my invitation," Starck said with a smirk. "When you are finished getting dressed – and I pray to the handsome lord in the highest heaven that I never have to gaze upon your unclothed torso again – report to me at the base of the main guard tower. You and I are going to be working closely together on this assignment... *very* closely indeed," Starck said. He dragged out "very" so it sounded like "veeeery." He gave Addison a menacing smile as he stomped out of the locker room.

Addison reached down toward his left pocket to find his rocks, but remembered that he was wearing his work uniform, not his trousers. From the corner of his eye, Addison could see Remy looking on with palpable jealousy.

"Look at you, Addster," Remy said, "getting assigned... I mean... asked to participate in an exclusive assignment from the new camp *wonder boy*. You should be honored..." Remy's voice trailed off remorsefully. Addison stared vacantly into his locker. He heard Remy, but he didn't have the energy or desire to respond. His heart was pounding with such intensity that the puckered fat around his waistline jiggled with each beat. No matter how deeply he inhaled, he could not get enough air. Feeling dizzy, Addison sat down to steady himself.

Starck had set him up. He wasn't yet sure for what, but he knew that he was in danger. "Addster, are you feeling healthy? You look as if you've just seen the specter of mortality," Remy said.

Addison spit out a sardonic chuckle. "I-I-I think I might have just seen the specter of my mortality," he said. His eyes flashed with anger and he barked out uncharacteristically, "And stop calling me Addster! You sound like a real swine's knuckle when you do!" Addison cinched up his smock and walked out of the locker room toward the main guard tower. Either he would make a mistake and give Starck a reason to punish him or Starck would get him alone and fabricate one.

As he walked, Addison kept coming back to one thought – why was Starck out to get him? He guessed that it had something to do with Otka, but what could it be? Sure, Otka was kind to him, but she had shown similar kindness to all of her customers. Did it have something to do with his rescue of the dog from the crystal pit? That was the day Starck made that threatening gesture at him. Addison forced himself to stop trying to understand the reasons behind Starck's anger; he needed to find a way out of this dangerous predicament… quickly. He was now an involuntary participant in some perverse game concocted by Starck – a game where the outcome was already predetermined. Although it had not yet started, Addison knew he had already been defeated. He was convinced he would ultimately be beaten as well. ■

CHAPTER TEN

❖

ADDISON STOOD AT THE BASE of the main guard-house. His left hand dangled at his side and nervously, absentmindedly, he twiddled his fingers as if he were rubbing his polished rocks. Starck was late. While he waited, Addison avoided looking at the guardhouse; the structure made him uneasy. It was an ominous-looking building of dark weathered wood with a roof of concave red beryl shingles. Perched atop long black stilts, it reminded Addison of a gigantic insect. A large rotating spotlight ("a giant prying eye," Nigel called it) was mounted in one of the guardhouse windows. Small wooden signs with the word "HALT" stenciled in black lettering above a skull and crossbones were placed in the ground in front of each stilt. Entering this area without SS approval was forbidden.

From his position at the base of the tower, Addison could see Starck talking to a group of campers erecting a prefabricated building at the western end of the camp. Addison also noticed with some surprise that no progress had been made on the mysterious structure being built just outside the camp's western barrier. The vertical supports for it looked lonely, like a cluster of denuded trees in a barren forest.

Starck continued to talk to the campers. Although the hum from the fissile plutonium power generator made it difficult for Addison to hear what Starck was saying, it appeared to be a typical SS harangue as Starck was waving his arms wildly as he spoke. Standing next to Starck was a blond-haired boy wearing a brown tunic and black lederhosen. Addison recognized it as the uniform of the Brock Lads – a well-organized group of brain-scrubbed youths that focused on building beautiful bodies through weightlifting, cardiovascular conditioning and healthy eating. Starck turned and walked back toward the guardhouse with his right hand placed paternally on the left shoulder of the Brock Lad.

When Starck reached the guardhouse, his chiseled face was flushed. "Maggot Hall!" he bellowed, "I am only going to articulate the details of this critical assignment once, so give me your undivided attention. Failure to carry out my requirements precisely as stated will result in a most harsh reprisal."

"Y-Y-Y-Yes, Lord," Addison said, his nervous stammer appropriate for a change. The Brock Lad affixed to Starck's side had an obnoxious little smile on his handsome little face. He instantly annoyed Addison.

"You will be providing assistance at the Arrival Station today," Starck said. "Our Leader has selected this camp to be the proving ground for some critical medical experiments. This research is so vitally important that the Minister of Health Services, Dr. Gleemen, will be personally supervising the experiments. The doctor has requested that we provide him with some fresh new campers to assist with this project. These *volunteers* will be transported here over the next three fortnights and your task is to register them as they arrive. You are to wear this garment whilst you toil," Starck said and he threw a balled-up camper's uniform top at Addison. Addison's reflexes were slow and the garment struck him on the nose causing his eyes to water. Addison wiped away his tears with the back of his hand. Starck laughed. "Aww, look at the infant weeping. Did someone abscond with your swatch of comforting cloth?" Starck asked mockingly. The Brock Lad laughed hard and loud; Addison recognized it as the typical counterfeit laugh that underlings give in response to their superiors' jokes (especially bad ones). He was surprised, however, that a preteen boy had enough savvy to pull it off. Starck smiled broadly when he saw the Brock Lad's reaction, obviously believing it to be sincere. Starck's smile quickly flipped to a scowl. "Dr. Gleemen requires that these *volunteers* be kept calm, unruffled and serene. Do you comprehend? They are not to be stressed, crumpled or agitated in any way. Say whatever you have to say and take whatever actions you need to take in order to ensure this. Do you comprehend?"

"Y-Y-Y-Yes, Lord" Addison said.

"I would love to personally supervise you for the first portion of this assignment, but I have to immediately attend to some important business with more intelligent and attractive people. Until I return, I am placing you under the supervision of my friend, Dolaf, here." Addison breathed a noticeable sigh of relief. "Do not be too relieved, vomit scraper; I will be joining you later." Starck pinched his chiseled chin and tilted his head upward, affecting a pensive pose, "And I have a strong premonition, *Addisoy*, that you and I will spend some quality time together when I return." Starck spun on his heels, launching a small plume of gravel and dirt in Addison's direction, and stomped away.

Dolaf picked up where Starck had left off; however, his squeaky preteen voice made his commands sound comical and Addison had to bite his lower lip to keep from smiling. "Listen to me, Maggot Hall. I am a surrogate for Lord Starck and I am to be shown the same respect you would show him. Do not take me lightly or else you will pay for your insolence when Lord Starck returns." Dolaf spun on his heels, but rotated too far and, for a moment, it looked as if he might lose his balance. Addison's eyes widened, hoping this little zealot would fall, but Dolaf disappointed him by righting himself. Dolaf straightened his shoulders (so wide for such a young boy!) and followed after Starck, extending his strides so he could trace the large footprints left by Starck.

Addison wiped away a remaining tear from his cheek and tucked the uniform under his left arm. He would wear it, of course – he didn't need to give Starck or his pocket-sized disciple an obvious reason to punish him – but he would put it on when he reported to the Arrival Station. The holographic time projection read 09:12. He had just enough time to return to the Menial locker room and use the waste elimination chamber. Once he got to the Arrival Station, he knew he would be forced to work without a biological or sustenance break for his entire shift.

When Addison entered the locker room, he noticed that Nigel's work smock was still hanging in his locker. His friend was officially tardy. Addison grew a bit more concerned, but he wasn't overly worried. In the four-plus years they had worked together, Addison couldn't recall a single instance where Nigel had been tardy to work. He figured that punishment for this blunder wouldn't be too severe – probably just a short flogging across the shins or upper back.

Addison left the locker room and walked toward the Arrival Station, which was located near the camp entrance. From a distance, he could see that Dolaf was already there, standing with his hands on his narrow hips. Addison put on the camper's uniform top. Gorgeous god, it was uncomfortable! If possible, it was made of an even harsher material than his Menial uniform. Dolaf saw Addison coming and walked to meet him.

"Glad to see you are punctual, Hall," Dolaf said, his high-pitched voice once again making his commanding language sound humorous. Dolaf pulled a small piece of writing foil out of the front pocket of his lederhosen and read, "You will be working the RU today. You are to input these new arrivals into the camp registry. Dr. Gleemen requires that these volunteers be kept calm, unruffled and serene. Do you comprehend?" He was using Starck's exact words, "They are not to be stressed, vexed or agitated in any way…" Dolaf stopped talking and looked over Addison's shoulder. Addison turned. It was Starck.

"Excellent point you are making, my muscular little friend," Starck said and he tousled Dolaf's blond hair. "I have just been speaking with Dr. Gleemen concerning this very topic. He wanted me to emphasize, Addisoy, that it is critically important that these volunteers be kept calm. He reiterated to me that his experiments will not be as effective if they are anxious, worried or apprehensive. Are you certain you understand?"

"Y-Y-Yes, Lord," Addison replied. Why did he keep putting an emphasis on the word "volunteers"? Starck spun on his heels and stomped back toward the main guardhouse.

"Are you clear on Lord Starck's clarifications, Hall?" Dolaf squeaked.

"As clear as a burlesque dancer's heel, you little lemming," Addison wanted to say. He had come up with that analogy during his morning commute (inspired by a remarkably underdressed holographic saleswoman) and he thought it was wonderfully clever. In fact, he had hoped to try it out on Nigel that morning. Now wasn't the appropriate time for it, however; he couldn't risk the possibility that Dolaf might tell Starck. "Y-Yes, I am," he simply replied.

"'Yes I am' what?" Dolaf asked.

"Y-Yes, I am, Lord," Addison said through his clenched, amber-colored teeth.

Addison took his position behind the RU. He rolled up his sleeves and folded down the coarse collar on the uniform top. He had been wearing the uniform for only a few minutes and already the areas of his skin not protected by his work smock were chafed. Addison heard the rush of an approaching transport. When it arrived, he sucked the air in shock. The transport was literally stuffed with passengers! Arms, legs, sides of faces, tops of heads, bottoms and torsos were pressed against the transport windows. A transport could carry twenty or so normally weighted people; this one had to be carrying at least three times that! The transport portal slid open and a pile of intertwined bodies spilled out onto the station platform. Handsome and holy lord, what a horrible smell! Addison put the sandpaper sleeve of his camper's uniform over his nose. A sickening waft of vomit, feces and urine emanated from the transport. Addison pressed the uniform sleeve tighter against his nose, so tight that the rough fabric scratched his skin; but the scratched skin was a small price to pay to get relief from such a ghastly stench. As the new arrivals lined up on the platform, Addison noticed two other oddities. First, these new arrivals were completely silent and their faces were expressionless – new arrivals usually talked amongst themselves and the Arrival platform typically hummed with soft chatter. These campers were so quiet that Addison could hear mayflies buzzing around the soiled transport at least thirty meters away. Mercifully, the transport portal closed and the transport pulled out of the station with a swarm of mayflies chasing after it. It was only after Addison removed his sandpaper sleeve from his nose that he noticed the other oddity – all of the new arrivals were extreme Cursed citizens. All were hideous looking; most were disfigured. Addison saw goiters, cleft palates, acute cases of Bell's palsy, albinism, craniosynostosis,[7] and a few disgusting anomalies that Addison couldn't identify. One man had a coin-sized orifice instead of a nose, which gave Addison an excellent but nauseating view of his wiry-haired, mucous-coated nasal passages.

As Addison gawked at these high SIN citizens, he noticed something else disturbing – none of the new arrivals was grotesquely obese. There were a few that could be considered overweight, but none of them even remotely compared to those in the current camp population. Didn't Nigel tell him he had overheard two SS talking about the camp expanding to include the "unsightly" as well? Addison's arms and legs broke out in gooseflesh. Even though the proof of what Nigel had heard was right before his eyes, it still didn't make any sense. What would a perspiration camp do for ugly people? Losing weight wouldn't make them more bearable to look at. There had to be another reason why they were sent. But what was it?

Addison didn't have time to ponder this any further – the new arrivals had been "coerced" into a tidy queue by a group of SS menacingly waving their batons. The first new arrival, a lanky fellow with a cleft palate, was heading toward Addison. What a disgusting curse, Addison thought. As the poor man got closer, Addison saw that saliva was dripping from the gap in his mouth, rolling down his neck and saturating his tunic. Addison took a deep breath and tried to concentrate. He couldn't let these grotesques distract him – one mistake and Starck would have an excuse to punish him.

A tall SS standing near the Recognition Unit put his hand out and stopped the lanky man with the cleft palate just a couple of meters from Addison by driving his forearm into the man's throat. The SS looked at the wet mark left on his spandex uniform top (a result of the lanky man's drool) and kneed the man in the groin. The lanky man grabbed at his crotch and dropped to the ground.

---

7   A genetic disorder of the skull that results in an abnormally shaped head.

The SS placed a stick of amplifying gum in his mouth, chewed vigorously for a few seconds, and spoke in a booming voice, "Attention! You have just arrived at Camp Sycamore – the oldest of the Beautification Retreats and soon to be the shining jewel of the Beautification System Network. First let me inform you that you are a most fortunate group of citizens. You are going to be given the chance to express your patriotism, and your devotion to Our Leader, by assisting our highly esteemed Chief Medical Officer in a critical research project. And if the honor of serving your nation isn't enough reward, we will be crediting your commerce accounts with a significant deposit upon project completion. While I can't reveal the actual amount, let me just say that you will have such a preponderance of credits to spend that my fear is that some of you might develop tendonitis in your right wrists from excessive procuring," the SS chuckled. No one in the queue even cracked a smile. The SS chewed a few more times and continued, "Your stay at this facility will not extend longer than a fortnight and you will be kept separate from the existing camp population. Yes, no need to fret, you will not be forced to engage in social intercourse with those blubbery bastards," he chuckled again. The new arrivals' faces remained expressionless. "The details of your assignment will be revealed to you shortly. If any of the guards can do anything to make your stay more comfortable, please do not hesitate to ask. Are there any questions?" He continued without pausing, "Excellent. Present your wrists to your fellow camper at the RU and as you are registered, please specify whether you would prefer a camp or river view from your private room." Addison gave the SS a confused look – camp or river view? Was this guy serious? Addison started scanning wrists. The queue was advancing slowly; he had only registered five new arrivals when the second transport whisked into the station. The scene was similar to that of the first transport, but the pong from this transport was even worse.

Assuming he was a camper, each new arrival directed their questions to Addison, questions that Addison couldn't answer. "What are they going to do to us?" "What is the purpose of this research?" "Can we have visitors?"

"Is it going to be painful?" Unable to answer their questions and anxious to keep the new arrivals calm (lest he violate Starck's order), Addison told them verbatim what the SS had told them moments ago. Hearing it from an unattractive man wearing an ill-fitting camper's uniform (rather than an Adonis wearing a tight black spandex one) apparently made a difference. Addison was able to allay the new arrivals' concerns. His job was to keep them "calm, unruffled and serene" and he was doing just that. He had to begrudgingly give Starck credit – dressing him in a camper's uniform helped put the new arrivals at ease.

As Addison scanned each arrival, they gave him their room preference. Addison repeated it; however, he had not been given instructions on how to record their requests. Was this how Starck was going to trap him? He brought this to the attention of the tall SS who was making the welcoming announcement, but he just snickered and ignored Addison's question.

Answering the new arrivals' questions caused the queue to move slowly, and while this didn't seem to bother the tall SS, Dolaf seemed quite agitated. Every so often he squeaked, "Increase your pace, Hall!" After a few minutes of this, the tall SS walked over and whispered something in Dolaf's ear. After that, Dolaf stopped berating Addison; the tall SS had apparently chastised him. The diminutive zealot looked chagrined.

Yet another transport arrived at the station and this new group of arrivals received the same well-rehearsed speech from the tall SS. Addison kept scanning wrists and never looked up. By this time, he had developed a good working rhythm – grab the new arrival's wrist, scan the wrist, wait for the confirmation beep from the Recognition Unit, then release the wrist. After a short while, he didn't even have to look up to see what he was doing. Grab, scan, wait for the beep, release. Grab, scan, wait for the beep, release.

As soon as the queue would dwindle, another transport would arrive. Addison lost track of how many transports had docked; he guessed about three per hour. As the day advanced, the combination of squinting into the sun and standing hunched over the RU had given him a headache so severe that he felt nauseous. Between scans, he rubbed his temples trying to relieve the pain. At least the sun was going down; he wouldn't have to squint for much longer. He glanced over his shoulder toward the guardhouse. A large man was walking toward the Arrival Station. The setting sun created a silhouette of the main guardhouse and the humongous one-eyed insect looked even more threatening. So did the gait of the approaching man, which Addison immediately recognized as Starck's bully strut. Keep your focus, he thought. Don't give him a reason to punish you. There were only four more new arrivals to register – grab, scan, wait for the beep, release. Addison heard heavy footsteps approaching from behind him. Dolaf screeched enthusiastically, "Lord Starck! Welcome back!" Addison could see Starck out of the corner of his eye, but he kept working. Maintain your concentration; you're almost finished, he thought.

"So Dolie, how has our vomit scrubber performed?" Starck said.

"He has been adequate, Lord Starck. He has executed his tasks in a minimally sufficient manner," Dolaf said.

"You will learn, my good-looking protégé, that lower caste members, with their limited intelligence, are only capable of achieving mediocrity. Only Blesseds, and on rare occasions a particularly gifted Favored, can perform with consistent excellence."

What rubbish! Addison thought. Dolaf just nodded, as if what Starck had just said was an irrefutable fact rather than an overt Face-ist opinion. When Addison looked up, three faceless silhouettes remained in the queue. Be careful, he thought. Starck will use even the smallest slip-up as an excuse to punish you.

"Dolaf, why don't you go enjoy the evening's entertainment in the officers' lounge," Starck said playfully. "The commander has arranged to have a few of the most fetching members of the Wakork bicepball spirit-amplifying dance regiment perform the ancient striptease ritual for the men. If it is anything like past performances, it will be a stimulating event." The words had barely cleared Starck's lips when little Dolaf took off running toward the officers' locker room.

Naturally, Nigel had heard rumors about what took place during these striptease rituals. According to Nigel, female single-digit SIN-ners walked around a stage wearing only their counterfeit copper tans and carrying a large sizzling steak on a glass platter. The sweet aroma of the steak, coupled with the lusty body of a nude woman, flirted with two of the seven fatal transgressions and created a potent sensual experience for the audience. It was called a "striptease," according to Nigel, because the cut of meat used was a strip steak, which produced a delicious aroma when broiled due to its high fat content.

While Starck sent Dolaf tearing off in an excited adolescent froth, Addison continued working. He looked up, grabbed a new arrival's wrist, waited for the beep, and then released. Two new arrivals remained. Grab, scan, wait for the beep, release. The last new arrival stood in line. He was going to make it. He had little doubt that Starck would still punish him, but he wasn't going to give him a reason to.

Addison looked up, grabbed the wrist of the last new arrival in the queue and froze. He held his breath and held the new arrival's wrist motionless, just a few millimeters short of the RU. Starck walked over, but Addison remained motionless. Starck shouted in an incredulous voice, "What are you waiting for?! Scan the wrist, Menial!" Addison cowered from the volume of Starck's voice, but still didn't scan the new arrival's wrist.

Starck lifted his arm high over his head and brought his baton down hard across Addison's shoulder blades. Addison yelped in pain and was shaken out of his shocked stupor. He scanned the wrist, waited for the beep, and released it. He glanced up at the newly registered camper with a look of deep remorse. The new camper avoided making eye contact and walked briskly from the registration area with his eyes cast downward and his feet pointed outward. Addison had just scanned the wrist of his friend, Nigel.

Addison was too stunned to move, too startled to breathe. Why Nigel? Addison felt disconnected from his body, an uninvolved witness to what had just transpired. He watched with disbelief as Nigel walked in his familiar gait away from the station with the other new arrivals. A few SS buzzed around the line, occasionally swatting at the new arrivals with their batons to keep them moving briskly. Addison's shock gave way to concern. What were they going to do with Nigel? What type of experiments were they going to conduct? Addison had no answers. While this troubled him, he had his own problem. His delay in registering Nigel had just given Starck an unimpeachable reason to punish him. ■

CHAPTER ELEVEN

❖

ADDISON STOOD IN THE MIDDLE of a small square room, squeezing the muscles of his buttocks in an attempt to contain his liquefied bowels. The room had one window, facing westward, and the fading sunlight that poured in swathed the interior with a dim orange glow. Under the window sat a small wooden table; a rusty shovel lay diagonally across it, anchored down by a cluster of long-since-abandoned spiderwebs. Addison guessed he was in a maintenance shed.

The floor was greasy – Addison could slide his feet from side to side as if he were standing on a sheet of dirty ice. The air in the room was stagnant; it smelled of sawdust and petroleum. It reminded Addison of his POP's toolshed. He grimaced as he recalled how his POP used to berate him for doing "unacceptable work" whenever he asked (forced) Addison to assist him with his endless series of small projects. That was the word his POP always used – "unacceptable." Was it Addison's fault he couldn't pound a fastener in straight or laser-cut a piece of wood along the prescribed line? He tried his best; he just wasn't good at it. Yet each and every time, his work was labeled "unacceptable." All these years later and Addison was still hurt by the unfairness of his POP's criticisms.

Starck had tossed Addison into this room immediately after he registered Nigel. He had been waiting in frightened solitude for what felt like a half hour. He guessed that fear was distorting his perception and that the actual time was less than that as the sun was still clinging to the horizon.

Starck had told Addison to remain completely motionless. "Do not even allow one of your underdeveloped muscles to involuntarily twitch," he'd said, and he had finished his warning with a dangling threat – "or else." Or else what? Or else I will put on a chrome tiara and dance around the shed like a whimsy pixie? Addison smiled. His birther would be proud that he was able to make a joke even though he was in this terrifying predicament. She would often tell him "when facing tribulation, make light of your situation."

Sweat ran down his forehead, stinging his eyes and dripping onto his smock. He had not removed the camper uniform top and his perspiration rolled off the collar like water off a Vegavis iaai's[8] derriere. This waiting was torturous. He decided that waiting for his pending beating was worse than actually receiving it.

How would Starck beat him? Would he use his baton? (He always seemed to be touching it.) Would he use his fists? Would he kick Addison the way he kicked that fat camper he pulled from the waste container? Where was Starck anyway? Was he purposely delaying his arrival to further torment Addison? Maybe he was involved in some other camp activity? Could he possibly have forgotten? Of the three possibilities, Addison knew that wasn't likely at all. Starck had manipulated events to get Addison into this situation; this was premeditated. There was not a chance in unheaven he would forget.

Addison contemplated peering out the window to check the time, but thought better of it. He wasn't sure his trembling legs could carry his weight. Suddenly, the door swung open and Starck stood in the doorframe with his legs spread shoulder-width apart and his hands on his hips. Addison was struck by the width of his shoulders; Starck's body clogged the entire doorframe. He glared triumphantly down at Addison, "Well, vomit scrubber, it is time for you and I to dance."

In spite of the pending danger, when Starck said "dance," it took all of Addison's self-control to keep from grinning as he thought back to his pixie joke from moments ago. Starck took a step into the room and continued in his deep voice, "For some unfathomable reason, my current coitus companion is *fond* of you," Starck paused, as if what he had just said surprised even him. He continued incredulously, as if he had momentarily forgotten who

---

8   A genus of bird that lived during the Late Cretaceous epoch that is closely related to modern barnyard fowl.

he was speaking to, "Isn't that the most baffling thing you have ever heard? She likes *you*, an underattractive Burdened! She revealed this to me after you pulled that engineered rodent out of the crystal pit. She had the unmitigated nerve to ask me if *I* would have attempted to rescue that mutated rat. Me! Do you believe it?! Does she believe I would take even the slightest risk of damaging my god-given gorgeousness? What a preposterous query!"

Addison was dumbfounded; so dumbfounded that he blurted out, "O-O-Otka is fond of me?"

Oh no! Starck hadn't given him permission to speak. He was about to apologize profusely, but Starck spoke again before Addison had a chance, "I know that is astounding information, but according to Otka, you have a 'sweet soul.' Gorgeous god, that woman is confounding! What does that even mean, 'sweet soul'?" Starck's demeanor softened; he looked genuinely befuddled, as if he had just been asked to produce scientific proof supporting the theory of evolution. It made him look vulnerable and allowed Addison to relax a bit. Maybe he would get out of this unscathed after all? Then Starck seemed to remember who he was talking to. He narrowed his eyes and glared at Addison. Addison's sliver of hope vanished as quickly as the saliva in his mouth. "What is a soul? Can you tell me that, puke cleaner?" Addison wasn't sure if he was supposed to answer or not. He quickly decided it was more prudent not to answer. "I have a brilliant idea," Starck said with a twisted smile on his face. "Why don't you show me your 'sweet soul,' so I can understand why my current coitus companion finds it so appealing? Let's see it, Addisoy," Starck stared at Addison expectantly. Addison fixed his gaze on Starck's knees. What could he possibly show him? And what would Starck do if he just remained silent?

"Well, naturally you are as dumb as you are ugly. You dare to disregard my order? I said show me your sweet soul… NOW!" Starck screamed. Addison leaned his body away from Starck, trying to put even a few more centimeters between him and this suddenly raging monster. "Well, if you aren't going to show me this 'sweet soul,' then I am going to BEAT IT OUT OF YOU!" Starck took out his baton, let out a deep roar and lunged at Addison. He brought his baton down hard on Addison's left elbow, instantly paralyzing his arm. Addison fell to the ground on his left side, protecting his injured arm. Starck brought the baton down on Addison's right elbow and rendered that arm useless as well. Addison rolled onto his back and flailed his legs wildly, trying to fend off Starck, who had positioned himself between Addison's legs.

Addison kicked his left leg weakly at Starck, who was smiling. (Luscious lord, he had gorgeous teeth!) Whether he was smiling at Addison's feeble attempt to fight back or he was enjoying what he was doing, Addison did not know, but he guessed it was a combination of both. Starck grabbed Addison's flailing left leg, tucked it under his right arm and squeezed, putting incredible pressure on Addison's femur. His leg was going to break! Starck reared back his left leg and kicked at Addison's exposed crotch. Addison twisted his hips, causing Starck to miss. His big black boot sunk deep into Addison's upper thigh. Addison shouted in pain.

"Discontinue your squirming! You are only going to protract your suffering!" Starck shouted and spittle from his mouth flew in every direction – this wasn't a man; it was a rabid animal! "Enough of this foreplay," Starck screamed. "The time has come to introduce you to your creator. You can complain to him for the rest of eternity for making you so ugly." Starck positioned Addison's body so Addison's face was aligned with his right boot. Starck drew back his leg. Addison closed his eyes. This was it. Starck was going to crush his skull. Addison was strangely calm, and noted with slight surprise that despite being just seconds away from his death, his life was not flashing before his eyes. Wasn't that supposed to happen? He was relieved that it didn't; it was not a life he was keen on reviewing.

As Addison braced for the kick, he heard a loud metallic thud. Something large and heavy fell next to him, causing the floor to tremble. What happened? Why hadn't Starck kicked him? Addison smelled espresso and jasmine, Otka's scent. He opened his eyes. Starck was lying beside him! What he had smelled was the sleeve of Starck's uniform – his massive arm had landed right next to Addison's nose.

❖

Starck was down, but he wasn't dead. Addison could still hear him breathing. Addison quietly got to his knees, afraid that he might somehow awaken him. The old rusty shovel was lying on the floor next to Starck. Someone had hit Starck with this shovel, but who? And why?

Addison glanced around the small room, but saw no one. He walked over to the door and looked out, but again saw no one. He tried to move the shovel with his foot, but it wouldn't budge. Whoever had knocked out Starck had to be strong; the shovel was heavy. Addison noticed a small translucent chip lying on the floor near the shovel handle. He picked it up and looked at it more closely. Sexy succulent savior! It was a fingernail! Addison guessed by its size that it was the nail to either a pointer or index finger. He considered putting it in his pocket, but changed his mind and placed it back where he had found it. He didn't want to move any evidence that might in some way incriminate him. The best thing he could do now was leave quickly.

Just then, Starck let out a raspy groan. Inverted third nipple! He was waking up! Addison tiptoed out of the shed and walked hastily toward the Menial locker room. Every couple of seconds, he glanced back to ensure Starck wasn't chasing him. Twenty meters from the locker room portal, Addison finally slowed down. He entered the room breathing hard and sweating. He quickly changed into his caste-designated light green tunic and left the camp. As he waited for the transport, he tried to sort out what had just happened.

Starck's anger was fueled by jealousy over the fact that Otka was fond of him? She liked his "sweet soul"? Addison couldn't believe it. But there was no denying Starck's rage. Still, Addison was puzzled. How could a perfect-looking Blessed like Starck be jealous of him, a completely inferior Burdened? This had to be some sort of precedent. Here was a man who possessed in absurd abundance all the qualities that Addison ached for and he is whipped into a homicidal frenzy over a "soul," a trait that wasn't even visible? Why did Otka find it appealing? And why did Starck even care that she did? Addison wasn't sure why. He was sure of one thing, however. He would gladly swap his "sweet soul" for Starck's finely formed face, massive muscles and beautiful blond hair.

Addison pondered a more intriguing question. Who had come to his rescue? Was it someone he knew or just a passing Good Samaritan? Addison had no clue. The only person he could think of was Nigel, but there was no conceivable way that Nigel could have sneaked away from the SS and helped him. Besides, Nigel's skinny arms could never have lifted that heavy shovel. Could it have been Remy? Addison snickered at the thought. That bootlicker would have sat his fat posterior on my legs to make it easier for Starck to attack me, he thought. The only plausible explanation was that someone who happened to be walking by took pity on him and decided to help. But who would be brave enough to assault Starck? One would either have to kill Starck or render him unconscious; to leave him in any other condition would be a death sentence for the aggressor. It was unimaginable to Addison that anyone could get the better of Starck in a physical confrontation. Could it have been another SS?

As he continued to wait for the transport, Addison absently rested his hand on a nearby billboard. Then he remembered – this was the rotting wooden billboard. Before he could pull his hand back, he noticed that the decaying relic had finally been replaced. Now printed on smooth acetate was a beautiful, five-dimensional, six-color image of a majestic lion sitting on a ruby red velvet pillow, looking down at a mud-caked pig sitting in a sty. The pig said, "Everything with an animal's face is equal," to which the lion replied, "That is what you filthy pigs would like us to think." Addison grinned. Despite its ludicrous message, he found this overt propaganda rather amusing. In fact, the pig triggered a memory. Addison recalled a story, written by an author from the Fortress of Britain (whose name he couldn't immediately recall), where an intelligent pig told a gathering of farm animals that "all animals are equal, but some animals are more equal than others."

Addison's thoughts wandered back to the possibility that an SS might have hit Starck. Could it have been an SS who was fond of Otka trying to eliminate Starck? Addison saw the way men gawked at her. Or maybe an SS had attacked Starck seeking revenge? Someone as arrogant as Starck was bound to have enemies. Addison might simply have benefited from someone Starck had mistreated. After all, even attractive people displayed hideous emotions – Starck had proven that on more than a few occasions.

Addison heard the rush of the arriving transport. He walked to the mounting platform, closed his mouth and eyes, and shielded his face with his hand to protect himself from the flurry of debris stirred up by the speeding caboose. Addison still felt peculiar... detached. He knew he should be experiencing a strong surge of emotions, but he felt nothing. He was completely numb. The events of the day had been so overwhelming, so shocking, that his mental circuit breaker had popped, temporarily shutting down all of his emotions to allow him sufficient time to absorb all that had happened.

Strangely, he wasn't the least bit tired. As he boarded the caboose, images from the day's events flashed through his thoughts. Nigel's face when they made eye contact at the RU... Starck's physique clogging the doorframe of the maintenance shed... Dolaf straining to step in Starck's footprints... His POP berating him for his unacceptable work... Starck's maniacal expression when he was beating him... The silhouetted guard tower... As the transport sped off Addison was so absorbed in reflection, he failed to notice a pushy holographic salesperson prattling on about "a freshly engineered Oxygenator with more effective element-bonding technology" just centimeters from his right elbow.

Addison walked toward the entrance to his living complex. "Orwell" popped into his head – he authored the story about the arrogant pigs. As Addison cleared the entrance portal, he noticed that the white light on his in-box was blinking. He queried the central postal server and was notified that a parcel was waiting for him. Who would send him a package? As he scanned his wrist to gain access to the storage chamber, he recalled that a few fortnights prior Nigel had persuaded him to order a signal-pirating device. "It will give you unlimited access to all the Blessed video feeds,"

Nigel had touted, "and all for the mere cost of a thirty-day-cycle's worth of espresso tablets. I've heard all the entertainment is uncensored. It's not only going to be fun to watch, it will be fun to talk about afterward," he had said with a yellow clay grin. So Addison ordered it; more to satisfy Nigel than from a desire to bootleg Blessed programming.

Addison retrieved his package and entered the waiting lift. He was surprised by the package's weight – it was unusually heavy for its size. He was alone in the lift and responded to the automated floor request with stammer-free composure. He entered his living unit, sat down on the edge of his sleeping platform, and waved his right wrist over the embedded security pad to deactivate the lock. The parcel top slid open smoothly. He removed the device and held it up to inspect it.

The device had two rows of three round chrome buttons under a small, rectangular, brushed metal screen. Remaining in the parcel was an instructional holographic chip, but Addison didn't retrieve it. He was sure he could get this device to function properly without watching it. Addison pushed a button on the side of the device and it began vibrating softly. "ERUDITION CONTENT" appeared on the screen.

Although he took pride in his command of the lexicon, Addison had no idea what *erudition* meant. He initially thought that he had accessed religious programming. A tiny man with dark eyes stood behind a Lucite lectern, preaching passionately. The man looked familiar, although Addison couldn't recall where he had seen him before. The man was peculiar looking; he had a tiny head, rodent-like facial features and the budding certainty of a receding hairline. (It was barely noticeable now, but Addison knew it would get worse.) He wore his thin black hair slicked back, in the style of an ancient financier or a personal injury litigator. As he spoke, his eyes darted from side to side rhythmically, as if controlled by a metronome. Then it struck Addison. This was the man from his bonfire dream! Addison slowly walked around the holographic image, studying the man closely. The hairs on the back of his neck prickled. This was absolutely the same man!

Addison sat back down on the corner of his sleeping platform and watched. The tiny man spoke in a baritone voice that belied his diminutive stature. "The Welfare Question provides the key to understanding the conflict and tensions that led to our nation's long-standing economic malaise. It is a fact that a majority of this nation's citizenry has limited knowledge of this Welfare Question. The purpose of tonight's program is to educate the Blesseds, and some select Favoreds, about this critical topic through discourse and interactive dialogue. Our first dissertation will focus on the Law of the Parasite. I will initiate this discussion by stating an immutable axiom – we can only live according to our nature. This applies to all forms of life, for all people. If they cannot live according to their nature, they will perish. In nature, there are creatures that can only live at the expense of the hosts – from the life of other creatures. Grapevine and grapevine louse – without a grapevine, the louse perishes. A tree and mistletoe – without a tree to support it, there is no mistletoe. One has to accept this law; one cannot change it. Pity, brotherly love and forgiveness are useless. There are no good or bad parasites, no decent or indecent parasites. The parasite always creeps up looking harmless and innocent, as if it belongs there. It acts, however, as an infection. At first a small cut, then swelling, then an abscess, then poisoning, and finally leading to the destruction of the entire body. The infested body grows weak, sleepy; it cannot resist any longer. Death soon follows. My fellow patriots, the Burdened and Cursed are the economic parasites among our citizens. We have completed a comprehensive study of the welfare records for the past ten annums and the fact is that more than ninety percent of the welfare recipients would be classified today as either Burdeneds or Curseds. As for those other ten percent, we can attribute their inclusion to flaccid motivation – a direct result of the economic hopelessness cultivated by this country's former leaders. The ancient holy writings tell us that where there is no vision, the people perish. When Our Leader took office and provided this nation with a clear vision for economic recovery, ninety-eight percent of these ten percent quickly transformed themselves into exemplary producers. As for the other two percent? Even our Chancellor's leadership couldn't reform these unfortunates. Multiple annums of defeatism had overwhelmed them beyond the threshold of rehabilitation. Although tragic, it is an excellent illustration of how quickly this country's economy could backslide without the firm but loving hand of Our Leader."

"My point is that this is natural law. The Burdeneds and Curseds cannot behave differently. They need a host to survive; if they exist, they exist at our expense. To eliminate them is not immoral since it is either us or them! In eliminating them, we commit no crime against life, or god, but rather we serve life's Law of Battle, which always opposes that which is an enemy to a healthy life. Our struggle serves to maintain life." Hoping to cut the feed, Addison pushed the same button again. To his relief, the tiny man was sucked into the floor and vanished.

Addison was angry. He could not believe what he had just heard. The Burdeneds and Curseds were economic parasites? What a heap of hooey! Well, he wasn't a parasite – he had never taken welfare; he had always earned his pay. There were thousands of "unattractive" just like him. This Face-ist propaganda was not only irresponsible, it was dangerous. No wonder the upper castes were exhibiting more animus toward the lower castes. Their pretty heads were being filled with ugly lies.

Addison stood up and walked over to his window. He bent down and peered out, hoping his partial view of the Luvista would soothe his agitation. Since he had left Camp Sycamore, he'd found it difficult to focus on one particular topic for more than a few seconds. He took a deep breath, taking in as much air as his lungs could hold (and discerning the odor of vaporized trash). He exhaled slowly. Upon receiving the parcel his emotional fog had started to lift. Watching the tiny, rodent-faced man had galvanized his thoughts, made him resolute. Addison decided that the next day he would seek out Pankewitz before he went to work. He would ask Pankewitz about the undercover escape operation that Nigel believed he was operating. Addison knew that Starck wouldn't stop pursuing him. His nerves, already strung tight, couldn't cope much longer with such impending terror. But he couldn't just leave Wakork; he would have to leave Alpdon. Leaving Wakork would just save him from immediate danger. By leaving Alpdon, he would escape persecution completely. For while Addison believed that some were created "more equal" than others, he also believed that all people, regardless if they looked like "pigs" or "lions," had the right to be treated with equal respect. Brock's regime regarded the lower castes with contempt. After witnessing the rodent-faced man's monologue, he was convinced that the treatment of the lower castes would continue to deteriorate until the nation finally came to its senses and usurped Brock's power. The more likely outcome was that Brock would maintain his power and ratchet up the persecution.

The lower caste citizens of Alpdon were not "pigs" but rather "frogs," helplessly floating in a pot of water on Brock's "stove." And the rising anger of the upper castes would embolden Brock to turn up the heat. Would Brock bring the water to a boil? Based on the tiny man's monologue, it was a real possibility. Nigel needed help; he wasn't sure what he could do, but he had to try to do something. Addison was going to have to find a way to get out of Brock's pot. ■

CHAPTER TWELVE

❖

THE AUTOMATIC WAKING DEVICE ACTIVATED, but Addison had already dismounted his sleeping platform and was preparing for work. He knew it was possible that Pankewitz was not involved in an escape operation. Or, if he was involved, that he would not be willing to help Addison. Taking "the unicorn by the horn," rather than waiting around and getting "gored in the derriere" as he usually did, made him unusually energetic. Unable to quiet his mind from the day's tumult, Addison had hardly slept; yet he didn't feel the least bit sluggish.

Addison's plan was to leave his living unit a few minutes early and wait for Pankewitz in the foyer. He knew that Pankewitz left for work around the same time he did each day; he had seen Pankewitz on the lift a few times. Addison needed to tidy up his mailbox. He decided to sort through his personal mail folder and delete the digital debris. (This had to be done every few fortnights to ensure storage limitations weren't exceeded.) It would also allow him to loiter inconspicuously in the foyer. He was slaying two pterodactyls by throwing one fist-sized rock! He thought his plan was wonderfully clever; however, he would only have fifteen minutes or so to carry it out. He couldn't take even a slight risk of being late for work. In fact, he would have loved to take the day off altogether – he was terrified that Starck might once again get him alone – but he didn't have that option. If he didn't register at Camp Sycamore by 08:35, he would be in violation of Alpdon's Productivity Laws.

The Productivity Laws went into effect soon after the SIN evaluations were completed to ensure that the country produced to its maximum capacity each day. Laborers who worked in any industry where goods were manufactured or laborers who worked in industries that supported manufacturing (raw materials, transportation, warehousing, etc.) were required by law to show up for work every day and on time. Each laborer was given a five-minute grace period; after that, the laborer was considered tardy. Five tardy arrivals in one year was a Prime Crime. The only acceptable excuse for missing a day's work was a "debilitating illness," which had to be sanctioned with a digital certificate by the Bureau of Health. (What constituted a "debilitating illness" was never defined.) Missing a day of work without a certificate from the Bureau of Health was also a Prime Crime. These laborers were denied vacations and had to work all holidays, even Brock's birthday.

About a year ago, without any communication, explanation or justification, Brock had extended these laws to include all lower caste laborers. Addison had no alternative; he had to show up for work at Sycamore today. If he didn't, he would be committing a Prime Crime. He already had three late arrivals this year; being tardy would put him perilously close to committing a Prime Crime.

There were thirty-eight solicitations in Addison's mail folder – more than a dozen were for some new sexual pleasure enhancer called "the CLIMAXimizer" that boasted the ability to create an "earlobes to shin bones" orgasm. Before he could read any further, the lift door slid open and three Burdeneds dismounted the lift, but Pankewitz was not one of them. Addison kept his head buried in his virtual folder and acted as if he was so absorbed with his task that he didn't even notice them. If he made eye contact with someone, he knew he would be socially bound to engage in WASP and might miss his chance to speak with Pankewitz.

When the three left the foyer and exited the living complex without even glancing his way, Addison was relieved. Then it occurred to him – how would he approach Pankewitz? Suppose others were with him on the lift. He was so nervous; he knew he would stammer more than usual. What if he couldn't get his words out?

The lift portal slid open and two more people appeared. Addison looked up quickly, saw that Pankewitz wasn't among them, and buried his face back in his virtual in-box. Moments later, the lift delivered two more people, but again Pankewitz was not one of them. Addison's nervousness increased. What if Pankewitz had already left? The holographic timepiece read 07:51. He would have to leave in nine minutes if he was to arrive at Sycamore by 08:30. Another lift arrived; Addison watched hopefully as the portal slid open, but still no Pankewitz. Addison grew more concerned. He glanced at the holographic timepiece – he had seven minutes left. Another lift arrived. Addison watched the portal expectantly. The door slid open. Alopecia! He cursed to himself. It was Remy!

"Greetings, Addster! Why aren't you at work yet?" Remy asked. Addison saw several beads of sweat on Remy's upper lip and noticed with disgust that his wetted-urinal-patty odor was already at midday strength. How did he generate so much perspiration so early in the day? He obviously wasn't engaging in an early morning exercise program.

"I-I was going to ask you the same question," Addison said defiantly, his eyes burning from Remy's cologne. Did he think such a heavy-handed application of fragrance was appealing? Heavy-handed – an inadvertent yet appropriate pun, Addison thought.

"You are correct in your counter-charge, Addster," Remy said, "but I have the proper authorization to be tardy. Last evening was my cohabitation anniversary. My coitus partner and I have been together for seven annums and we had an evening of celebration. We had sufficient sustenance, of course, and then we mounted our sleeping platform," Remy smiled mischievously, as if about to say something bawdy, "and I hate to be boastful, but our coitus was passionate and rapidly paced. We spent most of the night on our platform, but we didn't engage in much slumber," Remy said, wagging his chubby index finger. He laughed loudly. Addison could see that the ribbon holding Remy's jingler was so tight it looked like it was cutting painfully into his plump neck. Addison hoped it was.

Remy's bragging made Addison angry. How did Remy land a coitus companion? Addison had seen Remy's coitus partner, she was homelier than a giant-clawed ground sloth,[9] but someone was better than no one.

---

9   A megalonychid that first appeared during the early Oligocene epoch.

"Well, Addster, I am going to proceed to work. Will you be accompanying me?"

"N-Not just yet. I have to make some room on my server or else I am going to be charged for exceeding my allotted capacity. I will be along shortly," Addison said and then silently added, "you over-cologned sloth humper." Remy nodded and toddled toward the exit accompanied by the muted ring of the jingler buried in his fat neck.

"Fine morning, Mr. Hall," a smooth, deep voice said from behind him. Addison turned. Pankewitz!

"F-F-F-Fine m-m-morn-n-n" Addison found it difficult to speak. His larynx felt three times its normal size. He tried to talk again, but all he could manage was a series of rasps, gasps and gurgles.

"I beg your pardon, Mr. Hall, but are you attempting to initiate a conversation using the language of an AfriChile cave-dwelling primate?"

Addison took a couple of deep breaths. He had been so focused on trying to restore his voice, he had not heard Pankewitz's question. Addison closed his eyes (for some reason, this occasionally calmed his stammering) and tried again, "P-P-P Professor P-Pankewitz," he spattered, launching flecks of spittle that came to rest on Pankewitz's mothball-scented jacket. "I-I-I d-d-desperately need to get out of Al-Al-Alpdon. I-I-I h-h-heard that you have an underground operation and that you might be able to help me. I-I-Is there any way I can get involved in this? I-I-I am willing to transfer a substantial sum of c-c-commerce credits to your account for the p-p-privilege."

Pankewitz furrowed his brow and paused before answering, "Special operation? What special operation? I have not the slightest inkling of what you are referring to, Mr. Hall. And why in our remarkable-looking redeemer's name would you want to leave Alpdon?" he asked. "This is a beautiful country, chock-full of nature and culture, teeming with gracious people. And thanks to the brilliant restoration plan of Our Leader, our economy is improving rapidly. His strategy is infallible, Mr. Hall, and he will restore Alpdon's prosperity. Soon we will once again be the commercial behemoth of the RussoManchurian Empire!"

Addison was mortified. Pankewitz had no idea what he was talking about. Just a few fortnights ago, the Professor had stood in the lift with Addison and preached passionately about the maltreatment of the lower castes and the dangerous possibility that this maltreatment might increase. Now, his prophesy was being fulfilled and he had turned into a Face-ist apologist? What had caused him to flip-flop? Pinky-sized penis! Club foot! Addison's embarrassment was usurped only by his distress. He had been counting on Pankewitz's underground operation to get him out of Alpdon. What was he going to do now?! Cleft palate! HAIR-SPROUTING FACIAL MOLE!

The best way to get out of this uncomfortable situation was to pretend he was joking. He set his face in a forced smile. "F-F-F-Forget about it, Professor. I-I-I was just joking with you.

A-A-Apparently, I have a p-p-p-poor sense of humor. Wh-Wh-Who in their proper mind would want to leave Alpdon? S-S-Surely not I."

Professor Pankewitz nodded and headed purposefully toward the exit portal. A few steps from the activation pad, he abruptly stopped and turned back toward Addison. "Mr. Hall, I have been told by one of my neighbors that you are well-versed with our mail server. Perhaps you can provide me with some guidance? It is a fresh application and I am having difficulty navigating through my correspondence. Would you mind giving me a terse tutorial?"

Addison was confused. Was he serious? The current version of this application had been in use for at least a full year.

"D-D-Do you mean r-right now?" Addison asked. He had no desire to continue his interaction with this man after suffering such humiliation and disappointment, not to mention that he had to leave in four minutes if he was to get to work on time. Besides, Pankewitz made him uncomfortable; he had an inordinate amount of self-confidence for someone of his caste.

"My Primary Optimal Provider had a favorite aphorism, Mr. Hall. 'Complete your tasks in the present to avoid appearing indolent.'" Pankewitz walked back toward Addison. "The phrase isn't as pithy as some of his others, but it is a sound philosophy. Wouldn't you agree?" Pankewitz's eyes flashed quickly from side to side. He grabbed Addison firmly by the arm (what a grip!) and led him to the corner of the foyer. "Mr. Hall, I didn't mean to parry your earlier inquiry, but there was someone lingering in the foyer and it is imperative that I be discreet. You understand that don't you, Mr. Hall?" Addison nodded dully – he had no idea what Pankewitz was talking about. "I am not sure who informed you about our subversive operation, but I regret to inform you that the mission statement of the operation is to rescue and preserve the *creative capital* of Alpdon. No offense intended, Mr. Hall, but I am not familiar with your body of work. What is your artistic specialty?" Pankewitz asked sarcastically.

"I-I-I-I have no creative abilities," Addison replied sheepishly. "B-B-But th-th-there is an SS at Camp Sycamore who is terrorizing me. I-I-If I don't get out of here soon, he is going to kill me. I-I-I'm quite sure of it! H-H-Honestly, I need some help here. I-I-Is the life of an artist worth more than the life of a camp worker? I-I-If you believe that, then you are no better than Brock and his zealots," he said, surprising himself with his boldness.

"Mr. Hall, I am not going to engage in a debate with you over the relative value of an individual life. I hold that all life is sacred. But we are talking about choices here. My fellow patriots and I are putting ourselves at great risk. Our pipeline only has so much capacity; therefore, we have the right to decide who enters our program and who does not," Pankewitz said angrily. "When you are the one putting your epidermis in peril, then you can establish the criteria for program inclusion."

Pankewitz's harshness unnerved Addison. He had never encountered a lower caste member with such an authoritative presence. Confronted with Pankewitz's obvious mental superiority, Addison demurred. "I-I-I understand, Professor. I-I didn't know your operation was only for artists," Addison paused. "D-D-Do you know anyone else who can help me?" he asked. Where just moments ago his tone had been hopeful, now it was desperate, bordering on pathetic. He glanced down at his shoes (which were still horribly scuffed) and kicked at an imaginary pebble on the floor.

The white-haired man with the prominent nose paused briefly, then spoke in a voice that suggested to Addison that he already regretted what he was about to say, "You ask a lot of me, Mr. Hall," he said, then exhaled loudly. "Let me see if there is anything that I can do. I will talk to some of my colleagues. If we have the excess capacity and available resources to assist you, I will have one of my colleagues contact you surreptitiously. You understand what that word means don't you? Let me clarify it for you. You are not to talk to me about these matters again. This is critical! We will come to you if, and I stress only if, we are able to assist you. And remember, Mr. Hall," Pankewitz said with a vexed smile, "loose lips can endanger our trips. So please, no careless talk."

"N-N-N-Naturally, Professor. A-Anything you can do to help me would be greatly appreciated. G-G-Greatly appreciated!" Addison said. As Pankewitz left the complex, Addison allowed himself a quick, open-mouthed smile. He had done it! He had overcome his immense discomfort and asked Pankewitz to help him. For the moment, whether Pankewitz could help him or not didn't matter. Addison hadn't been graceful, but in this case, style points didn't matter. He had accomplished his goal; he had asked Pankewitz for help. Drenched in sweat, but feeling triumphant, Addison left the complex with his head up and walked quickly toward the transport station. He would have to skip the Caffeine Depot if he was to make it to work by 08:35, but he didn't care. He didn't need it this morning. He was on a high that would take five espresso tablets to replicate.

The cool breeze blowing off the Luvista refreshed his sweaty face and tousled his thinning hair. Addison looked down and saw that the breeze had also plastered his sweaty tunic against his flabby stomach. His mood quickly sank. He reached down and pinched his stomach fat with his thumb and forefinger – there had to be at least seven centimeters of fat! He might have willed himself to talk to Pankewitz, but he still was ugly. The older he got, the uglier he would get. By the time he made it to the transport station, his earlier triumph had been overwhelmed by his usual deluge of self-dep-recation. He waited for the transport in his usual depressed state, staring hard at his dirty shoe tops, hating the way he looked. He now wished he'd had time to visit the Depot. Suddenly, he could use the caffeine pick-up. The transport slid into the Wakork Station. An icy spark passed through Addison's bowels as he realized that if Starck had already recovered, there was a strong possibility that today Starck would once again concoct a way of getting him alone. ■

CHAPTER THIRTEEN

❖

ADDISON SAT IN FRONT OF HIS LOCKER completely exhausted. He had tried on two separate occasions to rise up off the bench, but both times he was afraid his tired legs wouldn't hold his weight. This day had been a long one; the holographic timepiece showed that he had worked two hours of overtime. He received no economic credit for these additional hours. The only benefit he accrued (and it was worth much more than extra credits on his commerce chip) was that his extra work at the Arrival platform had allowed him to scan wrists right through the end of Starck's shift. Consequently, he had avoided Starck for at least another day. He had evaded Starck for four days, but he knew that eventually his luck would run out. It always did.

New campers had arrived every day for the past half-fortnight. They were erecting prefabricated barracks on every parcel of empty ground at the western end of the camp. It gave Sycamore two very different looks. The original camp buildings, the converted military barracks, were constructed with solid looking, albeit partially deteriorating, red clay bricks. The new prefabricated barracks were built with a light-colored, flimsy-looking wood that looked as if a hardy sneeze would flatten one.

Addison also noticed that the mysterious structure located just outside the camp's western barrier was taking shape. Crossbeams had been attached to the vertical stanchions, the floors were laid, the walls were installed, and a large silo was being raised about twenty meters or so to the left of the structure. It was beginning to resemble some sort of factory. Addison had seen campers scattered about the new building; the new arrivals were working on this construction project as well.

Over the past half-fortnight, Addison had taken two walks through the new part of the camp, which was named Sycamore–Birch. He was looking for Nigel, and while he was eager to find out what had happened to his friend, he was nervous about making another trip. Entering Sycamore–Birch was not officially "forbidden," but it was dangerous to be traipsing around any part of the camp not normally patrolled by Menials without carrying an SS authorization emblem. Besides, he was sure Starck was still looking for a reason to punish him. He was fairly certain that Starck was making Dolaf keep tabs on him. In the past four days, he had seen Dolaf about a dozen times in different parts of the camp. He wasn't sure of his business, but why else was that little fanatic always showing up in the same part of the camp as Addison? It happened too often to simply be a coincidence.

Addison had wisely chosen to make his two sojourns through Sycamore–Birch at dusk, right before he went off shift. He reasoned that in the waning light it would be hard for an SS to identify him, even from a short distance.

The Sycamore–Birch campers all looked exhausted, overworked and underfed. What continued to disturb Addison was that their faces were devoid of emotion. It was the same look he had seen when he worked at the Arrival Station. Those spooky glassy-eyed stares gave Addison the impression that these campers had experienced something deeply traumatic.

Addison mustered up his remaining energy and slowly rose from the bench. He felt guilty that he had done nothing to help Nigel. His horrid self-image made it hard enough for him to look in the mirror; carrying this guilt around made it virtually impossible. He had to see if he could find Nigel no matter how remote the likelihood.

He walked slowly toward the locker room portal, as if he were trying to sneak across a bed of twigs and snapping one would give him away. He slinked past the SS locker room, past the trash disposal unit where he had witnessed Starck's murderous rage and headed toward Sycamore–Birch.

As Addison entered the new compound, he saw that the campers were standing in front of their barracks, in perfect formation and at strict attention. The SS loved making the campers stand at attention in either part of the camp. It was the end-of-the-day roll call. Addison kept his head down and scurried behind the formations, staying out of view of the attending SS. He scanned the campers' bodies in search of Nigel's unique egg-shaped one. It was no use – the campers' blue-and-gray-striped uniforms were so ill-fitting that he couldn't tell who was egg-shaped and who was just wearing excessively baggy bottoms. A few of the campers turned their heads and looked at him with that same vacant stare. Gorgeous god, those looks were chilling! More and more campers turned to look. This was bad. They were drawing attention to him. He decided to leave. He quickly turned around and headed back toward the original part of the camp, but it was too late. The SS attending to this barrack had spotted him. Addison's bowels contracted. He immediately straightened up and assumed the posture and demeanor of a Menial who was fulfilling an important SS order. He wiped off his hands, acting as if he had just risen from a fall, and began walking purposefully with his head held high. "To avoid the attention of the SS, always look like you are busy and set your face in an expression as if you are slightly annoyed, as if the workload you were assigned was just a bit too much," Nigel had advised Addison shortly after the two started working at the camp. "The SS don't care so much about what you are doing, but rather they want to see that whatever you are doing is burdensome." Nigel had been correct; this ruse had always worked in the past and it appeared to be working now. His heart swelled with admiration for his friend. He had a knack for appeasing these SS; the same knack he had displayed in appeasing the class bullies when they were in secondary school. Nigel had the ability to read people – he could tell immediately what someone wanted to hear by simply observing their facial expression or posture. Addison always thought his friend would have made a wonderful diplomat or a previously-owned-personal-transport salesperson. As he walked, Addison could feel the SS glaring at him, but the SS made no move toward him. In this fading light, he would have a difficult time identifying Addison.

Addison kept walking with long strides; he kept his chin high. Soon he was far enough away from the barracks and he relaxed a bit. He tensed up again when he realized he had a different problem. In his panic, he had continued walking west and now found himself at the camp's western barricade – the furthest point from the Menial locker room.

Addison was nervous, but he had an idea. He would find somewhere to hide until the sun set, then he would take the long walk back to the locker room. He could take cover from the spotlights along the way by hiding in the shadows cast by the barracks – there were more than enough to get him back to the original Sycamore grounds. He spotted a small prefabricated building against the western wall, fifty meters from where he was standing. The eastern side of the building was engulfed in shadows, blocked from the rotating spotlights because it buttressed the barrier. It was an ideal place to hide.

As he approached the building, he could see that the portal was open slightly and a sliver of light was visible through the crack. The building was made of the same light birch wood as the new barracks, but it was square instead of rectangular and much smaller. Addison peered through the crack, but couldn't see anything. He wedged his fingertips into the crack and gradually opened the portal a bit more to expand his view. He was not prepared for what he saw.

The room contained three rows of matte-finished chrome operating platforms placed four across, each illuminated with small white spotlights. Only four were occupied. Each one had a hydraulic lift system and parallel rows of deeply etched blood troughs, which fed to a drain at the foot of each platform.

An ornate cherrywood desk stood in the center of the room – a well-preserved antique that looked odd amongst the sleek metal platforms. An average-sized man with jet black hair and a thick black mustache was standing next to the desk, holding a chrome-finished cane in his black-gloved hand, and studying a holographic spreadsheet. He was wearing a starched brown tunic; his brow was furrowed and his lips pursed. He was a good-looking man, obviously a Blessed. If Addison believed the Face-ist ideology, this man would be exceptionally intelligent. Regardless, he looked smart just the same.

The first platform that drew Addison's attention was the one closest to the portal. A cherubic man, presumably a camper, was lying on his back and naked, with shiny chrome bands restraining his neck, waist, knees and ankles. He was trying to free his arms, which were pinned to his side, but he was only able to move them a few centimeters.

A distinguished older-looking man stood to the right of the platform. He was evenly tanned just the right shade of copper and wearing a tight white smock. Next to him was an oblong container of liquid polyurethane; next to that was a small table covered with a white sheet. Some shiny instruments were placed neatly on the sheet. The distinguished-looking man grabbed an implement that looked like a suction cup attached to a thin chrome handle. He reached down and held the camper's left eye open with his free hand. How unsanitary! The man's hand was unsheathed! Couldn't he have taken a few seconds to dip his hand in the polyurethane? The distinguished-looking man brought the suction cup down quickly, directly onto the camper's exposed left eye. The camper screamed and Addison saw his dimpled hands clench into tight fists. Moving quickly, the distinguished-looking man, who Addison guessed was a doctor, pulled up hard and lifted the camper's left eye right out of his head! As the eye was ripped from the socket, it made a sucking sound – like a foot being pulled from a muddy bog. The camper let out a yelp that prickled the tufts of hair in Addison's ears. It sounded inhuman. The distinguished-looking doctor muted his screams by stuffing a balled-up piece of cloth into the camper's mouth.

Strangely, the doctor held the eyeball motionless about six centimeters above the camper's open eye socket. Then Addison saw why. Thin red and white filaments stretched from the eyeball into the open socket. Holy and handsome god, the eye was still attached! The doctor reached quickly for a scalpel and cut the filaments the way a hungry man cuts the strings of cheese hanging off a forkful of raclette. When the filaments were cut, the distinguished-looking doctor picked up a small clear bag from the instrument table and placed the suction cup with the attached eyeball into it. He released the suction and the eyeball dropped in, making a slimy trail of intraocular fluid and blood on the side of the bag. The front of the eyeball spun towards Addison; it was a stunning shade of lapis lazuli blue. The distinguished-looking doctor lifted the bag up to his face. "What an exquisite color," he said, "soon it will reside in a face worthy of such beauty." Addison gasped quietly. They were harvesting body parts! The doctor walked over to a small chrome box sitting on the far left corner of the cherry desk. He opened the box and his hand was swallowed up in a plume of frosty vapor. He placed the bag in the box and closed the lid with his elbow, expelling a vapor cloud about a meter long.

Just then another obese camper – restrained on a platform in the far right corner of the room – started screaming, "Will someone please help me?! Our Father, who art in heaven, take pity on me and help! Holy Mary, Mother of God, please rescue me!" Startled by the volume of the camper's voice and his passé prayerful pleas, Addison lost his balance; he grabbed the portal to avoid falling. His hands pounded against the portal, creating an audible thump and causing it to slide open a few centimeters more. Addison held his breath. Had anyone heard? He scanned the room quickly. Gratitude to our gorgeous and granite-muscled god, no one took notice. Another doctor, older looking and paler than the one who had extracted the eye, ran over to the camper and stuffed a rag into his mouth. The camper's pleas were replaced with gagging noises; the older-looking doctor had apparently pushed the rag too far into the camper's mouth.

The older-looking doctor grabbed a scalpel and began cutting across the camper's forehead, along his hairline. The camper started screaming again, muffled by the rag. A frothy glob of mucous and saliva ran from the corner of his mouth and down his chubby cheek. The older-looking doctor continued slicing along the camper's hairline, down the camper's temple, and then over and around his ear. Addison gasped again – the older-looking doctor was scalping him! Despite having a disgusting body, the camper had thick and wavy auburn hair. The older-looking doctor tied the camper's hair up with a short length of copper wire. He continued slicing around the nape of the camper's neck until he ended up back at the forehead. Another white-smocked man entered the room. He was young looking, with an angelic face so smooth that Addison doubted the man had ever needed to swab it with crushed quartz crystal epilating paper. Addison presumed he was a nurse. The young-looking man walked over and stood next to the doctor, his fresh face making the handsome weathered face of the doctor look even older. The nurse reached down and grabbed a handful of the camper's hair at the forehead while the doctor grabbed a handful from the base of the camper's neck. Both men repositioned their feet by widening their stances. Addison watched apprehensively, his heart beating so hard he could feel it in the back of his throat. They were about to do something horrible; he could sense it. He was right. The older-looking doctor shouted a command in a language Addison did not understand and both men pulled upward in unison, yanking the hair right off the camper's scalp! The camper whimpered. Phlegm and tears ran over and around the cloth stuffed in his mouth. Addison was disgusted. Threads of blue veins jumbled like tangled fishing line, pus-filled sockets, globules of blood – the camper's entire scalp was an open wound.

The older-looking doctor walked toward the cherrywood desk examining the hairpiece. When he arrived at the desk, he said to no one in particular, "This is a tightly populated swath of sturdy hair. It will hold up quite well to the blond dying process." While the older-looking doctor was away from the table, the younger-looking nurse pulled a clear bottle of liquid off the instrument table and poured the entire contents on the camper's head. The camper started screaming as his head roiled and foamed. Hydrogen peroxide, Addison thought. How inhumane! The nurse smiled smugly, like a schoolboy who had just surreptitiously launched a spitball. The sight of the bloody froth that formed on the camper's head was more than Addison could bear. His stomach contracted and he vomited all over his shoes.

The mustached man with the chrome cane glanced over at the portal. His face turned red and contorted angrily. He appeared as if he were about to yell something at Addison, but before he could, Addison felt a sharp pain across his shoulder blades. He tried to scream, but the agony of the blow took his breath away. He tipped face-first against the portal, causing it to slide open. Addison tumbled through it, landing on his back. His body was now laying half in and half out of the room. Brilliant slivers of light danced across his field of vision like gleaming gnats, apparitions from the intense pain. Instinctively, Addison rolled on his side and covered his genitals with his hands, waiting for another blow. None came. He opened his eyes and looked to see who had hit him. No one was there. Whoever had struck him had already left. The mustached man with the chrome cane walked over and stood over Addison's prone body, glaring at him angrily. Addison recognized him as Dr. Leegmen, Brock's well-known Minister of Health. Leegmen shook his cane just centimeters from Addison's face.

"Listen, you troll-faced subhuman," he snarled, "I am conducting an important research project mandated by Our Leader and you are disturbing my *volunteers*. If you do not vanish immediately, I will drive my cane through your filthy hair-filled ear and impale that undersized brain of yours. Be gone!"

Addison got back to his feet and hurriedly walked eastward toward the main part of the camp and the Menial locker room. He looked down at his vomit-splattered shoes; now they looked even worse.

By now, the sun had set; Addison remained well-hidden by sticking close to the barracks. Between Sycamore–Birch and the original camp was a naked stretch of land about fifty meters across. If Addison were going to be seen, it would be there, because while the patch of ground wasn't directly lit, the glow from the nearby lights made it look like it was illuminated by a full moon.

Addison reached the halfway point undetected. He fought the urge to run; his pounding feet on the gravel would make a loud noise that might give him away. So he walked, quickly, swinging his arms hard while staying on the balls of his feet to keep as quiet as possible. When he was about fifteen meters from the original grounds of Sycamore, a booming voice from behind him yelled, "Hey, you! Halt all movement and identify yourself!" Addison turned. An SS standing in front of a portal to one of the Sycamore–Birch barracks had spotted him. Addison started running with long strides. Shards of gravel kicked up and lodged in his shoes. It hurt, but he kept going. He could hear footsteps heading toward him. Again the SS shouted, "I command you to cease your running right now!"

Was Starck the one chasing him? From such a distance and in the waning dusk, all the SS looked the same – tall and wide. If it was Starck, did he recognize him? After only a few seconds of sprinting, Addison's lungs and legs burned from fatigue. With an enormous amount of effort, he pushed through the pain. He spotted a group of campers heading back to the barracks; a slouching bunch of plodding shadows led by a short and stocky Menial that Addison didn't immediately recognize. Addison slid next to the last row of marching campers and walked with them toward the barracks. The SS ran past Addison and the campers and sprinted toward the Menial locker room. Addison saw that it wasn't Starck; this SS wasn't tall enough. Initially, he was relieved; but after a moment, he sighed with resignation. It wasn't Starck this time, but he was absolutely certain that Starck would eventually get him alone and destroy him. Avoiding Starck today merely brought him one day closer to this immutable fate. His desperation was growing; his only hope for survival was the slim chance that Pankewitz would decide to help him. Addison figured there were only two possible outcomes – he would either be rescued by Pankewitz or killed by Starck.

There had to be another way out of Alpdon, but he couldn't immediately think of any other alternatives. What made matters worse was that he didn't have Nigel around to help him come up with new ideas. Nigel was resourceful; he would be good at thinking up some other methods of escape. As he continued to escort the campers, he pondered approaching Pankewitz again and literally begging him for help. If he could convey the hopelessness of his situation, the Professor would have to help him; he was obviously a compassionate man. But the truth was he had already begged him. And while Pankewitz had said he would "see what he could do," Addison could read in the Professor's blue opal eyes that he had asked for too much. Asking him again would probably just worsen his chances. Maybe he could offer Pankewitz some type of compensation for his help. But as he took an inventory of his possessions, he realized the only thing of value he could offer was his new signal-pirating device. That wouldn't work – the opportunity to view such intellectually flaccid programming wouldn't appeal to an academic like him. Besides, Addison got the impression that Pankewitz was too principled to be influenced by material possessions or money.

Presumably out of options, Addison decided to do something his birther told him never to do – make a bargain with god. ("Do not put the lord, thy god, to the test," she would say.) Her warning flashed through his thoughts as he made his decision, but he was going ahead with it anyway. After all, what did he have to lose? His plan was simple. If he could make an "acceptable sacrifice," he would create an imbalance on god's divine scale and force god to help him or at least increase the possibility of god helping him. But he had to give up something he deeply cherished in order to make his sacrifice a worthy one. The first and only thing that came to mind was his morning espresso tablets. Starting tomorrow, he would only have one tablet a day. (The luscious lord wouldn't expect him to forgo them completely.) Such a significant sacrifice would surely get god's attention.

Addison arrived at the camp the next morning sporting a slight headache. He had only gotten one espresso tablet from the Caffeine Depot and a caffeine deprivation headache was building. ("Only one today, sweetie? Are you visiting another establishment behind my back?" Otka had said coyly with a wink.) Addison entered the campgrounds and was shocked to see that the Sycamore–Birch portion of the camp had been sectioned off with a twenty-meter-high red brick barrier topped with a few irregularly placed strands of razor wire. What was going to happen to Nigel?! How would he look for him now?! Addison's worry was sprinkled with shame-stained relief – the truth was he was afraid to return to that portion of the camp. ■

CHAPTER FOURTEEN

ADDISON'S AWAKENING APPARATUS ACTIVATED
as usual at 07:04. He dragged his weary body off his sleeping platform and
staggered clumsily into his waste elimination chamber. He banged his right
elbow on the sharp edge of the portal, but was too tired to feel the full brunt
of the pain. He just groaned softly; even making that sound took significant effort. Four days had passed since he'd stumbled upon Dr. Leegmen's
body-part harvesting operation. Addison felt morally obligated to tell
someone about what he had seen, but who? Leegmen was such a visible and
important member of Brock's cabinet that the idea of telling someone in
authority wasn't even an option. Nigel was obviously unavailable. Professor
Pankewitz was someone he believed he could confide in, but he hadn't seen
or heard from the Professor since he had asked him for help half a fortnight
ago. Telling Remy was completely out of the question – he would probably
waddle to the Sycamore commander and snitch on him faster than Addison
could say "over-cologned sloth humper." (He found that phrase clever and
thought of it often.) The only other person he could think of was Otka, but
he had two concerns about telling her. Firstly, their encounters were always
short and always in a public place, so it would be difficult to get her alone.
Secondly, she was a Blessed; he wasn't even sure he could trust her. For all
he knew, she might subscribe to all this Face-ist rot. In the end, Addison
decided to keep it to himself and hope that either Otka showed herself as
someone he could trust or that Pankewitz resurfaced. Gorgeous granite-
muscled god! He hoped that Pankewitz would return soon.

The queue at the Caffeine Depot extended all the way to the entrance
portal. It was one of the longest ones Addison had ever seen. The rapid
expansion of Camp Sycamore had brought a bunch of new SS to Wakork;
it looked to Addison as if most of them were waiting in this queue. To his
surprise, however, it moved quicker than he expected. In five minutes, he

was standing at the service desk giving Mimi his order. How ironic that a few fortnights ago just being in her presence would have caused his palms to sweat from nervous excitement. Today, he found her banal and her loss of self-confidence amplified her imperfections. Addison even noticed some new flaws – her skin was pale and blotchy; her mandatory jingler sat high on her neck as if she had recently gained some weight. He was also fairly certain that her once-marvelous breasts had shrunk – at least they looked significantly smaller under her tunic.

Otka noticed him and glided over next to Mimi. "Bright day," she said, flashing Addison her brilliant smile. Addison gave her a short nod and a close-lipped smile. Otka's presence had an immediate effect on him; his body responded now the way it used to respond to Mimi, but with much more intensity. And no wonder. Otka was absolutely beautiful; she didn't have a single discernable flaw.

Addison noticed that her nose was faultless. It was the ideal size – about as long as one-fourth of her total facial length, about as wide as one-fifth of her total facial width – and it was upturned at the optimal nasofrontal and nasomental angles. What a wonderful creation! Addison's nasal analysis had caused his gaze to linger longer than normal on Otka's face. She apparently mistook it for ogling. "Capture my image digitally, sweetie! With proper archiving it will remain untainted for a quarter millennium," she said flirtatiously. Addison went from intimidated to embarrassed. He snatched his lonely-looking espresso tablet off the chrome serving plate and headed for the Depot exit, taking long strides in an attempt to escape before his neck and face bloomed pink. He stomped on the sensor pad with his foot and the exit portal slid open. (Otka had recently replaced the voice-activated system with a contemporary weight-activated one.) Addison lunged through the portal – the way a sprinter breaks the finish line force field – only seconds before he felt the familiar tingling on his neck and cheeks. He popped the espresso tablet into his mouth, chewed it into small pieces, and positioned the pieces with his tongue between his cheek and gum. He was relieved – he had saved (red) face and escaped the Depot before he had once again blushed in Otka's presence.

A brassy fanfare trumpeted through Grand Square. Addison turned expectantly and watched as a nearby group of pine trees descended into the oxidized green copper dune they sprouted from, revealing the large, brushed-metal image panel. An authoritative-looking Blessed female, with her hair pulled back so tightly that Addison couldn't discern its color, announced somberly through overstuffed lips, "Please stand by in one minute for a special announcement from our handsome Chancellor." Her image dissolved into a digital counter that read 00:00:59. It began counting down.

Onlookers gathered around each of the four panels installed in the Square. When the countdown reached 00:00:04, the panel faded to black and then dissolved into a blurry image of orange, blue and yellow. Initially, Addison couldn't make out what it was, but then the picture coalesced; the crowd gasped. It was flames from a burning building. The image panned back, revealing the recognizable facade of the new parliament building. Shrieks of horror came from the crowd. Brock stepped into view, looking somber. He was dressed in his usual outfit – pearl jacket, brown tunic and black trousers. The image zoomed from a full body shot to a headshot. Brock's face looked tired. The word *weary* flickered through Addison's thoughts like the fast-moving shadow of a low-flying plutonium airbus over a walkway on a sunny day. Brock spoke,

"Citizens of Alpdon, a horrendous atrocity has been perpetrated against a beloved icon of our nation's glorious rebirth – our beautiful parliament building. As you can clearly see behind me, an inferno is insidiously destroying our adored building. More than an amalgamation of chrome bricks and mucilage, this structure is a living, breathing and sensual entity – as alive and attractive as any single-digit Blessed!" Tears rolled down Brock's face, running around his nose and soaking the short hairs of his truncated mustache. Some near Addison were sobbing as well. "And chillingly, the enemies of our country who plotted and then brazenly implemented this atrocity… this structural holocaust… reside not in a foreign country, but rather live and toil on our soil! And I use the present tense, for while we captured these latest perpetrators, others – many others, I fear – remain at large." Brock brought his right hand to his face and waggled his pointer finger for emphasis, "And I tell all of our attractive producers that our nation, and our improving way of life, will be at risk until the last one is apprehended and eliminated." Brock stopped talking and glanced back at the parliament building. Swarms of workers wearing bright yellow tunics were attempting to put the blaze out by aiming plumes of beige foam through the broken windows and onto the roof. When Brock turned back around, he was weeping more intensely, so much so that he had difficulty continuing his speech. A bubble of mucous formed from his left nostril, inflated quickly and popped. Addison was surprised that no one around him reacted; he had seen people wretch over far less repulsive things. In fact, during the final Great Debate held before the last election (which Addison watched from this same Square), Brock's political rival, General Kurt von Schleicher, breached his nostril with a finger while scratching his nose and many spectators gagged from disgust. ("Do you think the other prosperous and cultured nations will want to conduct business with a country that elects such an ill-mannered boor?" Brock had said.)

"According to Ernst Moehr, the Commander of my Security Agents and the man I have appointed to chaperone this investigation, three men posing as maintenance technicians gained access to my parliament building during today's pre-dawn hours. These scoundrels positioned incendiary mechanisms in various rooms of the parliament, concentrating most of their devices in and around the Office of Records – the central repository for the documentation supporting each citizen's SIN Evaluation. Although a thorough interrogation of the terrorists has not yet been conducted, it is obvious their goal was to derail our economic recovery by eliminating the records that underpin the scientific foundation on which my economic recovery program is constructed. And had it not been for an alert agent – horror of horrors! – they might have actually succeeded. This Security

Agent, a particularly fine-looking single-digit SIN-ner with dark simmering eyes and deliciously full ruby red lips, undeniably a superior specimen of a man, decided to recheck the credentials of these diabolicals when he noticed that one of the technicians, who had just moments before registered as a Favored, had a severely obtruded and asymmetrical proboscis and a puffy, flab-riddled derriere."

"He discovered that these three men were all classified as Curseds! How they registered as Favoreds has yet to be ascertained, but let me assure you, we will unearth their methods. Lord Moehr's interrogation techniques are extraordinarily efficacious," Brock smiled, "as he usually employs... how do I say this gracefully... the infliction of pain... violative and humiliating pain... to the most private and tender areas of the interrogatee's body," Brock's smile broadened. "This sexy Security Agent immediately apprehended these dreadful-looking and dangerous imposters and notified the Bureau of Elements.[10] As you can see, their talented workers are now combating the conflagration to save the life of this nation's precious icon."

When Brock spoke, it was in a disjointed cadence and with exaggerated mouth movements. It gave Addison the impression that he was uncomfortable speaking in the "heavy" language the Blesseds used to (presumably) demonstrate their superior intelligence.

Brock paused. His expression changed from sorrow to anger. "For those who doubted my assertion that this country was at war, think again! We are engaged in the most difficult type of warfare as we fight to rid our national body of an internal enemy, an insidious cancer – a hostile strain whose raison d'etre is to obliterate our existence." Brock's eyes ping-ponged from side to side. "I am the Great Physician and I will ensure that this cancer is eliminated. Like any accomplished physician, I must make certain that every last cancer cell is eradicated from the body, even if it means that I will eradicate some healthy cells as well. Remission will not be tolerated – it

---

10 The Bureau of Elements was responsible for putting out the few fires that still occurred; however, their primary responsibilities were to prevent flooding, icing, avalanches and mudslides and to maintain acceptable pollution levels in the water and air.

cannot be tolerated. The future of our siblings and our siblings' siblings is at stake. An absolute cure is the only acceptable outcome!" Brock's face was crimson. He took a deep breath and exhaled slowly through pursed lips. When he resumed speaking, it was in a calmer voice, "A few moments ago, I requested, and of course received, unanimous approval from my...," Brock grinned slightly, "I mean, *our* Parliament, the ratification of an Emergency Decree. This decree will go a long way in protecting this nation from future acts of terrorism. I will read it verbatim," Brock cast his eyes downward. "The articles 114, 115, 117, 118, 123, 124 and 153 of our Constitution are suspended until further notice. It is therefore permissible to limit the freedom to organize and assemble; to breach the privacy of written, verbal or digital correspondence; and to conduct searches and confiscations of personal property even if this is not otherwise provided for by present law. My administration will make use of these powers only to enable the protection of this nation's leaders." Brock paused, his face flushed, his eyes narrowed and his mouth open, as if he were about to say something. But then his eyes softened, the flush drained from his face, and he said in a gentle, paternal manner, "I simply want the best for you, my beloved and beautiful comrades, and I will do whatever is necessary, no matter how unpleasant, to give you what you so richly deserve. May our gorgeous god continue to smile upon this glorious country."

The image panels faded to black and the clusters of pine trees ascended from the oxidized cooper dune, hiding the panel from view. Addison paused for a moment, then resumed his walk to the transport station. He tried to make sense of what he had just witnessed, but he found it difficult; so much had been said so quickly. His initial impression was that Brock had said something critically important, but the fire, Brock's surprising display of emotion, and Addison's ignorance about legislative matters all jumbled his judgment. All he was able to retain was the indelible image of black smoke pouring out of the parliament building dome and Brock's effusive portrayal of the SA who had apprehended the arsonists. Did anyone else notice how Brock described the physical attributes of the Security Agent? He used the same terms a man uses to describe a gorgeous woman. He thought of Nigel. On numerous occasions, Nigel had tried to convince Addison that Brock secretly harbored same-sex proclivities. This display by Brock would have ignited a provocative exchange with Nigel. Addison sighed; he missed his friend.

Addison's workday was surprisingly mundane. He avoided Starck yet again. Today, he didn't even see Dolaf. Since the erection of the Sycamore–Birch barricade, Addison's job tasks returned to the normal Menial responsibilities. For some reason, the SS weren't using Menials for the supervisory work at Sycamore–Birch. Remy told him disappointedly that campers had been assigned by the SS to do the work the Menials normally did. ("We are missing out on a bona fide opportunity here, Addster. Can you envision the positive impression one could accrue by laboring in and around such a significant venture? It would have been an exceptional chance to gain some real visibility and advance one's career... an exceptional chance indeed.")

When Addison returned to his living complex after work, he was shocked to see a twenty-meter-high barricade encircling the Cursed complex. It looked similar to the new barricade at the camp; it was also constructed of red brick, but this barricade was topped with a lot more razor wire.

Addison was surprised... then confused. Why would they erect a barrier around the Cursed complex? Who were they trying to keep out? He decided to take a walk over to the front of the complex to get a better look. Construction scraps littered the area in front of the fence. Dried mucilage (Comely lord, that stuff smelled worse than ancient French cheese!), shards of brick, and fragments of razor wire all made getting close to the barricade difficult, but Addison ignored these impediments. What caught his attention were the official-looking signs posted to the barricade and spaced about twenty meters apart. Knots of people were clustered around each sign. Addison walked over to one.

ATTENTION! Chancellor Brock, in accordance with the Emergency Decree, has confined all Cursed citizens to this enclosure to eliminate the possibility of additional arson or assassinations and to thwart any schemes in progress to sabotage our economic recovery. This decree will also protect the fruitful and beautiful citizens of Alpdon against acts of barbarism and terrorism. Interacting with a confined occupant in any way will be considered a Supreme Prime Crime. As such, the punishment will be to extinguish with tremendous power and prolonged pain the perpetrator's life force in a public showground.

Addison was mortified. This was excessive! Not all of the Cursed population were conspiring terrorists! The handful of Curseds that Addison knew, Nigel particularly, and the numerous over-bloated ones he supervised at Sycamore were far from dangerous. Questions peppered his thoughts; questions he could not answer. How do you punish an entire caste for the misdeeds of a few? Were Burdeneds the next to be confined? Did any other citizens find this excessive? When were the educated and reasonable people of this nation going to speak up and put an end to this growing madness? Did this mean he no longer had to wear the jingler?

Addison turned away from the barricade and headed back toward his living complex, disoriented and unsettled, as if he had just awakened from a deep sleep in a strange place. About thirty meters from the entrance portal, Addison was nearly run over by Remy, who was walking hurriedly in the direction of the Cursed living complex. As usual, Remy appeared to be in good spirits. "Oh, this is first-class news, Addster…first class news indeed!"

"Wh-What is?" Addison said, irritated by Remy's cheeriness and sickened by his wetted-urinal-patty odor. After a full day's work, the "over-cologned sloth humper" smelled like an overused waste disposal facility at a sold-out bicepball stadium.

"The confinement of the Cursed citizens, of course!" Before Addison could protest, Remy continued, "Digitally document and archive my prediction, Addster; our professional lives will be greatly enhanced now… greatly enhanced! It's a mathematical certainty," Remy paused. His eyes widened and he belched with unabashed gusto, floating a malodorous air pocket of halitosis-tainted chocolate HastyTasty toward Addison, causing Addison to cringe. "Sorry there, Addster. I just finished consuming my evening meal. My birther advised me it's best to expel digestive gases rather than let them fester in your abdomen as they will erode the protective lining of your esophagus, stomach and intestines. Anyway, let me return to expositing on my prediction... Removing the Cursed caste from the population means there are now fewer lower caste citizens remaining to do the foundational labor necessary to keep our economy growing. And according to Our Leader, our economy continues to grow, Addster, at the rate of 2 percent per ninety-day cycle. This means that the need for foundational labor will also be growing. We will always have a job, Addster! They can't prosper without us!" Remy said happily as he resumed walking toward the Cursed complex. "I am going to go inspect that barricade again. I am amazed at the quality of the structure given how rapidly it was constructed. Did you see how the bricks lined up flawlessly? Each one is exactly a forefinger's width apart from the other. I checked it. Very impressive! Very impressive indeed!" With a look of anticipation, Remy waddled toward the barricade like a chubby child running for an empty swing. Addison shook his head – all he cares about is how this quarantine affects him. He has no concern for those sorry-looking people behind the barricade. What a selfish (stinking) buffoon!

Then it dawned on Addison that there was a more frightening scenario – one that Remy could never envision because his (hefty) head was perpetually buried in rose quartz sand. What if Brock enslaved the lower castes? Upon initial reflection, it would seem impossible for a nation as sophisticated as Alpdon to do such a boorish thing, but was it really that far-fetched? Brock's Emergency Decree laid the foundation for such a possibility. Once he made it legal to restrict personal freedom, the only question that remained was to what extent? If Brock had the authority to remove the Cursed citizens' right to leave their living complex, couldn't he simply strip all lower caste citizens of their rights? He could then easily force them to toil for no compensation, using them as the paving stones for the construction of his prosperous new empire.

Four fortnights ago, Addison would have scoffed at such a notion, but after discovering Dr. Leegmen's body-part harvesting operation and seeing how easily (and quickly) Brock was able to quarantine the Curseds, enslavement of the lower castes no longer seemed that far-fetched. ■

CHAPTER FIFTEEN

❖

"NO FOOD, NO PEACE, NO WAY! No food, no peace, no way!" the confined Curseds chanted from behind the barricade. Addison stood amongst a growing group of people who had heard the chanting, seen the ominous-looking searchlights, and took a detour from their evening commute home to find out what was happening. "No food, no peace, no way!" the chanting continued. An SA, standing on a wooden parapet on top of the barricade, yelled down at the protesters in a clipped voice, "Stop chanting and return to your living units at once! Failure to comply with my order will result in a most extreme punishment!" The chanting stopped immediately. After a few seconds of silence, some in the crowd started to leave. As Addison turned to leave, a gritty male voice, rasped to the brink of incomprehension, started another chant, "Brock's heart is rock and he flies on the serpentine trapeze. Brock's heart is rock and he flies on the serpentine trapeze." The SA on the parapet stood silently with his hands on his hips, obviously puzzled by this new chant. He looked down and shrugged his shoulders at the reassembling crowd.

The onlookers began murmuring to one another. "Was anyone able to comprehend what he shouted? What a raw timbre! It sounds as if his larynx has been mutilated." A powerful-looking Blessed man with language as coarse as the chanting man's voice said to no one in particular, "Did that lump of subhuman excreta say 'serpentine trapeze' or 'cervix full of fleas'?" The man looked around with a grin on his strong-featured face, apparently thinking that those within earshot would find his comment amusing. No one laughed, however. The only response he generated was an indelicate grunt from a fragile-looking Blessed woman who dry heaved.

A chorus of additional voices joined the raspy man and their chant became easier to understand, "Brock's heart is rock and he lies like the serpent lied to Eve; Brock's heart is rock and he lies like the serpent lied to

Eve." Some in the crowd near Addison chuckled; Addison did, as well. He wondered how many in the crowd knew that was an oblique reference to the Old Testament book of Genesis.

As the chanting continued, the crowd of onlookers grew. Tight and toned bodies started pressing up against him. A stab of panic pierced his gut and sweat pores burst open all over his body. Was he now claustrophobic? Had the stress of the past three fortnights loosened some long-suppressed phobia? The SA shouted again to the chanters behind the barricade, "This demonstration is concluded! Return to your living units immediately! Those that continue protesting will incur corporal punishment for their insurgency!" The chanting stopped again.

More onlookers joined the crowd and Addison was pushed from behind by a surge of bodies. He pointed his feet outward and widened his stance trying to stand firm against the surge, but it was too powerful. His torso was pushed forward, but something (or someone) was impeding his feet and he couldn't shift them to maintain his balance. Soon he was pushed to an angle of about thirty degrees. Sweat poured down from his forehead – from both the heat of the compressed bodies and from his growing anxiety. He shouted in a panicked voice, "I-I-I need some space!" But no one seemed to hear him, or if they did, they couldn't (or wouldn't) move to give it to him. There was another surge behind him and Addison's upper body was pushed to an angle of about forty-five degrees. Stay on your feet... If you fall to the ground, you'll be trampled! Addison tried desperately to lift one of his legs. If he could move his feet just a few centimeters, he could regain his balance. But they wouldn't budge. Another surge from behind tipped him to a precipitous angle of about sixty degrees, causing him to lose his equilibrium. He was falling! He struggled to free his feet. He screamed, "H-H-H-HELP!" Then, miraculously, the pressing crowd retreated a bit, loosening Addison's feet and allowing him to regain his balance. Addison guessed it had been someone's leg, or given the fact there were a lot of Blesseds around him, perhaps someone's heavily muscled arm that had been holding them down. His heart was pounding and his breathing was shallow. He felt dizzy. He needed to get out of this mob before it surged again, but it was too dense. He tried to turn around and found he didn't even have enough room to do that. Needle-thin penis, another surge! This time the crowd was coming towards him! Addison grabbed the muscular shoulders of the man in front of him to try to maintain his balance, but even this powerfully built man was at the mercy of the mob. He was pushed backward along with Addison. Now Addison was grateful for the press of bodies; they kept him from falling.

The chanting had stopped, but just as Addison became hopeful that the crowd would start to disperse, it resumed in a guttural, more defiant tone, "No food, no peace, NO WAY! No food, no peace, NO WAY!" More voices joined in and the chant grew louder, "No food, no peace, no way! No food, NO PEACE, NO WAY!" The crowd surged toward the barricade, apparently sensing that something was about to happen. Bodies pressed tighter against him, squashing his chest, making it difficult for him breathe. More voices from behind the wall joined in. The chant could now be heard clear across Grand Square, "NO FOOD, NO PEACE, NO WAY! NO FOOD, NO PEACE, NO WAY!" Addison closed his eyes and tried to ignore the pressure on his sternum. He breathed in deep and slow, hoping to stave off his escalating anxiety attack. Focus on your breathing, he thought. In through the nose... out through the mouth... In through the nose... out through the mouth... It was working – his heart rate was slowing. In through the nose... out through the mouth... In through the nose... out through the mouth. The wide-shouldered man in front of him took a small step forward, relieving the pressure on his chest. Gratitude to gorgeous god, he could breathe easier. A series of loud pops came from behind the barricade. At first, Addison thought it was bursting balloons or shattering crystal balls, but when he heard screams coming from behind the barricade and gasps coming from some of the onlookers, he realized it was gunfire.

Another round of gunshots echoed through the Square followed by more screams. "Holy Mother of God, they are killing us!" a female voice screeched. Despite the horror he was witnessing, the antiquated phrase she used surprised Addison. Holy Mother of God? Why not just recite a thou-, thy- and thee-packed passage from the King Jimmy scriptures? When this thought floated away, he realized that the gunshots had stopped; however, the wailing behind the barricade continued. Addison heard a man howling for his birther. How ghastly it sounded! "Birther, birther, please birther of mine... help me!" This was horrid... horrid! He had to get out of this crowd and out of earshot of this awfulness. Addison's anxiety ratcheted up. His heart was pounding and his breathing became labored. Soon, he was hyperventilating. No matter how deeply he breathed in, he couldn't capture enough air; it was as if his lungs had shrunk to half their size. He began frantically pushing people, trying to clear a path out, but he wasn't strong enough to budge anyone. He couldn't catch his breath and the little amount of air he could get was fusty. The crowd shifted, mercifully giving him some room. He dropped to his knees and began crawling through the forest of hairless and toned legs. The air was fresher at ground level, but it smelled of depilatory lotion and tanning cream. Still, he found it easier to breathe. The rough pavement lacerated his hands and knees, but he was too distracted to care. He took a knee to his nose and it started bleeding; the blood dripped into his mouth and tasted like an iron spoon. Finally, he saw an opening. Clear space! He dodged a few more pairs of tanned legs and dove forward. A cool breeze blew in his face. He had made it! His heart rate and breathing slowed. He rolled onto his back and breathed deeply. He was far enough away now that the din of the large crowd drowned out any sounds coming from behind the barricade, but apparently the incident was over as the crowd started to disperse. As people walked past him, he picked up snippets from different conversations:

A deep male voice, "Do you believe what just happened? The guard notified them numerous times to discontinue their chanting and those Curseds were just too brainless to heed his warning. I guess using 'Cursed' and 'brainless' together is redundant." The same voice chuckling.

A squeaky female voice, "Those whiners got what they deserved. Did you hear that one man crying over and over for his birther? Gorgeous god! Couldn't he suffer silently like a real man?"

A breathy female voice, "I haven't heard gunshots in quite a while. What a sexy sound a firearm makes when it ejaculates its bullets! Let's ambulate with alacrity to our living unit and engage in vigorous coitus. Hurry, my nipples are harder than Jupiterian diamonds!" The same breathy voice moaning.

Addison got to his feet, wiped his bloody nose on the sleeve of his tunic, and walked toward his living complex. The pine trees in the corner of Grand Square lowered into the oxidized green copper dunes and the video panels exploded to life with a triumphant brass fanfare. A Blessed woman appeared – the same one who'd given notice before Brock's speech during the parliament fire. Once again her hair was pulled back tightly. Perhaps it was different lighting or a different angle, but Addison could easily see that her hair was blonde. "Chancellor Brock will address the nation at 21:30," she said through swollen lips. The holographic time device read 19:45 as Addison entered his living complex.

After a quick shower, Addison sat down on the edge of his sleeping platform with a container of French Vanilla HastyTasty that took him three tries to open. Addison acquired the G-POP (General Population) feed, but it didn't matter – whenever Brock addressed the nation he co-opted all feeds, both general and caste-specific ones.

As always, Brock's speech started precisely at the announced time. He was sitting at his large, leather-topped walnut desk wearing his typical pearl jacket, brown tunic and black tie. When he spoke, it was in a calm voice. "Fellow citizens," he paused and ran his tongue over his lips. "A most unfortunate incident occurred earlier today in the city of Wakork." Brock paused and licked his lips again. It looked odd to Addison, as if Brock was trying to purge a bad taste from his mouth. "The Cursed citizens of Wakork, who were recently confined for *our* protection, brazenly attacked the Security Agents I assigned to their living complex. This is truly a case of attempting to bite the hand that provides you with victuals – the SAs they assaulted were the ones responsible for their care and feeding. What foolishness! But, then again, I am sure that no attractive Alpdonian is surprised by this. Ugly is stupid and stupid is ugly – it is axiomatic. However, this display will most certainly convert... it *must* certainly convert... the remaining heart-bleeding holdouts who have refused to believe that these parasites harbor ill will toward us. Trust my words, brethren... if they had the means and the opportunity, they would destroy us all! These Cursed subhumans, despite their obvious mental deficiencies, were able to stockpile a cache of lethal weapons, deadly tools and implements of destruction, which they used to attack my Security Agents." Brock stood up from behind his desk. His calm facade vanished. His face flushed. "In obvious self-defense – only after they were fired upon – did my Security Agents return fire at these... these... these unintelligent uglies!" Brock spit the slur out of his mouth with a spray of saliva, as if the phrase tasted bitter on his tongue. He licked his lips again. "Let me reiterate this critical point – they drew first blood. It was only after their initial assault that my three Security Agents, with tears in their alluring eyes, returned their fire. It was an irrefutable act of self-preservation. It was shoot or be shot, wound or be wounded, kill or be killed! My SAs acted justly and I defy anyone to attempt to prove otherwise!" Brock paused and continued calmly, "Not surprisingly, given the expert marksmanship of my officers, many of the insurgents sustained mortal injuries. Admittedly, the extinguishment of any life, even a subhuman one, is not an act to be trivialized; however, I can honestly say that I feel no remorse, no regret, and no urge to repent. These Curseds deserved to die and they received what they deserved. They were unprovoked. *They* initiated the violence and they didn't act alone." Brock paused again. "To that end, I have personally appointed Wakork's Gauleiter, Julian Scherner, to conduct a meticulous investigation of this most unfortunate incident to determine who supplied these rebels with the weapons. Do not misinterpret what I am about to say. Those who have ears to hear – listen! When the responsible parties are captured, I will punish them in a public venue using the grisliest method my Bureau of Justice can devise. I have ordered them to devise an execution process that will be painful, protracted and gory. The more blood I see, the happier I will be!" Brock shouted with a perverse smile. "Death by impalement, crucifixion or disembowelment – a Lucite Iron Maiden, a Pear of Anguish inserted in the anus, the Revolving Drum, Head Crusher, Skull Splitter, Judas Cradle – every technique and apparatus will be evaluated." Brock paused again and took a few deep breaths. The crimson drained from his face. He resumed speaking in a more controlled manner, "It would have been better for these traitors to have suffered asphyxiation from a compressed umbilical cord in the birth canal and emerged stillborn than to have exited the canal as a thriving newborn. What were their motives for initiating such a heinous attack upon my officers? At this early stage of the investigation, only our good-looking god knows. Soon however, I too will know."

Brock wagged his right finger as if admonishing a wayward schoolchild, "This administration will not tolerate rebellion in any form. To that end, I have assembled a new, elite State Police Force. These heroes of enforcement have been culled from my Security Agents and from the guards at the Beautification Camps. They are the best of the best; the richest cream skimmed from the cream that had already been skimmed from the top. Their singular mission is to root out and extinguish civic infidelity of any kind. Naturally, this includes those subversives who express their rebellion through violent acts of terrorism, but – and listen carefully, my good-looking brethren – this State Police Force will also be tasked with snuffing out those mutineers who spread and nourish this spirit of rebellion using religion or academics as their disguise. Those who speak and scribe to inflict their harm rather than commit tangible acts of violence are a more formidable threat to our nation because they have the ability to create martyrs out of every backslider we righteously execute for committing acts of terrorism. If they are successful in linking each insurgent's death to a cause deemed worthy by those countries that we engage in commercial intercourse with, they coat each insurgent with a sugary glaze, not only transforming their cause into an appetizing one, but more importantly, tagging me as a "tyrant" – marinating me in the stench of their rotting corpses and making me, and therefore our country, unappealing... dare I say... repulsive! Right now, we cannot afford to disgust our commercial coitus companions. On the contrary, we must endeavor to maintain excellent business relationships with all of them until we can assemble and train an adequately sized workforce that will enable us to once again manufacture superior quality products at fair prices."

"We are attractive individually; we need to ensure that we are attractive as a country. The prosperous nations must crave us the way every male with a distinguishable pulse craves a single-digit Blessed woman. I want them throbbing with desire to do business with us!" Brock was agitated – his salt-and-pepper mustache appeared almost translucent against his dark red face. He paused and took a long breath, "Tonight, I make this declaration. Any Blessed or Favored citizen who provides information that leads to the capture of one, any, or all of these conspirators will be handsomely remunerated. You will have the choice of receiving a four-color, six-dimensional portrait of me, embossed with my personally inscribed signature, framed in silver and bound in a red-sandstone-colored leather case. If you already possess such an enviable objet d'art – I know many of you are fortunate enough to have one – you will receive a hairline-to-ankle pneumatic skin exfoliation treatment that will make you look six to eight annums younger. You can approach any one of my SAs and give your deposition. I trust I have conveyed my offer with the utmost clarity. Be on the lookout and maintain your vigilance! If you observe something suspicious or even peculiar, say something! These conspirators are as slick as a swine slathered in lubricant and they want to deceive you my dear chosen ones of god, as if that were possible," Brock smiled. "Very well then my fellow good-lookers. I wish you all a pleasurable evening. May god continue to richly bless the eye-pleasing citizens of our beautiful country." The video panel faded to black.

Addison sat motionless with a heaping spoonful of HastyTasty suspended over its container. He was confused. Brock portrayed the Security

Agents as victims acting in self-defense, but Addison had been there. He'd witnessed the incident and he knew the SAs were the aggressors! Sure, they had been taunted by the chants of the confined Curseds, but they had responded to the harmless words with deadly bullets. In fact, as far as Addison could tell, the confined citizens weren't armed at all. Brock's rendering of the incident was far different than he remembered. There were hundreds of witnesses standing there with him. Surely others knew Brock was altering the facts. But why? Was Brock simply trying to exonerate the Security Agents from any wrongdoing? Or was there a more sinister reason why he had changed the account of what happened? ■

CHAPTER SIXTEEN

❖

ADDISON WALKED TO THE CAFFEINE DEPOT with the palm of his left hand placed firmly over his left eye in a futile attempt to stop a growing headache. Three days had passed since the Cursed citizens "uprising" (as it was immediately labeled by Alpdon's Chief Information Officer). Addison had not yet seen Pankewitz, even though he had kept up his end of his bargain with god for a fortnight. Why wasn't his sacrifice being honored? Was giving up most of his beloved caffeine still not enough to elicit god's favor? What more did he have to do to get the almighty (and all spiteful) to respond?

Addison's anger ignited. He decided that he was no longer going to kowtow to his guilt and stifle his blasphemous thoughts. Why should he? He had smothered them so many times before, but god never rewarded him for his constraint.

Addison used to pray religiously, begging god to help him become just a little bit better looking. Had god answered his prayers? Of course not! Addison scrubbed his teeth with toothpaste, sandpaper and bleach, yet they remained amber. He tried to eat healthy and avoid high-caloric foods, yet his cheeks got chubbier and his midsection flabbier. He applied all types of hair-restoring creams, salves, ointments, sprays and gels, yet his hair continued to fall out. His situation was even worse today because he grew a bit uglier each day. On top of that, he hadn't found a coitus companion yet; his one true friend, the only person who genuinely liked him despite all of his obvious shortcomings, had been taken away. "Let us all heap praise upon the one true god, our loving father, who art in heaven, who has never done a damn thing for me!" Addison said aloud. He felt relieved and liberated. He smiled with no concern about hiding his teeth. He finally had the nerve to express what he had suppressed since he was a child. His whole life, god had treated him like an unwanted orphan. He made sure Addison's basic needs were met – sustenance, shelter and security – but that was it. Anything extra – anything that might bring even a smidgen of joy to Addison's life – was denied him, while at the same time given abundantly to those god had already blessed, like Addison's early-blooming cousin.

Addison had finally confronted his divine tormenter. He was in good spirits as he entered the Depot and joined the queue. He was ordering three tablets today. To un-heaven with god and trying to curry his fickle favor! He wanted three tablets and he was going to order three. The queue lurched forward and he spotted Otka. She was standing at her usual spot behind the service desk, but she wasn't beaming her usual brilliant smile; she looked somber. Her flawless face looked incomplete without her smile, although her pouting face did make her lips look exceptionally pillowed. What he would give to kiss them just once! Would he give up his caffeine tablets? You bet the lord's divine derriere he would! He sniggered – blaspheming opened up a bunch of new phrases he could use – almighty's anus, holy creator's crotch…

He focused his attention on Otka. (Blessed birther's breasts!) He guessed that Otka was having man troubles; they always dogged these beautiful women. (God's grandiose gonads!) What had Starck done to upset her? Had Starck broken off their coital relations? A more probable possibility was that Starck had engaged in extracurricular coitus with another woman – the Blessed men were notorious for cheating on their coitus companions. He wished he received a commerce credit every time he witnessed a gorgeous woman weeping because her square-jawed coitus companion couldn't keep his bratwurst-fingered hands off some other gorgeous (and usually younger) woman. If I had a woman like Otka, I would be as loyal to her as a three-legged, two-toothed, one-eyed dog, Addison thought, believing his morals were superior to Starck's. If I had a woman like Otka…, he stopped himself. He would never even get a second look from a woman as beautiful as Otka. With this realization, the moral high ground Addison was standing on turned into a bog of envy; his self-righteousness got sucked into his all-too-familiar self-deprecating muck.

Addison approached the service desk. Mimi wasn't there today, but Addison took little interest in her absence. After he placed his order for three tablets, Otka said gravely, "Mr. Hall, I need to talk to you privately about a personal fiscal matter." Addison had a premonition that he was about to be humiliated and he took an involuntary step back. "It is of superlative and matchless importance that I talk to you forthwith," she said. It flashed through Addison's thoughts that while every Blessed made extensive use of the lexicon; Otka was particularly "long-tongued." "It is in relation to your commerce account. I received a transmission from the Bureau of Economics shortly after first light today that your commerce chip is fraudulent."

"What?! That can't be!" Addison blurted, so shocked by her comment that his subconscious didn't have time to seize his words and cause him to stammer. A sharp pain passed through Addison's bowels; depending on the magnitude, economic rape could be classified as a Prime Crime. But his chip couldn't be fraudulent; it was embedded in the radial bone of his right forearm. Obviously, he would have felt something if it had been tampered with. There was no possible way her accusation could be true. However... another possibility occurred to him... Did Starck have something to do with this? Had Starck concocted a scenario to get him alone and asked Otka to help him carry it out?

"Please step around the service desk and follow me to my administrative chamber," Otka said baldly. She spun smartly on her right heel and walked quickly toward her office at the rear of the Depot (the same office where Addison had recuperated during the Day of Shattering Crystal). As Addison followed Otka, terror caused his legs to quake. Watching her thrilling derriere sway from side to side as she walked provided him with no relief. Starck was waiting for him in her office – that had to be the reason for Otka's allegation. This monster was as diabolical as he was handsome! Addison could not escape. Otka had accused him of a possible Prime Crime in front of the dozen or so SS in the queue at the Depot; if he tried to escape, one of them would surely apprehend him. Addison's bowels burned, then loosened – he had a sudden need to use the waste elimination chamber.

Addison stepped through Otka's office entrance slowly... cautiously... and quickly glanced around the room. He saw no one; however, he dare not relax. Starck could still be hiding, waiting to pounce on him at any moment. Addison stood just inside the portal with his legs spread shoulder-width apart and his hands up in a defensive posture. Starck might attack him, but he wouldn't take Addison by surprise.

Otka turned toward him. "My apologies for putting you through that, but I needed a credible reason to get you back here." She paused. "Please relax, my dear man. You look more nervous than a virgin before an orgy. You are not guilty of economic rape. As I just said, I needed an unimpeachable reason to get you back here and that was the first pretense that materialized in my mind. Upon further reflection, it was an excessive pretense. Please accept my apology."

Addison heard Otka, but didn't respond. "Wh-Wh-Where's Starck?" he spluttered.

"Well, that is an off-topic question, but since I just accused you of a Prime Crime in front of all those souls, I will accommodate you and answer your random query. Starck is in the hospital. I am surprised you didn't know that. He recently received a devastating blow to the head while on patrol at Sycamore. The circumstances providing context to the incident are still unclear however he has been under medical observation ever since. He sustained a severe head injury and will need to convalesce for at least a thirty-day cycle."

Addison relaxed his stance. He wanted to chuckle, overcome with relief, but he didn't want to be disrespectful to Otka's coitus companion. "I-I-I hope he gets healthy soon," Addison lied.

"Not me, sweetie. That *scoundrel* can stay in there until he dies and decomposes for all I care. Do you know that the night before he was attacked I caught him with his hand in Cookie's 'jar'? I am sure you are familiar with Cookie, the Blessed proprietor of Ye Olde Tunic and Trouser?" Addison nodded; he had been in her store a couple of times. Cookie was striking – she was an emerald-eyed blonde with breasts the size of ripened nuclear summer pomegranates, a beautiful heart-shaped derriere that would arouse a eunuch and long legs with just the right amount of muscle tone. She possessed one of the most sexually alluring bodies Addison had ever seen.

"Do you believe they were engaging in flagrant fornication on a small chrome bench out in front of the store for all of Wakork to see?! They were flaunting their pubic hair in public and that adulterous Adonis had the nerve to proffer a bare-faced prevarication as an excuse for being caught in such a lewd predicament. He actually told me that Cookie had asked him to critique the results of her recent derriere-tightening procedure and as she pulled down her super-micro-mini shorts, she lost her footing and accidentally *sat* in his lap. Doesn't that burst the boundaries of credibility?! What a cask full of malodorous compost!" Otka shouted, obviously outraged. She continued in a calmer voice, "What I also observed – given their unique coitus position it was impossible for me not to take notice – was that Cookie is not a bona fide blonde." Otka's anger flared again, "That Starck… a fantastic-looking man with character as hideous as a triple-digit Cursed. What a swine! I am ashamed to say this, but I hope that crack to his cranium renders him impotent! I hope his TBI leads to ED ASAP! Wouldn't that be a righteous reward?! Oh, sweetie, I need to re-evaluate the criteria I use for selecting my coitus partners. Gorgeous men bring pleasure to my body, but misery to my soul…" Otka's voice wavered, and then trailed off. She turned away from Addison, but he could hear her sobbing. After about thirty seconds, she brought her hands up to her face and wiped her eyes. She spun back around to face Addison with a big smile – a dazzling disguise – looking as if she hadn't cried at all. She continued in her normal voice, "Unfortunately, sweetie, I must now impart some news to you that will turn your grin into a grimace. During the past half-fortnight, I have become intimate with one of the new guards recently assigned to Sycamore. His name is Cliff – I call him 'Cliffie.' My initial impression is that he is a man who possesses both masculine beauty and solid ethical filament. Time will be the definitive judge, of course, but I have an excellent feeling that Cliffie, unlike that bastardly, dastardly Starck, will be able to maintain his fidelity for the duration of our relations." A single tear ran down Otka's cheek. She deftly wiped it away with a flourish of her hand. Addison could see she was upset, but she was trying hard to conceal it. "Anyway, I'm sure you have seen him. He is a hulking man with scrumptious shoulders and expressive blue opal eyes. They look like blue crystal pools of tropical water; they are breathtaking. He is usually present in the Depot around the same time you are." Addison looked at her incredulously. If she would have added blond hair as one of his characteristics, she would have described practically every SS he had ever seen. "Well, it's not important that you know him. It is important, however, that you hear what he told me. Cliffie has been assigned to Brock's special police force – you know the one Brock mentioned? The richest cream skimmed from the cream?" Addison nodded; he remembered Brock's clumsy analogy. "He informed me that his unit will be supervising the erection of a new barricade encircling the Wakork Burdened living complex. Brock plans to confine the Burdened citizens the same way he has confined the Curseds!"

Addison gasped, "A-A-Are you sure Cliffie isn't pulling your leg?"

"Believe me, I am absolutely sure. My Cliffie is an expert on erections," she said coyly. "Besides, naked men never tell lies, especially right after they have climaxed," Otka said. "Our Chancellor has acquired indisputable evidence that Burdened citizens supplied the confined Curseds with the weapons they used in the uprising. They have moving footage showing Burdeneds smuggling contraband over the barricade. They have hand-scribed confessions from the perpetrators. They have flowcharts, pie charts, bar charts, line charts, fingerprints, blueprints, infrared scans, black lists and oral testimony from specialists in CSI, DNA and a few other important-sounding tri-lettered acronyms that I can't immediately recall. Their case is irrefutable! Cliffie… Cliff also told me that Brock will be extinguishing the life force of four Burdeneds tomorrow's eve, using a technique that will be severe, painful and fantastic to witness. With the next day's sun, barricades will be built around every Burdened living complex in Alpdon. Addison, don't you see what Brock is doing?" Otka's eyes were wide, her nostrils flared, and her face flushed; she looked fetching. For a moment, Addison was flustered... Did she expect him to answer her question? Before he had time to decide, Otka continued, "Brock is going to eradicate every Cursed and Blessed in Alpdon. This has been his plan all along. Take a look at this!"

Otka reached into her left breast cup and pulled out a small piece of folded writing foil. She unfolded it and handed it to Addison. It was a copy of an official-looking document bearing the seal of the Chancellor in the upper left-hand corner. It smelled of jasmine and espresso. Despite the gravity of the situation, the phrase, *"what a fortunate document,"* wisped through Addison's thoughts. He read it aloud:

"E-E-EUTHANASIA DECREE"

"I-I-I hereby increase the authority of certain physicians, to be designated by name, in such manner that any child up to the age of three, who according to human judgment is destined for classification as a Burdened or Cursed, *be accorded a mercy death?*"

Addison supplied the emphasis and questioning tone. "A-A-A 'mercy death'? Merciful to whom? Wh-Wh-Where did you get this? And why are you telling me all this?" he asked.

"I am telling you this because I care about you. Isn't that obvious?" Otka said, smiling. Addison noticed a hint of pink in her cheeks. Was she blushing? Addison was so astonished by her revelation that his mouth involuntarily dropped open. Otka paused, "What is causing you to affect such a surprised look?"

Addison didn't know what to say, so he remained silent. Otka gave him a few seconds and then continued, "Anyway, I got this information from an occasional friend – a toiler of prominence at the Bureau of Records – who is desperately trying to get me to mount his sleeping platform and subsequently mount him. Whenever he gets an official correspondence from the Chancellor, he gives me a first generation reproduction. He evidently thinks I'll be impressed by his access to power," she said indifferently, and she waved her hand in a manner that led Addison to believe that this fellow's scheme would never bear fruit.

"Wh-Wh-Why would Brock want to k-k-kill the future Curseds and Burdeneds? Doesn't he effectively accomplish his goals by just confining them?"

"Why would he want to eradicate the Curseds and Blesseds? Are you being serious or are you engaging in a tad of tomfoolery? Have you been living under a slab of Precambrian pink granite for the last four-plus annums? Addison, sweetie, you have got to arise and experience the flavor of the caffeine tablet. Haven't you assimilated the treatise Brock published right before he took office?"

It took Addison a few seconds to translate into common language what Otka had just said. This woman was easy to look at, but difficult to understand. "N-N-No, I haven't. I-I know the overarching principles of Brock's ideology, but I have no desire to r-read about the details," he said crossly.

Otka tilted her head and narrowed her eyes. Addison could see his anger had surprised her; he noticed she was lightly blushing again. "Well, anyway, I don't want to upset you; I just want to protect you. May I recite an excerpt for you?" she asked as she walked over to her desk and grabbed a chrome-finished printed version of Brock's thesis. "N-N-Naturally," Addison said, his eyes trained on her bouncing blonde hair as she walked back toward him.

She started to say what everyone, everywhere, in any age says when searching for content in any printed volume, "Why is it whenever you are attempting to locate a passage of prose…" Her eyes widened. "I found it!" she exclaimed as if she had just discovered a cure for male pattern baldness. It struck Addison that in his limited interactions with her, she responded with unrestrained enthusiasm even when she accomplished the simplest of tasks – she'd recently reacted similarly when she found a lip plumper she was searching for in her handbag. Otka began reading solemnly:

"The sooner this nation understands the concept of human inequality, the sooner it will return to its former glory. No one will disagree with this when we talk about physical appearance. It is obvious that the 'red skins' and 'yellow people' are different looking than the 'Negroes' and the 'white people.' And no one will disagree that even within these groups, there are differences in appearance. There are 'beautiful red faces' and 'ugly red faces' and this holds true for all."

"People differ in more than physical characteristics. What one person accomplishes with ease, another struggles at. When someone has a particularly sharp set of skills, we say that they are 'Blessed.' For instance, there are those who are 'Blessed' with a great body and those who are 'Blessed' with a sharp wit. This interrelationship must be studied, for a perfect god cannot do an incomplete work."

"The past era, which brought this country to its current state of decline, entirely ignored human inequality. Our former leaders pandered to those less fortunate because they wanted power, which they got and then misused. If this state is to resurrect itself and restore the economic prosperity we so foolishly squandered, we need to separate these unequal humans and prevent genetic corruption…"

"Genetic corruption?" Addison asked incredulously. "He is talking about genetic cleansing!"

"I am afraid he is, my dear. Let me finish. There is only a short passage left."

"For if one Blessed by god commingles with one un-Blessed, the offspring who takes half the genes from the un-Blessed will also be un-Blessed. Un-Blessedness is a disease like any other disease. We must destroy it – the same way we destroyed influenza, premature ejaculation and erectile dysfunction – if we are ever going to achieve and sustain long-lasting prosperity."

Addison's mouth dropped open again. Brock had actually written this? He was a lunatic! Aesop's fable of the wolf in sheep's clothing came to mind. However, Brock was no ordinary gray wolf; he was a rabid and perverted one – very unpredictable and extremely dangerous.

"You are in acute peril, cutie pie! You have to do something," she said, concerned. "You need a scheme of extrication!"

A scheme of extrication… He had one; he just hadn't thought that he would need it so quickly. He had to find Pankewitz immediately.

"Th-Th-Thanks for the information," Addison sputtered. "I really have to go. There is someone I really must talk to."

He left Otka's office and headed for the Depot's exit portal. Otka yelled after him, "Where are you running off to, sweetie? To whom do you wish to speak? Wait! Wait!! You forgot to procure your espresso tablets!"

Addison heard Otka, but didn't stop. He had forgotten to order his espresso tablets, but he dare not go back; he didn't have enough time. He would have to start the day with a caffeine deficit, which meant he would probably have a caffeine-withdrawal headache in about an hour. He would have to endure it until lunch when he could load up on the low-grade caffeine served in the Menial cafeteria. He hurried through the exit portal and ran to his living complex. He was desperate… frantic. He still had about ten minutes before he needed to board the transport for Shawcuzit. He had to try again to locate Pankewitz. Sweating profusely, Addison leapt into the open lift. He was going against the normal commuting flow and fortunately, the lift was empty.

"New arrival, please articulate your floor," the inviting female voice commanded.

Hair-sprouting facial mole! What was Pankewitz's floor? He had heard it that time Pankewitz rode with him in the lift and articulated his floor for him when his stutter befuddled the system. If he remembered correctly, Pankewitz had said his own floor number in an odd manner. Addison thought for a moment… he remembered! Pankewitz had started his floor number with a protracted "Aaayyy." But did he say "Eight" or "Eighteen"? He said "Eight." Addison had taken note at the time that Pankewitz had said his favorite number. He impressed himself with his ability to recall this information under such duress. Without stammering, Addison said, "Eight, please."

"Floor Eight recognized," the female voice replied.

As the lift rose, Addison wiped his sweaty brow with his hand and dried his hand on the threadbare carpeting adorning the lift walls. "Please refrain from soiling the walls," the female voice admonished in a notice-ably harsher tone. Addison's neck and face started to burn, but then he caught himself and smiled. He wasn't going to let a voice modulation sys-tem embarrass him —even a sexy-sounding female one.

The lift stopped on the eighth floor. Addison jumped out and franti-cally searched the row of entrance portals looking for Pankewitz's name. The Professor's portal was the fourth one he came upon. Addison waved his right wrist over the Recognition Unit, which was located waist-high on the right side of the portal. "Addisoy, Hall calling for Professor Pankewitz," an androg-ynous voice said softly. Addison waited. There was no response. He waved his wrist again. "Addisoy, Hall calling for Professor Pankewitz." Still there was no response. Frantically, Addison tried it again. This time, Pankewitz's dis-tinctive deep voice answered, "Greetings, my persistent caller. I am currently conducting critical commercial activities in our country's capital city. I will return to my living unit shortly. May this day bring you an overabundance of joy, peace and prosperity in whatever endeavor you choose." Addison's mouth dropped open. "Will return to my living unit shortly"? What did that mean? "Cleft palate, clubfoot, itty-bitty baby-maker and chronic plaque psoriasis!" Addison cursed loudly, not concerned if anyone heard him. He pounded the entrance portal in frustration and walked back toward the lift. He had to get to the transport station quickly if he wanted to make it to work on time. Starck was no longer around to terrify him, but he still ran the risk of getting his fourth tardy violation. Given his pending confinement, being one viola-tion away from a Prime Crime no longer worried him, but because it was his fourth tardy arrival, he would get more severe punishment – probably a few hours in the Standing Coffin.[11] He needed an uneventful day to figure out another plan of escape. The Coffin's insufferable heat and stale air would be a dreadful place to conjure up fresh ideas.

---

11 The Standing Coffin was a seven-meter-high, two-and-a-half-meter wide concrete box used to punish campers and Menials. The offending party entered from the bottom of the box. The box was then placed in the direct sunlight. Temperatures inside the box often exceeded 50 degrees Celsius.

At first pass, however, Addison wasn't sure if he had any other options. Worse yet, he didn't have much time to concoct new ones. If Pankewitz didn't return by tomorrow night and if Otka's new friend, Cliffie, in fact told no lies while he wore no clothes, Addison was less than forty-eight hours away from being confined indefinitely. ■

CHAPTER EIGHTEEN

❖

ADDISON WRITHED ON HIS SLEEPING platform like a worm on sun-drenched concrete, unable to find a comfortable position. A debilitating headache pounded behind his right eye making bright light difficult to tolerate and a train of thought difficult to maintain. Skipping his morning caffeine to try to find Pankewitz had left him with a nasty caffeine-deprivation headache. The five caffeine tablets he consumed during lunch and the three more right before he left for the day had done nothing to alleviate the pain.

Addison resigned himself to the fact that Pankewitz was not going to help him. Upon returning from work, he had gone directly to Pankewitz's living unit and heard, for a second time, the Professor's digitized voice crushing his hopes by announcing that he would "return" to his "living unit shortly." The vagueness of that phrase still annoyed Addison. Would he return the next day? Two days from now? A fortnight? Five fortnights? Once again, he punched Pankewitz's entrance portal in frustration – this time much harder. He now had a sore hand to accompany his aching head.

Trying to take his mind off his intensifying nausea, he reached over to the shelf next to his sleeping platform and grabbed his signal-pirating device. He wondered about Nigel. What was his current situation? Was he even still alive? Addison activated the device, pushed a random glowing button and accessed a home shopping program. The saleswoman hosting the program instantly captured Addison's attention.

She was a statuesque woman with blonde hair and a wrinkle-free, angular face that looked like golden porcelain. She was sitting on a tall chair (so high that her feet were not touching the floor); on top of her glossy crossed legs she held the latest status symbol in Alpdon – an autographed portrait of Brock framed in silver and mounted in a red-sandstone-colored leather case. It was the same portrait Brock had offered as a reward for information on the Cursed uprising's conspirators. It was an objet d'art that every citizen of Alpdon knew well. "Every Blessed living unit should be adorned with one of these," she said. Addison had no interest in what she was peddling; however, he was amazed that she was able to move her mouth enough to talk given the tightness of her face. She was beautiful, but in a contrived way. As Addison watched her, he half-expected her face to crack like dried clay. She appeared to be in her early thirties, but Addison guessed that she might be as old as sixty. Despite all of the appearance-enhancing scientific advances, the one thing that cosmetic surgery (available to Blesseds only), wrinkle putty, hormone infusions, astringent baths and thrice-daily skin exfoliations could never restore was the unsullied aura of youth. While this Blessed woman looked young, she comported herself with a weariness that was incongruent with her appearance.

Addison pushed another glowing button and by chance ended up again on the Erudition Content feed. The same rodent-faced man with the dark eyes and slicked-back jet black hair was speaking to a gathering of brown-tunic-wearing SA and black-tunic-wearing SS. Addison noticed that the SS sat in the front of the auditorium, while the SA sat in the rear. (He didn't know if this was significant.) The rodent-faced man spoke casually, with authority and a slight smile, "The winter before the glorious revolution, before Our Leader was installed as Chancellor, it came to my attention that some children in the town of Bychawa, a quaint, rural hamlet about 25 kilometers south of Bunill, did not even have shoes to wear as they walked through the patella-deep snow on their way to school. They had to walk from their living complexes with disposal sacks on their feet! At the same time, our former government made sure that some subhumans living in a state-run institution – subhumans that would later be classified as solid Curseds – had fresh Mercurian bananas to eat.[12] They were given one of these delicious bananas twice each fortnight to ensure that they received their necessary vitamins and minerals. I was also informed that a single citizen, who would be a triple-digit Cursed today, lived in a special care

12 A rare delicacy; the sugar in the fruit caramelized while still in its skin due to Mercury's proximity to the Sun.

facility just outside of Wakork at the taxpayer cost of 26,000 krams per annum. These krams were wasted on a life that had no meaning, no purpose and certainly no future! That considerable amount of mammon could have been used to prepare a dozen strong, healthy children born unto Blessed parents for a life of significance, productivity and abundant procreation. But I am not speaking of this as a kind of theft. Mammon is not an end in itself, despite what history tells us the capitalists believed. What we have here is a theft of spirit and soul. We tried to persuade the nation that our own greatness would come from sacrificing for the worst and most helpless among us. In the end, we went so far as to put the mentally and physically deficient before the Blessed and Favored youths. That is against nature and life! If our nation continued along this path, we would have wound up in a financial abyss. We went so far as to preach year after year to beautiful and prosperous families that they should have no children or, at most, one child. If they had more than one, we accused them of sinning against the nation and the spirit of this enlightened age because they had added more to the load of an already overburdened economy. But if some imbecilic Cursed whore and a genetically ill Burdened had a retarded child, this pathetic human being was not only a financial burden for its entire life, but it also took the labor of a person whom our society gave nothing better to do than to change this poor creature's diaper three times a day and feed it bottle after bottle of pabulum. That is a perversion of everything great and healthy. It is a sin against life and the spirit of our god's creation!"

Addison shook his head in disgust. Listening to the lopsided logic and twisted tenets made him physically ill. He randomly pushed buttons until the device shut down. He tossed it over his shoulder onto his sleeping platform, ripped down his pants and lunged into his waste elimination chamber, making it onto the commode just in time.

As Addison sat, he pressed his palms firmly against his temples, trying to squeeze the pain from his head. He sighed loudly. If Otka's nude friend was right, he was about to spend his last night as a free citizen.

Addison finished his business, left the chamber and hopped back up on his sleeping platform. He glanced over at the holographic time device.

It read 05:05 (the date Napoleon Bonaparte died). His awakening device would activate in about two-and-a-half hours. His headache had not subsided and he found it hard to keep his legs still. He rolled onto his side, put his hands together and placed them between his knees. He winced as the bones of his knee joints dug into the backs of his hands. If my leg muscles were better developed, this wouldn't hurt so much, he thought. He sighed again. Would this constant self-scrutiny ever end?

Addison's nausea continued to build. His mouth began watering so prodigiously that saliva leaked from his mouth and streamed down his chin. His entire body was soon covered in sweat. He hopped off his sleeping platform and lurched for his waste elimination chamber. He kneeled next to the chrome waste receptacle. His body retched and he vomited with a gurgling roar into the receptacle. He sat down next to it. He felt another surge of nausea. He quickly propped himself back up on his knees and vomited again, roaring even louder this time and even bringing up some bile. That was it. He knew it was over. He sat back down. How absolutely horrible it was to vomit! It was so horrible that you were willing to endure the slow and torturous drip of the building nausea in the hope that you could avoid that minute or so of total misery, even though you knew that as soon as you endured it you would feel so much better. Addison reached up to his sink, grabbed a gypsum-coated towel and wiped the sweat from his face and forehead. He spit some residual vomit into the receptacle then rested his forehead against the beveled rim. The cool metal felt good. His breathing, which had come in short bursts just moments earlier, gradually slowed back to normal. He closed his eyes and concentrated on the coolness of the chrome, which surprisingly gave him some relief from his headache. Addison was exhausted. He drifted toward sleep. As he teetered on the fuzzy line between slumber and consciousness, it occurred to him that he was about to fall asleep in his waste elimination chamber. Worse yet, he was using the commode as his pillow. An appropriate place to end an atrocious day, he thought. He fell asleep with a wry smile flitting across his vomit-coated lips. ∎

CHAPTER NINETEEN

❖

ADDISON WAS AWAKE, but he couldn't open his eyes. A crusty substance held them shut. He sat upright on the floor of his waste elimination chamber and a sharp pain radiated down his neck and into his shoulders. He rose slowly and turned toward the left, positioning himself in front of his only mirror. He strained to open his eyes, but the substance holding them together wouldn't yield. He reached up and stroked the area where his eyelids met. Addison groaned in disgust. He scraped the gunk off his eyelashes, removing a bunch in the process. Finally, his eyes opened. Addison leaned toward the mirror and examined them closely. How revolting! They were bloodshot, caked with dried pus and unbearably itchy. Conjunctivitis, he said stammer-free to his image in the mirror. He rubbed them vigorously with his fists. Oh, what relief! Addison was no stranger to this uncomfortable ailment; it had been a chronic problem during his childhood. His birther used to tell him that it was the result of rubbing his eyes with soiled hands. Could resting his head on his commode have caused this? His awakening apparatus activated, deflecting his thoughts. He didn't have time to ponder the reasons why; he had to prepare himself for his last day of work.

Addison left his living unit and paused for few seconds before summoning the lift. Should he visit Pankewitz's unit one more time? It was too time-consuming, he decided. Paying a visit to the Professor's unit might not leave him with enough time to stop by the Caffeine Depot and he needed his beloved caffeine this morning more than ever. His neck and shoulders ached, his back was sore, his eyes were sticky and he had his usual pre-caffeine morning skull-splitter. It wasn't possible to feel worse, he thought as he entered the crowded lift. He found a small patch of floor space between a tall, skinny man with a heavily pockmarked face and a short woman with a smooth cherubic face, a sulfur-colored smile and a protuberant stomach that jiggled when she exhaled. What was it with that woman? Every time he saw her, she was smiling. Why was she always in such a good mood? If he had a stomach like that, he wouldn't be smiling all the time.

The pressure built in Addison's ears; the lift was descending. It was so slow that if it weren't for this subtle change in pressure, you wouldn't even know it was moving. Why was everyone stealing quick glances in his direction? He looked down at his fly. That wasn't the reason; the mollusk-glue seal was closed. He quickly ran his hands over his face and through his hair in an attempt to dislodge anything out of the ordinary – maybe a wayward dollop of HastyTasty or worse yet, perhaps a pubic hair from the waste receptacle! How humiliating! He rubbed his now dampened palms more carefully over his forehead, ears, cheeks, eyelids and nose. Surely that got rid of anything unsightly stuck to his face.

Addison dismounted the lift, walked through the foyer and stepped outside. The hairs at the base of his scalp bristled. Placed sporadically around his living complex were neatly stacked piles of construction materials. Any hope he harbored that Otka's friend had been lying vanished. The building materials were undeniable proof that unclothed "Cliffie" had indeed been telling the naked truth.

Addison's steps were heavy and slow as he made his way toward the Caffeine Depot. He saw a small crowd gathered around one of the piles. A mound of clothes sat next to the pile and a large placard was placed on the ground in front of it. Addison stopped and watched the scene for a few moments. It felt good to stand still.

Onlookers were bending over, reading the placard, and then walking away. Most of the Burdeneds looked disturbed, while most of the Blessed and Favoreds were smirking. What could be written on that placard to elicit such diverse responses? He was curious to read the sign, but it would require traversing a slight incline to get to it and he didn't feel like doing it. As the crowd continued to grow, however, so did his curiosity. He gave up a long sigh and trudged toward the crowd.

As Addison got closer, a shiver, like a cold drop of rain, rolled down his spine. It wasn't a pile of clothes at all... Handsome lord, it was a man!

A slightly bloated man with an alabaster face... Sexy and succulent savior –
it was a corpse! As Addison got closer still, he could see a distinctive patch
of white hair on the man's head. He saw that the man was wearing a brown
corduroy tunic... Addison clapped his right hand over his open mouth.
God's grandiose gonads! Blessed birther of god's bulging breasts!! It was
Pankewitz! Pankewitz's face was a bit swollen, but it was definitely him – he
had that unmistakable aquiline nose. There was dried white spittle on his
full lips and an odd-looking blemish at the base of his left nostril. Addison
bent down to read the placard:

ATTENTION WAKORKIANS!
Here lies the body of Thaddeus Pankewitz.
Two days prior, a Security Agent, who is as vigilant as he is fetching,
overhead Pankewitz asking a transport operator to illegally help a group
of Burdened citizens abscond from our country. Although the identity of
these Burdened backsliders has yet to be ascertained, my agents are confident that they played a significant role in the Cursed uprising. Pankewitz
has been executed via an injection of hydrochloric acid into the brain stem
for the offense of conspiring to commit a Prime Crime. His cadaver will be
displayed for 24 hours as a dramatic and malodorous illustration of the fate
that awaits anyone who conspires against this country.
Long Live Bormann Brock!
J. Scherner

Addison felt as if his heart had been yanked from his chest. His anguish
was so great that it caused him to bend over at the waist and fold his arms
around his stomach. His last glimmer of hope had vanished. Guilt commingled with his despair. Was he the cause of this? Was it possible that
Pankewitz had been caught trying to arrange for his escape?

An urbane Blessed man wearing a jade-colored penis pouch and matching halter stepped up next to Pankewitz's slumped body and picked at the
blemish near Pankewitz's nostril. The size of the blemish grew and when he

took his hand away, it now looked like a large deflated blister. With a look of mild shock on his princely face, the Blessed man reached down again, placed his finger into the pocket of the blister and pulled. Addison yelped. Pankewitz's nose was a prosthetic! With some effort, the man yanked the prosthesis off of Pankewitz's face, revealing a perfectly symmetrical button nose. Spirit gum residue was stuck to the side of his nostrils and the bridge of his nose. The Blessed man casually tossed the counterfeit nose beside Pankewitz's body and continued on his way.

Addison was too shocked to react. It was undeniable; even in this post-mortal bloated state, it was easy to see that Pankewitz was a solid Blessed. With his real nose rather than the fake, hair-sprouting, protuberant one, Pankewitz was handsome. What a difference that nose had made to his overall appearance, Addison thought, surprised at his calm response to this startling revelation. Like a child who plays obsessively with a jack-in-the-box, Addison had experienced so many recent "pops" that the surprises no longer elicited a reaction.

Addison left the crowd and walked toward the Caffeine Depot, unable to shake the image of the handsome and lifeless face of Pankewitz from his thoughts. What reason did Pankewitz have for disguising himself? Could he have done it to put himself in a better position to smuggle those "creative types" out of the country? It seemed to be the only plausible explanation. But what would motivate someone to do something so selfless? (Those who performed such altruistic acts always baffled Addison.) After all, how did Pankewitz benefit from it? Addison noticed from their first meeting that Pankewitz was different. He seemed more capable than any other Burdened Addison had previously encountered. Pankewitz possessed an innate confidence. Was this confidence congenital or had Pankewitz somehow acquired it? Would he have displayed such self-assuredness if he had been a Burdened rather than a Blessed?

Addison entered the Depot and immediately noticed that Otka was not at her usual spot behind the service counter. For the past ten fortnights she had been standing in the same spot every morning. This morning – his last day as an unconfined citizen – she was absent. He realized there was nothing she could do to help him, but seeing her would have been a bright spot in what promised to be a dreadful day.

Addison stepped up to the service desk, resisting the urge to rub his itchy eyes. "Three espresso tablets, please," he said to Mimi, who was back at work.

"Sure. I am more than happy to assist you," Mimi said eagerly and a bit too loudly. She didn't put the tablets onto a chrome plate as she usually did. Instead, she placed them directly into Addison's hand. She wrapped her hand around his fingers and gave them a quick squeeze. This caught Addison off guard; he closed his hand and pulled it back as if he had touched a hot pipe. Mimi let her gaze linger on him longer than normal. Was she trying to get Addison to ask her out again? Couldn't she see he was no longer interested in her? Perhaps to compensate for the excessive volume of her initial comment, she said in a hushed voice with a smile on her pinched face, "Have a nice day."

"Thanks," Addison said. He turned and headed for the exit portal. Gorgeous god, she was so unappealing! It looked as if she had gained even more weight around her midsection. How pathetic she had become. How could he have been attracted to her just a few fortnights ago? As he approached the exit, he glanced over his shoulder at the service counter to see if Otka had appeared. She had not. He left the Depot disappointed.

Addison stepped back into Grand Square and fingered the tablets in his hand. She had given him four tablets instead of three. Did she make a mistake or was Mimi so desperate for a date that she had now resorted to pilfering in an attempt to gain his affections?

He eagerly looked at his espresso tablets – many times they were the highlight of his day. A flash of panic warmed his face. Would he still be able to get espresso tablets once he was confined? Even if they didn't have espresso tablets, they would have to have some form of caffeine. Even the cheap and chalky coffee tablets available at the camp would be better than nothing. He decided to stop by the Caffeine Depot on his way home from work and use all of his remaining commerce credits to purchase as many tablets as he could. Besides, Otka would probably be there; he wanted to see her one more time. Pleased with his idea, he popped all four tablets into his mouth. Four would deliver a large dose of caffeine, but he needed it after his terrible night's sleep.

He curled his tongue around the first tablet and positioned it between his cheek and gum. He did the same with the second and third tablets. Suddenly, he was gagging! Something was wrong with the third tablet. It dissolved too quickly and was now stuck on the back of his tongue. Either it hadn't been compounded with the correct recipe of ingredients or it hadn't been left in the tablet presser long enough. Of all days to get a defective one!

Addison turned and stomped back toward the Depot, determined to give Mimi a good tongue-lashing. She needed to be more vigilant when filling orders. He purchased premium tablets; he expected them to at least be potable. He spit the contents of his mouth into his palm, then abruptly stopped. One of the tablets was unraveling! He poked at it with his finger. Stunning looking savior, it was writing foil! He pulled it from the saliva and powder mush in his hand. He crammed the mess back into his mouth as best he could and licked his palm to make sure none of the caffeine was wasted. He unfurled the foil. Neatly printed in uppercase letters was the following:

MEET ME AT 21:00 AT KING SIG TRIB. I'VE DESIGNED A STRATEGY OF SOCIETAL EXTRICATION FOR YOU.
— OTKA

If he understood the note correctly, Otka was going to save him. Were his infected eyes playing a trick on him? He blinked hard, wiped away the pus that had accumulated in the corners of his eyes, and looked at it again. No, he had read it correctly.

Addison immediately knew the place Otka was referring to – the impressive five-dimensional King Sigismund III holographic tribute located at the northwestern entrance to Grand Square. Over the past few fortnights, Addison had experienced some shocking events, but this surpassed them all. He stuffed the saliva-soaked piece of foil in his pocket, then pulled it out and read it for a third time. He still couldn't believe it. Why had she decided to help him? The only reason he could think of was because she felt sorry for him. Could he accept her help even though it was out of pity? He decided that he most certainly could. He continued walking toward the transport station – now with an optimistic spring in his step. As he waited his turn to mount the transport, a rich brass fanfare sounded in Grand Square. A creamy female voice announced, "Chancellor Brock will address the nation at 19:30."

Addison entered the Menial locker room and saw Remy, first as always, changing into his work smock. He noticed that Remy's smock was much cleaner than his – probably because the SS assigned all the sloppy work to those Menials who didn't enjoy the taste of SS boot leather.

"What's up with you?" Remy asked. "If I didn't know you, Addster…" (You don't know me, Addison silently retorted) "… I would swear that is a smile on your face – or at least the gestation of a grin."

"A-A smile? Who's smiling?" Addison said, smiling. Even Remy wasn't going to spoil his good mood.

"I would additionally proclaim, Addster, that your visage bears a striking similarity to that of a man who knows he will soon be engaging in rigorous coitus," Remy said, flashing his buck-toothed, petrified-bone-colored smile, obviously enjoying what he perceived to be a rare moment of camaraderie.

Addison went from smiling to chuckling. "Y-Yeah, that's right, Remy. I have a flock of women eager for the opportunity to join me on my sleeping platform," he said derisively. "My biggest problem is figuring out which one I should engage with first. Be serious, Remster. Women don't look at me that way. In fact, they barely look at me at all."

"Well, Addster, there was that incident in the camp administrative offices... Don't you recall the time you tripped over a cobweb or a speck of dust or a mouse's eyelash and tumbled face-first into the lap of that heavily-breasted Favored secretary who operates the boot-buffing machine? She gave you a rather intense look if I remember events accurately!"

Addison's good mood allowed him to ignore Remy's jab at his occasional clumsiness. Usually just hearing Remy deliver one "Addster" would be enough to set his teeth on edge, but he took that and Remy's putdown, and he didn't have the urge to slap his bloated face. This was fascinating; he had to try this "good mood thing" more often.

As Addison pulled on his smock, Remy lumbered out of the locker room with a waddle available only to those with pudgy bodies. "That's it, Remster, you over-cologned sloth humper," Addison said (stammer-free) under his breath. "Go make your morning lap around the campgrounds to make sure every guard on duty sees you." He squatted down to emulate Remy's stature and said in a squeaky voice, "look at me, look at me," while he waved his arms in the air and paraded around the locker room like a convulsing velociraptor. He was enjoying himself, but then he stopped and lowered his arms. Would something horrible now happen to balance out this bit of good fortune? When he was a child, didn't his master birther[13] always warn him when he was laughing that tears would soon follow? And what was that allegorical tale she used to tell him about the fishermen? He remembered.

A group of fishermen were hauling in their net. They were celebrating and dancing about because the net was so heavy. When they pulled the net to shore, it was filled with rocks and seaweed and contained only a handful of fish. She always finished the story by wagging a liver-spotted finger at him and telling him in her croaky voice (the result of inhaling too many burning nicotine rods, and according to his master POP, from many years of "incessant gabbing") the moral of the story – joy has for its sister, affliction; if you rejoice prematurely, you can expect its contrary

---

13 Referred to in an earlier age as "grandmother."

to follow. "Never forget that, my lovable little baboon." She always called him her "lovable little baboon." When Addison entered secondary school, he queried an encyclopedic server and accessed an image of a baboon. He was crushed. Baboons were ugly! So ugly that their posteriors were actually better looking than their faces! Why would you put such a disparaging tag on a young boy? Had all those nicotine fumes cauterized the frontal lobe of her cerebrum?

Even though she knew nothing about child psychology, the point of his master birther's fable still stuck with him. The reality was that he was rejoicing prematurely. He had no idea what Otka's plan was. It was entirely possible that it was nothing more than a can of HastyTasty with a strand of razor wire inside. Addison became anxious; his heart rate increased and the palms of his hands moistened. After all, what could Otka do to help him? Sure, she could copulate sensitive information out of an aroused SS, but she couldn't change Addison's caste. He started to panic. The more he thought about it, the more convinced he was that Otka's plan would be a token one. Maybe not as hackneyed as the "saw in the strudel" scheme, but probably something equally as feckless. In fact, she might be offering to help him simply to allay her guilty conscious – similar to what had led Addison to walk around Sycamore–Birch searching for Nigel.

By the time he finished dressing, his good mood had melted away faster than a slug covered in powdered halite. Addison left the locker room and entered the grounds of the camp. He had blinked all of the pus from his infected eyes; they opened and closed without resistance.

He was supervising a group of campers repairing some of the barrack edifices. His group was already assembled and waiting for him in a single-file line by the guard tower. Addison counted them as he approached. There were eight campers! His lucky number! He looked over at the holographic time device in the center of the camp courtyard. It read 9:07. His heart leapt. The sum of those numbers was sixteen and that was divisible by eight. It was a sign! He thought for a moment, then came up with a routine that was sure to bring him some "god luck." If he alternately blinked each eye eight times at precisely eight minutes after each hour for the next eight hours, he would avoid being confined – either Otka would help him escape Alpdon or she would at least help him avoid his pending confinement. If he failed to do it, even once, then Otka's help would just be a token gesture and he would wind up confined with the other Burdeneds.

At the end of his shift, Addison had achieved his goal. He had alternately blinked each eye eight times at exactly eight minutes after each hour for eight straight hours. Unfortunately, doing his little routine over the course of the day had given him an excruciating headache and resurrected the nausea that had debilitated him the night before. He entered the locker room and immediately went to the waste elimination chamber. He crouched down next to the receptacle, careful to avoid the sticky patches of dried urine, and rested his forehead against the cool metal. He moaned with delight. Handsome lord! Lithe and lean savior, what relief! The sour smell of urine was easy to tolerate for such relief. Gurgling noises emanated from deep within the receptacle, like the distant sound of a babbling brook. The tension drained from Addison's ocular muscles. He wondered why his receptacle at home didn't make such noises; it was calming. Then something strange occurred – the receptacle started vibrating. Addison moaned again. This was even more soothing! The vibrations increased in intensity and soon his head was bouncing up and down off the rim of the receptacle. This was no longer comforting; it was painful. Addison lifted his head off of the receptacle and placed his hand where his head had been. The intensity of the vibrations continued to grow. Just then, a group of people charged into the locker room. The pounding of their boots made the receptacle shake with such force that Addison's hand bounced up and down.

The clamor of boots stopped and a scuffle ensued. Addison heard a high-pitched male voice blubbering, "My lords, it was an accident... it was inadvertent... you don't possibly think I would have done that on purpose... my lords, please! Show some mercy! I promise it won't happen again! I beg you in the name of my lord and our country's savior, Bormann Brock! It was a lone transgression and my record previous to this unfortunate incident has been impeccable! Without blemish! Please check the veracity of my claim... please!" A series of loud thumps interrupted the man's pleas. There was no mistaking that voice – it was Remy. It was obvious to Addison that a group of SS was beating him! Addison gasped in horror and accidentally sucked in and swallowed a pubic hair lying on the rim of the receptacle. He knew he should be mortified, but he was too engrossed in what was transpiring to care. The thumps grew less frequent, but Remy's moaning and pleading grew stronger. It was awful to listen to – "Oh, please, my lords... Oh, pleeeease! Stop it hurts! It hurts so badly! It hurts..." Although it was obvious that Remy was in great pain, his whining annoyed Addison. "What ever happened to suffering with dignity?" he mouthed silently – afraid of even whispering lest he be heard by the group and have their fury turned on him.

A few more thuds and Remy's pleading turned to throaty groaning, then to coughing and gagging. Remy was choking on something – maybe a rag stuffed in his mouth... maybe his own blood... or vomit... or all three. Addison heard the group of attackers exiting the Menial locker room. They chatted casually; some were even chuckling. They sounded to Addison like a group of laborers leaving a job site.

In what seemed like a long time to Addison, but was actually less than ten minutes, Remy's groaning stopped. Addison waited about five more minutes, wanting to make sure that the SS weren't going to return. He gradually opened the chamber portal. Merciful and magnificently muscled heavenly mediator! As he had guessed, it was Remy. He was lying face down with his knees tucked under his chest. An expanding pool of dark blood seeped from Remy's head; he was losing blood rapidly. If he wasn't dead yet he would be soon.

Addison hustled over to his locker and hurriedly changed his clothes, keeping his back to Remy's body the entire time. He didn't want to see it again. He sat on the bench and put on his shoes as quickly as he could. Even amongst all this horror, he noticed that they were still terribly soiled – he had never gotten around to polishing them. As he snapped the last buckle on his right shoe the puddle of Remy's blood lapped up against the back of the heel and soaked the brown leather. Addison was repulsed and annoyed. Now his shoes looked even worse. He bolted upright and ran out of the locker room, averting his eyes from Remy's body. As he left the camp, he noticed a holographic time device that read 19:04. He had less than two hours before he was supposed to meet Otka.

As he waited for the transport in the Shawcuzit station, he tried to push the disturbing image of Remy from his thoughts by focusing on Otka. Of all her outfits (she had an expansive wardrobe), which one was his favorite? Without question, it was her white super-micro-mini shorts and her perfectly hue-harmonized scalloped breast cups. That outfit created the illusion that he was seeing her most intimate areas when, in reality, he was not seeing them at all. It was exceptionally sexy. However, like an annoying lap dog snapping at your ankles, the image of Remy's head in a halo of blood nipped at Addison's thoughts. He repeatedly shooed it away by picturing Otka in her heavenly white outfit. When he saw her later would she be wearing it? More importantly, how would he view her after their encounter? Was she a hero who was going to save him or was she just trying to ease her guilty conscience? Her covert note had given him hope. It had put significant weight in his net. In a few hours, he would pull it to shore. Would it be loaded with rocks or fish? ∎

CHAPTER TWENTY

❖

A LARGE, GOOD-LOOKING CROWD was gathered in Grand Square. After dismounting the transport, Addison joined them. He looked at the people in his immediate area and he noticed that he was the only Burdened. He immediately felt conspicuous, but he wasn't about to leave; he would garner more attention if he did.

Many were dressed in their finest and skimpiest evening wear. Addison smelled the pungent yet pleasant odor of burning pine needles and strawberries. (It was the scent of a new tan extender being used by most Blesseds and many Favoreds.) In the past fortnight, this smell had been ubiquitous, especially in enclosed places like the Caffeine Depot and the transport.

Erected in the center of Grand Square, close to the area where the four-dimensional holographic tribute to Brock usually stood, was a large, rectangular platform about ten meters off the ground. Four wooden posts, about six meters high, were spaced evenly apart on the platform, each illuminated with a white spotlight. A Lucite lectern was placed front and center on the platform. A large group of SAs were scurrying on and around the stage like burly brown ants, apparently making last-minute preparations. The setting reminded Addison of a moving image premiere. As if on cue, four rotating spotlights came to life from each corner of the platform. A wispy fog crept off the Luvista River, giving the Square an intimate but menacing feel. Something unusual was about to occur and the crowd sensed it. Many of the good-lookers standing around Addison fidgeted about, apparently too keyed up to stand and wait quietly.

One man standing just a shade out of Addison's peripheral vision began shouting excitedly, "Woohoo! Woohoo! Woohoo!" at ear-numbing loudness, over and over again. Addison wanted to turn and tell him to temper his volume, but there was a better-than-excellent chance that the yelper was bigger, stronger and braver, so he decided against it. He kept his eyes fixed straight ahead and rationalized his reluctance to confront this yelping boob as a shining example of his social tolerance.

At 19:30, the four spotlights directed on the wooden posts slowly dimmed. A larger spotlight, aimed at the Lucite lectern, increased with intensity. The crowd gathered nearest to the platform cheered loudly. Curiously, many of them were wearing clear ponchos over their outfits, although there was no chance of rain in the forecast.

Seconds later, Brock appeared on the platform as if he had been dropped from the sky. Addison saw that indeed a clear parachute flapped behind him as he stepped up to the lectern. "What a glorious entrance! A glorious entrance... and so appropriate for the Savior of our country," Addison overhead from someone nearby. With a wriggle of his shoulders, Brock extricated himself from the parachute. As always, he was dressed in his pearl jacket, brown tunic and black trousers.

Brock grabbed a piece of amplification gum from a ruby red velvet pillow attached to the side of the lectern, placed it in his mouth, and chewed it indelicately, like a goat working its cud. As he started to speak, the crowd roared with such intensity and with such impeccable timing that Addison had the sense that what he was witnessing was somehow orchestrated, possibly by one of Brock's political marketers. Brock raised his right arm straight out with his palm facing down and held flat, attempting to quiet the crowd. His gesture only caused them to cheer louder – some in the crowd even mimicked him. Addison had never heard such noise! He placed his fingers in his ears to try to subdue the noise. A male good-looker standing to Addison's left (with a neck thicker than Addison's thigh) put his fingers in his ears, then pointed at Addison and laughed. Addison saw it out of the corner of his eye, but pretended he didn't. Brock lowered his right arm back down to his side, then made the gesture again. This time, many more in the crowd copied him. Brock brought his left arm up – both his arms were thrust out at ninety-degree angles. Instantaneously, the crowd fell silent.

Brock spoke, "Fellow citizens of Alpdon." He paused and a smile wisped over his lips. He continued speaking in an exuberant voice, "Soon – very soon, indeed – I will be able to address all of you as 'fellow *good-looking* citizens of Alpdon and it will be a worthy moniker for each and every one of you!" The crowd erupted with more cheers and applause.

Brock absently scratched his short mustache with his right pointer finger and continued speaking, "When I addressed you after the Wakork Cursed Compound rebellion, I promised that Wakork Gauleiter, Julian Scherner, would conduct a comprehensive investigation to apprehend the parties responsible for supplying those subhumans with the armaments they used in their uprising. In a briefing Lord Scherner presented to me this morning, I received the fruits of his investigation. It pains me to tell you, fellow producers of Alpdon, that many enemies of prosperity still live among us. *[Gasps from some in the crowd.]* Yes, there is a silent growth of malignant cysts in our midst! They stand among us and cheer my speeches, pretending to be patriotic conformers; while in their petrified hearts, these backsliders hate me and despise our country! *[Shouts of 'No, No!' from many in the crowd.]* But rest easy, my good-looking colleagues, for their days are numbered… *[loud cheers]* and that number can be represented on one hand!" Brock raised his open right hand over his head, his palm facing the crowd. They roared again. "Lord Scherner's investigation led to the capture of those responsible for enabling the Cursed revolt. But these men, who will receive their deserved and wonderfully gruesome punishment shortly, are only the tail of this devious serpent. My fellow attractive citizens, I have sobering news. Lord Scherner's investigation also revealed the existence of a well-concealed, well-organized terror ring that thrives throughout our Burdened population. *[Gasps of shock from most in the crowd, including Addison.]* Fear not, however! For as I have said in the past, I am the Great Physician! I will do whatever I must to eradicate this insidious cancer from our productive nation!" Brock pounded his open hand on the lectern. The crowd burst forth with its loudest ovation yet. After about thirty seconds, the cheering morphed into a chant of "Long Live Bormann Brock." Again, this sounded too well timed to Addison to be spontaneous. Over and over again the crowd chanted, "Long Live Bormann Brock." Brock backed away from the podium, tilted his head back, and with an orgasmic expression, let the crowd's fount of affection drench his pear-shaped body.

After a minute or so of absorbing their adulation, Brock stepped back up to the podium. The crowd instantly quieted. "Starting with tomorrow's new sun, to safeguard the producers of our recovering economy and our beloved nation from acts of subterfuge, savagery and sabotage, I am going to separate these Burdened parasites from our fruitful society. Did not our luscious-looking lord inspire the angelic-faced John, the most attractive of his twelve apostles, to proclaim that 'he cuts off every branch that does not bear fruit so that the others will be even more fruitful'? Furthermore, did not his apostle Matthew, the reformed tax collector with the broad shoulders and enviable golden tresses, under the inspiration of the lord declare that 'his winnowing fork is in his hand, and he will thoroughly clear his threshing floor; and he will gather his wheat into the barn, but he will burn up the chaff with unquenchable fire'? I am morally obligated – empowered by our perfect creator – to remove these barren branches, to eliminate this useless chaff. I assure you that I will not shy away from my divine duty."

Again the mob chanted, "Long Live Bormann Brock. Long Live Bormann Brock." After a couple of minutes, Brock brought his finger up to his pursed lips and the chanting abruptly stopped. He continued, "Now I will satisfy your lust for justice. The time has come to punish these traitors."

Four cowering men were led onto the stage shackled in testicle cuffs. The first man had closely shorn gray hair and a long beard that looked like it hadn't been trimmed in a while. From where Addison was standing, he couldn't see the man's face, but he could easily see his remarkably protuberant stomach. Addison had never seen a stomach so large before – it was as if the man had swallowed a twenty-kilo boulder.

The second man had a full head of black hair and was well built. From his angle and distance, the prisoner looked like he could be a Favored. Addison guessed that the man must have a repulsive face – maybe a horrendous birth defect – causing him to be classified as a Burdened.

The third man was bald except for a narrow dust-ruffle of hair at the base of his head. He had a wide and disproportionate derriere. It reminded Addison of what one would see if he looked at his distorted reflection in a mirth house mirror.

The last man was the most peculiar looking of all. He was tall, abnormally so, with narrow shoulders, gangly arms that extended to his knees and a tiny head topped with a shock of long brown hair. Apparently self-conscious about his height, he walked with his shoulders hunched as if he were trying to minimize his stature. Even from a distance, Addison could see he was hairy. His posture and his shagginess gave him the appearance of an emaciated ape. Some in the crowd evidently agreed; Addison heard some primate-like screams. The yelping boob standing beside Addison was actually aping an ape. He scratched his head with his left hand and his right armpit with his right hand while making a throaty grunt that reminded Addison of a constipated primate straining to gain relief. This guy was a real attention seeker – even for a Blessed! Addison stole a quick glance at him. As if to prove Addison's point, the yelping boob was using the gesticulations as an excuse to flex his densely muscled arms.

Each prisoner was blindfolded by an SA, placed in front of a post, and then spun around so they were facing the crowd. An SA bound each man's hands behind his back and around the post using pneumatic chrome wrist manacles. As each manacle was activated, it expelled the compressed air with a loud whoosh. Addison was surprised by how loud it was; they were obviously powerful constraints. The tall ape-man was the last prisoner to be bound. He fended off the SA by flailing his arms and bucking his body. Two additional SAs had to help subdue him and manacle him to the post. The SA who had initially attempted to secure the primatial prisoner cocked back his right leg, and with a grunt, drove it hard into the ape-man's crotch. The crowd howled with laughter. The SA then crouched down on his left knee, removed a piece of cloth from his left boot and used it to polish his right one. When he finished, he meticulously folded the cloth, placed it back in his boot and stood up. With military parade pomp, each SA goose-stepped toward the front of the stage, their boots slapping the floor in perfect synchronicity. Two turned and marched stage left and two marched stage right until there was a pair of SAs standing side by side at attention, like muscle-bound bookends, on each side of the platform.

Four long-legged Blessed women pranced onto the stage, each wearing basalt-colored triple-super-duper-hyper-micro-mini shorts and jasper-colored breast cups. Addison guessed these women were striptease dancers – they were in flawless shape, with blonde-hair and legs that looked as if they had been cast from virgin copper. Each woman carried a chrome javelin about seven meters long and positioned herself directly in front of a prisoner. All four women placed their javelins, point down, onto the platform, wrapped a leg around the pole and performed one complete rotation (further supporting Addison's theory about their occupation). The men in the crowd showed their delight by yanking up one side of their tight latex shorts and slapping their cupped palms against their exposed posterior cheeks. Addison had heard groups of men butt-cuffing before – usually when an attractive woman walked past a bunch of men toiling at an erection site – but the sound of several thousand men cuffing their tight derrieres at the same time was amazing!

Each Blessed woman handed her javelin to an SA and returned to the center of the platform. In unison, they turned their backs to the crowd, bent over at the waist and adjusted their shoe straps, giving the crowd an obviously scripted, but nonetheless appreciated, view of their exquisite heart-shaped bottoms. After their revelation, the Blessed women left the stage to another popping-corn chorus of butt-cuffs, now accompanied by exaggerated slurping sounds made by some of the more vulgar men in the crowd.

With javelin in hand, each of the four SAs positioned himself directly in front of a bound prisoner, about ten meters away. The media screens in each corner of the Square began a silent countdown from *20*. The numbers were large, white and three dimensional. They were set on a black background that blended in so perfectly with the obsidian sky that it appeared as if the numbers were suspended in the air. In fact, for a brief moment,

Addison thought he was seeing floating holographic numerals. Just then, one of the rotating spots passed over the media screen he was watching and he saw that it was an illusion.

The crowd chanted along with the countdown. When it reached *10*, each SA positioned his right hand on the middle of the javelin and raised it overhead to a throwing position. At *8*, the prisoner with the remarkably protuberant stomach thrashed his head from side to side as if he were trying to free himself from the post. Some in the crowd mimicked the prisoner's movements; Addison noticed that many were the same ones who had made the primate noises moments ago. He didn't need to look over at the Blessed boob standing to his right – every few seconds, he caught a glimpse of his bouncing head. Pockets of laughter could be heard throughout the Square, but Addison wasn't sure if they were laughing at the scared prisoner or along with those in the crowd who were mocking him.

When the countdown reached *5*, each SA shifted his weight onto his hind leg in an exaggerated manner. While the other three prisoners appeared calm with their heads hanging down, the prisoner with the protuberant stomach continued to thrash about. Addison admired the composure of the three calm ones and felt slight animus toward the squirming one. Couldn't he show some pride? Had the blindfold made him forget that there were about two thousand or so people watching him? As Addison watched, he wondered what he would do if he were in a similar predicament. How would he behave if he were on that stage, blindfolded and bound to a post, knowing he was going to die shortly but having no idea how? This question required no pondering; he knew without a doubt that he would be reacting similarly. He was also fairly certain he would be soiling and wetting his trousers. This realization, however, did nothing to extinguish his growing annoyance with the protuberant-stomached prisoner.

As the countdown wound down, Addison's anxiety ratcheted up as the gravity of what he was about to witness suddenly struck him. At the count of *4*, Addison clenched his hands into tight fists; at *3*, he clenched his teeth together; at *2*, he clenched the cheeks of his buttocks together; and at *1*, he did all three at once. There was no *0* – rather there was no numeral *0* – just an image of a human skeleton holding a scythe. As Addison questioned the relevance of such a graphic (wasn't it a bit campy?), each SA hurled his javelin. Addison shut his eyes to avoid seeing such horror, but he heard a single "thwack" as the javelins simultaneously pierced the prisoners' chest cavities and embedded into the wooden posts. The crowd roared with such gusto that Addison was compelled to open his eyes and take a look. He involuntarily squeaked from shock – all four men had been impaled. The power of the SAs' throws had collapsed the prisoners' chest cavities and torrents of red-ocher-colored blood poured from their wounds. Addison turned away, mortified and disgusted. He regretted his decision to look.

The rotating spotlights now turned toward the crowd. Wherever the beams of light landed, onlookers thrust their right arms out stiffly – again copying the odd salute that Brock had accidentally – or perhaps knowingly – invented moments ago. This continued for a few minutes. Then a deep male voice (possibly the rodent-faced man from the Erudition Content feed), announced solemnly, "Commander Brock has left the Square." The show was over. The rotating spotlights faded to black, but the four spots illuminating the bodies of the executed prisoners remained on.

Addison made his way toward the King Sigismund III, which was located at the southwestern corner of the Square near the entrance to the Favored compound. There was heavy pedestrian traffic coming from this same direction, traffic Addison hadn't anticipated. He frequently lurched from side to side to avoid colliding with someone. Some members of the crowd were still wearing their blood-splattered ponchos; Addison picked up the faint whiff of iron as they passed. Up ahead, Addison saw two poncho-wearing Blessed men nearly collide as they passed by one another. Both men stopped walking, raised their hands over their heads and bumped their ponchos together, chest-to-chest. Both laughing, they stepped back and did it again – this time much harder. Both men stopped laughing and were now just smiling. The third time was harder still and now their smiles were replaced by snarls. The fourth time, each Blessed man tried to knock answer he wanted, nodded apprehensively. "You're an idiot?" his POP said, obviously surprised by his answer. He bellowed with demented, criminal-like laughter, "Well, I'm certainly not about to argue with you."

"Are you satisfactory, sweetie? You don't appear to be thriving physically right now." A delicious voice, accompanied by a wonderfully familiar waft of espresso and jasmine, jolted Addison out of his painful memory. It was Otka, of course. Addison was dumbfounded. Those weren't rocks in his net after all; those were copper rockfish! (Clever, he thought.) Addison bolted up from his crouch, but he had risen too quickly. His legs felt flimsy... He fainted at Otka's manicured feet. She stepped back quickly – apparently not wanting the prolific perspiration from Addison's face to sully her shoes – and Addison's face hit the ground with an audible thump. Otka bent over and softly patted his sweaty cheek with her hand. "Arise, sweetie, arise!" she said, but Addison didn't move. She patted his cheek harder, but still Addison lay motionless. "Handsome lord! You are perspiring profusely," she said to no one in particular. She reared back and slapped his cheek hard, accidentally launching a drop of sweat that landed in her open mouth. She grimaced and dry heaved, but even her loud wretch didn't wake him. She reached back even further, closed her mouth tightly, and slapped him again. A small group of Blessed men gathered around to watch her and offer their encouragement. "Slap his face harder, you finely formed specimen. No need to fret. His ugliness won't come off on your hand," said one of the men. The group laughed. "Lean over again and strike him, beautiful. I want to steal another look into your breast cups," the most attractive man in the group said. Otka smiled. When she bent over again to slap Addison, she arched her back to give him a more direct view. She was never one to shy away from attention, especially from gorgeous men.

Another Blessed man said, "Face? I thought that was his blemish-riddled derriere she was slapping," and again the group laughed. Right then, Addison woke up – just in time to feel Otka's slap and hear the Blessed man's wisecrack.

"W-W-Was I passed out long?" he asked Otka as he got to his feet and the group of Blessed men dispersed.

"Oh no, sweetie, your respite was short; however, the time I have available for you is even shorter, so it is imperative that you listen to these critical mission details with the utmost vigilance," she said as she pulled a chrome commerce card from her gold-flecked turquoise convenience case. Addison noticed that the case matched her eyes.

He was surprised she had a commerce card. He hadn't seen one since the Bureau of Economics (in response to the increasing number of cases of identity theft) mandated about six years ago that each citizen of Alpdon have a commerce chip (or "fiscal flake") surgically implanted in their right forearm. Otka handed him the card. "Do you remember how to operate one of these?" she asked him in an authoritative tone that gave Addison the sense that if he just did as she said, everything would turn out all right.

"S-S-Sure... you present this for scanning instead of your wrist," Addison answered. He took the card from Otka with his right hand, grasping it gingerly between his thumb and forefinger and keeping it away from his body – like a young girl holding a bullfrog.

"Exactly!" Otka said, excited that he had answered correctly. "Just hold the card normally, sweetie. It's not going to nibble on your nipples," she said, smiling warmly.

"R-R-Right... sorry," Addison said, apologizing out of reflex rather than remorse. He switched the card to his left hand and tried to appear more nonchalant by waving it from side to side. The card slipped out of his hand and landed in a slight depression filled with water – the only puddle in a fifty-meter radius. Otka's smile flattened. She shouted at him in an infuriated voice, "Puny penis! Gorgeous god, will you *please* be careful?!" Addison quickly, nervously, retrieved the card and wiped it on his pant leg. "No, you buff..." It sounded to Addison as if she were about to say "buffoon," but caught herself. She took a deep breath and resumed speaking in a calmer voice, "No, you sweet-hearted geology buff. Do not rub the card against your trousers. The static electricity generated by the friction might render the critical information embedded in the card unreadable. Hold it up and let the breeze dry it." She smiled at Addison. He knew it was forced, but it looked sincere and he appreciated the effort she making to disguise her frustration.

"I want you to make haste to this address. Go directly there. Please don't dawdle, don't saunter, and don't mosey off on a scenic stroll. Stay focused. Get there as soon as you can and wait for me. I will visit you when I am able." She handed him a small slip of writing foil. Addison took it and squeezed it tight – so tight that the tips of his thumb and forefinger turned white. He stood there looking uncomfortable, pinching a commerce card in his left hand and a slip of writing foil in his right. "Read me the address," she commanded in a starched voice.

"S-S-S-Sure. 476 Landesberg Lane, Unit 7." (476… the year the Roman Empire was traditionally considered to have collapsed.)

"Are you familiar with this location?" she asked. Addison, momentarily absorbed in his historical musings, didn't immediately answer. "Addison? Are you familiar with this location?"

"S-S-orry. Y-Yes… It is northwest of here. That way," he said, pointing in the correct direction. He knew where it was; he had supervised some campers working on a land beautification project on that street about twelve fortnights ago.

"Correct," Otka said and her face softened. "Make haste, sweetie, and smile for our sexy savior's sake. I am going to be your Jesus."

"M-M-My Jesus?"

"Yes. If you put your trust in me, I will be your personal savior. I will lead you away from incarceration and deliver you from Brock's evil," she said. She spun on her right high heel and disappeared into the thinning crowd of svelte citizens. Addison stuck the slip of writing foil in his front tunic pocket and looked at the commerce card. Alopecia! Gorgeous god's groin! The chronic perspiration from his hand had dampened the card again! It had now gotten wet twice in the past five minutes. Would it even work when he tried to use it? He worried as he walked toward the Blessed entrance to Grand Square.

Addison passed through the lavish gate at the entrance – a striking white marble structure with six Dorian columns and topped with the likeness of the Roman quadriga. When he entered the Blessed Sanctuary – the area of Wakork set aside for the Blessed housing units – he noticed an immediate difference. The air smelled sweeter. (Nigel had told him that covalent ionic 4c-3E air purifiers were installed in every street light.) The ground was springier. (Nigel had told him the concrete was mixed with polyurethane not only to make walking more pleasurable, but also to give the ambulating Blesseds an effective lower-leg workout.)

Just inside the gate was a small patch of land cordoned off by a knee-high, slatted chrome fence. It was an area reserved for the beggars – the crusty gunk stuck in the corner of Wakork's societal eye. These pitiable people stood in what was called the "beggars' field" during the morning rush to work and the evening commute home, pleading for even a flash of attention from the good-lookers who passed by. Addison saw one woman whinny with delight when a passing Blessed man gave her a wave and a wink. Surprisingly, most of the beggars were quite attractive and wore exceptionally revealing out-fits. Consequently, most got the attention they so desperately craved. But it seemed that no matter how much attention they received, they always needed more. Even though Addison hadn't been in the Blessed Sanctuary in twelve fortnights, he recognized most of the beggars.

Addison walked a little further and found Landesberg Lane. Soon he was standing in front of number 476. The grounds for this property were spectacular.

A plush lawn the color of green tourmaline surrounded a semicircle of four waist-high holographic waterfalls that fed into a small holographic pond overflowing with different sized obsidian plates. A series of spotlights illuminated the waterfalls and the pond. The prismatic beams of light reflecting off the obsidian mesmerized Addison. He stood motionless star-ing at this impressive display. Obsidian was such a beautiful stone. It was his favorite of the three he had carried for so long in his pocket. Unfortunately, that was the one he had randomly plucked out of his pocket and given to Otka as a gift. Would it be rude to ask for it back? Given the ambivalence with which she accepted it, did she even still have it? He was shaken from his thoughts by an approaching SA. "What is an ugly man like you doing in a beautiful sector like this?" the SA asked, his voice dripping with accusation. "You traipsing about this compound is akin to… uhhh… analogous to… uhhh… Oh for comely christ's sake! You just look out of place. Now present for inspection your authorization emblem," he said sternly.

"W-W-W-Well, I know I am not supposed to be in this part of town… this sector," Addison lied, "b-b-b-but I am lost. I must have gotten turned around as I left tonight's lynching. And what a fine lynching it was! Did you happen to witness it?" The SA looked at him with obvious annoyance and didn't respond. "Well, I'm sure you did. Who would miss such a show? Anyway, I was so exhilarated by the brutality of this evening's display – a righteous brutality given their heinous crimes I should add – that as I walked home reflecting upon it, I became so absorbed in thought that I unwittingly headed in the wrong direction and wound up lost… Well, not exactly lost. I know I am in the Blessed compound, but I have no idea how I got here." Addison's neck and face burned; his ears burned so fiercely that he wondered momentarily if he had been stung by a passing swarm of bees. Bilateral cleft palate, he was a horrible liar! If the SA saw him flush, he would know for sure he was lying! Addison held his breath as the SA appeared to ponder the veracity of his explanation.

The SA pointed a thick finger at Addison, "I want you to listen to me with extreme concentration. I, too, was exhilarated by the lynching and I am feeling uncharacteristically magnanimous. I am going to treat you with unmerited munificence. I will take a rapid tour around the compound. If you are still present when I return, I am going to order a transport to pick you up and return you to your proper sector. Let me emphatically state that before you are returned to the uglier part of town, I will ensure that you never again mistakenly *wander* into this sector by dispensing some unforgettable negative reinforcement – reinforcement that will deliver agony to your bankrupt body. Do I make myself clear?"

"Y-Y-Y-Yes, sir… C-C-Clear as a burlesque dancer's heel," Addison said with a weak smile, hoping his freshly baked analogy would curry the favor of the SA. (SAs were infamous womanizers.) It had no effect; the SA just stared at him dismissively. Addison said quickly, "I-I-I-I'll make speedy steps back to my sector... don't you worry." Droplets of sweat crawled down his forehead, saturating his unkempt eyebrows. Did the SA notice? How could he not?

The SA glared at Addison, then smiled perversely, "I am not the one who should be worrying," the SA said as he rubbed his hand over his holstered baton. (Did all law enforcement agents learn that gesture in basic training?) The leather handle of his baton was well-worn and the shaft was peppered with dents, dimples and divots. He had obviously used it often. The SA spun on his right heel (was that move part of basic training as well?) and started to leave. Addison relaxed – incredibly, the SA believed him! Addison wiped his forehead with his hand and then dried it on his pant leg (careful, once again, to wipe by his knee). He looked down at the wet spot on his trousers. Handsome lord! He was sweating like a dyslexic at a spelling bee! About ten meters or so from the gold-bricked sidewalk, the SA stopped abruptly and turned back toward him. Addison's heart leapt into his throat. The SA had seen through his lie after all!

"Since only a triple-digit Cursed would be stupid enough to be standing here when I return, I am going to give this to you now," the SA said, smirking. He shoved his right hand into the pocket of his tight brown trousers and rummaged around until he apparently found what he was looking for. When he pulled his hand out, it was clenched in a tight fist. "Come here. You are fortunate enough to have encountered me on a day when I am feeling overtly charitable. Hence, I would like to give you something you will find stimulating," he said in a hushed voice. As he held his hand out toward Addison, he glanced from side to side as if he were making sure no one was watching. Addison stepped reluctantly toward the SA. Had his "dancer's heel" comment impressed him? What did the SA have for him? Perhaps it was a holographic projection chip of a dancing naked woman. Nigel told him that many of the law enforcement officials had them – usually a digital representation of their favorite striptease dancer or a current or former coitus companion. Nigel also told him they swapped these chips with each other like *Heroes of Face-ism* collector flakes.

He continued to approach the SA cautiously. "Hastily now, before someone sees me doing this," the SA commanded, shaking his closed fist back and forth as if he were about to throw some dice. When Addison got within arm's length, the SA pulled his hand back and punched Addison in the stomach. Addison dropped to the ground like a silver sack of spuds, gasping for air. The SA laughed and walked away. "How can anyone possibly assert that there are intelligent people peppered amongst the lower castes? That mental midget actually fell for that aged and wrinkled scam."

Addison lay on his side, his arms wrapped around his stomach, trying desperately to breathe. The SA could not have timed his punch any better, or worse, for Addison had just exhaled when the SA delivered his blow. Addison's lungs burned and a razor-sharp sting traveled from his sternum to his throat. Just one breath... he could endure the pain if he could just get a little air in his lungs. He rolled onto his back, pulled his knees to his chest, and discovered he was able to take a shallow breath. He exhaled slowly and tried again. This time a little more air. He exhaled slowly again. Finally, after a few uncomfortable moments, he had recovered enough to breathe normally. Soon he felt well enough to stand up. He got to his feet gingerly, resting his weight on his elbows rather than his bruised hands. He didn't know how long it would take the SA to make a trip around the block, but it was essential he be out of sight when he returned.

Addison pulled the commerce card that Otka had given him out of his tunic pocket, relieved it hadn't fallen out. He transferred the card to his left hand, then dried his sweaty right hand on his pant leg multiple times to ensure it was dry. He couldn't risk getting it wet again. He grabbed it again with his right hand and slowly held it up to the Recognition Unit. He held his breath and waited for the beep, but the RU remained silent. Maybe there was some dust on it. Without looking away from the scanner, he reached down and wiped the card on his pant leg. Hair-sprouting facial mole! He had wiped it in the same spot he had dried his hands! He rubbed the corner of the card. Itty bitty babymaker! It was damp! He found a dry patch on his trousers and wiped the card again. Large facial birth blotch! What had Otka told him earlier? Rubbing the card in that manner might cause static electricity to render the card useless! He was so obtuse! Here was his chance to finally experience some good fortune and he was doing everything he could to sabotage it. He held the card up to the Recognition Unit again, almost certain that it wouldn't work. He was right; nothing happened. The SA would be back at any moment. He had to either get the card to work soon or else find a good hiding place. He frantically waved the card under the Recognition Unit – back and forth, up and down, twisting it from side to side – hoping, wishing, praying that he could find the precise angle and distance that would make the card work, but still no beep. Flatulent father in heaven and stinking son of god! Why wasn't it working?!

Addison pivoted his head around looking for the SA – he was nowhere in sight, but he would be returning at any second. He brought the card up to his face and scanned it for a scratch, a nick, a blemish, anything that might be causing these repeated failures. He saw nothing. The surface was as smooth as a Blessed's forehead. He turned the card over and examined the other side. Printed on the back in large letters that ran the length of the card were the words THIS SIDE UP. Addison smirked. He had been scanning the wrong side of the card; however, he had no time to wallow in this fresh humiliation. With his hand shaking like a dry drunk, he waved the correct side of the card under the Recognition Unit. Rather than the beep he was expecting, the RU played an enchanting melody from a calliope and the portal opened.

Addison lurched through the portal into the living unit foyer. He found unit 7B and waved his card under the RU. It also played a short melody from a calliope – different than the one at the complex entrance, but equally beguiling – and the portal opened. When Addison stepped in, he was enveloped in such a potent scent of whiskey and musk that his eyes burned. This was definitely a scent for a man – a man with heaps of testosterone. Was this Cliffie's place?

The room illuminated automatically, the lights apparently triggered by a motion sensor. The unit was astonishing. The carpet inside was plush; Addison bounced up and down, marveling at how easily he lifted. He smiled with undisguised pleasure – a wide, open-mouthed, amber smile. The carpet looked like grass – in fact, at first Addison thought it was. Only after he pulled out a few strands and chewed on the ends did he realize it was synthetic. The unit was one large room, much larger than Addison's unit, but not as large as he expected. Against the left wall was a ruby-encrusted sleeping platform with a matching cantilevered sitting platform. In the far right corner of the room was a mysterious floor-to-ceiling cabinet of burnished chrome, about four meters across and eight meters high. *Zero Impact Cardio Chamber* was stenciled on the side of the cabinet in large black letters.

Addison walked over to the sleeping platform and pounded the pad with his fist. It sunk in about ten centimeters! Addison chuckled. This was amazing! No wonder Blesseds never had bags under their eyes! You couldn't help but get a great night's sleep on a substance as comfortable as this. Soft spotlights covered the ceiling like stars in the evening sky, giving the room a cozy ambiance. The light was both warm and functional. Addison had no problem seeing the details of the room. He looked at the commerce card; he was able to easily read *THIS SIDE UP*. And the rubies were magnificent! They glistened like oval dollops of dark red lava. He tried to pry a large one off the side of the sleeping platform, but the edges were beveled in such a way that it was impossible for him to wedge his fingernail underneath it. He tried some others, but they were all cut the same.

Placed on the right side of the room, closest to the entrance portal, were two narrow closets – one was a waste elimination chamber; the other, a food preparation nook with three shelves. The lower shelf was stocked with condom-mints (peppermint-flavored condoms that turned safe-sex fellatio into a refreshing treat for the fellator); the middle shelf was stocked with chrome utensils, chrome-plated plates and napkins; and the upper shelf was stocked with glass containers of Classy HastyTasty – a "top-shelf" version of the food staple available only to Blesseds. Addison walked over and grabbed a container

– French Vanilla Infused with the Essence of Caramelized Plantains. He tentatively lowered himself onto the sitting platform. He squealed with delight as he sank deeper and deeper into the cushion, until his thighs were swallowed up and no longer visible. Addison opened the Classy HastyTasty on his first try – this premium product didn't have the top-popping problems that plagued the standard one. He grabbed a chrome spoon from the middle shelf and took a mouthful. Juicy jehovah, it was fantastic! It was the most delicious thing he had ever tasted. And smooth… he let a spoonful luxuriate on his tongue for a moment before swallowing.

Addison ate quickly and had just placed the last spoonful into his mouth when the portal slid open. Otka entered carrying a small silver sack. She flashed Addison her big beautiful smile, "Greetings, sweetie!" Addison gasped. She was wearing his favorite outfit – her white super- micro-mini shorts and her low-cut white scalloped breast cups. (How did those things stay on anyway?) If possible, she looked even tastier than the mouthful of Classy HastyTasty he had just swallowed.

"How would you respond if I told you I was going to transform you into a Blessed?" she asked with a sparkle in her gold-flecked turquoise eyes. Addison laughed apprehensively, unsure how to respond to such a ridiculous question. It was so absurd, such an implausible thing to ask, that it could be nothing other than a joke. Are you ready to be transformed into a Blessed? How outlandish! Asking him if he was ready to grow a long tail covered with pink feathers would have been just slightly more preposterous. How could she transform him into a Blessed? Cosmetic surgery was not an option. It was not only a Prime Crime for someone in his caste to receive it, but it was also a Prime Crime for the surgeon who performed it on him and for any upper caste member who conspired in any way to arrange it for him. So how could she help him? Could she stick him back in his birther's womb and re-create him? Perhaps this was some type of trick question. Was she trying to make him look foolish? Addison would soon learn that Otka was not trying to make him look foolish. In fact, her question was rhetorical – she intended to do precisely what she had just asked. ∎

CHAPTER TWENTY TWO

❖

"**I AM PLEASED TO SEE** that you have made yourself comfortable," Otka said.

"Wh-Wh-Where am I?" Addison asked.

"This is my *father's* alternative living unit," she said. Addison was mildly surprised that she had used that ancient word. In this age, it was a derogatory term that literally described a man who impregnated a woman and then had no involvement in raising his offspring. The word was often figuratively used to describe a man who was carnal, immoral, and caddish. No matter which meaning she intended, it was lewd. "He used it for his frequent sexual dalliances, which of course my birther knew nothing about," Otka said with noticeable irritation. Well, that explains her use of the "f" word and the manly scent of the living unit, Addison thought. It was a living unit designed to put women in the mood for coitus.

"My *father* has just registered at a health resort up north to have his testicles tightened, lightened and lifted. I normally don't approve of elective surgery for genitalia because no matter how careful they are, no matter how fine a neutronic laser they use, procedures around these areas often cauterize the pleasure-rendering nerve endings and make subsequent sexual activities far less enjoyable. However, he showed me his testicles; they were unappealing, bordering on grotesque. They were wrinkled; they hung exceptionally low; and the skin was unnaturally dark, almost purple – just thinking about them causes a bit of bile to creep up my esophagus – so I supported his decision. Anyway, he will be spending the next sixteen fortnights at a recuperation spa – spending the majority of his time sitting on a wedge of ice, I would imagine – so, you will have the unit to yourself."

"My younger sibling will visit every half-fortnight or so. He attends secondary school nearby and often comes here to grab a quick snack or take advantage of the waste elimination chamber. He will be stopping by later so you will have an opportunity to see my younger sibling again. He's attending a seminar on proper skin maintenance tonight. Did you know it's much easier to stop a wrinkle from forming than to eliminate one once it forms? Were you aware of that? They have so many extracurricular activities for the pre-adolescents these days; it's quite wonderful. Why just last fortnight, he went to a workshop titled 'No Nicks, Burns or Rashes – Effective Techniques for Removing Body Hair.' What useful knowledge for him to have as he begins to sprout follicles on his chest, under his arms and about his penis." Besides "penis," Addison hadn't heard a word she'd said after "see my younger sibling *again*." He could not recall meeting her sibling, but it was possible he had. There were always good-lookers – both young looking and even younger looking – milling about her Depot.

"The time has come for me to reveal my master plan to you. Given your propensity for swooning, I am relieved that you are in a seated position – the shock you will experience after I disclose the details of my plan will most certainly cause you to keel over," Otka winked and smiled at Addison. Based on her outrageous proposition, he guessed she might just be right. "Because, sweetie," Otka said, pointing her finger in the air triumphantly, "you are about to be born again!"

"W-W-What do you mean by 'born again'?" he asked apprehensively, still concerned that Otka might be teasing him.

"What I mean, sweetie, is that I am going to re-create you… renovate your entire person… transmute you into a Blessed! A Blessed!" she exclaimed. "And I am ideally suited to accomplish this, sweetie. My caste has access to the tools and methods necessary to improve and maintain appearance. Additionally, I have male admirers in elevated political positions who will give me access to experimental implements, techniques and procedures that are not yet available to my fellow good-lookers. Harmonizing these with the expertise I have gathered and honed over a lifetime of always looking my sexy best *[she raised her hand over her head and struck a glamorous pose]*, I am going to buff-up your body, repair the symmetry of your face, and recondition your mind. You will not only… oh, I almost forgot… and add hair to your fleshed head. How could that have nearly slipped my mind? It's so obvious... but I digress... You will not only look, think and behave like a Blessed; you will actually become one!" Otka finished with a flourish of her still-raised hand, causing her breasts to bounce up and down – nearly popping out of her low-cut scalloped breast cups. Addison gasped, hoping for an instant to get a glimpse of what he imagined were glorious nipples; however, her breasts settled. Disappointed, he resumed breathing normally. Did Otka notice his reaction?

At that moment, the portal slid open and a precociously muscled boy entered the living unit. Addison jumped to his feet and a shiver ran through his body. Christ's crotch, it was Dolaf! Addison pointed at him and stammered "W-W-W-What is he doing here? Is S-S-Starck with him?" While Addison panicked, Otka stood there smiling. Dolaf walked over to her and wrapped his arm around her slender waist. She swept his blonde hair from his forehead and gave him an affectionate lick over his left eyebrow. "Salutations, my sexy sibling. It is my hope that you are feeling as good as you look," she said, giving him the Blessed WASP greeting even though Dolaf was still about six years away from his SIN evaluation. (There was little doubt he would be a strong Blessed.) "Was your seminar edifying?"

"You tell me," he said in his familiar squeaky voice. He tilted his face up toward Otka for her inspection.

"Fetching savior! This is excellent work. Your pores have vanished; your blackheads have been banished; and your oily skin is now pH balanced."

Addison sat back down and made no move toward getting up again. He still had no idea what was going on. Otka, evidently seeing his confused look, smiled broadly and said, "I believe we need to provide you with some additional information."

"I-I-I think so," Addison said. "He was... er... I mean is... Starck's protégé!"

Otka and Dolaf looked at each other and laughed. "Oh, you are wonderfully and adorably naive," Otka said, still chuckling. Addison wasn't sure if that was a compliment or a put-down. She continued, "He was

Starck's protégé, sweetie, because I enlisted this amazing-looking boy to *act* as Starck's protégé. I had a premonition that Starck might try to inflict mortal bodily harm on you so I placed little Dolie in Sycamore. I then asked him to keep his beautiful aquamarine eyes on you and either intervene or contact me in the event that Starck tried to harm you. From what Dolie told me about that incident in the maintenance shed, it's fortuitous for you that I did."

At that moment, Addison saw that Dolaf's right thumb was covered in a protective polyurethane casing and his thumbnail was missing. Addison bolted to his feet. "It-It-It was you? You're the one who smote Starck on the pate in the maintenance shed?" Addison said, surprising himself by saying "smote on the pate." Otka was starting to rub off on him.

Dolaf smiled. "Yes, it was me... and let me tell you, the corroded spade I used to *smite Starck on the pate* was exceptionally heavy." (He overemphasized the phrase that Addison had just used. Was Dolaf mocking him?) "It crushed my thumb as I put it down, which detached the protective calcium sheathing from my cuticle. Although I don't usually assume the posture of a martyr, I must say that I suffered intense discomfort for half a fortnight." Dolaf held his damaged thumb up as if he were hitching a ride. "It was not easy wielding that object. It is fortunate for you that I consistently engage in heavy resistance training." Dolaf brought his thumb down on top of his clenched fingers, rotated his hand skyward and flexed his bicep. An impressive muscle bulged from under his Brock Lad uniform top. Amazing, Addison thought, such a big bicep on such a small boy. Dolaf brought his arm down, walked over to the food preparation nook, grabbed two containers of French Vanilla Infused with the Essence of Caramelized Plantains Classy HastyTasty, and then headed for the portal.

Addison cringed. Why was he taking that flavor?

"Parting salutations, my stunning sibling. I'll be seeing you, *Addisoy*," he said over his shoulder as he exited the living unit.

Addison indeed felt fortunate – even though Dolaf annoyed him by taking two containers of his favorite flavor of Classy HastyTasty and mocked him by calling him *Addisoy* – the muscular boy had saved his life. Despite his gratitude, however, one question peppered his thoughts. Why? Why? Why? Why was Otka doing so much to help him? More importantly, what would she want in return? She obviously wanted something. In this age, acts of pure altruism were considered unenlightened, unfashionable, and even uncouth. Otka possessed none of those qualities. Additionally, whatever she wanted would have to be commensurate with the significant risk she was taking. The more he thought about it, the more he worried. What had he gotten himself into by accepting her help? What was she going to ask him to do? Although nervous about the answer she might give him, he had to ask. "Ot-Ot-Ot-Otka. I-I appreciate what you are doing... and what you are proposing. D-D-D-Do you mind if I ask why? Wh-Wh-Wh-Why are you doing this? Wh-Wh-Why are you helping me?" he asked, blushing from his scalp to his scapulas.

Otka flashed her brilliant smile, but left his question unanswered.

"W-W-W-Well?"

"Wells are used to extract fossil fuel deposits and potable water from subterranean streams, sweetie," she said, winking at him playfully. "Are you asking me why I am assisting you *again*?"

"W-W-What do you mean by 'again'?"

Otka continued to smile. "You have forgotten already the shelter I gave you after you fainted during that boorish Day of Shattering Crystal? It is conceivable – although I never would have done it, of course – that I could have carried you out of the Depot after business hours and placed you on a bench in Grand Square while the crowd was still frothing with patriotic frenzy. Need I remind you of what they inserted in the hideous buttocks of that short Cursed man? I heard he'll never be able to sit again without the assistance of a memory foam cushion ring."

Addison didn't know what to say. He had not forgotten about what she had done that day. How could he? Her question was just ambiguous. "O-O-Of course I didn't forget what you did that day..." his voice trailed off meekly and his blush deepened. All he wanted to do was run from her presence. He was embarrassing himself and he knew it.

"Oh, sweetie," Otka said apologetically. "I didn't intend to make you blush. I was merely having fun with you! I am fond of you; it wasn't my intention to discomfit you. I am happy to address your appropriate inquiry." Did he hear her correctly? Did she just say she was fond of him?

Otka brought her right hand to her mouth and tapped one of her front teeth with her pointer finger. "What would be a comprehensible yet pithy way to respond to your query?" she whispered in an offhanded way that Addison found sexy. (Of course, she could lance a boil and he would be carnally enthralled.)

Otka's face lit up, as if she was just struck with a brilliant idea. "Addison... Do you mind if I occasionally refer to you as 'Addy'? Addison sounds stuffy. I like to create a milieu of mirth and good cheer," Otka said. She winked again at Addison. It struck Addison that she was a flirting expert; she knew precisely how to stir a man's libido. Was she born with the ability to read what men wanted or had she cultivated it by observing the effects her words and actions had on men? Why did he care how she acquired this prowess? Did it matter? He liked it when she flirted with him. Why couldn't he just leave it at that?

Addison regained his focus and gave her a tight-lipped smile. He was pleased that Otka valued him enough to ask before assigning him a nickname. "S-S-Sure," he said. Remy had never once asked if the name "Addster" bothered him. His thoughts flashed back to the sight of Remy lying face down – motionless and probably lifeless – in an expanding pool of blood. Maybe Addison had been a bit too harsh with him. All Remy had been trying to do was fit in and feel accepted. Addison knew better than most the loneliness and shame you felt when you knew you didn't.

"Perhaps it is best just to vault into the meat of my monologue and forgo the verbal foreplay. You don't mind, do you, Addison... I mean, Addy?" she said playfully. "I am helping you, my dear Addy, because you are the absolute antithesis of all that Brock's ideology exalts! You are proof

Addison remembered this exercise from tertiary school. He closed his eyes and saw the correct sequence of numbers. He interrupted Otka, "3.1415926535897," he said softly. Addison smiled proudly, not because he knew the answer, but because he had said it without stammering.

"Well, sweetie, you are proving my assertion, aren't you?" she said, smiling.

Compensating for missing a chance to make him stutter, his subconscious now grasped his words firmly, and when he continued speaking, it was with much difficulty, "Th-Th-Th-That question isn't complex… it is simple memorization. B-B-Besides, th-th-th-that's just one example. B-B-Brock's CIO p-p-presented over one hundred questions and even provided testimonials from the authors of the tests. C-C-Come on, Otka, the evidence is o-o-o-overwhelming." Addison took a deep breath and relaxed his clenched hands, hoping it would be a few minutes before he was forced to talk again.

"Oh, how adorable! You are such an innocent-minded dear. You actually believed that outrageous drivel, didn't you?" Addison was grateful she didn't wait for him to answer. "And while I find it endearing, you are being naive, Addy. You must taste their pabulum and test its palatability before you ingest it. If Brock's propagandists can make an entire nation believe that the value of an individual is based solely on his physical attractiveness, how difficult would it be to raise doubts about a series of tests that citizens took, on average, twenty annums ago?" Otka paused. "The response is that it is as simple as removing these breast cups," and she mimed pulling them off. Addison's heart stopped; for a moment, he thought she was actually going to do it. "They forge questions; intimidate a few people into giving false testimonials… Brock discredited those evaluations, Addy, because they were a discordant note in the meticulously composed harmony of his dogma. Until they were abolished four annums ago, those tests were excellent barometers of cognitive ability. As I just finished telling you, you scored comfortably above average on all of them!" Otka paused again, as if reflecting. "When I first met you, my initial day as proprietor of the Caffeine Depot, I detected a spark of superior intellect in you. Well, *superior* is hyperbolical... I detected a *well-above-average* intellect. My intuition was confirmed when you gave me that lustrous chunk of black rock and then spewed all of that useless information about its origin all over me."

Addison cringed. He knew that giving her that rock was a bad idea the instant he did it, but did he have to hear about it again? His face and neck, which were slowly returning to normal color after Otka embarrassed him earlier, flushed warmly again. Otka kept speaking without changing her tone, either not noticing Addison's fresh flush or not wanting to amplify his obvious embarrassment. "Now I concede that that initial spark was muted – practically to the brink of extinguishment – by your diminished self-esteem, but it was still present. I decided then and there to get a look at your academic fitness tests. A little of this...," Otka turned away from Addison, arched her back, wiggled her derriere and then turned back around, "and I was reclining on my sleeping platform reviewing holographic representations of your evaluations. Getting those tests was as simple as taking glucose-rich confection from a child in the pre-toddling stages of ambulatory development. In fact, if my calculations are accurate, and of course they are," she said, smiling, "you have the intellect of a Favored, and with some liberal rounding of the fractional scores, you are not that far from a 'Bordering Blessed'! And Addy, sweetie, it is obvious that you are not even close to being classified as a 'Flanking Favored,'" Otka paused and frowned. "Sorry, dear. You might have interpreted that as a slur. My intention is not to belittle you; I am simply stating a fact."

Addison gave her a reassuring, close-mouthed smile. He took no offense. How could he? What Otka said was accurate. His SIN was 49 and that was an objective measure of his attractiveness; no amount of sensitivity on Otka's part could change that.

"Brock and his cunning information officers have perverted the Judeo-Christian scriptures to prove that their ideology is infallible. And in their warped ideology, the co-existence of intelligence within someone unattractive is not only illogical to them; they consider it blasphemy against their god. But notice that I said 'their god.' I did that purposefully, because the god they worship is not the one known as Yahweh, El Shaddai, Jehovah… the only true God."

"This true God is the One who was worshipped faithfully by about half the earth's population many ages ago and the One who is still intermittently worshipped today. The god that Brock and his disciples worship is not this God. Rather it is a deification of their own twisted values and only resembles the true God – resembles him enough, however, to dupe those who are so invested in the flesh that it never even crosses their superficial minds to verify the authenticity of the god Brock has concocted. Like the Roaming Catholics of earlier ages, they believe what they are told to believe." Otka paused, glanced upward for a moment as if she were gathering her thoughts, and then returned her eyes to Addison. "I saw you in church recently. If you attended church as a child, you naturally noticed a dramatic change to the liturgy. You saw that sexually charged representation of Jesus that was displayed audaciously over the altar?" Addison nodded. "Does that look to you like the Son of God as described in the Holy Scriptures? The one the prophet Isaiah described as a 'Man of Sorrows'? Does their Jesus look like he was, as Isaiah also described, 'acquainted with grief'? Isaiah wrote that Jesus 'had no form or comeliness that we should look at him, and no beauty that we should desire him.' Jesus wasn't even what the religious leaders of His day desired during those thirty-three annums He walked this planet. If that was the case so long ago, how much more is it true today – especially with our country's dearth of spirituality? Brock's followers think of their savior as a muscle-bound warrior who glides down from heaven on a gleaming chrome cross and pummels the mucous from Satan's proboscis. They don't want to worship a 'Divine Doormat' who purchased our salvation by obediently submitting to those who did the bidding of His enemy. He submitted in order to defeat Satan, while they believe he defeated Satan without ever having to submit. What is so distressing is that this wonderful plan, this divine gift of redemption that God has so mercifully provided for us, can only be understood by those who see beyond the flesh," Otka slapped her hand against her sternum, causing her breasts to jiggle in a way Addison found appealing. Did she do that on purpose or was that inadvertent, Addison mused, smiling inwardly at the irony of having such lustful thoughts while Otka explained the carnality of Face-ism.

"The concept of surrendering every battle to ultimately win the war is counterintuitive to them. Why? Because a spiritually blind person is incapable of seeing beyond today's battle. In her arrogance, she chooses victory today and to hell with tomorrow! Turn the other cheek? Only if it's while you are rotating your torso to deliver a good counterpunch!" Otka screamed, "HI- YAH" and punched at the air with an impressive right hook. Addison nodded his head and took a couple of steps back, afraid that she might accidentally strike him if she decided to throw another punch. Otka smiled and continued in a calmer tone, "What I find deliciously paradoxical is that these self-loving, soul-denying Face-ists have the audacity to use selective verses from the Holy Scriptures to support their ideology. What arrogance! However, these same Holy Scriptures serve to condemn them. When you gorge yourself on God's word, rather than lift a few verses out of context to boost your ideology, you learn that the true God attributes equal value to every human being, no matter their comeliness."

"The Face-ists label you a blood-sucking parasite – one who exists only at the expense of their god's elect. In the true God's eyes, you are as special, as valued and as worthy of life as a single-digit SIN Blessed! So I must protect and preserve you, Addy, because you are proof that Brock's ideology is built on a foundation of loose silt. Every time I look at you, Addy, my faith in the one true God is bolstered. Being in your presence edifies me!" Otka paused. Her face softened, she sighed and smiled at Addison. He knew that was all the explanation he was going to get for now.

"Now, sweetie, I am going to share with you my plans for making you a Blessed," Otka said. "I must confess, I am quite excited about this transformational journey we are about to embark on!" And Addison could tell that she was; her nipples hardened and appeared as if they might burst through the thin fabric of her breast cups. Otka reached into the small silver sack she was carrying and pulled out an instruction pod and an amber bottle with the image of a strapping horse on the label. Her nipples flattened when she resumed talking, "First, we need to pack your physique with lean muscle tissue. You are to begin ingesting these immediately," she said, holding up the amber bottle. "These capsules are hard to acquire as they are only made available to single-digit SIN-ners. They are potent – tremendously potent – but also tremendously effectual. They will manufacture high quality lean muscle tissue in a rapid time frame, but you must take these supplements precisely as explained on this instruction pod. This is critical. These are equine sterols and are formulated to build muscle on a beast that weighs about 750 kilos. If you experiment or deviate from the prescribed dosage, you will perish." Addison gasped.

"P-P-Perish? D-D-Die?!"

"Addy, you will not be in peril if you simply follow the instructions. Please don't fret. You are a smart boy – have you already forgotten what I shared with you moments ago?" Otka crinkled her nose playfully. "In conjunction with these sterols, you must also do the exercises that are demonstrated on this pod. You will need Dynamic Tension Bands for these exercises. My POP has a set in the cabinet under the sitting platform. These training techniques can only be accessed by single-digit SIN-ners. They are designed to amass the most muscle in the shortest amount of time. Do not misconstrue the meaning of my message. You will have to put forth a substantial effort on a regular basis, but your work will bear fruit sooner on this program. Oh... I want to also point out to you that there is an excellent chance you will develop prodigious acne on your back and buttocks and a better-than-average chance you will experience slight breast swelling. If either or both of these happen, don't be concerned. These side effects are not uncommon. They are minor inconveniences and are about as dangerous as an ingrown toenail, a blister or a benign colon polyp. You are going to have a phenomenal physique! Having to endure some breast swelling and an acute case of acne will be worth it given the eventual result, don't you agree?"

"D-D-Do I agree? Are you kidding me? I-It is most definitely worth it," Addison said sincerely. "I-I would give up a kidney and a lung to get a great-looking body!"

"Well, it is highly unlikely that these sterols will have a deleterious effect on the organs you mentioned," Otka said, "but you never can predict an individual's reaction to such a potent muscle-building cocktail. I did once hear about a man whose liver grew to three times its normal size from taking this exact combination of synthetic hormones..." her voice trailed off. She smiled, "why are we dwelling on the potential negatives? Soon you are going to have a body that will elicit desire from every Blessed woman and envy from every Blessed man!"

"I must abscond now, sweetie. I need to inform you that Brock's SAs have started erecting the barricade around the Burdened living complex and all Burdeneds have been warned not to leave their sector. Consequently, you cannot leave this unit for any reason. Is that clear?"

Addison contemplated answering Otka's question with his dancer's heel analogy, but he was uncertain how Otka would react. He decided it was prudent to simply nod his head to show he understood.

"I am afraid that I am not going to be able to visit you frequently," Otka said. "If I alter my daily travel patterns dramatically, it might raise suspicions. I hope you can entertain yourself. My POP subscribes to all the major media sources, so you should have no trouble passing the time. Besides, the prescribed workout regimen will absorb a major portion of your day. Once I add the mental agility exercises to your daily routine – in approximately three to five fortnights from now – you will have about as much free time as a paid coitus practitioner has when the floating fortresses are docked." Addison loved the way she talked; it was so stout... and so descriptive! Otka took two steps toward Addison. "When your transformation is complete, you are going to be indebted to me. I have already decided what I am going to request from you as compensation," she smiled furtively, leaned over and gave him an affectionate lick on his left cheek. "Remember, ingest those sterols *precisely* as detailed. Follow the training regimen *precisely* as prescribed. I will check on you when I am able." Otka turned around and left the unit – she left Addison swooning on the remnants of her espresso and jasmine scent and pondering a lingering question... why was she *really* helping him? Was it because he personified a religious icon to her? Or was she employing that logic to cover more malevolent motives? Would she commit multiple Prime Crimes just so she could bolster her faith? She was overwhelmingly attractive and obviously intelligent; Addison found it odd she was so concerned with ecclesiastical matters. She already had it all. What else could god give her? And what about her mysterious comment, "You are going to be indebted to me."? What was he going to have to do to repay her?

Maybe she wants me to perform some ghastly deed for her, Addison thought. Robbery, kidnapping, murder... maybe all three! Whatever she wanted from him, he would probably do – even if it were illegal and immoral. If she helped him build a great body, he would never be able repay her – it was that important to him. Besides, all Otka had to do was smile at him and he would be too intimidated by her beauty to turn her down.

He popped the digital pod Otka had given him into the presentation panel, sat on the edge of the sleeping platform and initiated playback. He reached down, lifted his tunic, grabbed a chunk of fat around his midsection and gave it a shake. His lips curled into a wicked smile. Suddenly, the little bit of remaining doubt in his mind vanished. If she helped him transform his repulsive body into a sexy and muscular one, he would be so grateful that he would be willing to do anything she asked. ∎

CHAPTER TWENTY THREE

AFTER SIX FORTNIGHTS ON OTKA'S PLAN, Addison physique had substantially improved. His body wouldn't make a Blessed woman stop in her tracks, but it would no longer send her running in the opposite direction. Addison achieved these results by adhering religiously to a daily exercise routine that he was both surprised and proud he had the discipline to stick with.

He set his awakening apparatus for 06:02 each morning. He had no reason for choosing that particular time. Could it be because it added up to eight, his lucky number? He no longer pondered such minutiae; he had more important things to think about. For instance, he was currently trying to figure out how to increase the peak of his left bicep so it matched the more prominent peak of his right one.

The sound the awakening apparatus emitted was unique – the intensifying moans of a woman becoming sexually aroused and then *apparently* climaxing. Addison wasn't sure if it was an actual orgasm. In tertiary school, his early blooming cousin had told him that women occasionally faked them. Addison could not understand why, but to ask would have invited ridicule. All these years later it still baffled him.

Otka explained to Addison through clenched teeth that the awakening apparatus was a gift from one of her *father's* coitus partners – a recording she'd secretly made during one of their more passionate encounters and then presented to him to celebrate their first (and only) fortnight of monogamy. "His coital encounters with that hussy were short-lived. Why he keeps it is completely illogical."

Addison liked the device. The woman's yelps of pleasure not only caused him to arise each morning with a big smile (and an aroused babymaker), it also motivated him for the first part of his daily regimen – thirty minutes in the *Zero Impact Cardio Chamber*.

This unique apparatus was outfitted with a floor-to-ceiling image panel that played a series of moving image montages once the portal was shut. The montages were designed to increase the heart rate of the person in the chamber, delivering a quick cardio workout. They included an oncoming speeding transport; large rats racing towards the viewer's face in a foaming-mouthed frenzy (the rats' attack point was about 10 centimeters over Addison's head; Otka's POP was apparently taller than he was); and a scene that made Addison's heart race – an effeminate male doctor with a pale pitted face approaching the viewer with a raised pointer finger slathered with lubricant and saying salaciously, "Lower your trousers, dahhling. Bend over and show me your beeeauuuuutiful bum."

After his cardio session, he consumed three espresso tablets. Otka's POP had a premium tablet press in the food preparation nook. ("My birther, Dolie and I never had the luxury of our own tablet press," Otka complained to him.) He kept an ample supply of the finest dark-roasted espresso beans imported from Eurafrica. After his espresso tablets, he took his first dose of supplements and began his resistance training. Using the Dynamic Tension Bands, he exercised his pectoral, latissimus dorsi, deltoid, trapezius, bicep and tricep muscles on even-numbered days and his quadricep, hamstring and calf muscles on odd-numbered days. He worked his abdominal muscles every day. After completing each workout, when his muscles were so pumped with blood that he was afraid (thrilled!) his skin might burst like an over boiled hot dog, Addison undressed, stood in front of the mirror and admired his body until his pump drained. After his mid-afternoon meal of French Vanilla Infused with the Essence of Caramelized Plantains Classy HastyTasty (even after six fortnights, it was still the most delicious food he had ever tasted), he took more supplements, relaxed by browsing the numerous media feeds for two hours, and stretched for an hour. He took his final (and largest) dose of supplements right before he mounted the sleeping platform for his evening's repose.

As Otka had forewarned, Addison's breasts had swelled slightly and his back was spotted with clusters of ripened pimples. He also had a nagging dry cough and he'd found a small lump on the side of his neck that burned painfully whenever he pressed on it; however, these side effects didn't bother him. After all, didn't the personal trainer on his instructional pod say over and over again that "with the absence of a burn there is no visible return"?

His personal trainer also talked about the importance of getting enough rest to facilitate muscle recuperation, so Addison mounted his sleeping platform early. Without fail, Addison slept well ever night. He guessed that his evening supplements included sleep enhancers – never before in his life had he slept through the entire night so consistently. He thought about asking Otka about this but decided against it, afraid that if she told him there were no sleep enhancers in his evening supplements, his chronic sleep problems would return.

It was after one such night of continuous sleep, when Addison awoke to the yelps of a (evidently) climaxing woman, that he saw Otka sitting next to the sleeping platform, wearing a large white smile and his favorite outfit – super-micro-mini shorts as brilliant as her teeth and a pair of low-cut, white scalloped breast cups. (Was that the edge of her areola or was it a shadow?) Gorgeous and great-bodied god! She looked fantastic (which amplified his already engorged babymaker)!

"Sweet morning, Addy. I hope you rested wonderfully."

"I-I did," he said groggily.

"Could you please dismount the sleeping platform for me?" she asked.

"B-But I am only wearing a sparse undergarment," Addison demurred. "A-A-And I..." he was about to mention the current state of his babymaker, but was too embarrassed. He tried to quickly subdue it, but focusing on it only ensured it would remain.

Otka looked at him expectantly, apparently waiting for him to continue. After a few seconds, she continued, "That is precisely why I want you to dismount the sleeping platform. I want to conduct a visual evaluation of your progress to date."

Addison dismounted the platform reluctantly, trying to keep his back toward Otka. Please go down, he begged his babymaker, but it just pulsed defiantly. Then he remembered the eczema sores on his lower legs. Alopecia and plaque psoriasis! Could Otka see them? Although they had faded a bit, they were still easily visible. Why couldn't she have just announced herself before entering? He would have been spared all of this humiliation.

Otka grabbed Addison firmly by the shoulders and turned him around. She smiled. "Well, I didn't realize the supplements and workouts would build *that* muscle," she said, staring brazenly at the bulge in his shorts. "In fact, it is not uncommon for the sterols to have a deleterious effect on a man's ability to obtain and sustain a state of arousal. I can't tell you how pleased I am to see that that hasn't occurred to you," she said coyly. She placed her hands on Addison's chest and gently pushed him backward until he was standing about three meters from her. "Very nice... oh yes... very nice, indeed. You are progressing ahead of schedule. Please turn around." Addison obeyed again. "Yes... yes... yes... your hamstrings are well sculpted and your trapezius muscles have more definition and mass than I would have expected at this stage. We still need to do some work on your calf muscles; they are lagging a bit behind. But overall, you are doing a magnificent job!" Without warning, Otka yanked his sleeping shorts down around his ankles. Addison gasped. "This is excellent... excellent! The cellulite at the base of your buttocks has vanished. Fantastic! This is not the same body that moped into my Caffeine Depot half an annum ago!" Elated by her effusive compliments and relieved she hadn't noticed (or at least mentioned) his eczema, Addison's face broke out into an involuntary open-mouthed smile. Quickly, however, he covered his teeth with his lips – even though his back was to Otka, he needed to be careful – the living unit was adorned with quite a few mirrors.

"You can get dressed now, sweetie, but I wouldn't complain if you took your time doing it," she said flirtatiously. Addison pulled up his shorts and with his back still toward Otka, jumped quickly back onto the sleeping platform and yanked the white gypsum-coated sheet over his crotch. Otka chuckled, "Your modesty is charming." Her expression quickly changed, as if she had flipped a toggle. She now looked determined and assured, "Now we must move on to some additional business. It is time to add mental agility workouts to your daily regimen. Your body is progressively approaching that of a Blessed. We now need to bolster your mental agility so you can consistently cogitate like one."

"This addition to your routine has two objectives – to rehabilitate your poor self-esteem, while at the same time building your mental acuity and nimbleness. As I have previously articulated, in order to become a Blessed, you will need to do more than just look like one. You have to swagger and ruminate like one... oh yes and copulate like one. But let us first transform you so Blessed women *want* to engage in carnal relations with you before we focus on your coital performance," Otka's face softened for a moment. She flipped the toggle again and her determined expression returned. It struck Addison that she looked gorgeous both ways. "I assumed correctly that transforming your body would be relatively unproblematic – I knew seeing the improvements to your physique on a daily basis would keep you motivated and help you adhere to the program. After all, success begets success. However, there will be no visual feedback from the rehabilitation work we perform on your self-confidence or from the training to sharpen your ability to think with agility. Hence, I have engineered a two-pronged solution to ensure your motivation remains ferocious because it critically important that you develop these two characteristics. Remember, we are transforming you into a Blessed, not simply trying to disguise you as one."

"First, I am going to utilize your vastly improved body to regenerate your self-esteem. This is obviously occurring already, but I am going to amplify its effect. Today, I am augmenting your daily supplementation diet with three amino acids." She gave the small silver bag she was holding to Addison. "Exact instructions for ingestion are included on a piece of writing foil inside the pouch. These amino acids will increase the nitric oxide levels in your blood and will increase the volume of your muscle pumps by 18.343 – that is an approximation – and extend their duration by a factor of 2.124 – again an approximation. It will also improve your vascularity, but it is difficult to quantify the magnitude of the benefit, so I won't even proffer an estimate."

Otka paused and smiled. Her face opened up in a playful, childlike way. Addison expected her to resume talking, but she just kept smiling, once even stifling a laugh. It looked to Addison as if she were about to say something outrageous. She was.

"Seeing the immediate and significant increase in the size of your muscles will expedite the rejuvenation of your self-esteem; however, I am afraid it won't motivate you to consistently do your cognitive exercises. To that end..." Otka paused and starting giggling like a school girl itching to share a secret. "I have an out-of-the-ordinary proposition. If thirty days from today you are able to pass a mental agility test that I will co-author with the Pastor from the Bureau of Cognition... another admirer of mine," she smiled wistfully, as if she had grown tired of being desired by so many men, "I will personally reward your performance with compensation that will be sexual in nature," Otka barely finished speaking when she started giggling again. Addison furrowed his brow and turned his back on her, supposing she was mocking him. "What is the problem, sweetie?" she said in a concerned tone.

"I-I-I don't appreciate being teased. Th-Th-That is an insensitive joke," Addison said in a wounded voice.

Otka approached Addison, grabbed his arm, gently turned him around and lowered her head so she was looking into his eyes. "Sweetie," she said sincerely, "I am not tugging on your limb; my proposition is legitimate."

"Th-Th-Then why are you laughing at me?" Addison asked.

"I am not laughing at you, Addy. I am chuckling involuntarily to mask the embarrassment I am experiencing from my rather brazen proposition."

Addison paused. It never even entered his mind that her proposal might be a serious one or that someone as beautiful as Otka would ever feel discomfited. "W-W-What is Cliffie going to say? More importantly, what is Cliffie going to do to me if he finds out?"

Otka sighed. "Don't worry about Cliffie's reaction. I recently discovered that Cliffie has been engaging in copious clandestine acts of copulation with other women since the day after our first carnal encounter. Once again, I have selected a prevaricating immoral cad as my coitus partner. Inverted third nipple! Congenital hairy facial nevus! When will I learn?! Will I ever learn?!" Otka flicked her head back disdainfully. "And as to the sincerity of my offer... How is this for attestation?" Otka yanked down her breast cups, quickly, angrily. Addison involuntarily squeaked. "Do you believe me now or would you like me to further prove the validity of my offer by removing my super-micro-mini shorts as well?"

"I-I-I believe you," he said, although for a moment he was tempted to say he needed more proof. He had only seen one naked woman before – the full-lipped and sexually open Dana from his tertiary school days. He still remembered Dana's body even though their (very brief) rendezvous took place more than fifteen years ago – puffy nipples crowning large firm breasts and a neatly trimmed triangular patch of tightly curled coal-black hair a few centimeters below her "innie" belly button. Addison recalled being shocked by that curly black patch since Dana's hair was blonde (naturally?). In fact, he only now realized that although Otka's hair was styled in a trendy manner – a shoulder length bob on the right side, short and layered above the ear on the left – it was about the same shade of blonde as Dana's. Would Otka's most intimate area look like Dana's? Would her hair down there be blonde or black, or (gasp!) would she be bare? If he passed her examination thirty days from now, he would no longer need to speculate.

"Well, sweetie, I need to be going." She readjusted her breast cups in an unrushed, nonchalant manner, as if she were putting on a pair of wooly mammoth fur-lined mittens. With her modesty restored, she placed another and much larger silver pouch on the sleeping platform. "In this pouch you will find everything you need to conduct your mental agility exercises. It is a simple exercise, but the Pastor at the Bureau of Cognition, after deluging me with overused and ineffective invitations to engage in consensual coitus, tells me this will dramatically increase your mental agility in a compressed timeframe. Toil vigorously and remain focused. Thirty days from now, if you score at the eightieth percentile or higher..." she stopped talking and flashed her remarkable smile. She burst out laughing and as she turned to leave, Addison noticed she was blushing. He had never seen her blush before and he found her vulnerability charming. With a desirous sigh, he grabbed the Dynamic Tension Straps and started his morning workout.

Addison released the Dynamic Tension Straps and rested his hands on his knees. Beads of sweat fell from his brow to the carpet and disappeared in the thick pile. Addison rubbed his bare left foot over the area where most of the sweat had vanished – he laughed – the carpet was dry. What an amazing substance!

Addison walked over to the full-length mirror, brought his arms up to his shoulders and flexed his biceps. He laughed again – were these actually his arms? He turned his back to the mirror, assumed the same pose and flexed again. They looked great even from the back. Just then the entrance portal slid open. Addison quickly brought his arms back down to his sides but made no move to grab his tunic; he wanted Otka to see him with it off. But it wasn't Otka, it was Dolaf.

"Well, well, well," Dolaf said with an assuredness incongruent with his youthfulness. "Don't you look smashing? My sexy sister is quite the magician! She has transformed you from a flaccid geek into someone tight, toned and sleek." Addison reached over and quickly put his tunic on…backwards. ,Oops, the body looks good but I see your intellect still requires significant work," Dolaf said smugly.

Addison narrowed his eyes angrily. He quickly removed his tunic and put it on correctly. The substantial capital Dolaf accrued from saving his life was depreciating rapidly and if this arrogant pre-adolescent continued to insult him, Addison wouldn't be able to hold his tongue much longer.

Dolaf had only visited on two other occasions to use the waste elimination chamber. However each time he left he grabbed a few containers of French Vanilla Infused with the Essence of Caramelized Plantains

Classy HastyTasty which only added to Addison's mounting annoyance. There were four other flavors yet he always took Addison's favorite. Did this pompous boy know that was his favorite flavor? Addison was fairly certain he did.

"You are missed, Addison," Dolaf said furtively.

"M-M-Me? M-M-Missed? B-B-By whom?" Addison asked, hoping that it was Otka who was missing him." He was disappointed by Dolaf's answer.

"Well not by my extraordinarily gorgeous sister, if that is what you were hoping for. I can see by your obvious dejection that it was. No, it's Brock's Security Agents. Apparently your disappearance from the Burdened ghetto has not gone unnoticed and they are eager to find you and return you to your 'proper' living quarters," Dolaf made quotation marks in the air, again Addison was reminded of Nigel.

"The SA are conducting thrice-daily inventories of all confined citizens and you have been officially classified as VILE."

"Wh-Wh-What! What does that mean?" Addison said.

"It is a loose acronym for Violation of Incarceration Laws without proper Endorsements."

"B-B-But do they have to use 'VILE'? It isn't even the actual acronym. Why don't they call it 'VILWOPE'? VILE is so mean-spirited."

"VILWOPE, or to be precise, VILWPE – 'without' is one word, not two, and as such the 'O' wouldn't be included in the acronym. What was I just saying about requiring significant additional work on your intellect?" Dolaf smiled mischievously. "Anyway, VILWPE is devoid of dash. VILE, on the other hand, is not a precise acronym, but it is clever, it's catchy and it's correct. After all, lower caste citizens comprise 97.342 percent of the incarcerated population and they are all indeed *vile* looking. Having answered your inane question, will you please allow me to return to my original point? Being classified as VILE means is that if they happen to locate and arrest you…" Dolaf ran his finger across his neck, copying Starck's mime after Addison (with a hand from Otka) rescued the dog from the crystal pit. Dolaf continued, "About an hour ago they were circulating a digital image of you around the Caffeine Depot, not looking your best I might add, and asking if they had seen you. They are apparently determined to find you so it is critical we take action swiftly. That is why Otka sent me here immediately."

Addison anxiously ran his hands through his thinning hair. He knew all this was too good to be true. Maybe not today and probably not tomorrow but one day soon the SA would burst through the entrance portal and return him to the Burdened compound. And somehow he knew it would be at night. These types of things always happened at night.

How foolish they had been to believe they could dupe Brock's regime. "Wh-Wh-When do you think they will find me?" Addison asked, knowing he was asking Dolaf a question he couldn't answer.

"If I am able to breach the National Database and alter your Master Record, the authorities will never look for you again; you will cease to exist as a Burdened," Dolaf said. He reached into his tunic pocket and pulled out an oblong chrome two-piece device that reminded Addison of an ancient ink scribing implement. Dolaf walked over to the media server and began rapidly twisting the top portion of the device back and forth.

"Wh-Wh-What's that?" Addison asked.

"It is a signal encryption decoder," Dolaf answered offhandedly as he continued to work the device. "With this appliance I can hack into the National Database of Records and with some minor edits I can alter your classification from a Burdened to a Blessed. The National Database however is protected with a quadruple encoded proton shielded nano-nuclear barrier and it is problematical to access. Just give me a moment here... What I am attempting to do is locate a digital needle in a humongous virtual pile of desiccated grass. By twisting the halves of this device in a random manner I am attempting to mimic the database's updating protocol, which cycles through several hundred or so every half second. If I am lucky enough to time it just right, and it will require significant good fortune, I will imitate the protocol as it receives an authorization signature from the digital barrier which will allow me to enter the database and access the master version of your record."

Addison had no idea what Dolaf was talking about but he took some comfort in the fact that Dolaf appeared to know what he was doing.

"Once I access the master record I can modify it; it will be as simple as swallowing a spoonful of French Vanilla Infused with the Essence of Caramelized Plantains Classy HastyTasty," Dolaf said with a wink. Flatulent father in heaven! He did know that was Addison's favorite flavor and he was taking it just to tweak him! But what could Addison say? This diminutive scamp was once again putting himself at risk to help him.

Dolaf continued to rotate his wrists back and forth with incredible speed and with such exertion that his porcelain face soon flushed the color of rosy quartz.

Addison noticed that the veins in Dolaf's forearms looked as if they were going to pop through his skin. What incredible vascularity for someone so young! After ten or so tense minutes of hard work Dolaf hollered a triumphant "Yes!" and a few lines of three-dimensional text slowly rose from the floor, stopping at about the height of Addison's waist. In shimmering yellow letters was the following:

HALL, ADDISOY
SIN=49
Commerce Chip Record Locater = 8675309
Wakork Burdened Complex Unit 10 G

Addison was surprised at the brevity of the record. "Th-Th-That's it? That is all the information they capture and archive for each citizen?"

Dolaf laughed, "Gorgeous god, no! They keep detailed data of every move you make; every move you have ever made. Each time you scan your wrist, they capture all the details related to the occurrence – the location, the time to the gigasecond, whether you are at an RU or conducting commerce. But that's not all. They also have the supporting documentation from your SIN evaluation, your medical records; your dental profile showing the location of all your cavities, the depth of the decay and the material it was filled with; all of your employment evaluations, the chemical composition of your last twenty urine and fecal samples; a list of all your coitus companions, a short record for you I'm sure, *if* one even exists; twelve generations of your familial psychological history; even your favorite foods (he winked again). The amount of data they have on you, if printed onto uncoated paper .005 millimeters thick, 10 centimeters long and eight centimeters wide, would create a tome 7 meters high. I am only accessing the summary record because it is all I require, and because uploading your entire record would take approximately three hours. Watch this," Dolaf said. He pulled on the top half of the chrome decoder, separated it into two pieces. He rapped the smaller piece hard against the frame of the sleeping platform bringing forth from the tip a thin stream of brilliant white light, six centimeters or so long. "It's an editing implement" he said in his familiar squeak.

Dolaf touched the tip of the implement to the number "4" in SIN-49 and then he carefully erased the triangular-shaped beak of the numeral until it looked like a "1." "There, you are now officially a Blessed," Dolaf said, obviously proud of what he had done. "This next part will require a tad more dexterity." Dolaf now touched the tip of the implement to Addison's address, *Wakork Burdened Complex Unit 10 G.* He twisted the bottom of the implement and expanded the width of the stream until it matched the height of the letters and then with a steady hand he erased the entire address line. Addison gasped. Dolaf smiled broadly, "Are you impressed?"

"I-I-Impressed? I'm not impressed; I'm worried. My record is incomplete! You just made things worse! A partial record will surely garner additional attention and that's the last thing I need. What are you going to do to replace my address, genius?"

"P-P-P-Please *Addisoy*, the moniker 'genius' is so overused that its meaning has been diluted, wouldn't you agree? If you feel strongly about it you can call me genius but I prefer that you address me by my given name. Besides, given my good looks everyone knows that I'm a *genius* anyway," Dolaf said. Addison clenched his jaw – now this arrogant imp was mocking his stammer? He had crossed the threshold of good natured teasing – that was outright malicious. Addison fantasized about taking Dolaf's implement and jamming it into the disrespectful boy's ear…but not until he was finished changing his record. "You must learn to be patient. I have not yet finished the task," Dolaf said and he twisted the bottom of the implement again, reducing the width of the beam until it returned to its original thickness. Then he meticulously wrote, 476 Landesberg Lane Unit 7.

When he was done he again smiled broadly. "What do you think? I would say that's the handiwork of a *genius*."

Addison was horrified. "Y-Y-Your not serious are you? I-I-I-It looks handwritten!"

"Why are ye fearful, O ye of little faith?" Dolaf said and he twisted the bottom of the implement again until it matched the height of the handwritten letters. He touched the beam of light to the handwritten text and steadily moved the beam of light from left to right. Addison watched, mesmerized. As the beam over each letter it instantly reformatted so that it looked exactly like all the other text in the record. When Dolaf was finished with the line the record looked uniform, as if it had never been tampered with. Addison bent down and inspected the record.

"R-R-Remarkable," Addison said, with reluctant admiration. "C-Can you fix the 'Addisoy'?" he asked.

"Why would you want to change 'Addisoy'? It is such a unique name and it suits you so well," Dolaf said, with an aggressive edge to his voice. Addison hands balled into fists. Favor or no favor, he wouldn't let him get away with this for much longer. "Actually, correcting Addisoy would be imprudent," Dolaf said in a softer tone, as if he were aware he was pushing Addison a bit too hard. "Every seven seconds, the central server matches all Commerce IDs to all registered names to ensure that an ID has not been duplicated. It is a fraud prevention mechanism. Altering it would allocate two names to your Commerce Chip ID and it would automatically be quarantined by the central server. The next time your chip was scanned every law enforcer in a five-kilometer radius would swarm to you faster than a lower caste male to a coitus-performing female humanoid." Dolaf put the chrome implement back together and gave it a protracted twist. The record retreated into the floor with a pronounced stutter. "Hmm, channel traffic must be high; performance is corroded today," Dolaf said and he arched his eyebrows in mild surprise. Dolaf put the chrome implement back in his pocket and walked toward the portal. He stopped and grabbed the last six containers of French Vanilla Infused with the Essence of Caramelized Plantains flavored Classy HastyTasty and placed them in his silver knapsack.

Addison had enough. "L-Listen, Dolaf. I appreciate all you have done for me, but do you always have to take the French Vanilla Infused with the Essence of Caramelized Plantains Classy HastyTasty? It's my favorite flavor. You just took the last six containers... six! And the next delivery is three days from now. Why can't you be more considerate and take one of the other flavors?"

Dolaf stopped a few steps from the portal and turned abruptly toward Addison. "Be more considerate? Addisoy you have testicles as big as Saturnian tomatoes! By assisting you, my sibling and I are committing a Prime Crime every day, and rather than be effusive with gratefulness, you have the nerve to ask me not to take your 'favorite flavor' of Classy HastyTasty?" He said, making quotation marks with his fingers. (What had become of Nigel?) "After all that we have already done and are doing for you, you have the impudence to say that? I have no idea why Otka is doing this for you. I have tried to warn her that you are not the 'sweet soul' she believes you to be but she vehemently defends her decision. My sibling is intensely beautiful and therefore brilliant, but she is so desperate for a monogamous relationship that she is letting emotion cloud her logic; she is imbibing you with noble qualities I don't believe you possess; I can read people *Addisoy* and I know you! It is my prediction however that you will ultimately reveal your true nature and she will see you for what you are... a self-centered insecure coward!" Dolaf pointed his finger at Addison and Addison took a step back. He was a meter taller than Dolaf and twenty years older yet this boy intimidated him. Dolaf could best Addison in a fight and both of them knew it.

"I-I-I am warning you, I am your elder. Y-You'd better show me more respect!" Addison said, trying to affect an authoritative tone.

"Or what, Addisoy? What are you going to do? I will tell you what you are going to do... absolutely nothing. Don't insult me and embarrass yourself with counterfeit bluster. It only serves to amplify your weakness."

Dolaf paused. "I fancy all the flavors of Classy HastyTasty, but I have just decided, *Addisoy,* that French Vanilla Infused with the Essence of Caramelized Plantains is my favorite. Every time I visit, which I assure you will be a lot more frequently, I am going to take as many containers as I can." Dolaf spun on his right heel and strutted angrily out of the living unit.

Addison burned with rage. "What a disrespectful little bastard," he said out loud. "I am an adult! He should treat me with more deference!" Addison reached down, grabbed the Dynamic Tension Straps and quickly did forty bicep curls without pausing, beating his personal best by five repetitions. Blood rushed into the muscle bellies of each bicep; he could barely bend his arms. He picked up a gypsum coated towel, with some difficulty reached up and wiped the sweat from his brow, and walked over to the mirror to admire his arms. "He thinks he's muscular, well he should take a gander at these!" With a bellow, Addison flexed his biceps and then kicked the sitting platform with his left foot. His big toe began to bleed but Addison was so livid that he neither felt the pain nor noticed the blood. ■

CHAPTER TWENTY FOUR

❖

"ACCESS MENTAL AGILITY PROGRAM," Addison said. Then he barked louder than he needed to, "Commence!" A word materialized a meter from his face. Addison squinted; it always took his eyes a few seconds to adjust to the brilliant three-dimensional white letters. The word was:

BEAUTIFICATION

Addison leaned over and using the pointer finger on his right hand he scrawled FAUCET on the holographic pad floating ten centimeters from his waistline. He smiled. That word was two more letters than the minimum. He was getting quicker. He thought briefly then leaned over and wrote NOTICE. He laughed out loud. This was getting easier! Then without pausing he scrawled:

NICE
CITE
BITE
BOUT
CANE

He glanced over at the timer. It read 12/30; he still had 12 seconds remaining of the 30 allotted for this exercise. He felt a slight surge of anxiety. He needed only two more words to pass this test but suddenly his mind went blank. He watched the timer countdown from 12/30 to 6/30. Then breaking out in a big smile he bent over and wrote:

TUBE
TUNIC

He glanced at the timer. It read 2/30. He did it again! He made at least 10 words of four letters or more from the word BEAUTIFICATION. And he had done it with two seconds to spare, which wasn't his personal best (two days ago he finished a test with 4/30 left) but it was close. BEAUTIFICATION morphed into the word VICTORY. Addison, basking in the glory of his triumph, moved his face closer to VICTORY to enjoy the pleasant warmth emanating from the holographic image.

He had been doing these cognitive quickening exercises twice a day for the past three fortnights and he was pleased with his progress. He had taken forty-two tests and he had passed all but four. He knew he stood an excellent chance of passing Otka's test, now only two days away, and he was nervous. Not because he was afraid of failing, just the opposite, he was afraid of what she would expect of him if he passed. After all, he only had one previous sexual encounter, a truncated one a long time ago. What if his spine... snipe... pines... penis couldn't "stand at attention for the duration of their parade"? That was always a possibility and now that the thought was in his head, it was a stronger possibility. Or what if she was disappointed with the size of his manhood? After all she had been with Starck and he was a large man; it was a near certainty that his babymaker would be proportionate with his stature. How would Addison compare? And how would Otka react if he was less than she was accustomed to?

Beads of sweat formed on his brow. His breathing became shallow and blood rushed to his neck and cheeks. But then something unprecedented occurred and Addison was struck with a moment of clarity. Why worry about a potential encounter with Otka? If he were that uncomfortable he could tell her he wasn't emotionally ready to engage in coitus. She would be initially shocked, a woman as beautiful as Otka was most certainly unaccustomed to having her sexual offers turned down, but he was confident she would understand, she seemed to be the type who would. Besides, she would probably be grateful that he let her off the hook. Or he could purposely fail the evaluation; there was no shame in coming one or two words short of the mandated number.

Addison's breathing returned to normal and his neck and cheeks cooled. He felt a surge of confidence, he was finally heeding the biblical verse that his birther quoted more times than he could have counted, "worry not about tomorrow for tomorrow will worry about itself. Each day has enough trouble of its own." Lord with the lovely locks, he wished he had a strand of hair on his head for every time she quoted that! When was Otka going to fix his hair anyway? She would have to repopulate his head with hair at some point. Addison walked over to the mirror, pulled his tunic up to his nipples and admired his lean midsection. He flexed his abdominal muscles by exhaling loudly and he squealed in breathless delight as they popped through his stomach's nearly translucent skin.

He couldn't believe that this was his body. What a physique, what a physique! He rotated his torso from left to right to catch a better look at his oblique muscles. A chime sounded. It was time for his supplements. He walked over to the food preparation nook and grabbed a hermetically sealed container preloaded with hydrogen gas. He placed the container in the shiny chrome Deluxe Oxygenator, a premium model available only to Blesseds, and pressed the "Commence" switch. He reached over and grabbed his supplements, which were neatly arranged on a nearby shelf. In a few seconds the Deluxe Oxygenator released a burst of hot air through its vented top and chirped. Addison reached in and removed his container of instant water. He placed the pills into his mouth and sipped the water, instinctively grimacing in anticipation of the bitter taste produced by his standard model, but this water, as always, was cold, smooth and delicious.

Addison walked over to the sitting platform. Before he sat down he tried again to pry off a ruby – it would be a great replacement for the obsidian specimen he had foolishly given Otka. His attempt failed again. I'll get one eventually he thought. It then occurred to him that he should try and get one from a less conspicuous area, maybe from a section of the platform closer to the floor, so neither Otka nor Dolaf would notice. And if one of them did? He could just lie to them and tell them he had no idea what happened to it. His two remaining rocks were still in his filthy pair of Burdened trousers, a safe hiding place since those as attractive as Otka and Dolaf would never sully their hands by rooting through the pockets of such a revolting garment.

Addison longed to go outside, take off his tunic and strut around Grand Square. He fantasized about encountering the Blessed couple he fell in front of outside The Eagle's Nest – he knew just what he would do... he would take off his tunic and polish her dirk-toothed cat skin shoes, giving her and her firebrick chinned companion an eyeful of his muscularity. He mused about contacting Fancy Nancy Arnott, Dana, other girls who had rejected him and classmates who had mocked him. The scenarios he concocted always ended the same way –those that had ostracized him now admired him. He always craved the approval of others and now, finally, he had a guaranteed way of getting it. Sure his hair was still thinning and his teeth discolored, but with a body as lean and muscular as his would anyone even notice? Wasn't a body more memorable than a face anyway? Women rarely talked about a man's handsome face but you always overhead them gushing about his sexy abdominal muscles, cute derriere or big, strong arms. (They always coupled the words "big" and "strong" when describing a muscular man. Why those two words? Why not use some clever alliteration such as "big and brawny" or "super-sized and strong"?) As Addison sat contemplating different duos of descriptors, his right hand wandered up to his left bicep. He flexed his bicep and cupped his hand tightly over it, "As hard as corundum and as dense as a diamond," he said proudly. He was in the middle of complimenting himself when the portal slid open and Otka walked in. Embarrassed, he quickly removed his hand from his flexed arm.

"Well, well, well... now that is an extraordinary illustration of narcissism. Given your condition when we started this program, I am impressed," Otka said in a playful voice.

Addison had heard the word "narcissism" before but couldn't immediately recall its meaning. Against his better judgment he acted as if he did. She used the word in a good-humored voice so it must refer to something positive. "Th-Thank you. I guess I do look good today. I had an exceptional muscle-to-mind connection during my workout today and apparently this intense training has engorged the two muscle bellies of my biceps with more blood than usual."

Otka smiled. "You are starting to talk like a Blessed... and there is no longer any doubt that you have the body of one. You will need to do some additional work on your verbal comprehension, however, sweetie. 'Narcissistic' refers to someone who experiences feelings of eros love toward themselves. The root of the term comes from the ancient Greek mythological character Narcissus, a sorry man who fell in love with his own reflection in a pool of water," she explained. "He couldn't pull himself away from his image and he eventually withered away and died. All that remained of him was an exquisite daffodil. You don't observe too many of them anymore. Who has time to nurture flora, there are only 86,400 seconds in a day and so many regimens to maintain to ensure you are regularly enhancing your physical appearance. I do miss the beauty of nature however; all the polished chrome gives the city a pristine feel but it doesn't feed the soul like meadow of gorgeous geraniums, a grove of blossoming begonias or an orchard of boysenberry bushes ..." Otka said sadly, her words trailing off.

"I-In hindsight, maybe it was folly to pretend as if I knew what narcissism meant," Addison said sheepishly. "Even a fool is thought wise if he keeps silent," Addison said, grinning thinly, quoting from the Book of Proverbs. His master birther used that phrase often, usually in response to something Addison's master POP had said. (They were lifetime cohabitants, so they were obviously fond of one another. Why then did they always treat each with such contempt?)

"You just enumerated verbatim a passage from the Old Testament Book of Proverbs, chapter 14, verse 28. Well done!" Otka exclaimed. Addison was thrilled that he had unintentionally delighted her. "The fact that you can quote that stanza of scripture so precisely illustrates that you are clearly no fool," Otka said and smiled warmly. "You are so different from any other male that I have ever met. You are authentic, honest; devoid of guile.

I find your lack of facade refreshing, even attractive. Practically every man I have ever conjoined with had a beautiful face, a fantastic physique and a large babymaker (a quiver passed through Addison's gut); but they all had one quality that I found troublesome. How do I best convey this?" Otka paused. "They were excessively confident, faultless; they revealed no trace of vulnerability. They were too polished, too at ease in their epidermis. They all said the most appropriate things and at exactly the right times – as if they were reading off some script that I couldn't see… maybe that's why so many of them had wandering eyes," Otka chuckled softly. "There is none of that with you. I just know you are the type of man who would remain devoted to me for my lifetime… you wouldn't get bored with me after only three measly fortnights. You wouldn't walk through Grand Square with your hand on my derriere and your eye on someone else's; and you certainly wouldn't call out another woman's given name during coitus like Cliffie did!" Addison could see Otka was still angry but even when revealing this ugly emotion she still looked beautiful. "Why do I continue to opt for coitus companions with brawny bodies and scrawny morals? Enough already! I am finished with macho men who compete with me for mirror time! I am finished with beautiful boys who admire their own bodies while they are touching mine! Now *that* is narcissism. I am finished with gorgeous guys who are acrobats on our sleeping platform and escape artists in our relationships!"

Addison, believing Otka was finished with her diatribe, was about to bring up the disrespectful behavior of Dolaf when she reached up and yanked off her breast cups.

Addison was astonished and again he involuntarily squeaked. Otka expression softened into a warm smile. She glanced down at her breasts and jiggled them by bouncing up and down on the balls of her feet.

Otka giggled and the tension she built up from her tirade appeared to drain from her. "Well, sweetie, you have now chirped like a titmouse both times I revealed my breasts to you… I wonder what noise you will emit when I do this." Otka reached down, hooked her thumbs under the band of her super-micro-mini shorts and then swayed her hips suggestively as she slid them down to her ankles. Addison's eyes widened and his jaw fell open, a trickle of saliva oozed from his mouth but he quickly slurped up. Cleft palate, how disgusting! Before he had time to blush, however, Otka said with a coquettish smile, "Don't fret it, sweetie, my unclothed body usually causes men to discharge bodily fluids." Otka stepped over her shorts. Her lighthearted response put Addison at ease.

"B-B-But I haven't passed your examination yet," Addison said. He noticed with titillation that Otka was follicle free from the neck down.

"That doesn't matter, sweetie. I know you will. I believe in you. And because I do, there is no point in delaying your... um... I mean *our* mutual ecstasy, is there?"

Addison nodded. Again he felt as if he should say something but Otka's nakedness had rendered him speechless. "Please arise, sweetie," she said with authority and Addison obeyed without pause; like a swinging watch her nude body had hypnotized him; he would have lowed like a Stegosaurus had she asked. Otka turned her back on Addison and keeping her legs straight, she bent over at the waist to retrieve her shorts. Flawless-faced birther of god! She (unintentionally?) just showed him everything! Otka turned around, twirling her shorts casually around her pointer finger. Addison unabashedly stared at her, feeling like a muddy swine standing in front of a string of AAAA quality pearls. His mind flashed back to that billboard at the Shawcuzit transport station. He was the filthy pig and Otka was the regal lion. All with human faces are not equal, it wasn't even close.

Otka walked over to Addison and handed him her shorts. "Please cover my eyes with these," she said and she turned her back toward Addison. Addison again ogled her perfect posterior; his heart pounding so hard that his bald spot throbbed. She had a small birthmark high on the right cheek of her derriere. For some reason discovering this made her even more desirable. He grabbed both ends of her shorts and tried to loop them over her head but was unable to reach. Otka was wearing six-centimeter heels and was much taller than him. She reached back and grabbed her shorts from

Addison and positioned them over her eyes. "Try tying it now, sweetie. And please make a double knot. I don't want them to displace if we get overly passionate," she said with a giggle. "Now one final request before we mount the sleeping platform. Please extinguish all the light sources and draw the graphite coated drape over the windows...be thorough please and make sure not a micrometer of light peaks through; I want it dark in here... absolutely black... like a capitalist's soul."

Her demands troubled Addison. There could be only be one reason why she was doing all of this – she was still disgusted by his appearance. Sure his body looked great, but nothing had been done to replenish his thinning hair, to beautify his face and to whiten his teeth. She obviously wasn't ashamed of her own nakedness; she had stripped off her clothes with the aplomb of a veteran striptease dancer. Addison's energy abruptly changed. Suddenly he felt self-conscious, unattractive, unworthy. Her physical perfection made him acutely aware of his imperfections. Without moving his feet, he inclined his body away from her. All he wanted to do was get out of Otka's presence. She apparently noticed. "Sweetie, you don't think that I am taking all these sight limiting measures because I haven't transformed you from the thyroid cartilage up yet, do you?"

"W-W-Well the thought did cross my mind," Addison said, speaking deliberately in an attempt to subdue his stammer and mask his mounting insecurity.

"Sweetie, I swear on my birther's incinerated cadaver that the only reason I want it to be dark is because it helps me relax, to decompress, to eliminate my inhibitions. I have a proclivity to affect unattractive expressions when I climax and I am self conscious about it. With the lights off and the room dark I can experience pleasure with no concern about how it makes me look," Otka said convincingly. If she wasn't telling the truth she was a superb liar. "And I know you want me to experience maximum pleasure, don't you?" she said as she seductively brushed her fingers across Addison's forearm. Addison nodded. It made sense. Even an extraordinarily beautiful woman like Otka had to occasionally deal with embarrassing situations after all she was still human, albeit a superior one.

Otka undressed Addison, lifted him up by the armpits and placed him on the sleeping platform. Her strength always surprised him. Addison was nervous but he performed adequately and although he climaxed quickly Otka did as well and they both crossed the finish line at about the same time. Fifteen minutes later, after Otka had given Addison a sublingual dose of recuperative vitamins, they engaged in coitus again. This time however Addison climaxed well before Otka and was unable to bring her the pleasure she so deftly brought him. As he lay on the sleeping platform fixating on this, Otka assured him that simultaneous orgasm was a rare occurrence and it was more probable that the Luvista River would "transmute into French Vanilla Infused with the Essence of Caramelized Plantains Classy HastyTasty" before that would happen again. Her analogy reminded him of Dolaf and as he lay there with Otka's head resting on his pectoral, he decided to tell Otka about Dolaf's repeated incidents of insolence. Right as he opened his mouth to say something Otka reached down and caressed his babymaker. As Addison enjoyed her expert handiwork he tried to recall what he was going to say but he couldn't remember and when Otka increased the pace and pressure of her touch it slipped his mind that he was about to say anything at all. ∎

CHAPTER TWENTY FIVE

❖

THE AWAKENING APPARATUS ACTIVATED. It was set to "flock of birds," only available on the premium model. It began as the peaceful chirping of a distant gaggle of birds (love birds Otka called them) and grew into a frenzied flock right outside their living unit. Addison took his right arm off Otka waist, straightened it out to admire his triceps, then rolled over and turned off the awakening apparatus. The holographic clock read 07:04. Those numbers were familiar. Did something of historical significance happened on that date? Whatever, he didn't care about such minutia anymore; he had more important things to ponder. For instance how was he going to improve the symmetry of his latissmus dorsi muscles? As he inventoried his physique yesterday he noticed they were disgustingly disproportionate.

Addison sat up and started coughing violently, jolting Otka awake. "My love, you need to get that diagnosed and treated. You have been barking like a mate-seeking pinniped for six-sevenths of a fortnight," she said groggily. Addison dismissed her concern with a wave of his hand, believing that his coitus companion was overreacting.

"It's just a cough. Why should I squander away valuable training time visiting the Bureau of Health when all they are going to tell me to do is consume chamomile tea tablets coated with crystallized honey? I have critical work to do. Have you examined the symmetry of my latissimus dorsi muscles? They are obscenely disproportionate. I must devote more time to exercising them. I need to shape the left one and build the right one. My back looks grotesque; how could you not have noticed?"

"Your physique is completely devoid of fault or flaw my love," Otka said, her voice muffled by her contoured memory foam pillow. Addison leaned over and licked Otka's forehead affectionately. He inhaled her jasmine and espresso scent, smiled wide and pearly white and then he turned and vaulted off the sleeping platform like a gymnast dismounting a pommel horse.

Their room was chock full of mirrors – Addison's idea; he loved mirrors – and he stood naked at in front of the nearest one. He rotated his hips to get a better look at his back. "You have irresistibly colored irises, my dear, but your eyes obviously don't function properly. Luscious-looking lord, it looks as if I have elephantitis!"

"You look amazing, my love. Why can't you just be happy with the way you are presently constituted?"

"Why should I be happy with the way I am presently constituted?" he asked, surprised. "There are still so many improvements I need to make! Did you see that guy at the Caffeine Depot yesterday? His upper arms were as big as my thighs! I am fairly certain he was snickering at me...he most definitely flashed me one of those 'sexier than thou' looks."

The truth was Addison had plenty to be happy about. Six fortnights ago Otka arranged for his facial enhancement procedures and a hair transplant and the results were outstanding..."They exceeded even my lofty expectations, "she had proclaimed to him, "Apparently my 'compensation' was sufficient," she said playfully. She made quotation marks with her fingers; Addison thought nothing of it. He had wondered how she was able to convince doctors to perform illegal cosmetic surgery on him; after all from the neck up he was still a Burdened despite his great physique. In the end Addison decided not to ask but based on her insinuation he guessed that she traded sexual favors for medical ones.

Addison stood in front of a mirrored wall, dipped his manicured fingers in some follicle balm, and smoothed down a clump of hair sticking straight up at the center of his hairline, the result of an unfortunately situated cowlick. Addison wasn't bothered by this, he was given a beautiful thick pelt of hair and the balm easily tamed the cowlick. He brushed his freshly dyed blonde hair off his forehead. He backed away from the mirrored wall and wondered for a brief moment if his new hair had been harvested off a lower caste member at Camp Sycamore. He felt a pang of guilt and then he quickly caught himself. Did it really matter if it did? Even if it had come from there, someone was going to get that hair, if it happened that it was him, so be it. They surely weren't going to reattach it to the lower caste person they took it from. His conscious clear, he leaned toward the mirrored wall and sighed with disgust, "Would you just look at these grooves on my forehead? They look like transport tracks," he said. "Where is the facial plaster? I'll eliminate them in just a few seconds. I'll have to be mindful of course not to look surprised or else the plaster will crease into ridges and my forehead will look even worse, as if that were possible."

"Addy, love of my existence (she hadn't referred to him as *that* before), re-mount the sleeping platform and I will show you what I think of your appearance." Otka threw off the gypsum coated sheet, revealing her naked body. Addison saw her in his peripheral vision but pretended he didn't. He continued to inventory his features in the mirror. Otka huffed, pulled the sheet back over her body and flopped onto her side so her back faced him. "Sexy Salacious Savior, I am feeling amorous this morning; I implore you, get back up here… pronto…hastily…NOW!" Knowing Otka couldn't see him; Addison lifted his left arm and rubbed a small lump under the skin of his armpit. He exhaled in pain as he pressed on it lightly, triggering another coughing spell. Over the past fortnight he found similar lumps in his right groin and behind his right knee but since they didn't affect his appearance or impede his workouts, he didn't worry about them. His coughing fits were more problematic as they affected his stamina and forced him to cut short his last three training sessions. There was some benefit however from this frequent coughing; the violent contractions from his hacking had improved the vascularity of his upper body.

Otka rolled onto her back. Addison quickly dropped his arm. Her hair was tousled and her face was flushed. She gave Addison an adoring smile. "I declare, you are a sexy stallion," she said in a breathy voice. With a sweep of her hand Otka removed the sheet so she was naked again. She slid her hands seductively over her breasts and down her thighs. Addison smiled back at her, showing off his pearl infused teeth. They still felt unnatural in his mouth; they were larger than his original teeth and occasionally his lips got stuck on them when he retracted a smile.

"Flex your abdominal muscles for me my love," Otka said. Addison put his hands on his hips and exhaled loudly; muscle tissue and veins exploded from the middle of his torso. She squealed gleefully. Amused at her reaction, Addison started laughing; triggering yet another coughing fit. Otka's expression turned from affection to concern. "I don't like the timbre or frequency of your tussis, my love. I am asking you... pleading with you... I am beseeching you – get it evaluated as soon as possible. Please. Please!" Addison never saw Otka assume such a subservient role before and he found it unappealing. As she spoke Addison noticed she had significantly more freckles on the left side of her nose than her right. Her face was asymmetrical! Why hadn't he seen this imperfection before?

He took a step closer to the sleeping platform and pointed his finger angrily at Otka. "I told you don't fret over it. Let this topic plummet, will you?!" Otka tilted her head and gave Addison a startled look, like a birther witnessing her toddler's first temper tantrum. Addison paused and then felt bad about his tone. "I'm sorry I spoke sharply to you," he said and he leapt back onto the sleeping platform. With foreplay consisting of two slaps on her derriere and a strategically placed tickle, he engaged her in coitus. He noticed that her body no longer excited him the way it used to early in their relationship. Addison was fairly certain Otka had two orgasms, although Addison wasn't sure if they were authentic and he didn't care much if they weren't. No matter how hard he worked however, he could not climax. Frustrated, he abruptly stopped. He was starting to get fatigued and he wanted to preserve his energy for his afternoon workout. Otka grabbed his derriere with both hands and pulled, "Keep going; I want you to experience orgasmic pleasure as well, my love. Wait... I have a superior idea. Please go retrieve a condom-mint, two chrome spoons of equal length, and a container of Classy HastyTasty, flavor doesn't matter, I am going to perform a procedure on you that..."

"No thanks," Addison interrupted and immediately Otka's face saddened. "Don't become vexed, this isn't your fault at all," Addison said in a placating tone, "I feel a cranium-cracker gathering behind my left eye. Let's dismount the sleeping platform and saunter over to the Caffeine Depot; the caffeine jolt from the espresso tablets will extinguish it."

Addison dressed while Otka fine-tuned her look for public consumption. He squeezed into pair of mini limestone colored shorts (thank the luscious lord for spandex!) and a white and copper striped halter top, his favorite outfit. He strapped on his polished brown shoes, pausing for a moment to admire his reflected smile on the squared toe of the right one. He smiled a lot these days. He then walked over to one of the mirrors and shrugged his shoulders, flexing his trapezius muscles. He was pleased – they practically touched his ears! The extended pause he added at the finish of the shoulder shrug exercise was paying big dividends – he added about a centimeter to his trapezius muscles in just the past fortnight! He decided to perform an isometric shrug and hold it until Otka was ready to leave. He had some time to pass, why not use it productively? When Otka was (finally) ready, they left her complex and headed toward the Caffeine Depot. Addison's trapezius muscles were so engorged with blood that when he shrugged they now actually did touch his ears.

Otka affectionately placed her hand on Addison's derriere while they walked. Addison liked the way it felt and he purposely shortened his strides to accommodate Otka's reach. As they passed by the northeastern entrance to Grand Square a Blessed woman coming from the other direction "popped her cheek"[14] at Addison. Otka took her hand off his derriere, wrapped it around his waist and pressed tightly against him. Addison looked over at Otka and saw that she was giving this brazen woman a nasty look. The

---

14 Like "wolf-whistling" for men, "cheek-popping" was considered a crass way for a woman to express her approval of a man's appearance. To make the noise, the index finger was inserted in the mouth, curled, and then pulled out quickly while the lips were sucked in. The distinctive noise was created as a slang gesture for the phrase, "I wouldn't mind popping your cork!"

woman shook her hands out in front of her large breasts (much larger than Otka's) deferentially, as if to say "my apologies," although it was obvious to Addison that she knew before she "popped" him that he was with Otka.

After they got their espresso tablets, Otka led Addison to a nearby park bench. Otka liked to chat while they consumed their morning tablets and today was no exception. They talked about a variety of topics but two dominated their conversations: for Addison it was his hyper-critical POP, his anger toward his POP for the way he consistently beat him down and the guilt he felt over this paternal anger; for Otka it was her philandering POP how the pain of betrayal led to her birther's abuse of grain alcohol nasal inhalers which ultimately dissolved her nasal passages and caused her to drown in her own mucus.

Otka told Addison of her overwhelming desire to enter into a monogamous relationship and succeed where her POP and birther had failed while Addison shared with her the excruciating envy he experienced whenever he saw a good-looking man. In tender moments Addison confessed his rage toward god for all his physical shortcomings and Otka revealed the pain and humiliation of being habitually cheated on, dating all the way back to secondary school when she discovered that her first coitus companion and finest friend were regularly fornicating behind her back. "He was the first in a protracted series of morally deficient men I've attached my trackless transport to," she had said.

Today, Addison asked Otka the question that had bothered him since she passed him the note disguised as an espresso tablet, and especially since she disrobed in front of him and first engaged him in coitus. He looked directly into her emerald and gold-flecked eyes and asked her, "Why Otka...what is the real reason you are helping me?"

"I already told you my love. In this society where superficiality is supreme and where we are told over and over again that god only values those who are attractive; you are proof to me that the god they worship, and the god they want all of us to worship, is not the true God. I am bombarded with this Face-ist nonsense on a daily basis... I need something, or better yet someone, to ground me, to ensure that I'm not swept up in this tsunami of apostasy and end up compromising the tenets of my faith. As you know, my faith is important to me." Addison thought back to his visit to Our Lady of the Immaculate Reflection and witnessing Otka's fervent praying.

"If that is the only reason," Addison said, "then why do you engage in coitus with me? Granted I am not complaining," he smiled, "but I need to know. Was cohabitating with me part of your plan? Obviously, you weren't attracted to me when I was a Burdened... no one was."

Otka broke eye contact with him and looked at the ground. "Well, I have to admit. There was another reason why I decided to save you, although do not harbor misgivings about the veracity of my initial explanation," she furrowed her brow and narrowed her eyes. Addison knew she was telling him the truth. "Seeing you enter my Depot day after day with your eyes cast downward, so nervous, so unsure of yourself, so pitiful and helpless... it hurt my heart and splintered my soul."

Addison interrupted, "I want to make sure I understand you correctly... you engage in coitus with me because you pity me?"

Otka sighed and looked up at him. "It is more complicated than that." She paused and once again tapped one of her front teeth with her pointer finger; this was apparently how she organized her thoughts. "When I was a girl my birther and *father* (the "f" word again... he didn't like it when she used such coarse language) procured for me an adorable albino Bengal tiger as a domesticated animal companion. Unbeknownst to them, the tiger was recently impregnated and soon she gave birth to a litter of four cubs. Three of the cubs were strapping, healthy, majestic looking specimens – pleasurable to gaze upon – and immediately after leaving the womb they were suckling their birther's teat and frolicking with one another. The fourth was an anomaly. He was approximately nine sixteenths the size of his siblings, his eyes were partially closed, his coat was dull, sullied and riddled with sores; he was unattractive and feeble and he could never reach his birther's teat because his stronger siblings kept shoving him away. While these comely cubs consumed colostrum, this pathetic sat in the corner of the pen, howling from hunger," tears rolled down her face as she spoke. "If I didn't intervene, he would have soon perished from starvation. He had not asked to be born, he had done nothing to justify his misfortune, and sadly he had no way of altering his destiny...but I did. I could give him a future even though it was providentially ordained that he should expire after only a few days. I became this cub's savior, in a sense his personal Jesus. I made sure he received proper nourishment by holding off his more powerful siblings and allowing him to suckle his birther. I also engaged in rough physical play with him so he could develop sufficient muscle coordination and tone," Otka paused and wiped a tear that was teetering on her angular jaw. "Needless to say, this cub and I had an extraordinary relationship... extraordinary! He understood what I was doing for him and he adored me for it...I have never experienced such love... I have never felt so needed... I have never been so content. Ultimately fate would not be denied and he developed feline leukemia. He succumbed to the disease when he was only two annums old, but I got to spend two lovely annums with him when it was predestined that he should live only a few days."

"The tattoo on your shoulder," Addison said.

"The tattoo on my shoulder," Otka echoed in a melancholy voice.

"I once overheard an SS at your Caffeine Depot saying that your tattoo was an indication that you were a bona fide 'tiger' when it came to nocturnal activities," Addison said smiling.

Otka wiped another tear from her eye and laughed. "Well that is not the reason, but as you can attest to, that isn't an erroneous assertion, now is it?"

Prior to Otka, Addison's only sexual encounter was with the immoral Dana in the Societal Ethics classroom, and since that lasted less than a minute he really had no reference group of experiences from which he could measure her prowess, however he decided to give Otka the answer she was expecting, "No, I would most definitely support that SS's decadent declaration." Otka's unique way of managing the lexicon was rubbing off on him.

"Despite my chic hair style, my modish style of dress and my intimate familiarity with the most up-to-date MOVA[15] techniques, I am a traditionalist my love and I want to share the duration of my existence with a committed cohabitation partner. I have tried multiple times to make it work with good looking – make that fabulous looking men – and never once has it coalesced into what I desire. And then a few fortnights ago I had an epiphany, thanks to Mimi from the Caffeine Depot," Otka paused and affected a distant look, "Poor Mimi. She is a wonderful person, but she desperately needs self-confidence. I wish I knew the reasons why, so I could help her..." Otka gave a reflective grin. "Pardon my digression. To resume... soon after I caught Starck fornicating with Cookie, I was observing Mimi as she operated the Depot's tablet press. She was creating black tea tablets and I noticed that the quality of the finished product was unacceptable – none of the tablets Mimi produced were holding their shape. I suggested to Mimi that she re-granulate the tablets and run them through the press again. Her response was enlightening, 'It would be a waste of time. The drought in Eurasia has affected the tea harvest and the latest black tea composite we received is below standard. I can run the materials through the press a dozen times, but the result will always be the same – *poor materials never yield good tablets*'. That was it!" Otka repeated the phrase slowly, emphasizing each word. "Poor... Materials... Never... Yield... Good... Tablets...! That pathetic sweetheart opened my eyes. The men I continually select are abundantly attractive but morally barren; they are all 'poor material.' My relational failures are a result of my defective approach. I try to take self-centered super gorgeous men and manufacture them into what I want... and not only has it failed miserably, it has made me miserable. Poor materials never yield good tablets. So now I am implementing a different strategy. I have decided to start with 'good material'; to select a man who is first and foremost faithful... but also sensitive, kind

---

15 MOVA is an acronym for the different ways a woman can stimulate a man's penis: Manual, Oral, Vaginal and Anal.

and considerate; and renovate his appearance so I find their visible qualities as beautiful as their invisible ones. I am excellent at appraising people and I knew that you would be the ideal man to apply my new strategy on… and I am delighted that my intuition, as always, was accurate."

Otka stood up, grabbed Addison's hand and pulled him too his feet. With their forearms entwined they headed back to Otka's living complex. It was such a pleasant day that Otka led him counterclockwise around Grand Square, the long way home. As they passed the Wakork Transport station another Blessed woman "popped" him. Addison smiled broadly. Two pops in one morning! What a fantastic feeling to be desired by such beautiful women! Addison glanced over and turned his head to follow her as she walked away. Otka gave his elbow a playful squeeze. Addison winced. He covertly rubbed his elbow and noticed there was another small lump right where Otka pressed. She leaned over said to him in mock anger, "cease and desist your flirting right now, you handsome fellow, or you will face calamitous consequences when we return to our living unit." Addison continued to watch the woman. As she walked away she hiked her super-micro-mini shorts up a bit higher, revealing most of her derriere. She turned back and smiled at Addison. He smiled back. She resumed walking but with a bit more sway in her hips. Oh, it was great to be alive! Otka suddenly stopped walking. Addison still watching the woman, stopped with her. He felt a slight chill; something was blocking the brilliant morning sun. Addison turned his head forward and an icy spark shot from the back of his throat to his bowels. Standing in front of them was Starck, and next to Starck was a remarkably attractive, voluptuous redheaded woman (for a change). She looked dangerous, pernicious, as if getting involved with her would deliver both ecstasy and heartbreak. Addison looked over at Otka to see her reaction but her face maintained a serene expression. Seeing Starck had not affected her on the outside although he guessed she was probably churning inwardly. "Hans! What a nice surprise! How are you? Are you feeling copasetic?" She said cordially to Starck. She leaned over and quickly pressed her cheek against his.

"Oh I am fine. Don't I look it?" Starck said coolly in his baritone voice. "My apologies, I am being discourteous; this is my companion Cytheria – colloquially I refer to her as Cyth." Cyth stuck out her hand and quickly clasped and released Otka's outstretched hand.

Otka didn't skip a beat and adhering to WASP she said just as coolly, "Nice to make your acquaintance, Cyth. It is my sincere wish that you are feeling as good as you look."

Cytheria smiled politely and gave the standard WASP response, "You are as thoughtful as you are attractive. I feel well, thank you."

"I am being discourteous, as well. Please greet my new friend, Helmut," Otka said. How crafty of her not to give his real name! Cyth gave Addison a handshake, but she focused her amethyst eyes directly into Addison's, widened them ever so slightly, and held his hand longer than normal. Was it possible? Was the coitus companion of a perfect male specimen like Starck actually flirting with him?

Starck was looking intently at Addison and a cold sweat broke out on Addison's forehead. Why was Starck staring at him? Had Addison's facial plaster clumped? Did Starck just see what Cyth had done? Protuberant proboscis! Did Starck recognize him? Impossible! Addison was completely transformed. There was no way Starck could know who he was; however, Starck's eyes remained locked on him. Addison finally spoke, "W-Well, we need to abscond Otka. I-It was an absolute joy meeting the both of you. You are a highly attractive couple," he said nervously. Otka nodded, but Starck would not let them pass. He pointed a massive finger at Addison.

"Helmut, you possess an impressive physique. You and I should engage in high intensity resistance training together in the near future – the more immediate the better. You know what they say, 'iron sharpens iron,'" Starck said, and he smiled at Addison. Addison felt a pang of jealousy. This man was fabulous looking – more attractive than he was. He sensed that Otka noticed it as well. Did she still harbor amorous feelings for him? He examined her face but still could read nothing in her expression; it was calm, natural, as if she had just encountered a familiar friend, not a former coitus companion. "Otka dear, I am still at the same living unit, you know the address... you spent more than a few evenings there," he said, winking his sparkling aquamarine eyes. "Give your friend my contact information so we can schedule a training session." Starck nodded, took his voluptuous redheaded friend by the arm, and they walked away. Addison was relieved. He was not only afraid that Starck might recognize him, he also felt like a complete fraud in Starck's presence. Otka had done a remarkable job transforming him, however while Addison was technically a Blessed, his good looks were simulated, forged, man-made – he was a counterfeit. Starck on the other hand was blessed with natural good looks. They were both good looking yet Starck possessed qualities that Addison did not; qualities that were hard to define but as real as a granite-hard derriere. He had an innate radiance, a manly aura, a self-assured countenance that supplements and exercise could never reproduce. Starck was more attractive than him and as Addison and Otka resumed walking he wondered if she noticed as well. How could she not?

Otka and Addison had walked ten meters when suddenly Otka grabbed his arm tightly and pulled him in a different direction. "Something is transpiring at the Burdened compound; let us go grab a gander!" A crowd was quickly gathering at the compound barricade. Addison resisted, he had no desire to see what was happening; he felt no attachment to the place or the people – a different Addison from a different time had lived there. He had been born again, he was a new creation. Or was he? The chance encounter with Starck revealed to him that his old insecurities lingered. He had put his past behind him but it wasn't sufficient, the Burdened Addison was a rotting corpse tied to his back and the stench was a constant reminder of his past. To become an unadulterated Blessed he needed to free himself from this cadaver and bury it deep enough in the ground so that he never again smelled the putridity of his former self.

Otka was persistent and he relented. Soon he stood with her in the middle of a pressing crowd. Addison flinched; someone was grabbing his right quadriceps. It was Starck's companion Cyth! She was standing in front of him, just off his left shoulder. She glanced back and winked. Handsome lord, she was flirting with him! Addison was ecstatic; the coitus companion of the one man he envied more than any other found him desirable! It was almost too fantastic for him to believe. Addison looked toward the barricade and saw Starck pushing his way through the crowd and toward the barricade, obviously to provide assistance. There was no possible way he could see their interplay.

The confined citizens in the Burdened Ghetto were chanting, "No food, no peace, no way. No food, no peace, no way."

"Why, that's word-for-word what the Curseds shouted during their uprising," Addison said to Otka, but loud enough so those nearby could hear. "Can't they author a more imaginative protest? The best they can do is to plagiarize one from a lower caste? Hey Burdeneds, change your chant to 'no food, no peace, no way, no originality!'"

People around Addison chuckled and Otka elbowed him in the mid-section, "That's a trifle callous," she said but Addison didn't hear her, he was enjoying the laughter his remark generated. In less than one year he had gone from doing all he could to avoid attention to now constantly craving it.

Cyth looked back at Addison and slowly and suggestively licked her lips, which were as voluptuous and appetizing as her body. She took a step backward so that her derriere was now pressed up against his leg. He leaned toward her and breathed in deep, taking in her scent of cinnamon and baked apple. Apple, the forbidden fruit, the irony of the second note in her scent didn't escape him. He glanced over at Otka. She wasn't paying attention to him; like everyone in the crowd except for Addison and Cyth, she was focused on the events unfolding behind the Burdened barricade.

The protesters chanted for about another minute then the loud commanding voice of an SA standing on a platform atop the barricade (obviously using amplification gum) shouted down the protestors. "Stop chanting and return to your quarters immediately or face the unpleasant consequences." After a few seconds however another chant arose from the

Burdened Ghetto, "Starve us or shoot us; either way we die. Starve us or shoot us; either way we die. Starve us or shoot us; either way we die."

"My love," Otka said nervously, "I am not keen on this at all. It's eerily similar to what happened in the Cursed Ghetto just a few thirty-day cycles ago. Blessed birther of god, this is chilling. Chilling! Do you concur?" Addison did not answer. "My love, did you hear me?" she paused but Addison did not reply. "Well, did you?" Still Addison remained silent, preoccupied because Cyth had arched her back to offer him a better view into her breast cups. "My love, are you listening to me?!" Otka said, tension mounting in her voice.

"Of course I'm listening to you," Addison lied.

"Well, isn't it?" Otka said in a frustrated tone.

"Yes… yes it is," he mumbled, but he had no idea what she had originally asked him.

The SA bellowed again, "If you continue to pose a threat to my SA, we will be forced to protect ourselves by employing whatever means are necessary." The protesters quieted. Then moments later another chant arose, "Bormann Brock lies a lot. Bormann Brock lies a lot. Bormann Brock lies a lot." There was a smattering of snickers from the onlookers; this was a spin on the "Long Live Bormann Brock" slogan which was currently peppering all forms of media. Another stern warning came from the SA, "Cease and desist immediately! Return to your quarters or face the dreadful consequences. You will not be issued another warning!"

New spectators flocked toward the barricade like horseflies to a heap of feces but Addison was so absorbed with Cyth that he didn't notice. The chanting grew louder, "Bormann Brock lies a lot. Bormann Brock lies a lot!" The swelling crowd pressed in on Addison. Addison's face turned red, not from anxiety and not from humiliation, but because Cyth was gyrating her derriere against his leg. He tightened his quadriceps and Cyth moaned. She reached back with her right hand and stroked Addison's left forearm with her fingers. Her scent was intoxicating. He recalled how Otka's espresso and jasmine scent used to excite him; now it was Cyth's cinnamon and baked apple. Otka turned toward Addison, "I am having such a feeling of *schon gesehen*.[16] Addison, are you feeling well? You are flushed and perspiring profusely. Addison? Addison!"

"I am listening, what do you want!" he said, his voice quivering slightly as Cyth ran her fingers slowly from his forearm to his bicep.

"What do I want? I asked you a question. Why aren't you listening to me?"

"Of course I am listening to you."

"If you were listening, please respond to my initial query?" she said.

"What was your question again?" he asked sheepishly.

"I knew you weren't listening. Please show me respect and listen to me when I talk to you. It is so maddening!" Otka said in an exasperated tone. Her tone softened, "Are you sure you aren't feeling ill? You are trembling! Let us return to my living unit and consult with a holographic health practitioner."

"There is no need to talk with a health practitioner... I am fine. Will you please stop worrying about me? I am your cohabitation partner, not your offspring. Stop smothering me!" he said, equally exasperated. Otka looked dumfounded. Addison saw her expression in his peripheral vision, but pretended not to notice. He had more interesting sights to focus on as Cyth leaned her torso back a few degrees more to give him an even better look into her breast cups. Addison bobbed his head up and down and from side to side, but he couldn't catch a glimpse of her nipple. He dropped his left hand and stroked Cyth's round derriere with the tips of his twitching fingers.

He was so excited, he was panting. He wanted this woman; he had to experience this sexy specimen. Otka was great, but why should he limit himself to one woman? He had to make up for a lifetime of lost opportunities. Lost opportunities? Try no opportunities! But he would never leave Otka... he could never leave Otka. She had done so much for him and he owed her more than her could ever repay. Besides, if he did, she might decide to turn him into the SA. He decided then and

---

16   The Bavarian version of déjà vu.

there that he would engage in coitus with someone other than Otka. If not with this voluptuous redhead then with someone else. These days he had plenty of options. Perhaps the ambiance coordinator in Otka's living complex – the one with the luminous citrine-colored eyes – who smiled at him every time she saw him... Or perhaps the new employee at Otka's Caffeine Depot... She had gigantic nostrils, but her gargantuan breasts and tiny bottom intrigued him and he thought of a few coital positions that would block those nasal canyons from his view. Addison was shaded from a passing cloud of guilt. Was he morally corrupt for deciding to do this? He thought for a moment, then laughed to himself. Of course not. It was just coitus; it was a biological need – no different than eating, drinking, urinating, defecating and sleeping. He happened to be one of those individuals who required more sexual diversity. Should he feel guilt because he had varied tastes? He gazed lustily at Cyth. How would this voluptuous redhead perform on the sleeping platform? How would she express her excitement? What was her favorite coitus position? Addison shook his head and grinned; further justification... Would he be fantasizing about Cyth if Otka was fulfilling his sexual needs? Of course not. And if he didn't take care of his needs, who would?

Addison knew if he was careful he could copulate with other women and keep it from Otka. She didn't believe it was in his DNA to stray. She judged him as "good material." Wasn't faithfulness one of the defining characteristics? And he did want to be faithful to her... initially. But as his options for extracurricular coitus companions swelled, his desire to be faithful shriveled. Again a question traipsed through his thoughts... Could he live with himself? Could he look in the mirror without feeling like a contemptible louse? That question made him smile given his previous aversion to his Burdened reflection. Of course he could look in the mirror now; he was gorgeous! Looking in the mirror raised his spirits! He wasn't going to allow the residual guilt from supplemental coitus ruin what he had spent a lifetime wishing for. And what was there to feel guilty about? He wasn't physically hurting Otka. It would just be some harmless fun between attractive adults – no different than taking a female friend out for a night of dancing. You moved your body in a sexually suggestive manner when you danced and that was in front of dozens of people! That is what Otka should get upset with him for, not a quick coitus session in private. Within a few short moments, Addison had used half-truths and flawed logic to hopscotch his way to a clear conscious – one that was now impervious to any further feelings of guilt or remorse.

"Addison, are you having a severe anxiety attack?" Otka asked. Addison didn't respond. Addison trailed his fingertips around the redhead's derriere to her bare stomach. He softly traced little circles around her navel. The redheaded leaned forward, pushed her derriere against Addison's leg and wriggled it. Addison's babymaker filled with blood and his chest filled with pride. He still couldn't believe that Starck's coitus companion found him attractive! Perhaps he was as attractive as Starck. Perhaps Otka took no notice of Starck's fantastic looks moments ago. As Addison thought of Starck, it occurred to him. What if Starck returned? This was still a formidable man and Addison did not want to upset him. He looked toward the barricade and saw Starck conferring with a group of SA and SS. He wasn't coming back anytime soon. And besides, if he did happen to see them flirting, Addison had an explanation – it was Starck's voluptuous friend who was the initiator! Surely she would admit to that. It never even occurred to him that Otka was referring to him by his real name and that Cyth might hear it and tell Starck. His growing desire had squelched his ability to think.

The chanting from the Burdened Ghetto continued, "Bormann Brock lies a lot. Bormann Brock lies a lot. Bormann Brock lies a lot." A burst of gunfire from the SA tower abruptly stopped the chanting. Somewhere behind the barricade a loud explosion reverberated and a plume of pumice gray smoke crept over the wall and into the group of onlookers. Spectators were rubbing their eyes and coughing from the acrid smoke. The air reeked of gunpowder. All that could be heard from the Burdened Ghetto were screams of pain and wails of horror.

Otka turned back toward Addison, tears filling her gold-flecked turquoise eyes. "This is ghastly, positively ghastly," she shrieked and buried her head into Addison's right shoulder. Addison took his right arm and put it around Otka's waist, then put his left arm around the redhead's waist and continued to trace circles around her stomach, expanding the diameter each time until the back of his fingers grazed her breasts.

Addison gasped in shock. Not for the carnage taking place behind the barricade, not for the lynching of Professor Pankewitz (which he probably caused), not because he decided to betray a brave woman who risked her life and her sibling's life to save his, and not because he was worried about the fate of his oldest and dearest friend – but because the voluptuous redhead reached back with her right hand started fondling his crotch. Addison bit his lower lip and moaned. He reached up and placed his left hand into the redhead's breast cup and rubbed his finger over her hardening nipple. With Otka's head on his right shoulder and Cytheria's breast in his left hand, Addison had at last become all he ever envied. ■

Breinigsville, PA USA
22 March 2010
234652BV00001B/1/P